LADY JAYNE
DISAPPEARS

LADY JAYNE

DISAPPEARS

JOANNA DAVIDSON POLITANO

Revell

a division of Baker Publishing Group
Grand Rapids, Michigan

© 2017 by Joanna Davidson Politano

Published by Revell
a division of Baker Publishing Group
P.O. Box 6287, Grand Rapids, MI 49516-6287
www.revellbooks.com

Printed in the United States of America

Library of Congress Cataloging-in-Publication Data
Names: Politano, Joanna Davidson, 1982– author.
Title: Lady Jayne disappears / Joanna Davidson Politano.
Description: Grand Rapids, MI : Revell, a division of Baker Publishing Group,
   [2017]
Identifiers: LCCN 2017025997| ISBN 9780800728755 (softcover) | ISBN
   9780800729745 (print on demand)
Subjects: LCSH: Family secrets—Fiction. | GSAFD: Christian fiction.
Classification: LCC PS3616.O56753 L33 2017 | DDC 813/.6—dc23
LC record available at https://lccn.loc.gov/2017025997

Scripture used in this book, whether quoted or paraphrased by the characters, is taken from the King James Version of the Bible.

Author is represented by Tamela Hancock Murray with the Steve Laube Agency.

17 18 19 20 21 22 23   7 6 5 4 3 2 1

To my dad who, like Aurelie's father, inspired a love of fanciful stories in my young heart and always had time to spend with the little girl who shadowed him.

PROLOGUE

Walk among the normal folk by day, but in your heart
know you are Robin Hood in disguise.

~Woolf Harcourt

LONDON, ENGLAND, 1861

"Well, Miss Harcourt. Are you, or are you not, Nathaniel
Droll?"

I squirmed on the chair across the desk from the old managing editor they called "Ram." How awful it was to hear
that precious name on the man's meaty lips, but of course
it was only a name to him. "That is a complicated question,
sir." The crinoline under-layers of my skirt poked my legs,
which grew warmer with each minute I spent in the offices
of Marsh House Press.

"So is switching the final chapters at the last minute. You
will forgive my doubt when a snit of a girl comes in here,
supposedly on behalf of a nationally famous author, yet

appears to be no older than his first novel. Have you proof of your connection to him?"

This would take a great deal of explanation. Perhaps it was time to retreat. But no, this had to be done. Turning back now meant the final installment of the novel would release in a few days, and the man of my dreams would find out how deeply I was in love with him. It was not possible to imagine an existence beyond that dreadful occurrence.

"Here is one proof." I set my notebook before the balding bulldog of a man who reigned over his desk full of papers and clutter. "Is it not the same type Droll has sent you for years?"

He whipped through the book with harsh fingers, tearing a page at the top, then shoved a pen and inkwell toward me across the desk.

Of course. I would need to show him my handwriting for comparison.

Leafing to an empty page, I drew the pen from its heavy well and wrote, *I am Aurelie Harcourt. I collected Nathaniel Droll's pay at 32 Headrow Lane in Glen Cora, Somerset.* The letters formed by my shaky hands had taller loops and were slightly less perfect than the rest of the writing in the book, but it was an unmistakable match.

He yanked the book toward him, inspecting it as seconds ticked by on the clock behind him. I focused on the ivory-topped fireplace in the room's shadows, counting the ticks.

Finishing his assessment, he leaned his heavy frame back against the chair and studied me, every button and tuck of my brown traveling gown. Thick fingers pulled at his jowls. "Well, well. I've always wanted to meet the great enigma who has earned me so much, and here he sits. A woman. A rather plain one, at that."

As if I was unworthy.

"Transcriber." My voice cracked. "I've been his transcriber for years."

"How is it you came to know Nathaniel Droll?" His eyes narrowed.

Could I refuse to answer? He hardly believed me anyway, that much was obvious.

"A long, uninteresting story, sir. But right now I am merely here to enquire about changing that ending." I waved a hand toward the notebook before him.

Holding his spectacles in place, he studied the book, then me, then back to the book, his left eye nearly disappearing beneath the folds of skepticism. "He's never done this before."

"This book is different."

He growled, squeaking his chair back and folding his arms. "Tell Mr. Droll he is lucky. First, because you caught us before we printed this installment. *Barely*. Second, because his fame has earned my pleasant side today." He lit an ornate pipe and puffed, exhaling tiny balls of smoke.

"I know it's a lot to ask, but—"

"Fortunately I'm a wonderful person." He waved the gathering smoke away from his face, grimacing at it.

A trapped breath released from deep in my chest. I'd succeeded. Everything was safe. "So you'll change it?"

"Well, that depends. If I hate this ending, I shall use the one he already sent. It has been approved, and this has not."

I straightened against the unforgiving spindles at my back. "I cannot let you print that."

"Oh, oh, oh, the little transcriber forbids me." He swiveled in his chair and tapped his pipe in a tray. "I'll not take risks with the final installment. Sales are predicted to break records at this house, and that ending *will not disappoint*." He slapped his hand on the desk to emphasize his words. "The first chapter sells the book, but the last chapter sells the next. Understand?"

"Yes, sir, but I must ask that you—"

"Where the devil did you come from, anyway?"

"Well, I—"

"We'll have to cut his pay, you know."

"That will be fine. But can I—"

"Just how old are you?"

Frustration eclipsed my self-control. "Two hundred and three. How old are you?" I shut my mouth behind the escaped words.

A few silent puffs came from the man behind the desk as he gave a wry smile. His eyes did not leave my face. "*Now* you are someone I care to speak with." He leaned forward, the leather chair creaking under his weight. "So, little thing. Tell me exactly how you came to be in possession of Nathaniel Droll's notebook. How his work bears your handwriting."

"I cannot do that, sir."

"I understand completely." He swiveled away from me, foot over foot. "And I can no longer consider printing your new ending."

Poised in the little wooden chair his assistant had brought, I bit my lip and gripped the arms. "I suppose I could tell you a brief version of the story. If you promise to strongly consider the switch."

He whipped around to face me again, eyes glowing, elbows anchoring him to the desk. "Nonsense. If we're to discuss Nathaniel Droll, I want every detail. Understand? Every little detail. I want to know who exactly is hiding behind that pen name and what his story is. Start with your part, and please do tell me about the imposters too. I've been dreadfully curious."

With a shuddering sigh, I glossed over memories not worth revisiting. Perhaps it would be sufficient to tell him only what happened in the last few months. That would cover the important pieces. With a fortifying deep breath, I slipped into my one and only talent—storytelling. "It started in Shepton Mallet debtor's prison, which is where I am from. That is, until recently."

1

Lady Jayne dreamed endlessly of escaping to something different, of living a fascinating and dramatic life—until she did.

~Nathaniel Droll, *Lady Jayne Disappears*

A FEW MONTHS EARLIER, SOMERSET, ENGLAND

It must have been the rain that felt so wrong that day, nothing more. It spit at my face and drenched me. I huddled close to the safety of the Shepton Mallet Prison walls as a carriage progressed toward me down the broken street, lanterns swinging. No, it was *everything*. Everything felt wrong without Papa. But this night, it was something specific.

Perhaps it was the sleek carriage, coming to fetch me to my new home, that looked jarringly amiss in this section of town after dark. Why hadn't Aunt Eudora come in broad daylight so we could stand outside and relish our reunion, hugging and sinking into shared grief? Surely she knew this was not an area in which to linger once the candlelit windows of decent folk were shuttered. Damp fog clogged my senses, choking my shallow breaths. She was not ashamed simply because of the pickup location, was she? No, I was *family*.

Family that had been abandoned by them for years, though. Perhaps I expected too much.

I squinted at the vehicle as it neared and I frowned. The outline of a top hat, not a lady's plumage, filled the foggy windows. Who else would come to collect me?

What if, *what if*—and this would make a brilliant scene in a future novel—it was not an old widowed aunt coming for the lonely girl, but her own beloved father, alive and well? The emotion of such a reunion billowed in me until I very nearly ripped open my trunks, right there in the rain, and pulled out a notebook to record the beauty of it.

Stop. I had to stop thinking about him.

The coachman reined in the puffing horses, who stamped their impatience in the foggy moonlight, and I held my breath, crouching back into the prison doorway. When the caped gentleman swung down into the rain, I longed for those blank pages even more. What a perfect villain, tall and dark-suited, a forbidding arch to his wide shoulders as he jogged through the puddles. Oh, to pin this man to paper with the exact words. But it was a generally understood rule among writers that the most brilliant ideas only came when one was not within reach of pen and paper.

Approaching, the man lifted his gaze to the prison, dark judgment etched deep in the brooding lines of his face. He removed his hat, nearly useless in the deluge, and swiped rain off his face with his sleeve. Upon spotting me in the shadows, his face darkened further, eyebrows hooding sharp eyes. He was more ominous close up. Threatening, even. I backed up until I hit the rough stone wall. And now, there was no one left to protect me. Not a single person who might report me missing to the constable. Like a kite with its string suddenly cut, I was alone.

The Lord is my shepherd, I shall not want.

I'd never had to depend so fully on the Lord before this, and it seemed now he was all I had.

My nails dug into the dirty stone at my back. The storm swelled and rain pattered against my shoulders, pouring down my neck and soaking my dress. Why were we not running toward the carriage and huddling under its roof? The man squinted against the shower, as if waiting for me to speak and explain my presence. Yes, he felt it too. Something was wrong.

My small voice cut through the rain. "You are from Lynhurst Manor?" Perhaps I'd been mistaken, and Aunt Eudora's carriage was still on its way.

"Yes, I am." Rain dripped off the clumps of hair plastered to his forehead.

"Oh." But neither of us moved. Was he waiting for my permission? "These are both mine." I indicated my two weathered trunks, which only deepened his look of confusion. "I am Aurelie Harcourt."

"Silas Rotherham."

Rotherham. So dark and sinister. Fitting.

After a few more awkward seconds, he reached for my elbow and propelled me toward the carriage. A head jerk toward the coachman sent the man scrambling toward my trunks. Certainly, those trunks were not of the same caliber as my new sapphire-colored dress, which billowed around my stockinged legs over layers of fabric in a sopping, yet stylish, mess. He must wonder which I was—rich or poor. Yes, that would explain the frown.

The first trunk thudded overhead as I mashed my dress through the too-small door and fell onto the front-facing seat, the man taking the one across from me. How did real ladies manage it every day? The dress was the finest article of clothing to ever touch my body, and despite having owned it for three days already, I did not know how to carry it on my slender frame. Even more so when it hung in wet yards of heavy cloth about me.

Perhaps it had been a foolish use of my scant funds, this costume designed to make me fit in when the rest of me did not. Even more foolish I'd been to give up my last pennies, assuming this wealthy family would hasten to meet all the future needs of a niece they had not seen fit to even meet before now. How fanciful I was.

But I had yet to locate Papa's savings, wherever it was. All those paychecks I'd gathered from Marsh House Press must amount to something that would sustain me. And with death freeing the man of his debts, I could use that money for whatever I needed.

I placed my soggy hat on the seat beside me and wrung my loosened hair onto the floor of the carriage. "It soaks right through a person, does it not?"

The man peeled off his wet coat, struggling out of the sleeves. By instinct born of a lifetime of recognizing need and rising to it, I reached across the space to assist him. When my fingertips touched his warm linen shirtsleeve beneath the coat, he pulled back, slinging his coat to the side, blinking at me with a mixture of shock and mild offense.

I jerked my hands away and backed into my seat with a thud, hurt warming my wet cheeks. Of course, this was a different world than Shepton Mallet Prison. Women were not for soothing and helping unless they were paid to do it. A grunt outside drew my attention to the window. The coachman yanked in vain at my second trunk, which had taken three men to hoist outside hours ago. I bit my lip, picturing its contents. He'd never lift it alone.

With a dark look, the man across from me stood and forged back into the rain to assist the coachman. Both men strained to lift the precious cargo between them, and they slung it with a thud and a crack onto the back. Lightning pierced the black sky as the two men ran for the cover of the carriage.

Mr. Rotherham hefted himself back inside, now coatless and dripping wet. Almost immediately the carriage lurched forward, reins jingling, and I collapsed against the leather seat. Just that quick, we were leaving behind the entirety of my short life.

Don't look back. Don't look back. Don't—

But I did. Fingertips clutching the window frame, I pressed my face to the glass for one last lingering glimpse of home.

"Have you left something behind?"

"No." I moved back into the seat, pushing my shoulder blades into the leather cushions. Leaving that place was the death of so many things.

The man recovered his breath for several moments, flexing until he found comfort in the tiny rear-facing seat. I fingered the flannel blanket beside me. He would not want me to hand it to him. But when his trembles convulsed into a full-body shiver, the sight compelled me forward, urging the blanket on him. He accepted it without glancing at me and pressed it into his wet clothes to soak up the rain. When he looked up, he pinched his lips in a reserved smile, revealing two fleeting dimples framing his mouth like quotation marks, and I finally relaxed a bit.

"I assure you," he said, "there are plenty of stones at Lynhurst. You need not bring any with you."

"They're books." I shivered, watching the shapes of thatched homes fly by. It must be utterly clear to him that I was a fake, not one who belonged at Lynhurst Manor. Up until a few days ago, my life had consisted of a one-room cell, my gregarious, boisterous father, and our three pieces of furniture. And stories, of course. He'd shown me how to thrive within our odd surroundings—reciting psalms, caring for the weak, loving people—but he'd never taught me to act as one of the elite class in which he himself had been raised. There had been no need.

Homesickness engulfed me. But how could anyone be homesick for such a place?

"Thank you for indulging me, with the books." I indicated the back of the carriage where my trunks lay.

"Of course. Books are essential nourishment to the mind."

This answer begged more questions, but I closed my lips. Any little word might be the wrong one. Lantern light bounced over his face as the carriage hurtled forward.

"I suppose they are the normal fare." The man's voice broke through my thoughts, deep and forced. "Miss Austen, Clennam, Wordsworth, and perhaps a few hymnals."

He really was quite poor at making conversation. "I prefer the serials."

"Of course." His slight frown, a mild look of judgment,

turned my stomach. As if my love of serial novels helped him to determine I resided lower than him on the social ladder. Wouldn't he be surprised to find that most of the books filling my heavy trunk were *blank*.

I pinched my lips to keep from spilling my delicious secret—the one that gave me more worth than anyone could guess. If only I dared say the words aloud. *Pardon, sir. Have you heard of Nathaniel Droll? Well, I happen to know the real man who masquerades under that pen name.* Ah, the look of shock that would splay over his arrogant face.

"Novel characters make the finest friends, so I can hardly fault your attachment." He straightened the hat that jostled on his head to the rhythm of the carriage wheels and smiled. "Flesh-and-blood people are more complicated and difficult to know."

"I should say not. So many people are closed up, all tucked inside themselves, yet they bloom open in beautiful ways if you would only take interest in them."

The flick of his eyebrow hinted at disapproval, driving me deeper back into my seat as my face heated. I had done it again.

I tipped my head back against the cushioned seat and allowed the carriage to carry me and my heavy thoughts toward a life where this disapproval would be normal fare. "I hope I did not offend you, sir."

"It was merely a surprisingly deep answer to what I believed a simple question."

"Life is deep, Mr. Rotherham." Oh so deep. Especially when it is a series of intense moments all piling on top of you, fighting for your urgent attention every day. "Which is why books are such a lifeline. Stepping into the pages of someone else's story means joining them in their normal life and pretending that you, for one liberating moment, will also become whole and healthy and wonderfully normal by the end."

His eyes, lifting into a pleasant crescent shape with his smile, assessed me with the softness of grace. "You've managed quite well in the life you were dealt. How were you not mired in sadness every day at a place like that?"

My first instinct was to inform him that Charles Dickens himself spent several years of his childhood in Marshalsea Debtor's Prison when his father languished there for numerous debts, for no one could doubt Dickens had made a success of his life in the end. But I merely waved off his comment with a simple reply. "There are many good days that outweigh the bad. And besides, imaginations are transportable. They even follow one into poverty."

His face dipped back into the shadows. Laughing? Or disapproving?

No matter. The stress of the week weighed me down much like the wet dress I wore. We'd only buried Papa days ago. "And might I ask who has the pleasure of escorting me?"

"I am a family friend staying at Lynhurst for the summer." He cleared his throat. "They did not feel they could trust so delicate a matter to a servant, no matter how faithful."

"I see." But I did not. What was delicate about the matter of bringing one's niece home?

Long, silent moments passed before the carriage paused for an iron gate to grind open. A crest seemed to seal the gates shut. Had we reached our destination so quickly?

I leaned into the window for a glimpse of the place, but the muted glow of lamplight showed precious little. Three

. . . no, four cupolas speared the dark clouds shrouding the roofline. Surely the estate couldn't be as fanciful and amazing as Papa's wild stories, but anything less would not have captured the imagination of such a man. Propping myself higher, I strained to see the outline of the fabled Lynhurst Manor through the muggy dark.

After endless minutes of rolling up the unlit gravel drive, the carriage veered left and halted mere feet from the great house. A large hanging light illuminated an arched stone entryway with double wooden doors not unlike the solid front entrance of the prison. Perhaps I'd feel at home here after all. The mansion's gray exterior wall extended far outside the little circle of lantern light, into what seemed to be eternity.

It was true, then. I'd hardly believed Papa's stories of this place, for what family could live in such wealth while their brother languished in poverty? A mere pittance of their wealth might have freed Papa years ago. Steeling myself against bitterness, I tried to summon an explanation, but could not.

At least the rain had stopped.

Mr. Rotherham alighted. As I pushed off the seat, he held up a palm to stop me. "You'd best let me prepare them first, Miss Harcourt."

I sank into the seat, the damp feel of my thick skirts beneath me. "Prepare them for what?"

He paused just outside the carriage, a rare smile flicking over his face. "We all rather believed you to be a collection of bags and trunks."

"I beg your pardon?"

"The solicitor had instructed Lady Pochard to collect the belongings of the distant relative who had died in debtor's prison."

Distant relative? I frowned.

"You can imagine her surprise when she finds out exactly what this relative's belongings include." He shook his hat and replaced it. "Wait here. I'll return for you when I've broken the news to her."

"Welcome back, Mr. Rotherham."

Silas strode through the double doors held open by the butler, who ushered him into the deeply shadowed hall tinged with lemon freshness on wood-paneled walls. A slight bow, then Digory's aged hand came out to accept Silas's coat. The weight of it jerked his arm down, but his face maintained the placid butler mask. "I trust your errand was pleasant."

"Pleasant as expected." He stamped wetness from his shoes and strode through the arched front hall to the drawing room where Lady Pochard waited. How was one to answer these meaningless questions, really? *A fine day today, is it not, sir? How was your walk? I trust you are in good health this morning.* He should tell them the day was terrible, he had witnessed a murder, and he'd walked to the moon, just to see what they would do.

What a stark contrast from the girl waiting in the carriage. Everything she said meant something, her sentences plump and juicy with originality. Fresh, and delightfully odd.

"Good evening, Lady Pochard. I'm surprised to see—"

"Well, have you fetched them?" Lady Eudora Eustice Pochard huddled in her wheeled chair in the bay of heavily draped windows. The fireplace glowed behind her, giving a soft yet eerie light to this red-and-gold gilded room of her ancestors. Oh yes, he had fetched them. Both trunks . . . as well as the additional piece of "baggage."

"Yes, my lady. Every last belonging of a Mr. Harcourt of Shepton Mallet."

"He is dead?" Digory's faithful-butler mask shattered.

"No! Mr. Harcourt—"

A daggered look from Lady Pochard sliced the end off his sentence. The poor man's Adam's apple bobbed, wiry hands working at his sides.

Silas tried again. "As to what I'm to do with—"

"I've told you. All the trunks are to be stowed in the rafters. Unless you have taken it upon yourself to look through the deceased man's belongings to decide their value is greater than attic fodder."

"I have only glimpsed one belonging, my lady, and you will hardly wish to keep it in your attic." Why did he tiptoe around the truth? It wasn't as if it was his fault, any of this.

"Out with it, then." The woman's aged mouth puckered. "I've no patience for your witticisms, Mr. Rotherham. Speak quickly."

He cleared his throat. "A girl, my lady. A young woman of nearly twenty, I'd say."

Realization dawned on the old woman's face in hues of white and ashy gray. "It cannot be."

"I brought her here, not knowing what else to do. If you prefer to dismiss her, perhaps I may at least take her to London where she might find more opportunities." Letting her loose in this area to grab at menial work for pure survival would suck the life out of her. But then, so would bringing her into this house.

"Isn't it scandalous enough to have a family member in

this predicament in the first place?" The woman couldn't seem to say the word *prison*. "I'll not have you taking the girl anywhere but this very house." She sat tall in her wheeled chair, as if she were a lady of great beauty, which she was not, at her age. "What has become of her all these years? Who has raised the child?"

"She seems to have raised herself, if there was any raising done at all. She climbed into the carriage alone with me, as if it were quite natural."

"You mean to tell me that this girl has been living with the *debtors*?" The woman huffed. "What a scandal. I suppose she's a wild little thing."

The bang of the front doors drew everyone's attention, then the creak of the inner doors. *Slap-click, slap-click* and then she emerged from the shadows of the hall to stand before them, shining wet hair plastered to her forehead and neck, falling in silky, disheveled tresses over her shoulders. In the light of the house, Silas drank in the full sight of her, wild and beautiful—huge brown eyes, cheeks cool and fresh like spring, perfect little lips pinched with tension. So this is what the darkness of the carriage had hidden from him.

"Just as I knew she'd be." Tears pricked the old servant's tired eyes. Digory leaned forward beside Silas, his hands clasped, as if he ached to throw his arms about the girl and protect her as he would a baby bird.

Lady Pochard leaned forward on her cane toward her servant. "Take care of this matter. And Digory"—her eyes pierced her butler with a look, shining with the awareness of all he'd likely witnessed in this great house—"tell her *nothing*."

2

For Lady Jayne, who possessed both wit and imagination, dead ends were merely an invitation to draw out her tools and carve a door into the wall.

~Nathaniel Droll, *Lady Jayne Disappears*

Shivers convulsed my damp body as I stood in the doorway of a dim, cavernous room, dripping on the green-checked tile just outside of it. The overly red space had two focal points—the giant white fireplace and the tiny lump of a scowling woman huddled by the windows. Her dress, the most becoming deep jade with black lace, was a waste of beauty on so sour-looking a person.

"I see you have welcomed yourself into my home," said the woman with silvery grace, "so I will not repeat the convention."

"They left me in the carriage." I shifted, and water dripped off the hat in my hands.

"Digory, ring for the chambermaids." Urgency lit her eyes as water pooled at my feet. "Pull them out of their supper if you must. The girl needs a bath instantly. And rooms. She will need a suite of rooms. What do we have available that is away from the main suites? She'll, of course, want her privacy."

What a diplomatic way of shuffling me off into hiding, away from my own family.

"Yes, my lady. I'll ask Mrs. Harper what will be best. Unless . . . unless you wish to give her the south tower rooms."

South tower? I bit my lip with hopeful pleasure. There had been a "south tower" in at least two of Papa's novels, including the unfinished work in progress.

"*No!*" A pop of the woman's cane punctuated her response, and she glared at me, as if assessing whether or not I might fit into a small closet or a crate. "You'd just as well put her in the cold stables as in that old tower. Find her something on the third floor."

"I just thought it would be nice to—"

"What part of 'no' was not clear?"

The man bowed deeply and backed out of the room, one hand under my elbow to hint that I was to leave with him, the other taking a candle. Silas Rotherham had retreated to the room's deep shadows, head down as if he did not wish to be noticed. I nodded my thanks in his direction, but he did not look up.

"I almost forgot to ask." The woman's voice carried out to us, drawing us back into the room that glowed with firelight and candles. "What's your name, child?"

"Aurelie. It's Aurelie Rosette Harcourt."

"Good heavens," she mumbled, eyes rolling back beneath her lids. "As if he were naming a woodland fairy." She tugged a lace handkerchief from her sleeve and dabbed her neck.

A swift defense boiled up, but I pressed my lips together to keep it at bay. Even if I knew nothing about being a lady, I had the higher ability of being a good and loving human being.

"All right then, Miss Harcourt. You shall stay for now, and how long your visit continues depends entirely upon you and your conduct. You may leave me now."

The servant's gentle pressure on the back of my arm propelled me toward the darkened hall again into the largest open space that ever could have existed indoors, now illuminated by the butler's candle. From tiled floor to wainscot-trimmed ceiling two stories above, meticulous designers had decked the space in lavish emerald-green wallpaper and dramatic life-sized paintings. The butler led me to the grand staircase with echoing footsteps, and then together we climbed on plush carpet.

At the first landing, he pointed with the lit candle. "This is where the family has their rooms. There are fourteen total in this wing." Several tall doors remained closed. "Ninety-eight total rooms in the house altogether."

"Nearly a hundred rooms?" All for one family.

"Yes, miss. Everything's in multiples of seven. That being the number of perfection in the Good Book. The whole house was built to reflect the faith, you know."

"How interesting."

"All except the land. They have 628 acres because the bordering estate refused to sell so much as a grass blade to make it an even 700. But, that's the Sutherlands. They were born with crowns and tiaras on their heads."

Rounding the balcony and climbing another set of steps, we reached a long hall of ivory-white doors steepled at the top with wood trim. The smell made me frown. No, it was not so much a smell as a lack of it. As if real life had been made sterile and fake.

"The south wing is behind us, toward the back of the house. At the end of the hall is the door to the west wing." He pointed toward a heavy wood door framed with scrollwork. "You'll have the grand ballroom and other things there, but they're hardly used anymore."

"I suppose I'm to stay in that wing."

"No, miss." But he smiled. "You'll be in the main house with the family, just one floor up." On the third floor, he paused before a white door. "I know Lady Pochard wouldn't like it, but I'll settle you into your father's old room. At least until she finds out."

"You know exactly who I am, don't you? Even though everyone else seems surprised I even exist, you knew."

This broke down a loosely constructed wall and his aged face relaxed into a smile. "Yes, child. I know you." His gentle voice pinched with age touched the same soft spot in my heart that Papa had.

"Papa loved you when he was here, didn't he? I'm certain I shall love you too."

In turn, he set the candle on a table outside the door and embraced me wholeheartedly, as a humble country farmer might hug his granddaughter.

Thank you, my Lord, for this single beautiful moment of love and acceptance from someone in this house. Like an embrace directly from you.

He moved back with a pat to my arm and, once again hooking his finger through the candleholder, pushed open the door to a grand bedchamber slightly stale with disuse. The candle illuminated a canopy bed with a soft sage-colored coverlet, and in the shadows stood a white fireplace and bay windows to the right. Two mauve chairs flanked the windows, either one ready to receive a reader into its embrace.

"It's perfect," I breathed. Not a trace of Papa's masculinity, but the room seemed to hold an air of his whimsical nature.

The butler lit a candle on the nightstand and left with the one he'd brought up. "I'll send around a girl to make the fire. It'll take the chill out before you climb into bed."

"Thank you. Oh, sir." I touched his shoulder.

The man turned, candle glow highlighting the angles of his old face. "Digory, please."

"Digory." I smiled. "What's in the south tower anyway?"

A smile tugged at one corner of his lip. "Now? Nothing but dust covers and old furniture, I'm afraid. But it's where we used to keep the guests who the lady thought might benefit from a little more . . . privacy."

"Lady Jayne stayed there, did she not?" I dredged out the name of Papa's latest heroine, and watched the man's face fall.

"It's best you not ask about her, Miss. I say that only out of concern for yourself."

With a quick nod, he backed out with his candle and closed the door on my other questions.

Finally alone, I stripped off my wet garments down to my slightly damp camisole and wrapped a knit blanket from the armoire about myself. If only I could strip away the creepy aura left by the man's answer about Lady Jayne. What a place this was, full of religion and darkness at the same time. So much was amiss.

Shivering, I huddled over an ornately carved wood desk and put nib to paper to write the letter that must be dealt with before I allowed myself the luxury of sleep. Despite all the grief and loss of the past week, there was one final death still to occur.

My Dear Sir,

I regretfully write to you this 23 day of April to inform you that you must now solve Lady Jayne's mystery yourself. After completing only 21 of the contracted installments in this work of serial fiction, the man you know as Nathaniel Droll has gone to rest in an early grave, having bled out his last word for your benefit before his beautiful soul departed to heaven. As the contents of this novel's remaining installments were disclosed to no one, it will be left to your most understanding self, or your kind readers, to guess for yourselves what has become of Lady Jayne.

Most sincerely yours,
Nathaniel Droll's transcriber

He would have loved the irony of so perfect a cliffhanger.

When a knock cut through my thoughts, I dropped the pen beside the page and stood to answer it, gripping the wool blanket more tightly about me.

"Water, miss." Two young chambermaids, girls of maybe fourteen, shared the burden of a large copper tub supported by ring handles. I opened the door farther, and they carried it to the empty hearth and were followed by another girl laboring under the weight of a cauldron of steaming water. I leaned against the wall, blanket clutched awkwardly around my nearly unclothed body, as a curly-haired maid stooped to create a fire in the cold hearth.

A steady line of mop-capped girls struggled to carry in water, all so I could wash. Another maid brought a stack of linens, the lace of a white cotton nightdress peeking immodestly from its hiding place between towels and blankets. My guilt was tinged with an eagerness to indulge in the treats laid out before me.

After the last pot of water had been dumped into the tub, the little maid who had carried it bobbed a curtsey and told me to ring if I needed anything, indicating a delicate coil bell near the door. "Best wait a bit for the bath, ma'am. The water's all kinds of hot."

"Thank you," I murmured, and then they were gone. I hadn't even needed to close the door myself.

My eager fingers tugged off the blanket and wet underthings so I could slip into the velvety warmth of clean bathwater. I sank into it up to my shoulders and closed my eyes, allowing the words of the hated letter to swim through my mind in a mental critique.

Sending this letter would not steal the identity of Nathaniel Droll from me. That had already happened when Papa died. But somehow my heart couldn't bear the finality of this action. Nathaniel Droll was the wonderful secret that had shaped so much of my life. It had kept me from feeling purposeless, discouraged, and empty. I moved the cloth across the goose bumps on my bare flesh. No matter how the world saw the little debtor's prison girl, I had a hidden sense of worth in this secret. And now I would only be an outcast living among strangers, and Papa a failed man who'd died in disgrace.

I rose and hugged a towel around myself as I stepped out. The hot bath had warmed my skin, and in a moment the bed would ease what the carriage and rain had done to my muscles. Donning the nightdress, I readied for bed and climbed into sheets thick enough to lose myself between them. Exhaustion pulled at me immediately, and I glanced around this room serenely for traces of my precious papa before sleep fell like a curtain on this first night here. With a smile, I closed my eyes and pictured him. Not the wilted giant on the cot in his final days, but the effervescent man with the booming voice who had lit up our tower room. Especially the night he'd begun Lady Jayne's story.

"And now, dear princess of the tower." He had dropped his massive frame down on one knee, gently lifting my hand and throwing his other arm over his head. "One wish I grant you tonight. What'll it be?"

I hugged my knees and rocked back into the sunlight streaming in our tiny window. "An orange. I've not had an orange in months."

"Ach, what a way to ruin it." He thumped his chest. "I'd planned to offer something far better than a mere orange, but"—he twirled his hand in the air and stood—"suit yourself."

Realization hit me at what he'd intended to offer. "Papa, the story!" I grabbed his hands. "You'll tell it to me now? Truly?"

He squeezed my fingers, eyes crinkling into that beloved smile. "I'm keeping my promise to you, Aura Rose. The next novel we write will be her story."

"What was she like, Papa? Do I look like her?"

Lifting the hair off my face with his free hand, he looked down at me and smiled thoughtfully. "So much so that it hurts, little one."

Another quick squeeze and I released him and went to fetch a blank notebook. "Shall we start now? This installment is due to be mailed in a few days."

"Ach, girl. Have I ever rushed to finish one?" He collapsed onto the broken throne-like chair against the wall and propped his feet up on the stool. I knelt on the stone floor at his feet, leaning against the table.

"Please, Papa. I'm ready to hear about her."

"She isn't going anywhere, child. She's taken up residence right here." He tapped his balding head. "And of course, she'll be in you too, before long. Ah, child. Once this story takes root and that woman invades your heart as she did mine, you'll be able to write her story as well as I. How I love that it's written in your own dear hand. That's a gift, you know."

I adjusted my legs beneath me. "Start with what she looked like. I want to hear that. No, begin with how you met."

He leaned down and looked at me, drawing me close and running a thumb along my ear. "This is your legacy, child. Hold on to it, will you? It's a living, breathing story that I'm passing on to you. Promise you'll take good care of it."

"Yes, Papa, of course. Now let's hear it!"

But still he hesitated. "I've put off sending it into the world with my other stories, for fear of the ripple effect it will have."

"Then why not tell only me?"

He exhaled the tension from his body. "Because, Aura Rose. This story is far bigger than you and me and your mother. It should be told this way, and you should be the one to pen it." Squeezing my shoulder, he threw his head back, revealing his whiskered neck. "All right, lassie, the story of Lady Jayne. Ready your pen, child, because the sparks are flying!"

It's a living, breathing story.

I'm passing it on to you.

Passing it on.

I snapped awake in the dark chamber at Lynhurst Manor, the extinguished candle a smoking stub on the table beside me. I must have drifted off. Scrambling to sit up, I clutched the covers to me and glanced about the room. Tree shadows waved from the window and embers glowed in the fireplace.

Nothing else in the room moved, yet his presence seemed powerfully real there.

I'd only dreamed it. Pulled it from my memory and relived it in sleep. Perhaps it was merely the guilt at my absence, for I'd been on an errand the moment he'd passed from this life.

Those words lingered in my mind, drawing me to the story I was about to cut short and pack away forever. But he'd never intended for it to be set aside, had he? *You'll be able to write her story as well as I. How I love that these words are in your own dear hand. That's a gift, you know.* Not a gift to him, though—a gift to me. Realization solidified in my mind. All along when he'd asked me to take dictation, he was offering the only gift he had to give me. The legacy of Nathaniel Droll's great name.

Slithering back down into the bed, my mind whirled with options. He wanted me to do this, but I wasn't the writer my father was. I blew the hair off my face and stared at the paneled ceiling where angelic scenes scrolled across the white expanse. I was not qualified in the least.

Yet here I lay in Lynhurst Manor, the setting for *Lady Jayne Disappears* and every book that had come before it. I'd now walk among people every day who'd known my mother, who'd been present when she'd disappeared.

I dusted my cheek with the tips of my hastily upswept hair and pondered the risk it might be to write under his name, to uncover years of buried family secrets, but I knew with immediate clarity what to do.

Pardon, sir. Have you heard of Nathaniel Droll? Ah, well, I happen to know the real man who masquerades under that pen name. In fact, it isn't a man at all. Not anymore.

It's me.

3

Lady Jayne's antidote for boredom was not entertainment but rather curiosity and imagination.

~Nathaniel Droll, *Lady Jayne Disappears*

I woke to a room lit with sunshine. Rising and pattering to the window bay past the now-cold tub of water, I stood barefoot and looked over the lawn, through a tangle of purple flowers climbing trellises toward the jutting wings of the house, each flanked with a tower at the end. Which one was the south tower?

Today I would take over *Lady Jayne Disappears* and create the next installment, for it would need to be posted immediately. That required opening a fresh notebook and filling its blank pages with words beautiful enough to carry Nathaniel Droll's name. But more than that, it meant unraveling what had happened here nearly twenty years ago. Visually tracing the pattern of vines winding over the wallpaper, I pondered the direction of the plot.

It was an ingenious novel, actually. One I'd enjoy working on. The prologue was the scene directly after Lady Jayne had vanished from the mansion, when the entire house slipped into a panic at her sudden absence, and then the story jumped back in time and told everything leading up to it, all the way to her disappearance in the final scene. Readers were pulled through each issue, guessing who and what and how as everything built up toward her mysterious disappearance.

Lowering myself to the rug, I lay on my back, arms spread above my head, imagining the woman who had captivated my father. The woman who'd given birth to me.

Jayne Windham, or simply "Lady Jayne," as the readers knew her, had come to visit a friend's country mansion. Lynhurst, specifically, but the book had not mentioned that detail. She often had vases of heather in her room and almost exclusively wore her favorite color—purple. She'd spent a glorious summer playing about Bath and Bristol, and then disappeared, leaving all her belongings behind, including her beautiful amethyst ring.

And her child.

That element made it even more confusing. It had seemed like he was telling the story of how they'd met, her appearing on the social scene as a lady of mystery and capturing his heart, but if the last time he saw her was the end of that summer, they'd have already been married with a baby. I picked at the plush rug. Perhaps Papa had made up the tale to give me a mother-story. For every girl, if she did not have a mother, sooner or later required an explanation as to why. This story, however, did not fit. Aside from the timeline discrepancies, the only way a woman would leave behind such things was if she'd been killed.

Ruminating on the story and letting the facts percolate, I glanced out of the windows. Somehow the sun had magically risen higher as I'd daydreamed. Hours must have passed, and my only accomplishment had been severe procrastination—inspecting wallpaper patterns and sweeping story facts into a pile to analyze. Not a single word put on paper.

How would I ever maintain deadlines? When Papa had been alive, his stories poured out chapter by chapter, without hesitation or flaw. Oh, that I would be so lucky.

Rising and pushing one of the wingback chairs to the decadent bay window, I lowered into its cushions with blank paper and looked over a flower-filled yard more elegant than my dreams of heaven. It was time to begin. Encouraged, inspired, I breathed in the magical beauty of my novel's setting and poured out the words that would paint the picture of my family estate. For nearly an hour I wrote, giving Lady Jayne a few mild enemies and some friends. My wrist ached when I released the pen.

How draining. And they required one installment per week. Pushing out of the chair, I forced myself into the motions of dressing for the day.

My underthings, stiff from last night's drenching, had been strewn about the chairs to dry. My new blue dress, however, hung in a damp mess from a rod behind the door. Just when I began to wonder if I was expected to breakfast in my stiff underclothes of the night before, someone knocked. Tying a colorful, shiny dressing gown from the armoire over my nightclothes, I opened the door. There stood a large pile of colorful dresses supported by a girl about my age with curly chestnut-colored hair and smiling eyes.

"I've been waiting for you to wake up. I have clothes for

you to borrow, and oh! I'm going to dress you up like a doll."
Shouldering into the room, the well-dressed girl swished the
items onto my unmade bed. "I've even brought you the most
beautiful underthings you'll ever see."

Underthings. That was normally not part of the second
sentence two ladies said to one another. "I am Aurelie." There,
that was a much more reasonable start.

"What a fine name for a pretty little thing. It makes me
want to put tiny rosebuds in your hair." She finger-combed
my wild tangles, sweeping them up with a dimpled smile.

"And who are you?"

She dropped the tresses and hopped onto the bed. "I'm
your new dearest chum." The bright smile showed perfect,
sharp little teeth and naturally pink lips. "I'm the old witch's
granddaughter, Juliette."

I perched on the edge of the bed with a tentative smile. I
should at least try to join in the camaraderie the girl offered
so easily and, well, without invitation. Her light-green gown
shimmered as she moved. Her undeniable, flirtatious beauty
was the sort that likely fit every man's ideal.

"She isn't really a witch, is she? I mean, she does possess
some redeeming qualities."

"The old woman? Hardly. She despises everyone and only
tolerates her family because she must. Have you a special
gentleman in your life?"

What a rapid shift, all over the place like a hummingbird,
making one work to keep up with her.

"No, I—"

"How perfect!" She sprang up and pulled me to stand
before her. "I have the ideal man in mind, and oh, he'll be
absolutely smitten when he meets you."

"Does that sort of thing happen?"

"Oh, of course Alexander will adore you." The girl held a full-skirted pink frock before me, hanging it from my shoulders and eyeing it. "And all of Somerset will be sighing over the fabulous new couple in the social set." I frowned and she lowered the dress with a smile. "You must think me vapid. I'm more intelligent than I look, that I promise. For better or worse. I can sum up a person in three quick glances, two if they're quite open in the face." She flung the dress on the bed and lifted another, fitting it against my shoulders.

"You can surmise that much about me in just a glance?"

"I know plenty. You're the news of the week, and servants have magical powers to hear through walls. Especially when they're told to keep to themselves."

By the time I was dressed to Juliette's satisfaction, her lady's maid shoving one knee into my back to tight-lace my corset, the staff informed us that breakfast had been put up. So we talked, mostly Juliette, of course, until the lunch bell gonged through the courtyard. By that time, my stomach burned with hunger.

"You must let me dress you up every day. I've had such fun." She looped her arm through mine and led me downstairs into the hall. "I hope your trunks are *never* returned."

Trunks? My trunks were *missing*? "What has happened to them?" The clothes could be replaced, but the notebooks? How was I supposed to finish Papa's novel without them?

"I only mean the accident last night. Grandmama told me about the carriage mishap, and your things being ruined. Only two measly trunks were saved, and they had almost no clothes in them. Just rags and a lot of books and papers." She wrinkled her nose.

I breathed slowly in relief, forcing myself not to smile. My trunks were safe. And storytelling, apparently, ran in the family.

At the main floor landing, Juliette led me to the left through another arched doorway, into a sun-filled room so bright a person had to shield her eyes upon entering. One wall was dedicated to tall windows covered with dark velvet drapes drawn back with red cords, but what caught my attention was the plate of food on a tiny table. I nearly pounced on the pyramid of little triangular sandwiches, wishing I could inhale them in one gulp.

"So the end of the story is that now you must be fitted for new dresses immediately." Juliette lounged comfortably on the sage couch, somehow still managing a becoming posture.

But dread coiled in me at the idea of so many dresses. Being indebted to the cold mistress of the house would not be wise, especially if I was ultimately to be cast out. I would need every penny I had. "Perhaps I should start with one or two."

"Or ten." Juliette winked, lips closing around another delicate nibble.

One bite into the vegetable-filled sandwich only inflamed my appetite. My fingers shoved a whole sandwich into my mouth while Juliette talked about taffeta and chiffon. Crisp celery never tasted so delightful.

"Juliette, did something happen to your grandmother? I've never known a soul to be bitter with no cause."

"Ach, who knows." She shrugged narrow shoulders. "There was much scandal with her husband and even her brother, I believe. Perhaps she was different before all that, but I couldn't picture it. And truly, it was a long time ago."

Two men ambled by the window in gray-and-red riding gear, whips in hand—Mr. Rotherham and an older gentleman I had yet to meet.

Juliette straightened. "Right there is one perfectly good reason for you to have a decadent new wardrobe." She pointed her sandwich toward the men. "I do so need competition with my Mr. Rotherham. He's too easily plucked from his low-hanging branch."

"He is *your* Mr. Rotherham, then?" Disappointment flickered, for his handsomeness had not gone unnoticed by my romantic little heart.

She shrugged. "Not really, but he could be quite easily." She poured weak tea and sipped it. "He's my brother Kendrick's oldest friend, and that's his excuse for being here. But of course Kendrick is in Bath at the moment, and as you can see, Mr. Rotherham is not." Another wink over her raised teacup. "Although I believe he's more enticed by the size of my fortune than by my many charms."

"I see."

"I don't care for him terribly much, but with everyone in London for the season, he's the only taste of romance within several shires. I must amuse myself how I can. And it would only double the amusement to have a little competition." She wrinkled her nose with glee.

"Then do you plan to court him?"

Juliette laughed at the nosy question, and my skin heated under the heavy dress. "Courting is not the big to-do you'd think. Its sole purpose is to keep girls reasonably pure and keep men satisfactorily confused. Give a man a puzzle, and you've given him a reason to exist another day."

Perhaps she and Rotherham deserved one another. He

was a gold digger, it seemed, and she a cold, hard lump of gold.

"So this perfect match you've selected for me, this Alexander. He is merely a game too, isn't he?"

Juliette nibbled a strawberry and smiled. "You're intrigued, aren't you? It's caught your interest. Admit it. Well, I'll have you two meet as soon as those new dresses are made."

By dinnertime, hunger still pinched my stomach. Juliette had dressed me in yet another gown, even though the first was hardly worn long enough to spill even a drop of tea on it.

"This one is more appropriate for dinner," the girl announced, swinging around a scarlet gown with black lace. "It's dreary, but perhaps that will catch Mr. Rotherham's eye. He's a bit dark in personality himself. Takes everything quite seriously."

In the stolen moments after Juliette had left to dress for dinner, I escaped to my room and hungrily reread the new installment of my book, the lovely words that had poured out of me that morning. I needed steel in my spine before attempting dinner with the whole family, and nothing did that like reminding myself of my secret talent.

But the words that met my eyes were empty. Meaningless chatter and useless, fanciful descriptions. How had I written this drivel? Hadn't I any sense as a writer? It read like the work of a child who thought herself a lovely, eloquent poet. Sickened, I shoved the book back on the shelf and forced my feet toward the stairs to go to dinner.

Juliette and I arrived in the drawing room first and perched on chairs as red as my dress, with walnut arms and backs. The shadowed room felt somehow cozy, and not unlike the tower room I'd called home my whole life. Maybe this dinner would go well.

"Let's make a game." Juliette moved up behind me. "First one to speak at the table loses. Shall we?"

"Why ever would I do that?"

Footsteps clicked in the hall. She bent close, her breath tickling my ear. "Because it's the only way a girl like you will survive what is to come now."

4

She managed to be the beauty of every gathering, because she clothed herself in confidence and made up
her face with a lovely smile.

~Nathaniel Droll, *Lady Jayne Disappears*

Within minutes, the other family members gathered in the
drawing room and paired off to go into dinner together
amidst pleasant chatter. My arm was caught by a young
boy no taller than me, with serious green eyes and freckles
over his nose and cheeks. Silas Rotherham escorted Juliette.

The couples filed into a long room of intricately carved
wood and tall candles and stood behind their seats. Situated
in the center of the long table, I faced a low, austere fireplace
with a gold-rimmed mirror above it. I caught sight of myself
from the chin up—smooth hair gathered behind my head,
soft tendrils loose on white skin as if they'd escaped by accident, eyes large and scared. No wonder Juliette thought
me in need of guidance.

The last to enter was Lady Pochard, my aunt Eudora, walking with the aid of a cane and the severity of a queen. She paused her royal entrance behind me with a crinkle of fine clothes and the aura of peppermint. Surely she wouldn't make me leave this minute or shame me before the family. Not a woman this genteel.

"It occurred to me last night that I did not suitably welcome you into my home."

I turned to the heavily powdered face, unsure what was expected of me at the moment, and dipped a curtsey for good measure. The others stared as the woman patted my shoulder with stilted movements and dropped a kiss on my forehead.

Silence followed the gesture. Aunt Eudora hobbled to the head of the table and took her seat, signifying that the rest of the family should take theirs.

As the aproned maids served soup, Aunt Eudora spoke to me. "I'm pleased to have you meet my family. Beside me are my daughter, Glenna, and her husband, Garamond." The middle-aged, overdressed pair would be my first cousins, and likely Juliette's parents. "Their eldest, Kendrick, is detained in Bath. Their other children are Juliette, across from you, and Clement, your escort. Of course, you've met Silas Rotherham, guest of Kendrick." Rotherham's gaze flicked over me with quick evaluation, long lashes hooding his eyes. "This is Miss Aurelie Harcourt, a relation who will be staying with us for now."

Glenna's eyes snapped to mine, radiating with quick judgment that would wither a crowned princess, then fading again into a serene look of a wealthy woman.

"Harcourt?" coughed the little man at her side, studying me with sudden interest.

Juliette clapped, drawing a pointed look of annoyance from the head of the table. "Isn't she a pretty thing, Mr. Rotherham?" she asked her companion in a stage whisper. "So innocent and unworldly. It's as if she's grown up in the woods."

Apparently her little game of silence had been abandoned as her attention flitted on to the next interesting thing.

Mr. Rotherham hunched over his soup, brows drawn, clearly uncomfortable. But he did look up at me after a moment. His eyes, serious and penetrating, jumbled my nerves. Yes, he belonged in my novel, but certainly not as the villain. With that handsome physique and shadowed face, perhaps he was Lady Jayne's secret beau. At this thought, a smile touched my lips. This man, a romantic? It'd be much like embracing a stone wall. Or maybe Lady Jayne was just the right woman to unlock this wonderfully mysterious puzzle, unleashing the power and passion pent up in those steady gray eyes. For any stone wall was merely a well-sealed dam.

Conversation floated politely around me as the first course passed to the second, and I watched the others for how to arrange my linen napkin and balance my glass aloft with my fingertips. Poor Garamond, with a nose and ears bigger than his face, worried over his "dainty little woman" whom he seemed to believe was in danger of straining herself with the serving utensils or under-eating. But the radiantly plump woman, with rosettes dotting her dress across her abundant bosom, could likely lift her husband over her head.

The courses arrived one by one to the mostly silent room. When a server placed a plate of pheasant before me, I immediately cut into it, relishing the way the tender slice fell away. The soup and bread had only tantalized my gnawing appetite.

Juliette lifted her glass toward Aunt Eudora. "Grandmama, you must insist that the woman come from Bristol tomorrow. A girl needs her own dresses."

Aunt Eudora sighed with the patience of a thousand hardships. "When I can produce a woman out of thin air, Juliette, I will present her to you." She turned to Glenna, who sat beside her. "Why did we allow her coming out so soon? The girl is far better suited to ornamentation."

Cheeks warm, I swallowed my bite and spoke. "You needn't worry about dresses for me. I don't enjoy them quite so much as other girls."

"A young lady who is not dying for dresses?" Garamond spoke up, mouth dotted with garnish. "Is she broken?"

"Really, if you only give me access to a library, I shall be more than happy to amuse myself. Reading makes me forget that I'm wearing anything at all."

A fork clattered and someone choked on a bite, and Aunt Eudora leaned back and rolled her eyes. The other diners fell silent.

My already-warm face heated even more. What, were ladies not even to like books?

Rotherham's low voice broke the tension. "Reading is the perfect way to engage and excite your mind while appearing to merely pass the time." He met my gaze with the barest trace of a smile on his solemn face.

Light chatter resumed around the table now that I, the oddity, had been safely tucked into conversation. Yes, Mr. Rotherham made such a fresh character. He was quiet and brooding, yet with some undeniable redeeming qualities to round him out. Perhaps he had come to Lynhurst to woo Juliette for her fortune, but there had to be a reason. Was his mother ill, desperately in need of medical care? Maybe a sister with an illegitimate child languished in some secret corner of his house, needing protection and financial assistance. One thing was certain. I had read far too many books.

Rotherham stared openly across the table, as if still trying to label me, yet constantly reassessing his findings. His voice broke through my thoughts. "And the maiden found her escape into books, the worlds created by the pen of some stranger who would creep into her mind and rearrange the furniture."

At this, my gaze snapped to his sparkling gray eyes. I'd never heard those words voiced aloud, but I knew them oh so well. "You read Nathaniel Droll." And that particular quote had been from a chapter I had penned during one of Papa's illnesses. "I had no idea gentlemen polluted their shelves with serial fiction."

"Good literature is good literature, whether it is marketed toward the poor for ha'penny an issue or the aristocracy for a fortune." The corner of his mouth tipped up in a fleeting smile.

Good literature. He had called my little thoughts *good literature*. I had come to dinner with no desire to engage with Mr. Rotherham, but hearing him quote my own writing had enticed me into conversation anyway. He'd found the one topic that trumped my insecurities.

"What, exactly, do you like about his writing?" I couldn't help it. Every detail of his assessment must be coaxed out and revel in.

He ran his fingers along his jaw. "I suppose I ought to say

he has a fresh style and brings characters to life. And he does, but to be perfectly honest, I'm enraptured by Mr. Droll for reasons I cannot explain. It's as if he laced his words with an addictive substance that draws me through the pages until I'm surprised to find myself at the end of the installment."

"Really." His words needed to be written down. In large letters. Somewhere I'd see them often, just so I would believe them. "And who was your favorite character?"

"Call me dark, but I rather like the villains. No one crafts a murky figure like Nathaniel Droll. It makes one wonder what sort of company the man keeps."

I bit my lip to keep from revealing the truth. I longed—I *ached*—to spit out the secret, but I offered a rote reply instead. "Not the sort of company anyone of this household keeps, that is for sure." For who among these perfectly presented family members would ever talk to the prison inmates who made up Papa's and my entire stock of friends?

Which is exactly why I needed to introduce the world to them through the novels. Yes, it was brilliant! The decision swelled to an overwhelming desire that nearly drove me from my chair to find my notebooks. Oh, if only the world could see the prison, and the people who lived there, as I had. Well, soon they would.

I'd put everything about prison life into those books. Crippling disease. Death. Slimy newborn babes. Open sores. Sewer rats. The grit of real life to me, but completely foreign to this family.

"Whatever his experiences, they must be incredible for his mind to spin such tales." Silas reached for his water glass. "Perhaps it is his interesting life that makes Nathaniel Droll the genius writer he is."

Garamond leaned toward Silas, waving an empty fork with a frown. "It isn't the writing that's so fantastic, when it comes to Nathaniel Droll. It's the mystery of the man himself. He's only famous because no one knows who he really is. Superb marketing trick, isn't it?"

Glenna popped a bite of bread into her mouth and blotted the crumbs from her lips with her napkin. "No, no, no. Why ever do you insist on talking when you don't know anything? And you never know anything. Honestly, Garamond. You're sharp as custard." The napkin then descended on her poor husband, blotting every trace of food from his face. "Why, a man's come forward!"

I swallowed the green bean already in my mouth and coughed. Another gulp and it was down. "Come forward? You mean to say, someone has revealed himself as Nathaniel Droll?"

"Isn't it splendid? He has made himself known to the publisher and plans to come forward publicly rather soon, I believe. I cannot *wait* to know who he is and why he has hidden himself for so long. What a story his life must be."

After forcing the rest of my food down, I followed the other women into the drawing room while the men disappeared down the hall for billiards. Juliette perched at the piano, highlighted by the glow of a dozen candles above and beside her and, in the stillness of several moments, transformed into a lovely work of art as she closed her eyes and drew magically beautiful sounds from the instrument. Was it truly the same girl who had flounced into my room, all dimples and gaiety?

But the sounds faded into background music as my thoughts once again crowded in. Who was this man claiming my father's *nom de plume*? Could the publishing company

have concocted this mess to generate more excitement? I had
to tell someone he was an imposter.

No, because that meant revealing that the real Nathaniel
Droll had died.

"I suppose you've left a man pining for you at home, have
you?" Glenna nestled herself onto the couch beside me, her
deep voice near my ear.

"I have no attachments at present, Lady Gaffney."

Again, that evaluating gaze roamed my stiff body, as if
noticing every possible flaw and immediately assessing everything she could lay eyes on. "What a pity for a pretty girl
like you. Quite pretty. I daresay you'll turn heads away from
everyone else in the household, even my own dear Juliette."

A palpable ire, a female rivalry, rose between us with the
few words spoken, and the many words left unsaid.

"I have no intention of turning any heads, Lady Gaffney."

"Which is precisely why you will."

Digory brought in a tray with biscuits, wine, and tea, and
the women rose for refreshment, redistributing around the
room. When they each exited the room one at a time that
evening, their lights disappearing down different hallways,
I circled back to reality long enough to smile goodbye, take
a candle from a table, and drift out into the grand hall. Finally, freedom. Alone, I could sink into deep thoughts to my
heart's content.

I veered away from the stairs, slipping down a narrow
hallway toward the section that should be the south wing.
It was late, and I should return to my bedchamber, but my
mind overflowed with questions.

This is what Papa had pictured as he wrote. Suddenly
I could not imagine tearing myself away from this place.

Papa had spoken of Lynhurst Manor so much that it had settled into the dear parts of my memory as if it were my own childhood home. Great yawning caverns of rooms lay through each doorway off the hall, empty and enticing, but there was one part of the house I *must* find—the infamous south tower.

For research, of course.

But then the hallway turned east. Frowning, I followed the path past closed doors and great windows draped in sheer curtains. The hall ended at the rounded wall of a tower, and I ran to it, but it proved to be a disappointment. A mere storage closet for the servants' personal items, the delightfully creepy space seemed a complete waste. Turning back, I spun and my candle light illuminated another hall. Had it been there before?

This one angled south and west, tapering off into darkness. Shoring up my courage, I crept down the slender hall with cobwebs stretched over the gaps between stones and bare windows splintering at the sills. At the end of the lonely, moonlit passage, another tower curved into the hall, the door open and enticing with the foot of a bed visible just beyond.

Upon entering, the feminine aura of the place wrapped itself around me. Dusty glass surfaces and rose-colored trim dominated the round room. Certainly, this was the south tower where Jayne Windham would have stayed, if Papa's stories were true.

"You certainly would have lived like a fairy-tale princess in this room." My mumbled voice did not echo. Likely the only place in the house where that was true. I perched on the rosebud coverlet and absorbed the lovely emptiness, ideas spinning. It could have been a jealous rival or a former suitor who caused the disappearance. Maybe it was a kidnapping. Perhaps someone had snuck in from outside. Sheer curtains sparkled over the ground-level windows, letting in a full dose of moonlight. But that still did not explain how all the pieces fit together, and where I came in.

I pivoted to look at the place where my mother had supposedly spent her final months. *My mother.* That had been such a foreign concept while growing up, but a vague idea of warmth and femininity accompanied all thoughts of the woman who had given birth to me before she'd ceased to exist. Even when Papa began sharing her story months ago, the woman still seemed like a fairy in the woods, ethereal and fleeting. That's when I admitted it to myself—I did not believe in my mother. At least, not the one in my father's story. That magnificent woman had been his grandest fairy tale.

Drawn to the cherrywood armoire gracing the north wall, I walked to it and parted its doors, letting in the nighttime glow. There, hanging in shimmering perfection like forgotten ghosts, were the most luscious gowns. *Purple* gowns, every last one. Suddenly her presence in the room nearly overwhelmed me, as if she called out to me to find her killer. As if some part of her lived here still.

I moved back, panic rising in my throat. As I pivoted away from the door, a tiny sparkling object caught my gaze. There on the glass-topped dressing table sat a delicate, ornate gold ring with a light purple stone, blanketed in dust.

An amethyst, like the one in my father's book.

She was real. Lady Jayne was real.

And something very real had happened to her.

A tingling fear invaded my body and propelled me from

the room. Candle in hand, I slipped out the doorway and down the hall.

Footsteps sounded deep in the shadows, echoing against stone. Paranoid, I turned and walked back the way I'd come. The footsteps sped up, *click-click*ing with rapid beats, and I hastened my steps. But the sound grew closer. When I turned with the candle, I spotted the outline of a man moving along the passage toward me. Fear gripped me. Overcome with the notion of ghosts and horrible murders in these very halls, I abandoned all caution and sprinted, hand out before me.

At that moment a wall rose up and collided with my body. I crumpled with a cry, fingers pressing into the pain in my temple. Blackness swept over me and muted my senses. Moments passed. Then light flickered on the hallway walls, brightening with approaching footfalls. Turning over and planting my hands behind me for support, I watched a figure close the distance in seconds, and there he stood, his dusty gray suit hanging open over me, muttonchops lining his jaw. "What are you doing here?"

"Only exploring. I've just arrived." My arms shook under the weight of my upper body and my vision swirled.

Angry eyebrows lowered. "No. What are you doing here . . . at my home? Isn't it enough that you've already stolen my work from me?"

"I've stolen nothing, that I promise."

A long growl radiated from his broad chest.

"Sir, might I ask who you are? I thought I'd met the whole family."

His jaw twitched, muttonchops jerking. "I am Nathaniel Droll. And I want my stories back."

5

The bright lavender dresses she wore were simply an outward display of Lady Jayne's personality, an expression of the color and joy that overflowed from her soul.

~Nathaniel Droll, *Lady Jayne Disappears*

"Rise and get up, sleepy!" Juliette's voice jarred against the sharp throb in my head as the sound forced me out of sleep. It was morning. I twisted onto my side, legs tangled in the sheets, and groaned. Had I managed to get myself into bed? No, it was the maids. Digory had been there too. Flashes of memory from the previous night swirled through the flood of pain. The room with the purple dresses. The man in the hall. I jerked as a shiver climbed my spine.

Before I could string together the words to ask questions—and really, what on earth could I ask without sounding like a madwoman?—Juliette approached the bed and flung an armload of bright fabric onto it. "I've brought you a dress for the day, but only one."

"I'm sure it's lovely." Would the girl remain all morning? I massaged the splitting pain in my forehead, eyes closed.

"I do hope you're feeling better today." Her voice softened and the bed sank at the edge under her weight. "How's your head?"

Forcing myself up, I leaned against the headboard and continued the gentle massage. "Still attached, it seems."

Juliette giggled, eyes sparkling. "Good. You'll look much better in the gown I brought for you today. Aren't you going to ask me why I brought only one?"

I opened my eyes and fingered the gown—a green-and-yellow affair with stripes that somehow managed to be feminine. "The dressmaker from Bristol. She's coming today."

"Yes! She's bringing a full swath of samples and fabrics and everything you could want." Juliette took my hands. "We're to start right away."

"Without breakfast?" My stomach growled.

"I suppose we could manage a hasty breakfast, if you need one." Disapproval shadowed her lovely face.

After gingerly dressing with the help of a chambermaid, whom I forbade to yank my hair into a formal design, I led the way down the stairs. The pounding receded with my slow steps and long inhales of fresh air pouring through open windows in the great hall.

In the morning room, Glenna and Garamond stood near the sideboard, Glenna leaning over to spoon more oatmeal. "Yes, but she simply does not belong. You cannot shove a bird into a rabbit nest and hope it survives. I'll talk to Mother about it presently, in very strong terms."

Garamond's eyes widened as he spotted us, his finger jamming into his wife's fleshy arm.

"You needn't always shush me, you know. I'm more than a mantelpiece decoration in your life. My opinions needn't—"

One final shove stopped the flow of words my curiosity desperately wanted to hear but my soft heart wished to shut out.

"Good morning, Mama. Father." Juliette brushed into the room, smile in place.

I only followed because she'd gripped my wrist like a shackle and yanked me along. Juliette fit in here. Mask in place, she could glide about as if she'd heard nothing. I, however, would need a dark room and a good cry before I could appear such.

A slamming door in the great hall broke the tension. Footsteps clicked on the tile and voices carried in to us. "I'll announce your arrival." Digory appeared at the door. "A Miss Flossy Payne to see you. May I say you are at home?"

"Oh, of course we're at home! Tell her to meet us in Miss Harcourt's suite immediately." Laying hold of my hand, Juliette pulled me out the door and up the stairs again, plates abandoned. When did wealthy women have a chance to eat?

The whole affair felt awkward and somehow degrading as the two women spun and measured my body. *My* body. Had Papa really wanted all this for me?

"And our wonderful Miss Wicke will do the embellishments." Juliette took a servant girl by the arms and swung her out of her shadowed corner where she'd stood like furniture. "She does our sewing, and she makes the most lovely adornments on the gowns."

The slender young woman, with hair severely parted and

pulled back, tolerated the girl's embrace before backing into position again. Her plain face held the gravity of one who had endured a hundred burdens already, but carried none of the lines of age.

"I knew a man named Harcourt once." The dressmaker from Bristol, a pleasantly eccentric woman with frizzy hair, broke into my thoughts.

Juliette spoke up before I could answer. "He isn't likely any relation to Aurelie. My cousin comes from far away, with no relations around besides us."

I did not correct the mistruth.

"Ach, 'twouldn't be the same one, then. Pity. A clever one, he was. The man swooped in and out of my life just that quick, but I still remember him, clear as ever. Must be five and twenty years past or more." Her eyes sparkled with the evocative memory. "Wouldn't mind happening upon him again."

"A romantic tryst. It sounds fabulously dramatic." Juliette smiled, dimples brightening her lovely face.

"The man's middle name might have been romance, for the way he swept me away." A wide grin spread over her face. "Such stories he told."

"Oh, do tell us about the trysts," Juliette urged. "I must know the whole story."

"I'm sure she has enough to do, measuring for dresses." My small voice cut through the terrible conversation barreling toward things I did not wish to hear. It couldn't be Papa she spoke of, could it?

Juliette flashed me a pert look with a question in her eyes at my rudeness. "We've nothing else to do while she measures. Why not let her tell it?"

The story of the woman's romantic three-day tryst unfolded, including long descriptions of a man with a grand presence, hearty laugh, and money to spare. It sounded like no one but Papa. But this woman couldn't be my mother. Couldn't. *Flossy Payne. Lady Jayne.*

No.

When the woman finally made her exit, a trail of cockney-tinged words following her down the hall, I shoved the story into the attic of my mind. I buried it in a dark corner and covered it with many sheets, never to be revisited except in some rare, unforeseen need.

"Now we must find Father in the library and send Miss Wicke into Bristol for all the things we'll need."

After dressing, I followed Juliette and Miss Wicke to the library, the room I'd craved since arriving, but it turned out to be wholly disappointing. Lined with half-sized bookshelves, the space was dominated by an ivory-and-black fireplace, taxidermy on the walls, and a large walnut desk where Garamond Gaffney sat. In this room, where books should be overwhelming and abundant, they were a mere afterthought.

"Father, Miss Wicke must use the carriage to buy things for Aurelie's gowns. Please tell her it's all right, would you?" Juliette spoke with the confidence of being granted her request.

And of course she was.

"Where do you plan to make your purchases, Miss Wicke?" The balding man dipped his pen in the ink and wrote on the documents before him. Agreeing to his daughter's whims had apparently become such a habit that he needn't even give it his exclusive attention.

The young maid stepped from the shadows. "I might find

most things in Glen Cora, but I'm not certain they will have all the specialty items Miss Juliette has requested."

"Of course, of course. Go to Bristol if need be. Bring the notes to me, and I'll pay them."

Bristol? I stepped forward. "Perhaps I should accompany Miss Wicke. I might be able to offer an opinion on things. And I'd so enjoy a day outdoors. My heart craves the sunshine."

At this, Garamond dropped the pen into the inkwell and looked up with a patronizing smile. "If it would do your heart good, my dear. Only that leaves Juliette alone for the day."

A voice came from the shadows of the library. "I would be honored to escort your daughter on the horse trails." Rotherham shifted against a bookshelf, where he paged through a red leather volume.

"Agreed. Well then, be on your way."

Why was that man everywhere, in the most intimate parts of this family's life? How had he earned such a place, and why ever did he want it?

I persuaded the ever-silent Miss Wicke to drop me off on the way to Bristol in front of an overflowing curiosity shop and return for me after her errands were completed. Doubt flitted over the woman's puckered brow, but she did not spend her few words on trying to dissuade me.

Clutching a notebook wrapped in brown paper, I pressed through the town toward the familiar rows of crumbling houses and streets bowed up the center like an inverted spine. How fortunate to find a means of escape today. Future visits would have to be made to post all the coming installments, but those could be arranged when the time came.

Thank you, sovereign Lord.

Nearing the prison, memories cinched my gut, sending my heart into overtime. How had Papa so easily slipped into the background of my mind since leaving Shepton Mallet? Life had started over at Lynhurst, but returning here, even to the outer gates, his death seemed suddenly more real and recent. The wound split open, fresh and raw, the ache caving in on me.

With a shuddering breath, I turned left before reaching the prison and walked down the narrow Headrow Lane to number 32, the familiar thatch-roof cottage with crumbling stone walls that belonged to Shepton Mallet's only physician and coroner, and one of the few friends Papa and I had from the outside—for no one entered Shepton Mallet unless paid or forced.

Climbing the steps and dodging the broken one, I knocked on the door. A bang and clatter sounded inside, and the door swung open.

"Well, well. She has returned." Jasper Grupp's fingers slithered over his two-day stubble, blue eyes snapping with interest. "Just as easily as she set me aside for a sleek carriage ride with a top hat."

"I need my mail, Jasper. If you would." I had once found those intense blue eyes ringed with midnight sky utterly captivating.

His mouth turned up in a devilish smile. "You don't look like you need nothing, your majesty. All fine and feathered in that costume."

"I'd like to speak to your father." Heat radiated from my overdressed body, perspiration gathering across my belly and neck.

He turned and thunked his broad back against the door frame, arms folded over his chest, watching me. "Take and plunder at will, my lady. You know your way about the place."

I hesitated at the door, considering retreat. But I needed the royalty payment that would certainly have arrived. Chin high, I grasped my wrapped notebook and moved past him.

But he grabbed my package as I glossed by, spinning me around and hissing in my face. "What a liar. Fix your hair and wear anything you like, but you're no better'n me. Never was. How long before they know it too, prison rat?" Rage fueled by pain streamed out of his ice-blue eyes and flared his nostrils. His dirty hand squeezed my wrist, his other hand still clutching my wrapped book.

I pounded my heel into his foot and yanked the package from his grasp. As he coiled in pain, I shoved past him into the one-room hovel. "My father was always a gentleman. Throwing a man in prison doesn't change who he is."

He straightened and followed me inside. "Neither does a woman's dress."

"Well, look who's returned to us so soon!" Jasper's father thudded down the ladder from the loft and landed with a floor-shaking thump between us. I relaxed in his jolly presence as Jasper backed into a dark corner. "Right glad I am to see ye, my girl. Have ye got something for me?" His voice vibrated off the walls, filling the little home.

I shoved the wrapped book into the man's hands, glad to have it away from Jasper. "I have this for you to post, Mr. Grupp, and I believe a letter may have arrived for me."

"Of course, of course." The man pawed through papers on a narrow desk against the wall and returned with the familiar long envelope from Marsh House Press. "'Ere ye be, lassie." He shifted and looked me over as a shepherd looking over a returned sheep for injury. "Folks miss ye in the Mallet. Miss them stories and yer healin' touch. A few claim that little hand on a man's brow cures up the meanest infection."

"Thank you." Meeting the old man's friendly eyes, I felt tears prick mine. What sort of girl actually missed debtor's prison? But I did. So badly. A few days at Lynhurst, in the life I'd dreamed of, and I ached for the old one. What an ungrateful wretch.

As Jasper glowered in the corner, a decision solidified in my mind. Death had occurred, whether or not I'd chosen it, and life had pivoted. I turned to Mr. Grupp, heart full. "You have no idea how I miss you, and all the others. You've been such a kind friend to Papa and me all these years, and I cannot thank you enough."

Gray eyebrows arched up. "That do sound like a goodbye of sorts."

I nodded. "I believe it is. I will have these letters directed to a new address closer to my new home." My gaze flicked with meaning toward Jasper, then back. "But I do appreciate your cherished friendship. It will never be forgotten. *You* will never be forgotten."

"A fine kettle it is, losing all the excitement in our lives, and me favorite girl, too. These mystery packages ye bring are the only thing of consequence happening about the place. And you steppin' into this house is the prettiest thing to happen to this ol' hole. We'll miss ye, won't we, Jas?" The older Grupp gently squeezed my shoulder. Then in a kind whisper, "Ye do what ye need to, little Aura Rose."

Jasper gave a pinch-lipped smile from his corner where he watched the exchange.

Giving the old man a quick hug that crunched the envelope against me, I left the pair and stepped back into the cloudy outdoors, delighting in Mr. Grupp's words. They were true—just beyond those walls, arms would be thrown open to me in welcome. The sick would ask for me and my stories. My life would be poured out for those who needed comfort.

But I couldn't make my life at the Mallet anymore, for I owed no one a farthing. Instead, because of my great luck, I must return to Juliette, my cold aunt, and the echoey house where I must scheme to stay on, despite not being wanted. Having not a single penny allowed a person to live with all the freedom in the world, and having everything sometimes meant a person had nothing at all. For in truth, it was a slow death to find one's self utterly unneeded.

The sound of footfalls behind me tugged at my thoughts, but I continued. The clops neared until a hand yanked my arm and spun me around. "There's a thin line between love and hate, you know. And you're standing on the wrong side of it."

"Hate me all you want, Jasper. I'll not have anything to do with you."

"But I will have much to do with you."

"What we had is fully in the past. What possible thing still ties me to you?"

His eyes narrowed. "Oh, I wish you hadn't asked that, princess. Would you really care to hear the answer?"

6

In her unwillingness to stand out and possibly appear foolish, Abigail instead became entirely invisible.

~Nathaniel Droll, *Lady Jayne Disappears*

Rain chilled the air outside the closed-up curiosity shop where I waited for Miss Wicke to return and pushed Jasper's threats from my mind. The man was only a bitter, jilted suitor wishing to make me squirm. He couldn't truly do anything dangerous to me, could he?

But he did possess a remarkable ability to deceive. I myself had experienced his expertise in this matter.

The approaching carriage stood out among the wagons and horses in town. Eager to sink into the cushioned seats, I lifted my skirts above the puddles and sprang toward the vehicle as it stopped. Rain had drenched everything. As I reached out for the glossy black door, a boot came from above and crunched my hand. I cried out and the foot jerked and kicked me, sending me reeling back from the carriage door. With an awkward pinwheel of arms, I stumbled back and fell into the muddy road, limbs tangled in crinoline and fine fabric.

"Miss! Oh, please forgive me." The coachman jumped the rest of the way down from his perch atop the carriage and hovered, helping and patting. His face creased with more worry wrinkles than a hound. "I was coming to open the door for you. You shouldn't have walked through the mud alone. Truly, I'm sorry."

Miss Wicke's pale, wide-eyed face peered down from the carriage window, watching the scene unfold. Mud spatter cooled my cheek and I simply looked at them, taking in their expressions. The two of them looked for all the world like the moon had crashed into the earth. I splashed the mud and giggled. "Well now, that's one way to justify a hot bath."

Tension cut, the coachman pulled me to my feet with an embarrassing *shlep* as the mud released me. Miss Wicke threw open the door, and together they delivered me, sopping wet and mud drenched, to my seat in the carriage after covering the cushion with burlap.

Puffing out a quick exhale, I smiled at the little seamstress and collapsed into the seat, tailbone throbbing where it had struck the ruts in the road. "And now I am well equipped to describe a woman falling into a puddle, if that should come about in a story."

Miss Wicke gave a tiny smile. "You're not really a lady, are you?" But then she whipped a finger to her pinched lips, cheeks reddening. "I do not mean—I mean to say—"

"Quite all right." I held up a hand to wave off her concern as the carriage jerked forward, sailing past the paint-chipped storefronts of Glen Cora. "I most certainly am not a lady, especially at this moment. And I delight in that fact."

"Might I ask something, miss?" The woman's face had eased into a more natural expression.

"Of course. Nothing bonds two women more than stripping away all that makes us dignified, right?"

We shared another smile, and the seamstress studied me. "Who are you, exactly?"

Who was I? My father's daughter, more than anything. A lifelong resident of Shepton Mallet. An interloper among my family. But especially, I was now Nathaniel Droll. "I'm not entirely sure how to answer that."

"It's just that, well, Lady Pochard isn't given to charity. She rarely has relations come to stay."

Head back against the soft leather cushion, I sighed. "Suppose I make up a story about who I am. It'd likely be more fascinating, and more romantically beautiful." Until Jasper had threatened to spill where I'd come from, I'd had no idea to be ashamed of it.

The girl's smile invited the story. I launched into a touching tale of the young working-class woman who hides from the wealthy man who loves her so he doesn't marry her and lose his inheritance.

The seamstress perched on the seat, hands clasped and tucked between her knees. "What a beautiful tale. Please tell me at least some of it's your true story. You make me want to run right out and find that man and tell him where you are. And then witness the reunion."

I sighed and glanced at the girl in the swaying carriage. "I only wish I had a worthy man who loved me. My real secrets are nothing wonderful."

"I understand, truly. I have ugly secrets of my own."

The heavy words caught my attention, stimulating the part of me always sensitive to story ideas.

Easy silence settled over us for several minutes, but my head spun with possibilities as colorful as the bright green fields we passed. Was she an illegitimate child of aristocracy? She spoke so well, carried herself with grace. Maybe she was a cousin, born to someone at Lynhurst as well. I gripped my knees. Ah, the beauty! Two relations separated who later find one another as friends and kindred spirits.

The closed face across from me did not invite any personal questions, though. Perhaps if I began with something less personal. "Now I have a question for you, Miss Wicke. Who on earth is Silas Rotherham, and why is he hanging about?" It had niggled at my mind for days.

"I'd love if you would call me Nelle, as if we were chums. And Mr. Rotherham. Well, he is an old family friend who never had occasion to improve acquaintances with the family, until suddenly . . . he did. He came at the start of the London season to visit his old school chum Kendrick. Leastwise that's what he claims, but he asks an awful lot of questions about relations, fortunes, and the like."

I considered the words. "Such a silent man. As if he's judging everything and finding fault. Yet it sounds as though he's the one with the fault."

"He's hardly different than any other man swayed by the temptation of what's right before him."

"Surely the family is suspicious of him."

She smiled. "Hardly. Sniffing around for details on the family's fortune is a purely acceptable motivation, if you're a prospective suitor."

"So he merely wishes to discover the amount of Juliette's fortune? That seems like a simple goal that would not keep the man here an entire summer."

"Yes, but if one hopes to *influence* that number, he might find himself, you know . . . deeply interested in the matters of the household." Her prim smile conveyed much.

Back at Lynhurst, heat climbed my face as I was forced to repeat the story of my "mishap" to every servant I passed. The sludge still hung in heavy chunks on my dress, and my skin had become tight with it. But still, it was only mud. Why couldn't they stop exclaiming over me as if I were bleeding profusely?

Holding up my skirts to keep the grime away from the pristine tile, I snuck through the halls toward the stairs. As long as I could make it past the main part of the house without being seen by the family, it would be all right. The chambermaids would begin carrying water up to my suite before I even reached it. I could bathe away my disgrace, don fresh clothes, and once again take my place among my family.

Ahead, the hallway spilled into the grand entrance with a clear escape up the staircase. It was empty, but the library doors stood open. I held my breath to sneak past. Silas Rotherham and Garamond hunched over papers inside, low murmurs and pipe smoke floating about.

Once past the doors, I sprinted lightly toward the stairs, the toes of my ankle boots tapping across the tile as I watched the doors of the library. Five feet from the first step, I collided face-first with a pillowy mass and stumbled backward, nose smarting from the impact.

"Oh!" Glenna's shrill voice echoed in the two-story hall. "Oh, my heavens!" She pawed desperately at her dress where we'd hit and backed away. Desperate hands flitted around her marred frock.

I lunged back, feeling like a leper, and bumped something hard behind me. *Crash.* A blue vase shattered on the floor around my feet, the pieces rocking, then coming to rest in the silent hall. Fresh-cut flowers lay in a puddle of water. I shook.

The men charged out of the library like a rescue brigade, Garamond flitting around his distressed wife. Digory and a handful of lace-capped servants streamed from doorways, blocking my escape. One of the maids dropped to her knees before Glenna and scrubbed the dress with her apron as if the mud were flames.

"Get this wild girl away from this house at once. I shan't be attacked in my own home."

Hot and perspiring from scalp to foot, I stiffened, arms held away from my muddy clothes.

Juliette rushed in, steadying her mother by the arms. "What's happened? Are you hurt?"

"Look at the sort of madwoman your grandmother has welcomed into our home. Just look at her."

Gazes turned toward me, and Jasper's words of condemnation rang through my hassled mind. The odor of raw mud tinged my nostrils and a chill from wet stockings climbed my legs. I'd have given anything to disappear in a poof and reappear before a huge horse trough, where I might jump in fully clothed and bathe.

And then the image of the man from the night before swirled and took root in my mind. *I want my stories back.*

Nathaniel Droll, the pen name, in the flesh. But no one else had seen him. No one. Perhaps I really was mad. Dizziness pulled on me, toying with my balance.

Suddenly Nelle was there at my elbow, propelling me toward the servants' hall. As we hurried out, Rotherham glanced around with politely veiled disgust. To my surprise, his look was not directed toward me and my muddy clothes, but toward Glenna.

Tears pricked my eyes as we climbed the servants' stairs together, behind a maid hauling a copper pot with water sloshing onto the uneven steps.

"Something told me I should remain with you. I'm sorry I didn't heed it."

Tears fell then. "It was God, I'm sure. He knew I'd need you."

Closed in the quiet bedroom upstairs, Nelle helped me untie, unlace, and unbutton, laying the muddied clothing across chairs as it was shed. "A house full of fanatics, and you're the only one who talks about God that way. As if you really believe he's floating about, ready to pull us up from a fall. It's quite nice, you know."

I sniffed and released a calming sigh, shaking away the need to cry more.

"And that was devilish rude of her, what she did. But she's always been that way. The woman should be on the stage. I heard she gave quite a performance last night when you fell in the hall."

"You heard about that?"

"Of course, miss." She smiled, turning me around to undo the ties of my chemise. "It drew quite a crowd. Especially when Glenna and her set of lungs reached the scene. Drew every last servant in the house, I expect."

"I don't recall seeing any of them."

"Oh, you wouldn't, miss. That's what happens when you have a concussion." She pulled my hair together and piled it onto my head with a comb. "It's probably better you don't remember. That woman's dramatics would have made you want to fall through the floor with embarrassment. Any little upset, and she cries as if the roof's falling in."

I laughed with relief and swiped a palm across my face. It had been a hallucination. I'd struck my head on the wall and hallucinated the whole run-in with Nathaniel Droll. I stepped behind the divider hiding the tub from the rest of the room and peeled off the loosened chemise. I sank into the warm water, easing my chilled body in as low as it would fit.

Her voice grew louder to reach beyond the partition. "This house simply *oozes* religion, but has precious little of God. They've even built their own chapel right on the grounds— which, I might add, has likely never heard a sermon on decent human kindness."

Nelle appeared to place a fuzzy towel and dressing gown on the chair and remove my wet clothes from the floor, then disappeared again. How like Jesus serving his followers. And how unlike the family that was supposed to love me as one of their own.

"It goes far beyond what you saw today, Nelle. So very far." I scrubbed mud from my arms until my skin was red. Jasper's threats again floated back to me, mingling with my aunt's introduction of me as a mere "relation." "Did you ever hear of Lady Pochard's younger brother, Woolf Harcourt?"

"Lady Pochard has a brother? She's never spoken of him."

"She wouldn't, of course." Pain constricted my chest at the admission. Poor Papa. "He died a pauper in debtor's prison. Even with all that wealth, the woman would not extend help to him. I am that brother's daughter, and I spent my entire life with him in Shepton Mallet Prison until his death. There, that's my story. See? Far less fit for a fairy tale."

"Well, it's something of a fairy tale, coming from Shepton Mallet to a place like this."

"Will you keep this a secret? My aunt is quite ashamed of it. I am becoming so too, I must admit."

"As well she ought to be!" Her voice softened. "But not you. Shame is reserved for those who disappoint God, not people."

"What words of wisdom."

"Have you seen the way she treats poor Lord Gaffney? The man isn't the shrewdest bloke, but he never gets the kind end of her glances."

"Whatever has he done to her?"

"He married her daughter, that's what. He was the house steward when they still had the London townhouse. A gentl'man, but still very much in service."

I couldn't stop a grin from stealing over my face. Glenna, the stuffed peacock afraid to besmirch her gowns or her reputation, had married a servant. Papa had been right—the walls were bursting with stories. And I must remain among them as long as humanly possible.

Skin tingling from the warm bath and fuzzy towel, I stretched out alone across an open space on the pale rug in my room, wrapped in clean clothes with a notebook and pen before me. Something about Nelle captivated me. It wasn't her looks—which were better than ugly and less than splendid—but her remarkable love. Gratitude mixed with awe compelled me to pen a new character into my novel—Lady Jayne's close friend, Abigail. Nelle had confided that she had always been lost in the background. I had the power to change that, to immortalize the sweet girl in a novel.

Beautiful women rarely find true friendship among their own gender, but when they do, it speaks highly of such a friend's great worth. Abigail was one such friend to Lady Jayne. A girl with gold-spun hair and delicate grace, she was oft called plain by the world, if she was called anything at all.

And when Lady Jayne's suitor happened upon the pair in the entryway one day, he paused in hanging his greatcoat and took in the sight of them. Lady Jayne smiled coyly, but it was not his love who drew his stare this time, for he was already well-acquainted with her beauty. It was the unusual girl at her side who radiated contentment, a quiet joy that overrode her plain features for reasons he could not determine.

What an odd twist that Charles Sterling Clavey should find Abigail somewhat attractive, but it made me appreciate the man.

Kneeling beside my chair, I ended my writing time by praying for Nelle's future spouse. My deeply romantic heart carved out a picture of the kind, affirming man who would recognize in Nelle the beauty of a lovely soul and cherish her as he ought. To that one man, Nelle would never be invisible.

Dressed in a lilac dress a half hour later, I crept down the stairs in soft slippers and met the family in the drawing room. Perhaps none of them would bring up the incident with Glenna. But as we pulled out the heavy dining room chairs, Glenna turned to me, made-up face sparkling with dangerous delight. "Aurelie, I'm so glad you feel well enough to come to dinner. I'd like to make a request of you."

7

She slept very well at night, owing to the fact that she never took her bitterness into bed with her.

~Nathaniel Droll, *Lady Jayne Disappears*

Pheasant and mashed potatoes awaited us on the sideboard in the dining room when we entered. The buttery smell did heavenly things to my senses, despite the nerves twisting my stomach.

"Dearest, let her be seated first." Garamond's whispered words reached the entire room.

"But it's such a marvelous story, and she simply must share it before I burst."

Aunt Eudora's lips pinched in sour disapproval—a trademark expression, to be sure, for the wrinkles around her mouth so easily slipped into the pucker. The old woman took her time being seated and directing the staff as they served the food to each person. Several long moments passed, in which I eagerly hoped the matter would be forgotten.

But Glenna never forgot another woman's moment of downfall. "Miss Harcourt, do tell us the whole thing. And start with whatever happened to drench you in mud in the first place. It must have been a dreadful story." Glenna's awful smile looked as though it would crack her face.

I cleared the mashed potatoes from my throat. "It was a simple misstep into the carriage."

"Come, now. There must be more to the catastrophe than that."

My gaze lifted and met Silas Rotherham's gray eyes, and the tenderness I found there comforted me. He offered a small, private smile and I returned it. My throat tight, I silently commanded the tears to stay back.

He restoreth my soul.

He leadeth me in the paths of righteousness for his name's sake.

Verses repeated often by Papa, redirecting and refocusing me. Releasing the tension, connecting me to God, fading the evils of the world into the background. And suddenly a calming power swept over me, cooling the heat of embarrassment. Offering strength. Tell a story—that's all Glenna had asked me to do. The one thing I did well.

It's always a choice, Aura Rose. Happiness is always a choice.

My back straightened, shoulder blades hitting the chair back, and the story flowed like clear water poured from a cup, just as Papa had taught me. Starting with the comical splash into the mud, I wove through the details until Glenna's voice broke through my near trance.

"And then she broke the blue-flowered vase in the hall." She clapped. "The priceless one Papa brought you from London."

She turned her animated face toward me. "Truly, it was like a game of dominoes, was it not, Miss Harcourt?" As if she were magnanimously making light of the situation for my sake.

Aunt Eudora's eyes blazed toward me. "You broke my Royal Worchester?"

"I'm so sorry. I bumped it by accident and—"

Her frown cut off the rest of my apology. "Do you think it possible to refrain from ruining my belongings while you accept my hospitality?"

I ducked my head. "Yes, my lady." But uncertainty pulsed through me at my ability to keep such a promise, and at the hopelessness of my fate in this house.

"It looked as if she'd rolled around in the mud." Glenna's voice trilled into laughter.

Garamond, always the man at Glenna's side, laughed heartily, encouraging his wife's witty remarks. Harder and harder he laughed.

Then he was sputtering and coughing, fumbling for his water.

"Oh my. Oh, Garamond." Glenna rose and uselessly delivered a set of uneven pats to his back. He coughed and blotted his face, waving her off. Finally he rose, eyes watering, and charged out of the room to collect himself in private, Glenna on his heels. In a moment I also left with graceful strides, heavy skirt whishing on the carpet.

Reaching the empty great hall, I lifted my dress hem and ran, thankful for solitude. My exposed ankles felt the coolness of freedom as I flew down a narrow hall.

Perhaps I should simply return to my bedchamber. I'd done enough damage for the day. But a few paces more revealed a light streaming from the west, where my memory had painted nothing but a wall. The mystery of it coaxed me down the narrow hall to a haven of plants through double glass doors. Pushing inside, I stepped down into a glass-walled sanctuary of fruit trees, flowering plants, and vines that crowded toward the low ceiling. A piece of heaven it was, hidden away down a hall that had seemed to yawn open just now from the darkness. Inhaling deeply of the floral air, I ducked under low-hanging branches to a metal bench against the far windows, where I curled into the hard seat, knees to my chest, and talked to the One who accepted me already, thanking him for my rescue, and for this secret moment of beauty.

God, I truly do not belong here.

Where did I belong, if not here at Papa's dear Lynhurst Manor?

With Papa, that's where. I fit into his world, by his side. We worked like elements of a steam engine that hummed in efficiency together down the track. Without Papa, I had only our shared story to comfort me. Eyes closed, I tried to push myself into the world of Lady Jayne's tale, but it kept escaping my grasp. Uncertainty wet-blanketed my creativity.

As the setting sun glowed orange and red against the bright green landscape, lighting the water in the tiny fountain beside me, footsteps approached.

Mr. Droll?

I shook my head, but I couldn't dispel the premonition that I was about to glimpse this man again. The doors creaked open and black-suited legs carried a man obscured by foliage through the conservatory.

Concussion. It had been a concussion before.

It was Silas Rotherham who ducked under the branches. Of course it would be him. Releasing my breath and forcing myself to concentrate, to not make a foolish move, I masked my childish fears and focused on a flowerless lily plant at my feet.

With a long exhale Mr. Rotherham sat on the bench, dropping a bunched-up linen napkin on the table beside me. Split-top rolls tumbled out of its folds. Was it that obvious I was starving? Enough that he felt the need to feed me. My body heated beneath the heavy fabric of my ill-fitting, borrowed gown.

For moments we sat, his relaxed posture denying any awkwardness existed between us. Finally he drew his gaze up. "Have I ever told you how to rid yourself of distressful ants?"

I blinked. We were discussing ants?

"Do away with the uncles."

I spit out a laugh, muscles relaxing, and shook my head. "They are my cousins, actually." What an odd sort of man.

"Cousins. That's the first bit of information I've gotten from you." He held out a roll as if we were seated at a formal table and I had just asked him to pass them.

"Is he all right?"

"Gaffney? He isn't choking anymore, if that's what you mean."

I covered my face with my hands. "I certainly have a talent for mistakes, don't I? He looked so pitiful when he ran from the room."

Adjusting himself on the seat, Mr. Rotherham thought for a moment, ignoring my comment. "He reminds me of a character in another Nathaniel Droll novel."

"Simon Long, in *Tempest and Trouble*." That had been one of Papa's fast and furious novels, dictated with clarity and rapid ideas I could barely keep up with. Perhaps Mr.

Rotherham's observation of the two men's similarities was closer than he would guess. For very likely, the balding little man at dinner had inspired Papa's fictional character.

Rotherham glanced at the ceiling as he recalled the words of the book. "'A man gentle to the point of stupidity, who clung to his wife with a childish obsession.'"

Not the exact wording, but a decent paraphrase. I reached for a roll as I spoke. "What of Juliette? She sometimes strikes me as Estella, from Dickens's *Great Expectations*. A bit cunning and worldly."

"You cannot judge someone who is merely a product of circumstances. Nothing they could help—either of them." His defense slipped out quickly, quietly. As if he'd thought it through before and circled back to that conclusion several times.

"Both of those women have brains. If you've known Juliette for half a day, you'd know she's well equipped to make her own decisions."

His chin jerked, and he frowned. "Whenever I read *Great Expectations*, I pity Estella. We are all driven by our most important experiences, but Estella never had that privilege. She inherited Miss Havisham's and was taught—no, brainwashed—to act on them."

I studied his face, the shadowed planes that hid such depths. Did he really think of Juliette that way? A helpless victim of her circumstances, as Estella was? "Don't you find her a bit foolish to let others control her that way?" I bit into the soft roll, relishing the food about to reach my starving belly.

"She is both controllable and headstrong, neither of which are appealing traits. But Pip saw something of value in the girl, to the point of obsessing over her."

I forced down the bite and cleared my throat. Obsessing. Could Rotherham possibly feel that way about Juliette? "Pip seemed to want her wealthy life as much as he wanted her."

"Of all the characters, Pip was the most misguided one, working so hard to join the wealthy. He could never possibly fit in, no matter his efforts."

Poor Pip, who only wanted to belong somewhere, to someone. I frowned as I finished my bite and swallowed. "All people learn to be the way they are, including the rich. Why couldn't Pip?" And indeed, why not myself?

"But you see, he couldn't have belonged. In his very nature, he was never one of them."

My very nature. That's what was broken, what would never belong. It was not Glenna, not my cold aunt Eudora, not even the demands of society itself. I was the one in disrepair. "Mr. Rotherham, Pip was so alone and unhappy. Is it so terrible of him to want to belong?"

"Silas. Call me Silas. And no, I suppose it is not entirely terrible." His warm hand hovered tentatively over mine on the bench, fingertips grazing my skin, ready to pull back if I demanded it, which I did not. I welcomed the comforting touch of this surprising ally.

Finally he wrapped my hand in his. The contact was solemn, as if born of a deep need to convey his thoughts through both word and touch. "It's quite all right to not fit in sometimes. It's desirable, actually."

Thoughtful, I reached to the side for another roll, anticipating more of the crusty delight even though I'd filled my belly, but only crumbs remained on the napkin.

Silas's quick smile revealed his fleeting dimples again. "You've eaten them all. Shall I find you more? Perhaps the braised pudding I saw on the sideboard when I requested the rolls."

The thought of braised pudding—or any sort of pudding—tickled my taste buds, but I shook my head. "I am currently full of rolls and deep thoughts. No part of me shall go hungry."

He leaned close, still clasping my hand with his. "I do so love asking you questions. I am always rewarded with an answer richer than chocolate."

"Tonight, every thought I have slips out before I can think. You have made my tongue glib with your kindness."

"Have I?" He smiled serenely, nestling one finger into my fist to loosen it, and placed a little chocolate piece in my palm.

Chocolate. And a smile richer than fudge.

"Do not say no, Miss Harcourt. You needn't ever stand on pretense with me. Let this be a sweet ending to a troublesome night. And I thank you for the conversation."

He rose, gaze still on me, and ducked under palm fronds to back out of the tiny space we'd shared. With a backward glance full of warmth through the leaf fingers, he straightened his suit coat on his shoulders and left the room.

I released my breath as the room stilled in his absence. What a complicated novel character. He was disarming, yet elitist. Serious, yet playful. And any man who could melt my embarrassment and provide me with a momentary sense of self-worth in the face of ridicule from my own family deserved at least a measure of my respect.

With long, slow strides, Silas meandered through the silent hall with no rush to return to the men. It was only another game of billiards, which would be repeated nearly every night. But that girl's words hung on him, weighty and rich, and he meant to ponder them alone.

How did she always do that? No matter what intelligent thought he put forth, she turned it upside down, made him think. He never wanted to leave her presence. In the words of Nathaniel Droll, she "climbed into his head and moved the furniture around." Dust had settled over his stagnant beliefs, arranged just so in his mind. Yet she made sure they shifted just a little—or fully stood on their heads—every time they talked.

"Pardon me, sir." Digory slipped out of the shadows and extended a long envelope with a red wax seal. "This has come for you, sir. I thought it best to wait for a private moment."

"Thank you, Digory."

How had he not seen the man? The butler blended into Lynhurst as if he'd grown out of the gold-papered walls—just a part of the great house, like the gilded mirror or the ornate doors. The man had likely witnessed a great deal over the years.

Silas tucked the letter inside his suit coat and rocked back on his heels. "I've just come from a pleasant conversation with Miss Harcourt, and I wanted to thank you for the rolls." Hands in his pockets, Silas focused on remaining casual. "You remember the girl's father, I imagine, don't you?"

"Of course I do. Mr. Harcourt was one of the most extraordinary men I've had the pleasure of knowing."

"It's a shame he was cut off from this family. All because of a woman." Drop just a few of the pieces he'd overheard to imply he knew everything, and . . .

"Aye, the man never knew a stranger. But no one in this

house could forget what happened with poor Jayne Wind-ham."

Silas blanketed his shock with a placid expression. Who on earth was Jayne Windham?

I couldn't face Glenna. Not yet. Anger heated my belly at the thought of that woman. No, not anger—deep embarrassment. I curled into a chair before the windows in an unused drawing room toward the rear of the house with an empty notebook. The writing part of my brain quickly strung together harsh, pointed sentences that would pierce the woman's bubble with remorse and validate me. If only I had the courage to speak them. How vindicating it would be. Then I could move forward and stop smoldering over the whole thing.

While those sharp sentences zinged around my brain, pushing for release, the notebook before me caught my eye. A solution filtered into my mind. Dare I? This installment did need to be completed immediately. Thoughts firing, I fitted a new nib on the pen, hardly believing what I was about to do.

Shadows moved as the wind blew trees outside the window and my heart sped up. Glancing about to each corner of the room, I saw no one. But why did I feel a terrible presence upon me? Nathaniel Droll had been a hallucination. Nothing real at all. Firming my jaw, I set myself to writing.

Lady Tabitha Toblerone used confidence like honey, drawing important people into an acquaintanceship whenever she could, since she lacked Lady Jayne's youth and beauty. And on

the night of her masked ball, her own schemes
were thwarted when her rival, hidden behind
a bejeweled purple mask, radiated beauty only
magnified by the costume meant to cover her.

Corseted to a dangerous degree, Tabitha
watched Lady Jayne through squinted eyes that
poured malice upon her impossibly exquisite head.
Something about this woman was wrong. No one
possessed beauty so flawless unless such a blessing
was tempered with a life of hardship or lower-
class living. Lady Jayne most definitely had a
secret, and soon she'd uncover it. That thought
alone brought the miserable woman comfort.

Our poor Lady Toblerone, finally overcome
with jealousy, took herself out of the party and
hastened down the hall with gentle pat-pats
from her slippers. She had only one salvation
where Lady Jayne was concerned.

Fumbling in the near-dark hall outside the
kitchen, she slid open the door of the dumbwaiter
and plunged her arm into its great cavernous
space, the movement as habitual as whisking out
orders to her staff. Her fingers found the hidden
stash and drew out a handful of golden delight.
Peanut brittle. Filling her mouth and chewing,
she breathed through her nose and the hard
breaths drew sharp pain under her corset. After a
few more painful breaths, she performed a feat
of fantastic agility to undo a portion of her dress
and loosen the stays below. One must always
make room for what was important.

The salty treat excited her senses and calmed her nerves. After consuming the quantity needed to fill her belly and her obsession, she hurried back to her guests.

With the grace of a born hostess, she descended royally on them, charming smile and perfect posture in place. The gathering sailed smoothly, her daring emerald and lace gown drawing looks of amazement, as she'd intended. Emboldened by the impact she had on her peers, the woman swept from cluster to cluster, giving grand little speeches and even speaking before the entire party.

And after all this show and pomp, it was her maid who finally informed her, well after the party's conclusion, that her gown had not been fully closed in the back, her lacy camisole exposed to the world the entire night. Thus her animosity for Lady Jayne swelled to a dangerous level, igniting the dark side of her creativity as a new, more permanent plan swirled and took root. Only one sure way existed to fully cleanse her little corner of the world from the insidious young woman who had invaded it. And now Lady Toblerone reached for this solution in her desperation . . .

I heaved a sigh as the scene came to a satisfying end and rose, crossing the room to the other windows that overlooked the fountain. Controlling one's temper was perfectly doable, as long as a girl also knew how to write about the villains in her life and give them their due. For a writer, revenge was best saved for an empty notebook where the pen was, indeed, a mighty weapon against her foes.

Footfalls in the hall snapped me from my writing trance, heightening my senses. A man's boots echoed on tile, striding toward my little haven and threatening to intrude upon it. Yet I was the intruder, sneaking into this room into which I had not been invited. Someone must have seen me framed in the window.

Ducking out of sight, I glanced around for a hiding spot. To the left stood a smaller side door and I exhaled as I sprinted to it on silent feet. As the main doors creaked open, I slipped through the side door and closed it behind me.

Stealing up the steps to my bedchamber, my heart fluttering with wicked excitement at my escape, I kicked off my little shoes and prepared for bed, splashing my face with water in the washbasin and tying back my long hair. *And what adventure will you have for me tomorrow, God?*

After nearly a half hour had passed, a cold realization grabbed me and squeezed. My notebook—I'd left it on the window seat in the drawing room.

Flinging a pink-and-gold wrap around myself, I darted out of the room and down the stairs. No one used that space. Dust covered every surface. No one would see my misplaced notebook. I repeated these thoughts as I flew toward it, shaking.

In the desolate room sat my book, opened on the cushions exactly as I'd left it. With a giddy laugh tickling my chest, I snatched the wayward object and paged through it as I headed again for the stairs. Keeping this secret was taking a toll on my nerves. As I thumbed through to see how many pages I'd filled, my eye spotted unfamiliar writing on a lone sheet. I spread the pages open at the spot, curious. The few lines in perfect cursive chilled me to my core.

At this point, you should be beginning to understand the murder. You need not look further than Lynhurst for the killer, but you'll have to search carefully and guard yourself well. Keep digging into the past until you have it right. What I really want to say is this: Go and run away—make off now, dear.

Yours truly,
Nathaniel Droll

8

One unfortunate part about life among the gentry was that those who brimmed with confidence were always the wrong ones to do so.

~Nathaniel Droll, *Lady Jayne Disappears*

That night, visions carried me through never-ending hallways, passages that disappeared, and a shadowy old man chasing me about the house. I awoke often with anxiety that plunged me in and out of sleep like a drowning woman, until finally I threw back the covers and plunked onto the cool floor. This attempt at sleep would only leave me exhausted and fearful as the dreams multiplied.

Lighting a tallow candle on the nightstand, I bit back fear and collected the book from the floor where I'd thrown it the night before. Walking to the window with it, I set my candle on the ledge and thumbed through the pages until I found the writing. Tiredness pulled at me, but I knew the writing before me was real. With steady fingers, I ripped the page from the book and slid it between two other notebooks on the shelf.

So she'd been murdered after all. But who at Lynhurst might be evil enough to kill her? Perhaps Mr. Droll simply wanted me to take the story that direction, to—

Stop. This was madness. Nathaniel Droll did not exist. Well, except in the wild imagination of a young writer who'd hit her head. I hugged my knees to my chest and glanced about the shadowed room.

What would Papa do with all this? *Upset the plot. When life twisted your gut, dive into your story world and twist the plot.* But in my middle-of-the-night frazzled state, I had no idea where to take the next installment.

The walls are literally filled with stories, Aura Rose. They hide in the cracks until a keen eye slows down long enough to pay attention to them. My overtired brain could nearly hear Papa say those words. How many times since my childhood had he uttered them? As if Lynhurst were the only estate with juicy—

Then my roving eye saw it. In the pattern of perfectly dovetailed stones, one sat farther out from the wall. Jumping up and dropping my notebook, I ran to it and tugged, digging my fingernails into the dirty crevices around it. In slow jerks it came loose until I could slide it out from its space and push my hand into the dirty cavity. Nothing but settled dirt and chilly stones.

I replaced the piece of wall but did not give up. Going over that wall in laborious detail, I felt for more hiding spots. Then, ducking behind a vast wall mural, I found another. And in this cavity lay a tin box. I drew it out and flipped open the lid bound to it with rusty hinges to find stacks of letters. Oddly folded scraps of paper and various trinkets and ribbon filled the little thing.

Holding the first letter up to the barely cresting sunrise, I gazed upon my own mother's handwriting for the first time. For it was her name scrawled with fine, feminine cursive at the bottom.

> *The worst has happened. Please, my love. Tell me you can fix everything. This is the last note I will be able to leave you here. We must escape immediately if we are to have any chance together.*

I stared at the page, taking steady breaths and absorbing the implications. Their love *had* been forbidden—so much so that they needed to hide their communication. I picked up the rest of the little missives and read note after note, heart pounding at the words.

> *My fear increases nearly as much as my affection for you. They both grip me with a power that threatens to overwhelm. Please tell me my worries are unfounded.*
>
> ~
>
> *Are you growing concerned? I am, but perhaps I am only paranoid. With our moments together so few, I try not to dwell on it, but surely you see the coming threat. Let us hold each other close in our minds when we cannot do it in body.*
>
> ~
>
> *Your heart resides in my chambers, my love, because that is where you left it when we last met. Do not forget to return and claim it.*

~

I am bursting with joy as we embark upon this secret journey together. Perhaps one day reality shall dash this all away with its chilly waters, but for now, I shall cherish each precious moment with you and make that my reality.

~

Good morning, sunshine of my heart! Come spill your golden rays on me this day. I will walk about in the garden and hope to see you.

~

Time spent with you is never wasted, even if nothing but conversation is accomplished. Whatever you think of me now, after what we shared yesterday, I want you to know how deeply I delight in the brief moments spent in your company.

My heart ached for this pair so deeply in love who were kept apart by small-minded people who could not have understood real love. They'd been allowed only stolen moments together and secret letters. How had they ever managed to marry? They must have been another Gretna Green romance. But even as my mind trailed down that possible path for their story, I knew there was far more to the tragic romance than a mere elopement. But with all that had blocked their path, they couldn't possibly have married any other way. Unless . . .

My mind scrambled to collect all the facts and sort them out from what I'd only assumed. Father had told me about Lady Jayne and their love, but marriage—had he actually mentioned that word? Not once had he called her his wife, only his "love."

My hands shook. The tale became tarnished in my mind as I acknowledged the subtle insinuations now occurring to my reluctant heart. I could not equate the famed Lady Jayne with such impurity, and my writer brain immediately dreamed up the most lovely justifications for what I could not explain in real life. Heroines must be above reproach, and I could not include even a hint of impropriety on her part.

As my mind spun with possibilities too wild to be reality, a knock sounded on my door. Shoving the letters into the box and hiding the whole thing beneath my bed, I hurried to answer.

"Here to help you start the day, miss." The chambermaid bobbed a curtsey and swept into the room. After dressing with the help of this hapless young girl who was wonderfully terrible at tight-lacing my corset, I turned to her and smiled. "Minnie, have you served long in this household?"

"Yes, miss. Ten years this fall."

"What of the other servants? Have any been here twenty or so years?" This would be one way to narrow down the person indicated by that note. The killer would have been here twenty years ago when Lady Jayne had come, and if Nathaniel Droll meant for me to find the guilty one here and now, it must mean he or she remained at Lynhurst.

"Digory has served here his whole life. Most of the others have had a shorter stay than myself. But you can check Lord Gaffney's books, if you'd like. He keeps records of the staff."

"What a brilliant idea. Thank you, Minnie." Of course. He'd been the house steward years ago, and certainly he still retained that level of management, even though he now wore the title of son-in-law.

I readied myself with haste, grateful for a day with looser

constraints about my ribs. Pausing at the doorway, I turned and locked my chamber door, pocketing the heavy key. If Nathaniel Droll wanted to paw through my things, I wouldn't make it easy.

As my stomach growled, I took myself down to the morning room and into the lovely aroma of fresh toast and stewed fruit. Silas and Garamond hovered near the sideboard, speaking in hushed tones over their plates, and Juliette glided toward me, arms outstretched in welcome.

"I knew I'd find you here eventually. Wherever there is food." She offered a brief embrace, then led me toward the sideboard. "Honestly, I'll never know why you insist on eating so much. It's as if you're already thirty and completely finished caring about your appearance. Why, look at my figure." Hands lighting on her corseted waist, Juliette turned this way and that, sneaking sideways glances at Silas Rotherham to see if he, too, heard the invitation to appreciate her figure. "Neither of us can expect our trim figures to last without a little effort."

No sense. The girl had no sense. How could one live without eating? Besides, my figure was more slender than hers. I plunged a silver spoon into a bowl of eggs and heaped them on my plate. Salivating, I tucked a stack of sliced cheese on the side, dropped crusty bread on top like a cherry, and followed Juliette and her single teacup to the couch in the center of the room.

"Don't you delight even a little bit in your waistline?" These last words Juliette whispered, hand flat against her cinched belly.

I smiled coyly and popped a bite of crust into my mouth. "Very much. I delight a great deal in filling it up and testing its capacity." Generous bites of bread and jam followed.

Silas coughed and sputtered, covering a coy smile with his hand and clearing his throat. So they *had* overheard.

When the men excused themselves to embark toward Bristol on business, the awareness of opportunity sparked. As soon as politely possible, perhaps a few minutes before, I escaped Juliette's company, begging the need of solitude. But my deeper need was to quench the thirst of my curiosity, with the study now unguarded.

Slipping between the doors left ajar, I avoided looking into the eyes of stuffed game that bordered the room and focused on finding the staff logs. The neatly organized desk made the search quick and simple. I pulled the ledger from the cabinet and perched on a stiff sofa to read. Flipping through pages, Garamond's typewriter-perfect writing outlined the basic facts of the staff. Skimming the list, I tore out a sheet of paper and recorded the names of every staff member serving before the year I was born and when Lady Jayne had disappeared from Lynhurst. And one by one, every name came off the list as I found a record of their service end-date. The only name remaining was Digory.

But of course, there was the family to consider. I wrote down each name: Aunt Eudora, Glenna, Garamond, Kendrick, and Juliette. Clem would not have been born yet, and perhaps not even Juliette. She had to be at least a year or two younger than me. Tapping my pen against my chin, I crossed out Kendrick's and Juliette's names. If they had been alive then, they would have been mere children.

Tucking the paper into my purse, I snuck out of the room and into the garden through the patio doors for the solitude I'd requested. A lovely floral aroma greeted me in the heady noonday sunshine, and I slowed at the edge of the patio to breathe it in. There were some things about Lynhurst that made it feel like the haven Papa had described.

Soft whinnies drew my gaze toward the stables. Yes, a perfect way to spend my coveted alone time—rubbing the soft noses of horses and looking into their large, serious eyes. I lifted the hem of my pink morning dress and ran, only to lose one of my kid slippers along the way. Limping into the straw-littered building on one shoe, I blinked to allow my eyes to adjust as the earthy smell of animal rolled over me. Before I could make out the dark shapes of horses, a roughened hand grabbed my arm and yanked me back, my shoulder bumping the rough walls as fingers bruised my arm. "Finally left your little castle to be part of the real world again."

"Jasper." My erratic heart recovered as my mind worked to fit this man from my past into my present location. "You have no business here."

"Of course I do." His knowing smile showed white teeth against a dirty face. One bony arm reached over my head to lean against the beam and he moved close, towering over me. "Got business with the princess of the castle. You wouldn't happen to know where I might find her, would you?"

"Stop playing and run home."

"I shall, but I'd like my pockets to be a bit heavier when I go." He leaned back and pulled out empty pockets, scattering crumbs on the ground.

Panic squeezed my chest. With a frown, I pushed past him toward the door. I did not have access to my family's money. Did he really think I would? I was a guest. A barely welcomed one at that.

"I've a loud mouth, you know," his voice called from the

shadows. "And quite a bit to say about dear Princess Aurelie that would shock everyone."

Irate, I spun in the doorway. Why should it matter if my father had died a debtor? "I will not let you do this. Go home, Jasper. Those secrets are all past history."

"I'd call it more of a 'present' condition, seeing as how Nathaniel Droll still seems to be writing."

Hot waves chased an icy chill over my skin. *That* secret.

"'Lady Jayne's voice carried like a sonnet through the empty house and lifted the spirits of even the lowest servant.'"

My stomach turned, hearing my carefully crafted words from the latest installment on his twisted lips. Why had those silly words ever felt beautiful to me? Like a child who has applied her mum's face powder and color and thinks herself beautiful, I'd fooled myself horribly when I'd sat down to fill Papa's notebooks with my writing. Everyone else had the privilege of keeping their thoughts and words buried in a journal by their bed, but not me.

"Yes I did, I took a peek in your package. I figured to myself how this might come in handy, knowing what the little ice princess was always posting to London." He stepped toward me, worn boots scuffing the hard-packed floor as he hemmed me against the wall with his body. "And knock me over, it was a book. A rather famous one, I understand."

"You cannot tell a soul." I hugged my middle.

"Wouldn't dream of it." Palms up, he feigned innocence. "But just to make sure it don't slip out, you know, I might need a little reminding."

I balanced on my one shoe, bare toe from the other foot on the ground to aid. "What is it you want?"

"Oh, I imagine fifteen pounds sixpence would do the trick."

"You saw the money." My most recent payment, the one delivered through Jasper's father, had been exactly that amount.

"With quarterly payments like that, you can afford for one to disappear." His words filled me with ire. "Especially without dear Papa to waste it all away as soon as it comes."

I hated his face. Every last dirt smear and stray hair on his shaggy head. The murders of Papa's mystery novels suddenly made sense—the hate that drove a person to want to wipe another off the earth completely. "I'd rather throw the money in the Thames."

He squinted, the whites of his eyes standing out against the darkness. "Just this one check. Not another shilling shall I ask of you. A fine deal, considering all I know, and all I could do to ruin your pretty little life. Would you like me to tell them about the little babe you hid away? Or the many times the constable locked you up for quick-fingering?"

I balanced on my bare foot, digging my heel into the straw littering the ground. None of it was true, but Jasper Grupp had the ability to make anything he said sound so.

"What'll they do to you then? Throw you out on your ear, I'd wager." He moved closer and brushed a dirty thumb along my jawline. "But don't worry. I'll be right there to catch you when no one else will." He fingered the ends of my hair.

"Wait here. And don't let anyone see you." I limped through the thick carpet of grass to my other shoe, slid it onto my dirty foot, and ran back to the house. Through a garden entrance that led to an unused parlor and up the stairs, I sprinted on my toes to my bedchamber and stopped to catch my breath against the doorframe. What good had I ever seen in Jasper Grupp? Once upon a time I'd seen only his pain. Someone who needed my help. Something in him had moved me to act, to give of myself more than usual.

I should have left this particular hurting person alone.

Snatching the check with its blank payee line, as my father had insisted when he began this scheme, I ran back to the stables and held it out, my fingers reluctant to let it go.

"This means you will not say a word."

"Word of honor, princess." He covered his lips with one dirty finger, backing into the stable shadows. "No one shall know your secret."

But the sour taste of his visit did not depart with him. Doubt still gouged my gut. His look of silent victory had unnerved me in a way I couldn't release.

Horse hooves on the packed ground behind me made me jump. A tall man in dark, neat riding clothes strode with the confidence of ownership into the stable, leading a tall brown stallion. "Beg your pardon, miss. I did not mean to interrupt a meeting." Perfectly shorn blond hair reached light eyebrows. His face, young and bright, beamed with remarkable self-assurance. He must be about my own age. The light in his face was so like Papa's—it drew me in.

"It was a chance encounter with an old acquaintance. Nothing private."

His raised eyebrows made me wonder how long he'd stood in the doorway, holding his horse by the bridle and listening. Why hadn't I heard them approach? Or had fear thrummed up to my ears and covered the sound?

"What's your business at Lynhurst?" he asked.

More footsteps swished in the grass outside. Someone was coming—a distraction that might save me from answering. I stalled, chewing my lip. A shadow crossed the doorway, then Silas Rotherham stood there, his form briefly blocking the sun.

"Ah, there you are, chap." The stranger clapped Silas on the arm. "I was just making myself acquainted with this rather skittish young woman who happens to find herself in my stables." He led the horse past them both into an open stall.

"Kendrick, this is Miss Harcourt. Miss Harcourt, Kendrick Gaffney of Lynhurst. He is Juliette and Clement's older brother, and my schoolmate from Master Chumley's."

"Ah, and now I'm suitably charmed to make your acquaintance." He dusted his gloved hands against each other and extended one, which I took hesitantly. He turned to Silas with a wide grin, as if I had suddenly disappeared. "I suppose you have renewed your acquaintance with my dear sister, have you?"

Silas dipped his head in agreement. "A bit, of course."

"And she was very happy to see you return?" He elbowed Silas.

How terribly awkward. This was not a conversation for me to hear. Especially after what Juliette had told me about Silas.

"Shall we go, then? I'd like to greet Father before the day is too much past."

Silas turned to me. "Would you care to join us back to the house?"

"You mean to say, she isn't in service?" Kendrick frowned, his gaze assessing me. "I thought for sure she was one of my sister's little kittens rescued from the storm and tucked neatly into our warm home."

"Miss Harcourt is a relative come to stay. Although I rather say she's become your sister's rescued kitten, even if she did not pull her out of the storm."

Kendrick cocked one eyebrow and leaned back, arms folded over his chest. "A relative, you say? Why, I thought I'd met every last boring one of them."

A fleeting smile on Silas's lips portrayed the nature of his thoughts. "All the *boring* ones, yes."

Perhaps he was thinking of the puddle hopping and mud. Or of waistlines and rolls. Either way, that he found me amusing was pleasantly obvious.

At least I was of some use to one person in this house.

"Wonderful, then. Of course she must accompany us."

We strode together through the yard, thoughts racing through my head. If only I could grasp one of them and pull it into my command so that at least I might speak in this awkward silence.

But before I could manage a word, Silas laid a gentle hand on my arm. "Actually, Miss Harcourt, I need a word with you. Privately."

9

A good book will enable you to both lose yourself and find yourself.

~Nathaniel Droll, *Lady Jayne Disappears*

A rare gem among women—that's what Aurelie was. Silas watched her hair sway against the back of her gown as they neared the bricked patio with white metal furniture and curling vines. Every part of her seemed surreal, from the innocent yet intelligent eyes to the personality that glowed from the inside. And with little-known background, she seemed even more a fairy-type creature.

At the patio she turned with a question in her eyes, that placid face like a spring breeze. No matter that Kendrick had thought her a servant or Glenna laughed at her muddy fall, her face remained the same. As if her thoughts always ran deeper, and were more important, than what happened around her.

"I merely wanted to know that everything is . . . that you are . . . safe."

She dipped her head, obvious shame pinking her cheeks. "Quite all right, thank you. Just a little run-in with someone I used to know. He won't be coming around again." Briefly lifting her face for a polite nod, she pivoted to leave.

"I think I've figured you out. Why you're so calm." His voice paused her steps and turned her back to him. "It hardly made sense at first. You have all manner of barbs thrown your way and endure insult upon insult, yet you carry yourself with the grace of a duck."

She frowned. "A duck, Mr. Rotherham?"

Why hadn't he said something safe? There were plenty of options—What book are you reading? Do you think it'll rain today? Is that hat considered blue or *light* blue? Instead, he jumped directly into the deep end with a splash, chasing off every living creature in sight.

"You know." He made a graceful swoop with one hand. "Up and over, right off the oily back."

"I see. You think I stand out here, in a world of pretense and masks, because I am able to cover up my feelings?" Amusement tipped the corners of her lips.

Of course. This one was different. She sat and he sank into the seat across from hers. She didn't flitter off because he said the wrong thing. No, she jumped right in and swam beside him.

"Not cover up. Just . . . remain detached. Deal with them within yourself. I wondered about it, until I recalled that . . . that trunk of rocks. Or books, as you claim. That's your secret, is it not? You know how to escape into your own world whenever necessary."

"On the contrary, books *enhance* everything for me. I do not write to escape the world but to untangle and understand it."

"Write? You write stories, then?" Of course she did. He should have guessed.

Her toes scuffed crispy leaves on the ground, her face reddening as if she'd shared too much. "Little fables and fairy tales. Mostly for people in Shepton Mallet. It offered them a wonderful distraction."

Perhaps she was afraid he'd ask to read it and find it lacking. She'd never think her work better than it was. Not this girl.

A loud exhale trembled the delicate clematis beside his face. "I admit I'm an escapist when it comes to books. I become drunk on story, on words, as a buffer against reality." If only she knew how often. If books were alcohol, he'd be the worst drunk in history. "Growing up, we lived in a swampland in an abandoned house until my father's business became successful. Insects, a big lonely house, and plenty of people eager to look down on us. When reading, a boy could nearly pretend other people did not exist for a time."

"How could you pretend that? The best books draw the curtains back on a person's life and allow the reader to glimpse each part and understand it fully."

A smile flickered over his face. "Tell me one of your stories. I'd love to hear it."

She fidgeted, hands on her knees, then relaxed. "I suppose I could tell you one of the stories heavy on my mind at the moment." Flicking a glance toward the stables, she settled into a comfortable, wide-eyed, sky-gazing pose as if it were a well-grooved chair she reposed in every day and launched into a story.

"It's about a little boy. He had a kind, wonderful father but a mother who was not altogether motherly. She all but removed herself from his life, as if she deemed it unworthy as soon as she'd created it."

He forced a gulp down his throat that was thick with tension. Yes, she possessed that remarkable writing knack—the ability to, in a few sentences, re-create his own experiences as clearly as if she'd been there. Acute self-awareness drove his gaze down toward the polished, pointed toes of his boots, then out over the expanse of fresh green grass.

"The lad grew up, forming himself around the large hole in the center of him. He was, to all observers, whole and healthy. But inside he was deteriorating as quickly and helplessly as his mixed-up household."

His hand gripped his knee, and he frowned with the intensity of his thoughts. What sort of ghostly creature was this? How could she know that much about his past? He squeezed until his knuckles felt ready to pop out of his skin.

"Finally when he became an adult, the boy stopped aching for the right sort of household and realized he was meant to create his own home one day. He began reaching out to women he thought to marry. Not in the normal way one courts, but with intensity and dire thirst. As if he hardly cared who quenched that thirst, as long as he could drink his fill immediately."

Is that how she viewed him? Desperate? His jaw hurt from clenching. How soon could he remove himself from her presence? How could he do it gracefully, keeping his thoughts under wraps? It was never his strongest ability.

She trailed on—the young man in her story met a girl and everything changed, but the details were lost to Silas's fuzzy brain as he processed what he'd already heard.

The story died on Aurelie's smiling lips as she closed her eyes and tipped her head back against the chair. Allowing a few moments of silence as one would at the end of a piano recital, Silas tensed his muscles until she spoke again.

"A rather dark story, but I'd like to think it will have a happy ending one day." Her dazzling eyes burst open and met his gaze. "It feels a waste of time to become attached to a story without a nice resolution. I hope it met your expectations. What did you think of it, Mr. Rotherham?"

With a mumbled excuse, he stood, bowed, and moved swiftly toward the house.

Silas's reaction to Jasper Grupp's story left my heart raw, but so had the mere telling of it. A dread had also settled into the pit of my stomach at the suddenly tenuous bond with my only ally in the house.

It was not until evening that the ideas for my current novel began to spark again, and I composed the next installment of *Lady Jayne Disappears* in my mind. I barely spoke at dinner as my characters talked back and forth wildly in my head, clamoring for attention with their clues, both real and false. My thoughtful mood intensified as Juliette played the piano for us all after the meal, her magical touch carrying me into another realm.

Finally at bedtime I hastened to my chamber, prepared to shape and solidify the new ideas. With wind whipping the sheer curtains, I poured the story onto the page, watching the characters unfold as they talked and reacted to one another. I also walked Abigail through debtor's prison and introduced the readers to a taste of life there, making clear that each person in the prison owed only a minuscule amount of money which would never be repaid, since their imprisonment kept them from working. Later I would show how the jailer ran his prison as a business. My own precious papa had greased the jailer's palms with some of his book money to keep us fed and living in the tower, lifted away from the disease and squalor of ground cells.

The familiar *clock-clock-clock* of footsteps below the stairs echoed hours later, sending chills up my arms. Who wandered the halls this late at night? It must be nearing midnight.

Curiosity distracted me. I reread the same sentences many times, trying to dive back into the world of my story, but the bumps and scrapes below pulled me back out. Finally I rose from the chair, pushed my toes into brown day slippers, and snuck down the stairs with a greasy tallow candle clutched in my right hand. The second-floor hallway lay quiet and still, as did the main floor. The noises continued in the distance, as though someone moved through the interior of the house. I followed the sound down a windowed tunnel and into a grand foyer with ivory-handled doors ahead. It was like an entire secret building attached to the house. Had it appeared from nowhere? Perhaps I was losing my sanity. Again I recalled the dusty old man in the hall.

Hesitating only a moment, I pulled one door open and extended my candle into the dim room. A gigantic open space lay beyond, lined with pews and stained-glass windows that cast a prism of moonlit colors. The chapel. At the front another candle glowed, illuminating the bent form of a woman in white.

Aunt Eudora.

The woman touched her candle to several others on a wooden ledge, bringing a soft glow to the ivory room. Peaceful and eerily beautiful, the scene drew me, not allowing me to look away.

When my slipper scuff echoed in the room, the old woman jerked as if coming awake. I sucked in my breath. *Pull away. Close the door.* Slowly she turned until our eyes met and held.

"Come in, Miss Aurelie Rosette." Her voice echoed in the chapel.

Propelled forward in automatic obedience, I closed the distance between us and sat on the altar steps beside her. Had she been praying? Without the family around her and stiff, fancy clothes perfecting her posture, she looked tiny and vulnerable.

Her wrinkled hand appeared from under her dressing gown and swollen knuckles grazed my cheek. The too-large eyes rimmed with redness searched mine. "He was never fit for this earth, your father. The world where creditors must be paid, daily tasks completed, and promises fulfilled. He was too far above the mundane tasks that keep life functioning." The gnarled hand traveled back to my loose hair, gently fingering the strands. "And I suppose you are too." How different she was here, with a loose braid down her back and emotion clouding her face.

"You loved Papa, didn't you?"

The weathered cheeks creased back in a smile. "Like my own son." Emotion tripped her words. "Mother had nine dead babies after me and before your father. When he came,

I was fifteen years old. His birth made me not only a sister, but a sort of mother too."

Yes, that's how Papa had painted her—the mother who had replaced the one who'd died in his infancy. This soft woman lit by candle glow, draped in a white nightdress with pink ribbon, was the sort of aunt I'd assumed would be greeting me upon my arrival. And here in this midnight meeting of candles and muted stained-glass colors, it seemed impossible that she could be anything else.

"Why did you let him remain there, then?"

The old woman tipped her head and twirled a strand of my hair around her finger. "My child, it is as I said. He was not fit for this world. It was far better to keep him out of it, to keep him from ruining himself with greater sins."

Chills prickled me. What had he done?

"But you are another matter altogether. Had I known he intended to keep you, to bring you to that place, believe me. Something would have been done." Tears welled in the corners of her eyes. "I suppose you tell stories, just like he did. He would have taught you that, if he gave you nothing else."

I nodded. This woman's suffering tugged at the corners of my bitterness, prompting something akin to forgiveness.

"Tell me a story, won't you? Calm my old heart."

My tension eased. I could tell a story. It's what I always did in the face of illness, death, all sorts of pain. "All right, then. Have you heard the tale of the duck family of Knoll Pond?" I swept into a fairy tale and wove it together as it came from my mouth. A family of ducks once lived together in a small lake, each with a distinct personality. The story progressed, and the woman's face relaxed. Her eyes even closed.

But somehow, the sight of her calmness irked me, pulling

out the bitterness I had nearly tucked away moments earlier. This woman did not deserve peace and comfort. Did she even understand what she'd done? Did she realize the full weight of her choices? She'd played God, in a way. Chosen our fate. Decided what was best.

The story of the ducks took a decidedly pointed turn as a little gosling was accidentally born into that family. He did not look altogether different at first, just a little. But as he grew, it was obvious this gosling-turned-goose was different. With a long, graceful neck and striking beauty, he did not fit in with the ordinary ducks. They thought this was wrong, especially when other animals laughed at their odd-looking family. "When embarrassment overwhelmed them, they tricked the goose into a hunter's trap so that he would be taken away and they could return to their peaceful life, coexisting with the other animals of the pond. Their evil hearts—"

The old woman grabbed my wrist with surprising force, squeezing the feeling out of it. Her eyes darted frantically. "I was only trying to protect him. I knew what he'd done— what he'd continue to do if he were released. I couldn't bear to watch it happen over and over, ruining his life. I should have taught him when he was young, but I spoiled him so! It's my fault, so I *had* to protect him." Gray eyebrows drew together as the woman's shoulders shook, then her head dropped forward in a posture of utter despair.

I rested a hand on one trembling shoulder. I'd gone too far. What was I doing, trying to exact revenge? Regret bathed my bitter heart, cooling it again. This was the beloved sister Papa had spoken of so warmly. He wouldn't have wanted this.

Slowly, Aunt Eudora's head lifted, her gaze going straight

to the altar before us. "This is between you and me. And God. You deserve to know about him, but no one else must." She looked at me. "Do you understand? No one. Especially my grandchildren. They are not wise enough to handle it well." Her gaze flicked down. "Perhaps I never should have allowed you to stay."

So many crevices of this story begged to be explored. To be exposed to the light. "What happened to my mother when she disappeared? Did she run away? Did she—"

"It isn't a story that bears repeating, child." But as my hope crumbled, Aunt Eudora's anger melted into the worn lines of pity. "It is best if you do not know the rest. Suffice it to say that you were born, and that's the only event you need be concerned with."

She'd died. In childbirth. That explained her hesitance. The realization struck me hard and heavy. But no, it was my father's story she'd wanted to bury. It was something he had done, and Aunt Eudora felt the need to keep me from that knowledge.

"You might as well have this too." She unpinned a great teardrop pendant from her shawl. "It was my grandmother's, and I meant to give it to my brother's bride one day, to honor her into the family. Clearly, you held the highest place in his heart, so it should belong to you." It took several tries for her trembling fingers to pin it to my dressing gown. The weight of it, tugging down the fabric, matched the load I carried in my heart. "I truly loved him, you know. Despite . . . everything. You should keep this, and do not sell it, even if you are someday destitute."

Her words constricted my chest worse than a corset, and remained with me on my walk back upstairs and during an entire night of fitful sleep. The information sparked ideas, new possibilities and outcomes. But it saturated my heart with dread. Wild dreams of Papa filled my troubled sleep, from which I woke over and over again before finally glimpsing the orangey light of early morning through dry lids.

Nelle would understand. That realization poked through my haze in the morning, drawing me from bed. I dressed, bending awkwardly to tighten my borrowed corset rather than call for a chambermaid. My own worn corset had fallen apart in my fingers when I'd scrubbed it in the tub, and it was no wonder. It had seen daily use for more years than I could count on one hand. I resigned myself to Juliette's borrowed corset, with the rigid bands that constricted my gut. My frame was much slighter than Juliette's. How did the girl fit into such a piece? Wiggling the laces a bit looser under my chemise and the green-striped dress, I allowed one slow breath into my squeezed lungs and left to find breakfast, and then Nelle.

But it was Juliette who claimed my attention first in the morning room, with a dangerously eager glow to her face. "Aurelie, dear, you must hear my brilliant scheme."

10

Secrets are like elaborate gifts. They are held close until
the proper time, and then they are given with sweet
uncertainty and hope.

~Nathaniel Droll, *Lady Jayne Disappears*

Juliette approached with a presence that commanded me to
remain, despite my desire to flee, and took my hands. "I've
finally decided how you can meet your gentleman. It'll be a
benefit, with all the best of Somerset in attendance. And if
you find my match so disagreeable, you'll find another." The
girl's marigold-colored dress lit up the already-sunny room,
but her smile nearly overpowered it. "Kendrick will have to
talk Mother and Father into the idea, but I know they'll go
along. And once they're in agreement, Grandmama will have
to let us do it."

"I have nothing to wear to such an event. None of my
dresses would be finished in time."

"Do you really think you'll not have anything to wear?

It'll be my pet project, after my own dress. Besides, it isn't a ball, it's a benefit. That makes all the difference when trying to convince Father."

"Who exactly will this benefit?" I perched on the edge of the settee, balancing a small plate on my knees.

"Why, the poor in Liverpool, of course. We're sending it to the workhouses."

"You wish to send money to the poor?" My heart swelled with hope.

"No, silly. Not to the poor themselves. To the ones who run the workhouse. It surely costs an awful lot to feed all those people."

"Why not send it directly to the people who need money? Or better yet, to pay the debts of men in debtor's prison, so they are free to work again?"

She focused a pitying gaze on me. "I shan't call you foolish, since you don't know any better, but squandering charity on the debtors really is the worst idea. Oh you poor dear, the world just isn't that way. You've some romantic notion of all men being honest workers, if given the chance. But they're there for a reason, you know." She leaned forward and patted my knee, but I tensed and wished with painful desperation to yank away from her touch. "There's so much to teach you about the world. In the meantime, I imagine you in a cornflower-blue dress and a drop-line necklace for the benefit. Or would you prefer a Persian blue? Either way it must be blue, with that lovely hair and skin. And I have it on excellent authority that Alexander dearly loves blue."

I forced a polite reply. "As long as it sufficiently covers me, I'll consider it to have done its duty."

As soon as Juliette sailed out of the room and on to tackle

her next project, I relaxed and pushed her from my mind. It was people like her I needed to enlighten with my writing. Thus urged forward in my work, I asked a maid how to find Nelle's cottage.

Clement stepped up, discarding his plate. "I was about to take a walk there myself. Allow me to escort you. It's called Florin cottage."

"I would appreciate the guidance." I carried a handful of berries and toast into the garden.

In the yard, Clement paused to snatch a few radiantly pink flowers, grasping them in a bunch. I smiled. Did he perhaps have a crush on Nelle? That he frequently made the trek from his house to hers was soon obvious, as he led us quickly along the way.

"You've traveled this route often, I see."

"Often enough. I've lived here long enough to know all the paths, though." He strode on without looking around. "Nearly ten years or so."

I frowned. Only ten years? Did that mean I should cross his entire family off my list of suspects? 'Did your family live elsewhere before that?"

"In the city. Only Grandmama and Grandfather lived here with the servants before that. When we came, half of the house had to be uncovered and cleaned for our arrival."

My mind spun. That removed Glenna, Garamond, and Kendrick. Only Aunt Eudora and Digory remained.

But neither made sense as Lady Jayne's killer.

As we arrived, the quaint little thatched cottage amidst wildflowers captured my attention. Boxes of flowers lined the windows like long lashes and a stone walkway led to the door. I knocked, but no one answered.

Voices and girlish laughter floated from nearby, and Clement romped around to the back, his long legs carrying him through the grass. Behind the house, white sheets on a clothesline flapped around Nelle, who worked to pin them in place. A small blonde girl of about five or six spun around her, bubbling with laughter. When she spotted the visitors, the girl shrieked with delight and ran to throw her arms around Clement's skinny legs. The youth took her hand and twirled her around so her little skirt flared. "Good morning, Dolly."

Nelle straightened and froze, staring at me like a wild animal sighted by a hunter.

"Clem! I've learned a new song. Would you like to hear it?" Tucking rumpled hair behind her ear, the girl smiled up at him.

Clement whipped out the flowers he'd brought with a flourish. "Dahlias for the Dahlia." The girl again exclaimed and caught them up, spinning around with them.

Hand in hand like two playmates, the pair disappeared into the little cottage's back door, leaving Nelle and me alone.

Hands pressed into the small of her back, she walked forward, wind whipping her apron.

"Well, now you know my secret." She grasped my arms when she reached me, brow furrowed over intense eyes. "Will you keep it, please? I can't bear to lose her. Or my home."

"She's your daughter?"

Nelle offered a small smile, a look of blushing pride directed toward the back door. "She is. My little Dahlia Evangeline."

"Nelle, she is gorgeous. Absolutely nothing to be ashamed of."

Suddenly awkward, Nelle focused on the ground, then back on her clothesline.

I filled in the pieces. "The father is of questionable background?"

"The father is *missing*." Nelle whispered and then returned to pinning sheets. "For all he's worth, there is no father. Which is why she must remain a secret."

"And Clement?"

"Yes, Clem has been a wonderful playmate for Dahlia. I'm thankful every day that he stumbled upon us years ago. He always brings her dahlias from the yard when they're in bloom, and she finds it so humorous that he continues to do it nearly all season."

"I like the boy all the more."

"But no one else must know." She paused, dropping the remaining pins into her pocket, and returned to me. "I've come to trust Clem, but the others . . . if they ever have reason to dislike me, it'd be over for us both. We'd be in the workhouse before sundown. Or worse."

"I understand." I embraced my friend and stepped back. "Is he quite loathsome, then? Her father?"

She shrugged. "No more than most. I come from such a loving home with doting parents. I'd no reason to doubt anyone, least of all the gorgeous man who attached himself to me."

"I won't tell a soul, I promise. But might I come visit you both sometimes?"

She brightened a little. "If you like." She led me into the house, lifting a basket to her hip. The dark, single-room structure was filled with evidences of home—crusty bread on the counters, mismatched but clean furniture crowding the room, and two tumbling children at play. Clem chased Dahlia, tickling her into hysterics and knocking over a chair.

I told my friend everything about the night with Aunt Eudora, and what she'd said. While I spoke, Nelle pulled open the oven door, letting a sweet doughy aroma into the room, then shut it again. "And Nelle, I must ask you another favor. An important one. Will you be a postal address for me?"

Nelle watched me, suspicion raising her brow.

"I have something that needs to be posted once a week. A package. I can bring it right to you. And then I need to have things sent here. I'll give you postal money for everything. I only need an address. One that is not my own."

Her frown deepened. "What's this about, then? I'll need to know if I'm putting my own skin on the line."

"I suppose it's only fair. You've given me your biggest secret, I'll give you mine. But you must promise that it'll never leave this room."

She nodded.

I lowered my voice to keep it from Clem's hearing. "Have you heard of Nathaniel Droll?"

"Of course! I've read every piece of *Lady Jayne Disappears* so far. The staff at the house takes turns buying a copy to pass around."

I gripped my friend's hands, bursting with the news. "Nelle, I know Nathaniel Droll."

"What?" She jerked back, then took me by the shoulders. "Truly, you do? No. Really?"

"Really."

She shook her head, hands on her forehead. "I cannot even begin to grasp such a thing." Laughter burst from her.

The joy of sharing a small piece of my secret eased the

ache that had hovered since talking with Aunt Eudora. The possibility of Papa being responsible for Lady Jayne's disappearance years ago seemed remote and unrealistic in the light of my friend's gushing delight. It was contagious—addictive. "What's more, Lady Jayne was a real person. A guest at Lynhurst."

She laughed, unbelieving. "What a secret."

"Her name was Jayne Windham, and she stayed in the south tower." In my billowing excitement, I nearly spilled my other secret, but shied away from revealing my connection to the missing woman. It felt like a silly childhood wish that was too embarrassing and private to say aloud. Somehow, it was shameful to admit not having a mother, as if I were not quite a fully formed person.

She dropped onto a chair. "I feel as if I've been touched by royalty. Lady Jayne was here, and you—oh, you know Nathaniel Droll!" She fanned herself with her apron.

"Listen, Nelle. I need you to post the installments to the publisher and to collect the royalty checks. And you mustn't ask questions about his identity." At the moment, I honestly had no idea how to frame the answers anyway. "Everything will be sent right to you, and I would simply retrieve it when I visit. I'll include one other little 'thank you' too. I'll bring the notebooks to you unwrapped. If you have time to read them . . ."

Her grin nearly broke her face. "You mean it? I'll read a Nathaniel Droll installment before it's published?"

"Yes, ma'am, you will." I took up my friend's hands again. "That is, if you'll help me. Please, I really need it."

Eyes shining, Nelle stood and embraced me. "Of course, my dear friend. I shouldn't have questioned you." Wrapping her hands in her apron, she again opened the oven and pulled two loaves of bread from it. Steam poured from the split-crust tops. She carried them to the wide window where delicate curtains blew in the breeze. "I see you've noticed them." She indicated the billowing material. "That is *my* secret, if you can call it that."

I stepped over a stool and dolls to the front window and fingered the lace and elaborate eyelet design across the scalloped bottom. "Nelle, you made this? It's unbelievable." The perfect stitches looked like the monthlong work of an army of women. "Why, you could go into business for yourself. You would have the most elegant ladies asking for your trim work."

She dropped her gaze, eyelashes dusting her cheeks. "It would be presumptuous of me, trying to push above my station that way. They'd all know about Dahlia in short order, and then no one would come."

"Why order your life to please people who do not even care for you?"

The girl swiped off the counter with her apron, then pulled it over her head and sat across from me. "After the choices I've made, it hardly seems I deserve to ponder such a dream."

In those watery eyes, I saw the depth of my friend's longing. This is why I'd felt so compelled to pray for Nelle's future husband. His role took on even greater importance. He would be the father of her secret child, and he would set about righting the lies she believed about herself and her worth. How great was God to use husbands so often in that task. But for now, until the man appeared, it was put to me to remind the girl of truths she already knew. "As someone told me, shame comes from disappointing God, not people."

She gave one short laugh and stood. "The one return I cannot argue."

A screech cut the solemnity and two playmates barreled through the kitchen. Dahlia stumbled into Nelle's legs, swaying the slender woman.

"What a little bubble of joy." I smiled.

"That boy brings it out in her. She's the quietest thing until he comes around." Nelle lifted the girl by her arms and set her on her feet. "Time to settle, darling."

The lower lip protruded, threatening a rebuttal.

I rested a hand on the girl's slender shoulder. "Have you heard the story of the warrior prince? Come, I'll tell you." Settling on the floor, I invited the two to join me. Dahlia perched on my lap, the sudden weight of her surprising me. Clem sat beside us, arms around his bent legs.

"It seems you and Nathaniel Droll are birds of a feather." Nelle smiled at me. "He with his stories and you with fairy tales."

I launched into the story of a warrior prince looking for the stolen source of his power. Brushing the girl's hair off her moist forehead, I sank into the homey comfort of friendship and shared afternoons. Here, I felt like royalty welcomed into a common home with joy and awe. A few hundred meters away stood the house of my true family, where I was merely the tolerated intruder.

When the story ended, the girl's eyes shone and Nelle wore a placid smile. "Thank you for visiting, and for the story. Truly, I'm grateful for any company I can offer my sweet Dahlia." Nelle pulled me up from the floor. "There, and now it feels we are close chums, doesn't it? We have each shared our intimate secrets with one another."

Heart overflowing with gratitude and sweet friendship, I left Florin cottage with a prayer on my lips. This prayer for Nelle's husband would have to be even more specific. He would have to be more than a "good" man—he'd also have to be an able and willing father to a child already born. Very few men would fit that need, which meant all the more that prayer would become vital. And I would shower my friend with it.

On the walk back to the main house, I remembered the benefit, and suddenly it presented me with new and wonderful opportunities. Surely there was a man among my family's acquaintances who would be exactly what I had prayed for. While Juliette watched out for my perfect match, I would seek out Nelle's.

11

Were the whole world blind, Lady Jayne would still
stand out among the common grass as an exotic flower.

~Nathaniel Droll, *Lady Jayne Disappears*

The benefit loomed ahead as a happily pivotal moment, pro-
viding a veil of distraction from my worries. I might meet
Alexander, the long-discussed man I was meant to love, and
begin a sweeping romance. Or I might find the perfect man
to introduce to Nelle.

I spent more than a half hour readying myself for it when
the night came, which seemed an absolutely ridiculous
amount of time for such a task. Possibilities for the event
played through my mind as I tucked and adjusted, agonizing
over stray wisps of hair.

But then Juliette and her lady's maid spent three hours
redoing me into something else entirely. With bold peacock
feathers sprouting from my partially upswept hair, the beautiful blue dress Nelle had created somehow seemed gaudy. The

iridescent fabric shimmered when I walked—which wasn't often, with an overtight corset and heavy underlying fabric. Juliette met my eyes in the mirror. "You shall make your grand entrance just before eight o'clock, when I'll have stationed myself at the door as hostess, then everyone will be able to compare. We look so vastly different that we'll each have our own camp of admirers with few who straddle the fence."

"Can I not just sneak in from the drawing room?" This whole affair had become far too complicated.

"I won't let you waste all this beauty on 'sneaking in.'" She cupped my bare shoulders with cold palms to turn me, her eyes meeting mine. "When you walk down those stairs, I want you to smile. Not because you're happy, but because you might be happy one day as a result of this night. Smile as if this is your future love's first glimpse of you, and he'll be immediately smitten."

"I'm not sure I'd care for a romance that begins that easily."

"Love needn't be complicated." The chilly fingertips rose and cradled my jaw. Her angular face softened. "You wear your entire self on that beautiful face, dear cousin, and some man will know immediately when he sees you that he's found the perfect woman in a crowd of pretenders." Chin tipped, she studied me with a vague smile. "Keep that sweet charm, for it isn't every girl who's born with it." She stepped back and wiggled her fingers into elbow-length gloves.

"Every girl is born with the ability to be herself. Many simply unlearn it because they do not like who that is, and they think no one else will either." I shoved my fingers deeper into my own gloves. "Perhaps you'll find the man you long for in the deepest part of your heart, if you display who you truly are."

"Who I am?" Her lips quirked into a wry smile. "My dear, I'd never want the man who'd be attracted to that." The candid words settled over us, squeezing my heart. Juliette pivoted to the mirror, examining the subdued curls around her face. "If I ever catch a man's heart, it'll be because I've wheedled it away from him." She paused her primping and studied our faces in the mirror, raw vulnerability shadowing her features in a momentary flash. It was quickly and intentionally masked by a hard smile. "When they've all gone, I'll find you. Then tell me which one you think Alexander is, and if you're correct, you'll know for certain he is your perfect match." Juliette twirled in her shimmering gown of maize and exited.

Alone, I fingered the iridescent blue dress. Sweeping the edge of my shoulders and dropping to well below my throat, the beautiful collar line had been trimmed with an exquisite teardrop design of lace and crystals. A bit like a walking lampshade stuck with a feather, but the overall effect in the mirror was remarkably stunning. I was a new girl. It would have been a proud moment for Papa to see me this way, dressed by his family and waiting in his own room to attend a party at his beloved Lynhurst Manor. If only he could escort me through the night, making light of my mistakes and easing the social tension.

I fluffed the peacock feathers blooming from my hair. Had I really agreed to appear before strangers this way?

Perhaps a small alteration. Plucking the feathers from my hair, I fitted the pendant from Aunt Eudora into their place in my upswept waves and turned in the trifold mirror. Yes, much more fitting. Feathers and bright colors belonged on a girl like Juliette. But the delicate sparkle of the gems seemed like a subtle part of me that had always been there.

In the grand entrance, I tried to honor Juliette's request. Chin up and shoulders back, I met Kendrick on the stairs and descended on his arm. I smiled at nobody in particular until Kendrick's flushed face registered in my peripheral vision. He stared openly at me. "Who knew my sister had buried such a beauty in the guest room. You are more radiant than moonbeams."

And in that moment, I could not be comfortable. The top of my gloves tickled my arms to distraction, and the long gown seemed constantly a hair away from tripping me. I'd tumble down the stairs. Too many eyes stared at me from below. But forcing my shoulders back, blades together, I held myself tall and descended.

The faces of the men below all seemed about the same—scrubbed clean and shaved, hair dark with oils, politely interested expressions. Who among them might be my great love? I couldn't pick a single one out of the lot of duplicates. My Alexander must not be among them. He certainly didn't strike anything special in me if he was.

As my blue slipper touched the marble floor, I remembered with a panic that I might be expected to dance, but I hadn't a clue how. Not a step.

"Aurelie, I'd like you to meet Lord Carney." Juliette appeared, gliding about in her natural element among the well-dressed guests. Her serene face looked the way mine might if I were to lie back in a warm tub. The dark-haired man on her arm seemed the perfect male counterpart to her loveliness. "His family has recently purchased a country house near Bath, and his father runs an oil business in America." His lips had the perfect shape. Absolutely perfect. "Lord Carney, this is my dear cousin Miss Aurelie Harcourt."

I nodded to the man and whispered to my cousin, "Am I meant to dance with him first, then?"

"We're not to dance tonight. Grandmama threatened to snuff the whole party if we did. Light fare and conversation, then we're chasing them all out before midnight."

Cool relief pulsed through me. No dancing.

"As much as I love the color blue, I've never seen a girl who carries it as well as you do, Miss Harcourt."

I offered a polite nod, examining his handsome face for some sign he was my perfect match, this man who liked blue.

"Ah, dear Aurelie." Glenna's voice stiffened me. "I'm so glad you've made a few acquaintances. I was afraid our Juliette would outshine you completely, especially with a background such as yours."

"Mother!"

At these words, Lord Carney gave a grim smile with gentlemanly aloofness and moved away, ending the formal introduction. Her mission completed, Glenna offered her own prim smile and turned.

"Was that Alexander?" I whispered the question that had hovered for many minutes already.

Juliette glared at her mother's back and turned to me. "Is the man swooning over you?"

I shook my head, watching the man's retreating back.

"He was only meant to ease you into things. I have far better in mind for you." Her eyes sparkled as she glanced about the room, her gaze stopping on a familiar figure huddled alone near a far pillar. "Just look at poor Silas, hanging about on the fringes. He's such an unsociable creature, even if he is nice to look at."

"Perhaps he's uncomfortable."

His wavy hair was tamed, his posture perfect, and from the outside he fit in with the others so well—yet there was a gentle strength to his face, a rugged authenticity that went unmatched in this crowd.

"You know, he asked after you today. He wanted to know exactly who you were, and how you were related. He took a keen interest in your affairs."

"What do you mean, my affairs?" It felt as if he'd punctured my precious privacy and looked at the most embarrassing aspect of me. And then he'd gone and judged me by it.

"His invasive questions became off-putting, even to Papa. He wanted to know if part of Papa's good fortune, as he put it, would someday pass to you. When he said it would not, he wanted to know if you had any fortune from your family of origin. It was far more than a passing interest, you know. He wanted details."

Heat burned in my chest. How could he ask such things? A few kindnesses thrown my way like breadcrumbs hardly afforded him the right to ask such questions. As if he were window shopping for the right combination of pretty face and fortune for his wedded bliss.

"He seemed quite convinced you had money, but I've no idea why."

I eyed the man through the forest of well-dressed partygoers, and his face lit as he entered into conversation with a man approaching him. He thought himself high quality. Perhaps to women like Juliette, he was. With a deep breath, I thanked God that Papa had had the good sense to teach me the true measure of a man's worth. Irritation simmered on my warm skin when I thought about how I'd admired him a moment ago, and even defended him to Juliette.

No matter. If he continued digging to understand my exact fortune, what he found would chase him away faster than a fox pursued by a hound. A wry smile lifted my lips. The joy of poverty—it provided a convenient buffer against the wrong sort of man.

When Silas Rotherham saw Aurelie next to the yellow-clad Juliette, he began to doubt their relation. Juliette's hair had been curled above her head in unnaturally perfect loops, true to modern fashion. Aurelie's looser hair, wild and exotic, floated thick and fluid about her petite face, matching the personality that sparkled through her eyes. One could never tame that girl, which was truly a blessing.

Maybe that was the answer—she *wasn't* really a relation but was bound to this family from some past wrong they committed against her own. But no, she had called them her cousins. She could spin a wonderful story, but she wouldn't lie, would she? She had too honest a face. So unlike her cunning, confident cousin.

The drawing room doors opened again to admit a woman whose familiar posture, graceful and statuesque, drew his attention. Her coiffed silver hair seemed too perfect to be real, but he knew it was. He'd tested it with his own hand as a child, which had immediately earned that hand a slap.

He closed the distance between them, nodded in greeting, but her wide, genteel smile dimmed as she saw him.

"Mother. A surprise to see you here." Silas leaned in to kiss her cheek, but she blocked it with a folded fan and offered her hand instead.

"So this is where you've buried yourself away. And for the entire season, I might add."

"I'd rather your new damask curtains be on display for your friends, not me."

"Your father mentioned you were seeing to business of an urgent matter." She held her arms wide to indicate the party, pursing her lips into a patronizing, polite smile. "Truly, I see the urgency."

"Perhaps we can discuss it when I return?"

"I suppose." She tapped his cheek with her fan and followed it with a kiss that did not quite touch his face. As if he was not deserving, and offering anything more affectionate would only encourage his subpar efforts.

"At last, I find you." Kendrick's arm dropped about Silas's shoulders from behind. "Pardon the interruption, but I believe this gentleman has left my sister to hostess alone."

Silas hesitated, suddenly uncomfortable. "I cannot welcome guests to someone else's home."

"Oh, come now. She's too stubborn to ask you to be her official escort, but I'm certain she sees you that way."

"Mother, I'd like you to meet Kendrick Gaffney of Lynhurst Manor. Kendrick, this is my mother, Lady Rotherham of Berkshire."

The drawing room doors burst open with a flourish, interrupting the introductions, and a finely dressed young man with a wily gait strode into the room, a butler running after him to catch up his coat and hat.

That face seems most familiar. But where would I have seen it?

But the name he uttered to the butler—Jasper something—struck no memory.

12

Most rumors about Lady Jayne came from men who could not have her or women who could not compete with her.

~Nathaniel Droll, *Lady Jayne Disappears*

"Another awkward moment of hostessing." Juliette leaned toward me, smile still in place. "A guest who brings a friend I've not yet met. Do I introduce him, try to find a suitable conversation companion for him? Or do I merely let him wander until he is introduced to me by the—truly rude—acquaintance who brought him?"

"If you did not invite him, ask him kindly to leave."

Her lips twisted as she assessed the man with his back to us. "I suppose that's one answer. But I rather prefer to keep him here. One always hopes for diversity in her dinner parties. Besides, I find the man . . . interesting to look at."

When the familiar face spun toward us, I spit my drink

back into the goblet and coughed. Did he wish to torture me all my life?

With slicked hair, a well-fitted suit, and a clean-shaven face, Jasper fit in as well as I did.

"If he's to stay, it's my duty to welcome him, isn't it?" Without waiting for an answer, Juliette left my side in a breath, dress whispering along the tile as she went to meet him.

Private conversation between the two led to a playful volley of touches back and forth. Jasper's eyes glittered dangerously as the beautiful girl absorbed every trace of his attention. Jaw clenched, I imagined stalking over there and cuffing him with an open palm. It'd leave a red mark.

How dare he.

How dare he.

"Has she stolen the man of your dreams?" Silas's deep voice tickled the hairs around my ears. His body was close behind, near enough to brush if I wobbled on my unsteady legs. His aura of some elite-class scent lingered after he stepped back.

"Of course not. Whatever made you think that?"

"The disdain in your eyes is enough to poison a whole herd of elephants."

"He's the one who receives the look. Not Juliette." I bit my lip hard, too hard, hating my glib tongue. I'd said too much, and now he'd ask something I couldn't answer.

But he did not do the expected. "Good. I should hate to have to pry you apart from him later. He is far from worthy of you."

I angled toward his face that was smooth as oil. Were all men wretches? "How can you assess a person's worth by a simple glance?" Or perhaps the amount of one's fortune.

"You do the same. Something about what reading does to the mind. A good book allows you to examine the life of another. Are you saying that a girl who analyzes book characters does not also read people in real life?"

"Performed on real-life people, it's called judgment. Something I try not to partake in." I moved away, but he followed, close at my elbow.

"What is the difference, other than a kinder label?"

I turned. "You take great pains to draw similarities between us, Mr. Rotherham, but there are more differences between us than stones in this house." The heated words, useless and silly, felt good to my frazzled nerves. Life was not kind. People weren't, either. I had grown tired of being gentle in this world of games and selfishness.

He moved around to face me, gaze digging into mine. "Why do you insist on hating me so suddenly? Have I so severely wronged you?" Why did he see through everything with such unsettling depth? He'd seen my fear and anxiety, as always.

"I do not hate anyone, Mr. Rotherham. But I do dislike shallow judgmentalism of any kind. Pardon me."

Pushing through the crowd, I strode through the drawing room and onto the terrace separated from the room by two thin curtain panels. What was I doing? How could I let Grupp shake me so? I wasn't myself.

To think, only a few short years ago he'd proposed. I'd considered it, back when I believed him to be a damaged but repairable wreck. Now . . .

Thank you, God, for protecting me from him when I knew no better myself.

I could have been his wife by now. Closing my eyes and

lifting my face into the moist breeze, I exulted in God's protection. I sank easily into a conversation with him, baring my heart and asking for help with the current predicament, which twisted my insides.

The sound of footsteps jostled me from the prayer and I turned toward the open doorway. A dark figure beyond the curtain walked intentionally toward me. I glanced around, then lifted my skirts, perched on the rail, and swung my legs up and over. I dropped onto lush grass half a story below, ankles stinging. The pursuer above me stole onto the terrace and easily cleared the rail in a side-jump and landed before me, polished boots thudding inches from my dress hem.

"Jasper, what is it you want?" Anger simmered below the surface at the sight of his face, but remained controlled, soothed by the talk with my heavenly Father.

"Only to show you my new clothes." He held out the overcoat by the lapels, spinning in the grass. "You paid for them, you know."

I pinched my lips together.

"I've kept your secret, as promised. But now I need you to do a little something for me."

"Not another farthing will I give you."

"Only because you haven't any. Your wonderful papa gave every farthing to come through his greedy little fingers over to the prison guard. That grand tower, high as his pride . . ."

My defenses rose, but I pinched my lips shut. I had yet to locate any trace of money from Papa thus far. But he couldn't have squandered it so, could he? It meant we never would have left Shepton Mallet, and surely that wasn't his intent.

Jasper smirked. "Besides, it's not money I want this time. It's about a girl." His laugh tipped him backward. "Always about a girl, isn't it? Well, I need you to put in a good word for your old chap. Stoke the flames, as it were."

Juliette.

"She cannot even know that I know you." What would Juliette do if I revealed my true background? How many allies would I find at Lynhurst then?

He shrugged, hands in his trouser pockets, pushing back his overcoat. "What's to say she needs to know a thing? All I need is female chatter." He made a chicken-cluck motion with his fingers. "Start her talking, keep her excited about a certain young man she met tonight."

"You're deplorable."

"And I'll need an open invitation to everything at this lovely house. I aim to dance my way right into polite society *and* endear myself to the most beautiful woman alive. All that's needed is the costume and a few of the right friends. The other details are filled in by the wonderful imaginations of the people with whom I shall now be closely acquainted." With an exaggerated swoop, he plucked a fistful of tall grass and presented it to me as a bouquet. "And I know you'll oblige me, what with you being so lovesick over me after I rejected you."

I squinted. "Liar."

He dropped an arm around my stiff shoulders. "Liar, debtor, storyteller. All one and the same, love. And don't be a spoiler and tell anyone of our deal. My storytelling skills aren't as fine as your father's, but they have a much stronger wicked streak. I'm certain I could come up with quite a story to share with your family. Or perhaps, with all Nathaniel Droll fans."

Panic cinched me at what I couldn't control. And somehow

his words marred the beautiful vision I'd carried of my beloved papa in a way I couldn't rectify.

My muscles did not relax until later that night, when I'd stepped out of the constricting gown, lifted the pins from my aching scalp, and poured my emotions into *Lady Jayne Disappears*. A new side character appeared—the ragged street vendor who robbed a gentleman of his money, timepiece, and fine clothes to walk among polite society for an evening as one of them. I even included a few specifics from our dinner that night for a taste of authenticity.

The miserable man introduced himself as Arthur Hobbs III and enjoyed his good fortune, gorging himself on fine seafood and the attention of beautiful women. He partook of two helpings of shrimp soufflé and cauliflower.

By the end of the night, however, this street vendor in disguise discovered an unfortunate allergy to seafood, of which he'd consumed a great deal. He turned a putrid shade of green and his throat swelled, causing a most embarrassing to-do at the dinner table in the presence of his newfound love interest. He ran in sheer humiliation from the room, hacking and sputtering over the guests. His foolish lie turned around and bit him in the end.

It wasn't until I'd slid beneath the sheets that night and extinguished the candle that poor, faceless Alexander again came to mind. Juliette had forgotten to have that talk she'd promised after the benefit. It was just as well, though. I had not seen a single man fitting his description. My mysterious perfect match would have to reappear another night if we were to accidentally but providentially meet. In the meantime, he'd remain a frequent visitor to my dreams and conscious wonderings. Never in my life had I been told a stranger would be my perfect soul mate, and the little piece of my mind that didn't believe it also wanted to be proven wrong.

To have a partner again—a best friend. Someone with whom I could be Aurelie Rosette Harcourt, and nothing more. The pleasant hope for my future carried me into a gentle sleep.

As the weeks turned hot, I began waking early, in the cool of the morning, to dream and write. But on one particular Thursday, a shrill sound in the distance burst my sleep, pulling me from bed. Glenna's frantic voice echoed up from the second floor, contrasting with the pleasant lilac scent wafting in the open windows. Springing from bed, I flung my dressing gown about myself and ran to the landing.

"He's spying on us, Garamond. Nathaniel Droll . . . spying on this house!"

And that's how I knew the next installment of *Lady Jayne Disappears* had been printed and delivered in almost no time after I'd posted it to the publisher, thanks to the modern railways. It was jarring, realizing that the words I'd dreamed up in my head and penned in the quiet of my own room were now being made public to whoever happened to pay their shilling for a copy.

"There now, little woman. Don't take it to heart. I'm sure he isn't writing about you, dear. Many women in our class would have much the same clothing and food. Not to worry over the similarities. Perhaps you should refrain from reading this novel altogether. Yes, I believe that's a wise idea."

"But Garamond, I *know* he's been here. I know it! He's written some very startling details into his account that cannot be overlooked."

The candy. It must be the peanut brittle she spoke of. I stifled a giggle, picturing the woman's face. She'd never convince her husband that the insidious "Tabitha Toblerone" was in fact patterned after herself. Not without admitting her secret obsession. Fortunately she hadn't seen me in the hall that day I'd spied her dipping into her secret dumbwaiter stash. Tickled with amusement at the sight, of course I'd been compelled to include it in one of the installments.

My smile froze as the truth dawned on me. Why hadn't it occurred to me that my family would read Nathaniel Droll's novels? Anything I wrote about Lynhurst, my family, or awkward situations would reach their eyes eventually. This could be dangerous, or it could be immensely amusing. As long as they never discovered his identity.

I dressed in a simple pink gown that I could manage myself and slipped downstairs, past the heated conversation on the second floor.

In the morning room, Silas poured himself tea at the end of the sideboard. It was the first I'd seen of him since the benefit, and the memory of my sharp words suddenly nipped at me. I joined him and selected a crusty orange Danish. Hopefully I was not breaking a social norm by approaching a gentleman uninvited.

"Good morning." I smiled, hoping to melt through the ice of that night. "I thought perhaps I'd join you."

"Of course." Fingertips gently pressing against my back, he led me to the sage-colored sofa washed in sunlight, and we sat together.

"You've been dining in your room?" I bit into the Danish, but it crumbled dry and powdery in my mouth. I chewed it anyway.

"I've been in London, delivering Mother home and seeing to some business."

Good. At least I had not been the cause of his absence.

A pinched smile turned his lips up. "You're looking more like yourself than when I saw you last."

I dipped my head. Did he refer to my dress, now a simple pink print, or my bearing? "I owe you an apology. I was cross about other things and you happened upon me in the right moment. Wrong moment, actually."

"I found it refreshing." Again, he turned the tables on my expectations, glancing up at me with a lightly stubbled yet fresh morning face. "For once, the girl with such deep thoughts has let some of them seep out into the world. I was glad to hear you saying exactly what you thought, even if it offended a bit in the moment."

"It was unladylike and uncontrolled. Hardly a positive trait."

"But it was honest. A *very* positive trait."

"Saying every honest thing that came into my head would cause a lot of trouble."

"Or it would mend relationships and connect you to the people around you." He set aside his plate and turned fully to me. "Nothing's to say you cannot tell your aunt and your delightful cousins exactly what you think when they ridicule you and force you into awkward situations."

"My father once gave me a rule for writing." Squinting, I imitated his exact tone. "'Always learn the rules before you break them.'" He watched me steadily, the calmly amused expression glowing on his face. "I aim to learn the ways of polite society before I decide which rules to break."

"Why do you need their rules? Like Dickens's Madame DeFarge—she immediately knew what was broken in her world and refused to be a part of it."

"What of Charles Darnay, who had to live as an aristocrat for years to know for certain he must reject it? Besides, I'd never want to be Madame DeFarge. I haven't that level of cruelty in me, no matter what sort of social evils I fight against."

Silas's gray eyes flicked back and forth, absorbing my face in a glance. "And do you fight against social evils? What a shame if you were too busy adapting to the rules to fight them."

"I'm hardly a revolutionary, but there are certain social ills that tug at my heart. I have my own way of fighting them." The urge to spill my secret was nearly overwhelming.

"I'd like to hear about your efforts."

My skin warmed. "I must protect my efforts with secrecy for the moment."

"That sounds very specific. Now you have left me wondering."

"What about you? Surely with all this talk you have done your share to fight wrongs."

His eyes twinkled. "I must beg secrecy as well. For other reasons. But I do promise you that I have my own way of righting wrongs I see in this world." He shifted, draining the last of his tea. "So at least tell me what sin in this world you wish to fight against most ardently."

That answer was easy. "Debtor's prison. It's a terrible way to compound a simple problem. Not to mention the conditions of the prisons. If people knew what really happened inside those walls, it might prompt them to overhaul the entire system."

"Certainly, it's a bit overdramatic to throw a man in prison for mere debt, but the crime must be punished. It isn't as if we still hung the debtors or shipped them off to foreign parts. We simply slap their wrists and take their toys away for a time."

Haunting images flashed through my mind. Disease that peeled away the skin, desperate hunger for those who had nothing to pay their jailers, and rat-infested cells stuffed with half a dozen people. But he wouldn't know that. No one on the outside did. Not yet, at least.

"Your eyes tell me you disagree passionately."

"Most passionately. Mr. Rotherham, have you ever stepped inside a debtor's prison?"

"I suppose I haven't, but it isn't like they are on a remote island. They're right here in England, all over. I know of them without having to visit one."

Desperation welled up in me. Desperation to be understood. "Knowing *of* them is not the same as understanding them. Believe me, you would be appalled at what occurs inside."

He fingered his teacup, considering me. "This has truly shaped you, hasn't it? How much of your life did you spend at Shepton Mallet?"

"Every single day of it, up until now."

I carried the memory of his face, gentle and spellbound, up to my bedchamber as I readied to write again. Perhaps I could re-create that image for my readers in this next installment, if Charles Sterling Clavey happened to grace the page with his presence.

Settling in at my desk with the next notebook, the most prominent words in my head were those my mother had penned to Papa. They haunted me with an eerie fear delicious enough for a novel.

When Lady Jayne moved about the drawing room with the others, her gaze flitted to Charles Sterling Clavey, no matter where he stood. The gentleness in his strong features drew her in a way no other had. Their longing glances and hidden smiles beamed back and forth, gliding over all the oblivious guests filling the space between them. Why her benefactor had forbidden them to speak, she had no idea. But no human limitations could tear them apart any more than she could tear her soul in half.

When the guests drifted away, some retiring to their suites upstairs, Lady Jayne took herself with a measure of secrecy into the yard tinted blue in moonlight, crumpling a piece of paper in her hand. If anyone glanced out the windows, they would see her lilac-colored gown stealing through the dark, but she had to take the risk. She thirsted miserably for the briefest contact with Charles.

Pausing at their willow, the kind tree that had

so oft shielded their amorous embraces, she tucked the note into the great gaping hole in its trunk and retrieved the note left for her. With rapid steps, she slipped back to the house and entered through the silent patio doors, her slippers muting all footfall. Charles's note to her she'd crumpled in her fist, to be enjoyed in the privacy of the south tower where no eyes watched her blush as she savored his words. As she hurried—

I froze. More unfamiliar writing greeted me as I had turned the page, shocking all ideas from my head. It was signed "Nathaniel Droll."

I slapped the book shut and pivoted on my chair, looking back at the closed door. I'd locked it when I'd left, hadn't I? Of course. It had become habit to lock it and test its security with each exit. My gaze flew about the room for another entrance. The fireplace? But hot ashes glowed in its mouth.

Thumbing through the pages again, I paused to read Nathaniel Droll's message to me.

The villain in this story knows how to cover up a vast array of motives. Suspect everyone, consider every possibility. The only thing I know is this: Ghosts are real, and may one never die.

Nathaniel Droll

Ghosts aren't real.
Ghosts aren't real.
But Nathaniel Droll was.

13

They found Lady Jayne wise for keeping her secrets so tightly, but she knew in her heart that the real wisdom would be in not having any to keep.

~Nathaniel Droll, *Lady Jayne Disappears*

Swift feet carried me to Nelle's cottage that afternoon, where the aura of simplicity and real life banked my nightmares. I'd had to finish writing the installment in the sunny morning room to escape the ghostly aura of my chamber, praying no one walked in. Now I handed her the book with one particular page torn out and tucked away.

"Nelle, have there been any stories of Lynhurst being haunted?"

She smiled, wiping a bread pan before putting it away over her head. "Do you plan to spin them into your fairy tales? But yes, of course there are. What country manor house has no ghost stories? People this wealthy always find it difficult to leave this world completely behind."

"So you believe they are true?"

Her laughter filled the cottage with silver tones of mirth. "As much as I believe in your fairy tales. The only one that even sounds believable is the old master's ghost, Lord Pochard. When his daughter Glenna married below her, it broke his heart. They say it killed him within a day. Supposedly he lurks about the place whenever one of his own is about to enter into a terrible marriage with someone below them."

"Poor Garamond." I sighed with a smile, my somber mood lifting. "He thought he married above his station."

Nelle smiled. "The poor man painted himself into that corner."

Rain sheeted over the vast estate on my return, walling us all indoors for the rest of the day. A moment in the morning room to snatch a luncheon sandwich had trapped me into an afternoon of whist, the entire family seated in chairs of different heights around an oval sofa table. Even Aunt Eudora graced the room with her regal presence. My mind wandered, gaze nipping about the room at the portraits hung about. But surely I would not see the man from the dark hallway among those faces, that awful manifestation of my delusion. He did not exist.

And suddenly, his name rang out on Glenna's high voice. "Have you read it, Mother?" She swiveled on her high back chair to speak to the older woman framed in the bay window. "Nathaniel Droll is writing about Lynhurst. The south tower. The neglected drawing room. Even the orange grove. There's no mistaking the setting."

Must the woman obsess so much about it? I fanned my cards out before my face.

Aunt Eudora grimaced. "If those insipid books really are set here, we'll rain the law down on poor Nathaniel Droll's head for making a fool of this family. But until you have proof, I'll thank you to put aside your superstitious notions."

"Kendrick, have you read it?"

"Enough to know it's rubbish." He lobbed the conversation onto the next person with a dark look not usually worn on his face.

"Aurelie, we should hear your input on the matter." Glenna discarded and then leaned toward me magnanimously, as if proud of herself for stooping to include the oft-forgotten girl. No matter that it was the last conversation I wanted to be part of. "You are a fresh mind to this household. What do you think of old Nathaniel Droll's work being set here?"

As if the light of a train had swung directly into my face, I froze. Cards and numbers swam in my vision. What to say? I had to pass the conversation along. Quickly. "I cannot say I've ever purchased a single installment of Nathaniel Droll's fiction." I dropped a seven onto the growing discard pile and retreated back on my ottoman.

Silas's gray eyes fixated on my face then. The gaze scorched my neatly packaged deception. The man ran his thumb over his fanned-out cards, contemplating me rather than the game. My jaw tightened, but he remained silent, allowing me to keep my secret. Again, a complicated character.

"Why don't you read a selection, Mother?" Juliette's words made my skin cold. "It would be a nice diversion this evening. You have not read us fiction in months."

"No sense straining your sweet voice, darling pixie." Garamond patted his wife's pudgy hand.

"No, it's a wonderful idea. Digory, bring me the installment from my night table."

My back stiffened as I hung over the piles of cards on the table, dangling my discard. Would my face give me away as they read? Within one more round of plays, Kendrick won the hand and then rose, adjusting his jacket. "And now, if you'll excuse me, I shall spend my time in far more valuable ways than allowing my ears to be assaulted by drivel."

I ducked my head, cheeks burning.

"What on earth is so pressing, Kendrick?" Glenna frowned from her throne in the center.

"Nothing at all." He fitted his hat on his neatly combed hair. "But I'd rather muck the stables than listen to this." With a jaunty smile, he departed.

When Digory returned with the requested booklet, the rest of the family dispersed throughout the room with Glenna holding court in the grand wingback by the fireplace where her voice could project across all the listeners. With animation that made the dialogue snap and the characters stand up from the page, Glenna read the installment. It turned my insides in an odd mix of pleasure and anxiousness to hear my own words read aloud. One of my most clever lines brought no reaction from the audience, but a flippant section that had popped into my head in a minute garnered laughter. I forced myself to join in.

Oh, how witty was this Nathaniel Droll.

Only Garamond remained silently watchful from his chair, pondering the words.

"The butler did sound a bit like our Digory," Clem admitted. "I could see his face as you read that selection."

"You're all batty. As if Nathaniel Droll would take an interest in this old family." Juliette sat back on the sofa, somehow maintaining perfect posture even while lounging.

"I'll have you know, dear daughter, that once we were a popular name among the—"

"Among the elite in London. Yes, I know, Mother. Once upon a time. But we aren't in London now, are we?"

The listeners reached no conclusion in the end, each leaving for his bedroom with a closing statement to ponder.

In the wee night hours, I shot up in my bed, aware of a presence in my room. Trees bobbed outside the window, their fingers pointing toward me. I looked about.

"If you wanted them to know you wrote it, why not simply scrawl your own name across the manuscript?" The crater-faced man in the dusty gray suit scowled from the corner chair.

Fear stabbed my chest. "What are you doing here?"

"I thought the point of a pen name was to remain anonymous. Yet here you are, parading before everyone that you are the author. Despicable, I say." He puffed on his pipe and exhaled great plumes of smoke. "If you're going to write such drivel, at least take my name off of it."

"I've done my best to hide it from everyone. If they guess . . ."

"It'll be because you *told* them, you fool girl." His puffs intensified. "You had Lynhurst written all over the last installment. You think they won't guess?"

I sucked in a breath, my stomach rolling over, as the details of the latest piece flitted through my memory. It depicted clear scenes from their recent dinner party, from the brand of wine served to quotes from the toast made by a tipsy Garamond.

"But they can't possibly—"

He snorted. "Better start running, princess." His voice suddenly became Jasper's, oily and low.

Panic rose, choking me. I clutched the blankets to me as moisture gathered on my skin. What had I done?

Seconds later the dream was yanked away, my eyes flicking open to the reality of early morning. Dream. It was a dream. I breathed hard, buried up to my chin in blankets. None of that had been real.

But that warning was.

I lurched onto my side, tugging the blankets with me. What an idiot I was. An utter fool. But what could I do about it now? Nelle had already posted the manuscript.

Restlessness jabbed at me until I rose and penned a letter to the publisher in the harsh red light of early sunrise. *I would be most appreciative if you would remove a few details from my latest submission.* Then came a list of the telling details. It needed to be posted immediately—in Bristol if possible, where a train would speed it on to London that day, only a single day after the installment Nelle posted would reach them. Rain already dotted the window and dark clouds hovered low. I'd need the carriage.

As I glided past the window and caught my reflection, something moved in the back garden. A person? Yes, definitely. Chills rose on my bare arms. Shrinking back, I shrouded myself in the curtain. But it was only Juliette who moved through the shrubs, obscured by the stone wall around the garden, but clearly visible from my third-floor bedroom.

Juliette never rose this early.

Jasper Grupp's lanky frame danced past the same shrubs, then caught Juliette up and swung her around. The pair walked along the path, playful touches back and forth, marking them as more than mere acquaintances. Was that a fresh gown, or the one she'd worn yesterday?

Dressing quickly when the chambermaid came to assist and lacing up my ivory half-boots, I gathered my skirts and raced down the stairs. When I'd almost reached the bottom, Juliette pranced through the side door, pulling off her hat with a trail of ribbon.

"Why, good morning, miss early bird." She radiated like the sunshine that broke through the passing clouds.

"Juliette. I've never seen you up this early."

"Why would I waste this glorious morning in bed?" She twirled, hat in the air, and came to rest before me, face solemn. "I trust you have seen nothing of interest. Nothing that you might mention to the family." Her cutting glance warned me.

The weight of responsibility settled on my shoulders. Now. This was it. Time to say something about Jasper. "Nothing I'd tell the family. But, Juliette—"

The moment snapped closed as she whipped away with a casual gesture of dismissal. "I hope you've nothing planned for next week, because I've secured us an invitation to the Naughtons' dinner party on Wednesday." She strode through the grand hall and hung her hat on the mirrored rack. "It'll be a stylish event. They always have the grandest parties."

"I think I—"

"Oh, do tell me you will go. I'd hate to make excuses after maneuvering the invitations in the first place."

"Well, no, I will go, but—"

"Oh, good." She crossed to me and framed my face with her hands, squishing my cheeks a little. "I do so love to dress you up." A frightening spark lit her eyes.

Sweeping her scarf off her neck and across my face, Juliette ended the conversation. With a few confident clicks of her boots, the girl reached the stairs and jogged up without a backward glance.

The first attempt was a failure. But there'd be others, of that I would make certain. I pivoted away from my cousin's retreat, guilt hanging heavily about me. Breakfast would help.

The morning room, usually quiet, bustled with servers placing trays and arranging teacups on the sideboard. I'd never come to breakfast quite this early. But there was much to do. I needed to talk with Juliette soon—perhaps I should prepare my speech—and the letter absolutely must be posted to the publisher that day. I'd snatch breakfast to take along.

Grabbing a Danish and an orange, I stepped back into the tunneled front hall, where Digory held out a hat for Silas. Settling it on his dark hair, Silas turned to smile a good-morning.

"Are you traveling to London again?" Perhaps this was a way to get the letter there faster. Pocketing the orange, I slid the envelope out.

"Just to Glen Cora."

Close enough. "Would you be willing to post a letter for me?"

"Of course." He accepted the envelope, fingered the edges, then looked back up at me. "In fact, why don't you come with me? This trip is, after all, because of you."

14

Sharing with another soul the pain from your past dilutes its hold over you.

~Nathaniel Droll, *Lady Jayne Disappears*

"Digory, would you please tell the ladies of the house that I've gone out and taken Miss Harcourt with me?"

"Of course, sir."

He leaned toward me, offering his elbow with an inviting smile. Perhaps a trip would clear my crowded mind and allow me to think. With a nod, I took it and followed him to the front doors and out into the cloudy morning, curiosity swirling. At least the rain had slowed to a misty trickle.

"A bit like our last carriage ride." His jaunty smile encouraged mine as he took the rear-facing seat.

As I climbed in, my mind ticked through possible destinations for this trip that was "because of me."

We rode through the hilly landscape, now bright green with fresh precipitation. I clung to the letter in the silence that followed, fingering the red wax seal as my thoughts returned to my own mission. What if this letter didn't reach the publisher in time? What if confronting Juliette would ruin my chance to stay at Lynhurst? My nervous fingers discarded the letter and picked at the orange peel until the rind lay in bits across my lap. I absently pieced the orange and ate each sliver.

"If it's all right, we'll make my stop first and then see about posting your letter in town."

Anxiousness clawed at me, but I nodded. When the carriage turned off the main road into the village of Glen Cora, waves of homesickness passed over me, temporarily minimizing all thoughts of the letter. Where on earth did he intend to take me? A few more turns down a familiar alley, and the carriage rolled up to Shepton Mallet Prison, the stone-and-metal gates looming before us.

"Why are we stopping here?"

"Because an intelligent, well-spoken girl challenged me to visit the place I had so many opinions on." Pushing up from his seat, he reached for the door and stepped down with the aid of the footman. "And now I have the finest escort I could have asked for." His smile was warm as he turned back to help me down. "Won't you please show me around your home?"

Odd sensations of warmth spiraled through my chest at the invitation.

After climbing down, I lifted my skirt hem over the rain that had pooled in the uneven street, one hand on my chest. Memories made my heart pound. Why hadn't he warned me of his destination? At least I'd worn a soft brown print dress with a simple ribbon hem—the plainest of the dresses created by the woman in Bristol. Imagine if I'd worn the beautiful gold or red gown. I'd be scorned right out of the cell block. A double knock on the little door in the gate brought the guard running, his ratty coattails flapping behind him as he swung out on the gate.

"Why, lookee what we got." The heavily whiskered man ran a finger under his crooked nose and sniffed, but stepped back to allow us entry. "Never thought to see you again."

"It's that easy to enter the prison, is it?" Silas whispered the words as we stepped over the threshold and into the muddy courtyard.

"Easy to enter, not so easy to leave. For the prisoners, anyway." Flooded with the familiar sights, the tall stone buildings and broken fountain in the center of the courtyard, I hardly knew where to go first. Suddenly beset with the urgency I'd always felt in this place, I glanced around. Who might need a visit most? Which sickness was currently the worst?

But I was not alone, and I was hardly the same girl who'd left. Would my visits be as welcomed as when I was a daughter of the Mallet?

My feet directed me toward the tallest building, carrying me on the path I'd walked millions of times. What better place to start than my own home? It was the best cell by far, and perhaps it would ease this poor gentleman into the reality of life in prison. After I'd gauged his reaction to this one, I could decide if I dared take him to see actual prisoners.

Ducking into the main entry, we climbed the circular stairway, hopping over the broken steps. Halfway up, Silas held a handkerchief to his nose. Not a good sign.

But when I pushed through the door at the top of the stairs, a sense of *home* surged over me, purging all other thoughts. I rushed into the empty space, hands out to feel everything I'd once held so dear. The large bed with the three quilts, the one-doored cabinet on the wall, even the vibrant blue curtain meant to brighten the room—everything was exactly as I'd left it. *Thank you, Lord, that they have not yet filled this cell.* Lynhurst seemed less real in my mind as I wandered from item to item in the cell, running my hand along everything and taking it in. Yes, Lynhurst was a dream, and this place was my reality.

"We were fortunate to be here. It's by far the best cell at the Mallet. And these blankets are a rarity as well." And that's when Jasper's words returned to strike me with all their ugly implications. I glanced about this tower at the items I'd always taken for granted. "No one else has furniture, nor such lavish space." I said the words almost to myself. "We were quite lucky."

But luck had nothing to do with it. Not here.

A wave of truth came crashing across my mind, stealing the sweetness of the moment. As I stood there in that tower cell fitted with the comforts no other cell possessed, I suspected I had found Papa's savings. Never one to plan for the future, he must have paid the jailer a ridiculous sum for immediate comforts, sentencing us to a lifetime in . . .

I shook off a building dread and moved toward the stove. I couldn't bear to sully the tender memories with thoughts such as those. It wasn't as if he'd purchased anything unnecessary. "We heated tea here, and I slept here." I ran my hand tenderly along the broken pipe stove and the narrow bench with a high back. Papa's thick black coat hung from a hook at the top of the bench, covering an oval frame that ought to hold a mirror. "We took our meals here." My fingertips brushed the three-legged table surrounded by two squatty benches.

Then onto the backless chair where Papa sat, pulled close to the stove when he told me stories. We'd cuddled away the winters there throughout my childhood, and although I'd never known what it was to own a new dress, I knew love. Extravagant love. My father's presence remained there, ingrained in every piece of wood, reflected in the dirty window. They were precious memories, no matter what he'd done with his money. How dearly I wished I could experience those moments in real life again.

But suddenly they choked me. Loss gripped my throat, striking a vague panic. Never again would I live here. Never again would I see him.

It was too much. I had to leave. I'd suffocate.

Bunching the blankets and coat to my chest, I hurried from the room, hoping Silas Rotherham had the sense to follow.

I stumbled down the steps, forcing my trembling legs to hold me up. I'd been doing so well these past weeks, thinking only positive memories and hopeful thoughts, but in a matter of minutes, everything had been undone, like a corset with the ribbons yanked out.

Yea though I walk through the valley of the shadow of death, I will fear no evil: for thou art with me.

The shadow of death loomed heavily over me in the narrow tower stairwell. I reached the bottom and shut my eyes. In those few seconds alone, I drew deep breaths and let the painful tingles pass over and then leave my body. Silas's footsteps slowed on the final steps and approached from behind. Warm arms encircled me. His heart beat against my shoulder blades as he drew me back against his solid chest. How inappropriate and scandalous. How unladylike.

But I couldn't break away. I counted the rhythmic beating

to one hundred and my muscles relaxed. There was nothing wanton about the way his arms supported me, offering strength from his soul to mine through this simple physical contact. My own father could have held me so. A few more deep breaths, and my emotions normalized.

I turned my head to look up at him. "Have you seen enough?"

"Hardly." Endless patience softened the planes of his chiseled face so near mine. "I'd like to see everything, to leave knowing exactly what this place is like. Whenever you're ready to show me." He took the coat and blankets from me and held out a hand to indicate that I should direct him.

Lifting my skirt hem above the mud and securing my hat with the other hand, I led him out to the courtyard and then toward the building in the far east corner, nearest the back wall. The door hung on one hinge and opened into a damp little hovel lit with meager light pouring through small windows. Four rooms filled the space with debris littering the floor. And now, after weeks at Lynhurst, I stepped down into the pungent, stale air of the cells afresh. This is what it must be like for Silas, visiting for the first time. It softened my judgment toward him.

"Step down here." The doorway, worn down by hundreds of pairs of feet, had become a rutted mess. "Rosa lives here. She has had four infections this year and has not been completely well in ten years at least."

Silas had to duck in the low rooms as I led him toward one of the doorless cells. The familiar pile of rags moved, a bony hand rising from the mass.

"My own dear Aura Rose, is it?" The raspy voice had surprising strength.

I grasped the hand, squeezing gently, and helped her stand. The rags fell about her, covering her form in the shape of a pieced-together tent-like dress.

"Ah, you've brought a guest! Won't you make the introductions so I can begin flirting with this handsome man?" She cackled gleefully.

"Rosa, this is Mr. Rotherham. He's a houseguest at my aunt's home."

He bent to shake her hand, but she drew him toward her. "None of this, none of this." Pulling him down to her level, she threw her arms about the man, leaving a dusty imprint across his black suit.

Please don't pull away. Don't be disgusted.

But he smiled a little, a rare occurrence that revealed the dimples above his mouth.

"I was a fine-looking woman once. Afore all this mess happened to me. Age, and sickness. Avoid it at all costs."

"My body ages, but I hope my heart does not."

She cackled, shaking her head. "Good boy, good boy."

"Can I bring you anything while I'm here?" I felt the woman's turban-wrapped head for fever, and found she had only a slight one at worst.

"A lemon-balm cake with custard sauce." She said the words slowly, deliberately, as if they held the flavor she spoke of. Her tongue snaked out and licked her lips.

"How about a blanket?"

Her high-pitched grunt of approval led me to pull one of the blankets from Silas's arm and drape it over the woman's shoulders. If only it were warmer and softer. What had made these rags seem so lavish to me only weeks ago? Just a handful of nights under a thick, whole comforter had altered my attitude.

Back outside in the gloomy daylight, I looked Silas over. He hadn't brushed the dirt from his jacket, but worry shadowed his features.

"Are all the cells this way? This . . . dirty and bare?"

"This building is one of the nicer ones. Only one inmate per cell. I'm easing you into the reality of Shepton Mallet."

He said nothing, but his face clearly asked, *So it gets worse?*

"Rosa is fortunate enough to have former neighbors who care for her and send her little tokens. That's how she has her own small space."

"And whom does she pay for these privileges?"

"The man who let us in. This is not his civic duty, you know. It's a business."

Silas's Adam's apple bobbed as we crossed the courtyard again. Even after that glimpse, he still wanted more, so I would give him what he asked. Crossing to the long ivy-covered building to the west, I pushed open a door and stepped into another dim room. The high voices of children greeted us in the dark.

"What a shame these poor children must suffer for the debts of their fathers." He whispered these words. "What of the children who have other relatives? Are those few lucky enough to at least be shipped off to live with them?"

I paused in the corridor and faced him. "Yes, they are shipped off. And they are *unlucky* enough to grow up without their parents."

Stalls without doors lined the long building, the barred walls dividing one family home from another. The tiny rooms reeked of disease and human odors.

I turned into the first cell. "Good morning!"

Mrs. Shipton and her four children turned dirty faces in

my direction, wide eyes a stark contrast against grimy skin. "Ahhh, Aura Rose. Aura Rose come back to the Mallet." She stood to throw her arms around me, her back warped into the sitting position she often assumed all day. The youngest, three-year-old Micah, catapulted himself toward Silas, welcoming the stranger in the way of young children. His dirt-encrusted body landed against the man's legs, his arms cinching around his knees.

The actions stunned the onlookers into frozen silence, including Silas. Then Gerta, the eldest, broke the moment. "Have you gotten an ending to the story of the frog yet, Miss Aura?"

"Of course I have. That ending has been rattling around in my mind, waiting to spill out."

The girl smiled shyly and a younger child charged at me, arms open. Collapsing together onto the bed, sinking the mattress to the floor, I dove into the story. But a quick glance at Silas jarred my momentum. He'd lifted Micah into his arms, carefully wiping a stark white handkerchief across the dirty sores on his face. His tender smile put the boy at ease, and soon Micah sank onto Silas's shoulder, playing with his neck cloth. Silas wrapped his arm more securely around the tiny frame, as if exuding the same comfort to him that he'd tried to give me moments ago. Wonder poured from his eyes toward the tiny boy.

The sight fractured my heart. Taking in the scene in quick sips, I permanently embedded the image in my mind. Whatever his flaws, the man had a heart. One remarkably like my own.

After the story, I lifted the Danish from my pocket and set it on the table before Mrs. Shipton. "For the family."

"Why thank you, Aura Rose." She set upon the pieces greedily, shoving a piece into her mouth and handing the remaining ones to her children. "Lucky for us Father is in the courtyard at the moment or this would have to be divided six ways instead of five."

We finished our visit and stopped at the next cell, home to the Eides. A couple in their late sixties, they'd come up short one month when the meat business had been bad for more than a year. I quietly explained to Silas the struggles that had landed them in this place, where they clung to each other still.

Mrs. Eide huddled under the same plaid shawl she'd worn into the Mallet six years earlier, though the body underneath it had grown considerably weaker and more bent. She leaned on her tall husband on their shared bench.

"I'd like you to meet Silas Rotherham. He's a friend of mine."

"Oh, Aura Rose!" Tears pooled in the woman's eyes as she struggled to rise, holding out a hand. "What a delight. Come let me love on you."

I hugged the couple together and then nudged the woman's sleeve up to inspect her arm. "Have you changed the dressing?"

"Until I ran out of clean strips. But it does feel much better now. Really."

Lifting the hem of my skirt and locating a clean section, I ripped a strip from my garment and wrapped it around the woman's arm, pinching the open wound together.

"Still all right?" I turned to Silas as I worked.

"Actually, I'd welcome a small break. Something's come up that must be attended. I will see to my errands and return for you shortly. Would that be all right?"

My heart plummeted. But like a drowning man, he needed to surface for air sometime. The misery and reality were enough to overwhelm any outsider. I nodded, dismissing him, and turned back to the task. Even if he did surrender early, he'd done remarkably well. Better than I'd anticipated. I needed to focus on that.

But I suspected there was no errand awaiting him.

15

Too often we cut away essential elements of ourselves
to fit into a mold and discover those elements were
vital to who we are, and our improvements have only
made us more ordinary.

~Nathaniel Droll, *Lady Jayne Disappears*

Silas Rotherham stepped down the dank hallway and out into
daylight. Was it really still daytime? It seemed like eternal
night in that dungeon. Approaching the carriage waiting
outside the gate, he tossed the coat onto the seat and flipped
a coin to the coachman. "Go to the Briar Avenue bake shop
and bring me a lemon-balm cake with custard sauce. And
throw me your handkerchiefs. Here's another piece to get
yourself some new ones." He flipped a second coin, then
retreated back into the prison.

Walking into a building identical to the one he'd just left,
he moved down the row of cells, glancing at the husks of
humanity trapped in each. Inmates stared at him with empty

faces as he passed. So different than when Aurelie had swept through these same halls. She'd lit up the space, infusing life into worn-out bodies.

Finally he stopped at a cell with several dirty children lolling about. The smaller ones rolled over each other with squeals. A hairy man with thick, overgrown muttonchops hovered in the back corner, a lifetime of failure weighing down his shoulders.

"Good morning, sir." Silas smiled at the man, then his children. "Would you like an orange?" He pulled the fruit from his wide pocket, eternally grateful he'd placed it there, yet wishing he'd overloaded his pockets with them. No, overloaded the *carriage* with them.

A small girl took the orange gingerly, but the father smacked it onto the floor. "Take nothing from strangers, Hattie. We haven't the money to pay for tokens."

"It's a gift. From Aura Rose."

Her name worked like a password. The man's eyes brightened. "Aura Rose?" He retrieved the fruit from the floor and considered the orange treasure.

"Does everyone here know the girl?"

He nodded. "She prayed my beautiful Lily into heaven last year, sang to her the whole time." A tear made a path through the dirt on his cheek. "She came through every day to check on her, cleaned the infection, and gave her food."

Silas tried to swallow past the huge lump in his throat.

"Then she told them wild stories of hers. Just wild enough to keep my little ones afloat when they lost their mama."

"What of Aura Rose's mother? Who was she?"

The man paused, blinking at the straw on the floor. "Don't believe I ever heard tell of her having a mother. I suppose she must have at one time, but heaven knows who she is."

Silas traveled down the row of cells, stopping at some, talking to the residents about their illnesses and about the enigmatic Aura Rose. Two things struck him—that the residents had been flooded with preventable diseases and unnecessary infections, and that no one knew anything about Aura Rose's personal life. A few told snippets of her stories or described the healing touch of her hand, but none knew anything about the girl herself. How amazing, how humble, was this girl who broke herself into a million pieces and distributed them to any who had need.

Finally Silas emerged into the courtyard again. Before he could choose the next course of action, the guard flagged him down and handed him the requested delicacy from the coachman. He thanked the man and turned to the building containing Rosa's cell. The woman had asked for such a small item. For this day at least, Silas would ensure the woman got her simple wish.

He ducked back through the door and into the cell where the moving pile of rags huddled in the corner.

"Rosa, are you awake? I've brought you something."

The warted face appeared in the dim light, blinking at him. "Ah, the handsome one, back for a second date. Come in, and shut the door behind you." She pushed herself up onto her legs. "Can't have the chickens getting out again."

"Of course." He made a motion to shut the nonexistent door and held out the treat. "Your dessert, madam."

Her eyes flew open, hands twitching over the white box. "Oh, oh . . ." Tears pooled in her glossy eyes. "It's real, ain't it?"

He opened the box and she reached in, but her hand

trembled so hard she couldn't grasp the cake. Urging her to sit again, he knelt before her and broke off a piece, setting it on her lips. She gobbled it up hungrily, and he repeated with another piece. His stomach turned as he watched this woman, a human with a childhood, likes and dislikes, skills and interests, who devoured this food as a hungry dog. When the last piece had disappeared into her mouth, Silas stood, but she grabbed for the box. "If you've no need of it, might I keep it?"

He lowered it back to her lap. "Of course."

"I want to look at it every day, and remember that I've tasted heaven today." She winked at him. "And seen an angel."

When he pivoted to the door, Aurelie hovered in the shadows, her finely freckled face a mix of intense emotions. Had he trod on her territory? Crossed a line? Perhaps she thought him foolish. He'd brought the woman a silly luxury item, when what she really needed was clean clothes and a bath.

"Have you more to show me? I'm ready now." He approached her, rubbing at the grit on the back of his neck. A bath would do wonders to remove the traces of this place on his skin, but nothing could erase what he'd witnessed, or the heavy realization that Aurelie had been absolutely right.

With a silent nod, she led him to another tenement with long rows of cells. "I have a few more I wish to visit."

She moved among these broken pieces of humanity, binding wounds, cleaning faces, and drawing smiles. The aura of peace and comfort glided with her down the hall like lamp glow. He felt an odd sense of honor to be in her presence. With her pure skin and neat clothes, she did not appear to belong. But neither did she belong at Lynhurst, among the flirting, the insincerity, and dramatic wardrobes. All the efforts of those people, and the people he'd always known, suddenly seemed so trivial and off the mark. They cared greatly about many small things, making them seem large, when truly big things like life and death and family love filled this place.

Finally they left the building when his stomach growled. It must be well past lunchtime, and he'd hardly eaten breakfast. The jailer met them at the door with a hearty handshake for Silas.

"So what did the fine gentleman think of my Mallet?"

"Far from my expectations." His solemn answer poured forth from his over-squeezed heart.

With a laugh the jailer clapped him on the back. "Glad you approve. I run an efficient ship here, and no one gets away with nothing. Not a bit of waste goes on, neither."

"You provide their food and other needs?"

"Aye, that's me."

"What sort of food do you give them?"

"Aw, you'll like this, sir. I use me brain. We have horse feed brought in from the races in Bath. Buy it on the cheap when they're through with it. Corn and oats and such. We soak it in water over the stoves, and we have food for weeks. I struck a deal with the market on Fox Haven Court for carrots and potatoes that go bad before they're sold. Not real bad, of course. Just bad enough that they won't bring the full shilling asked for 'em."

"They get no meat? No bread?"

"Oh, some do. Depends on how well they grease me fingers." He rubbed his thumb and forefinger together with a wink, as if Silas would appreciate his shrewdness.

"I see." Without more to say, Silas led a white-faced Aurelie by the elbow from the prison and back onto the street where the carriage waited. Outside the gates, she leaned her narrow shoulder against his arm, almost as if by accident. Surprised by her touch, he dared not shift away or even breathe too hard. Her tenuous favor toward him would likely not last, but he would do nothing to upset it.

She leaned on him until she'd stepped into the carriage. He climbed in after her, suddenly filled with an overwhelming urge to shield her forever from the evil of this world—not the disease-ridden prisons where she walked about like a miracle, but the parts like Lynhurst that sought to exclude and devalue her.

The carriage jerked and bumped over the rough alley and turned down the main street of Glen Cora before either of them spoke. The letter had been posted, and the vehicle now turned toward Lynhurst.

Aurelie watched him with bright eyes from the shadows. "Now how do you feel about debtor's prison, Mr. Rotherham?"

"Would it be dishonorable of me to call your home a miserable stink hole?"

Her face lighted with the glow of a hundred candles. "It is never dishonorable to speak the truth."

"Have you always walked among the sick that way?"

"Always. I know it isn't seemly for a woman, but I think I was born with an overwhelming urge to *do*."

And an overwhelming love for people—although he did not dare say anything that forward aloud. It was one simple trait women were meant to have inherently, this extravagant love, but there were a great many of them who had evolved so far past what they were originally created to be. "You miss it a little, don't you?"

"Prison?" She tilted her head back. "Would you find me odd if I said yes?"

"Wonderfully odd." He smiled in the dark.

"It's cleansed my spirit to return there." The rattling vehicle nearly drowned her soft voice. "Even though it hasn't been long since I left, I've never been gone from the Mallet even for a night before. Thank you for arranging this visit." Tears lit her eyes, shining in the dim space. "Somehow it solidifies who I am and my purpose." She ducked her head. Her posture compelled him across the space separating them. Perching on the edge of her seat, he angled toward her, his face close enough to smell the almond scent of her hair.

There in the privacy of the dark, the outside world and its opinions hardly mattered. He slipped his arm around her hunched shoulders, drawing her doll-like face to his chest. The heat of her emotion radiated onto him, and he held her tighter. For all the youthful years he spent craving a comforting touch, it healed some unseen thing in him to be able to bestow it so freely on someone else.

"It was my pleasure. And in a way, you do belong there. Not because you are a debtor, but a rescuer. A healer. You are magnificent in that role, as if God created you as a special being expressly for that purpose." He snapped his jaw shut. That thought should have remained in his head. He'd alienate her before they even reached Lynhurst.

But she melted into his embrace. When would he remember? She was not anything like the others. He anchored her tiny frame against himself, his lips brushing the glossy strands of her hair and eliciting a pleasant tingle from them.

When she stirred, he unfolded his arms and straightened against the seat back. She tipped her sweet face up to look at him, dewy eyes drawing him in, tugging irresistibly at the protector in him. Her mouth twitched in a pure smile, and with the outside world a blur in the tiny window, he drew close, watching those lips, unable to pull away. How could mere lips be so expressive? In a flash, he imagined skimming them with his own. What sort of passion would they return?

But this wasn't the time.

He could so easily ruin everything, maybe losing this beautiful, unnameable friendship between them. Or maybe he'd come close to the most perfect kiss he'd ever experience, and everything that lay on the other side of it.

Silas firmed his jaw. No, the timing was awful. What flitted over her rosy face—fear? Worry?

Now returned to herself, the girl's delicate chin tipped up and her mouth thinned, indicating she intended to push past whatever emotion had overcome her at the near kiss. It took several moments for her to speak again, but when she did, she had collected herself. "Dickens wrote so much about Marshalsea Prison and somehow the world thought it all an exaggeration. He is a man of fiction, after all. But he wrote from experience, for he himself lived there as a boy."

"Perhaps you should write your own commentaries on prison life. Explain to the outside world what occurs there." An easy slide across the seat offered a calming distance between them. "You do have a wonderful way of spinning stories."

Her noncommittal smile made him want to encourage her even more. Convince her.

"I've thought of it."

"Then why aren't they done? Have you so many other pressing engagements at the moment?"

Face slanted toward the window, she shrugged, allowing the silence to hang.

"All right, then tell *me* one of your stories. I never seem to have my fill of them."

With a sleepy smile, she leaned her head against the wall of the carriage. "Have you heard the story about the princess and the knight?"

Amused, he shook his head. "No, but I would love to."

Animation filled her lovely face as the story took on its own life in the carriage rattling down the open road. As the story poured forth, Silas focused on breathing in and out, achieving normalcy again within himself. What had so intoxicated him about this girl? She couldn't be of this earth. No one really loved the way she did. Not without an audience.

A fleeting ache squeezed his gut. What would it be like to have that immense love directed toward him?

The carriage delivered us to the front door of Lynhurst Manor as the first glow of sunset tinged the horizon. Had it really grown that late? I stepped out and nodded my thanks to the coachman.

Silas landed on the gravel next and shoved his hands into his pockets. "It was a lovely time."

Somehow those moments of being supremely comfortable together only led to increased awkwardness afterward. Had I nearly let him kiss me? I'd never been that relaxed—and yet remarkably alive—in my life. Not even when crafting the perfect scene. And now we had to walk back into Lynhurst, sit across from one another at meals, and pretend the whole blessed day had not happened.

But it would never be forgotten. It would spur my work, driving me to it with even more purpose and love for the truths I'd write about.

The early-warning dinner bell sounded, sending us scurrying into the house. At least we were free from awkward conversation for the moment. I climbed the stairs to my room and dug through my wardrobe for a dress that fit my mood—serene and soft, and far from flashy.

But Papa's coat tossed over the corner of my bed caught my eye. Papa. My wonderful, dear Papa. I walked to it and buried my face against the smooth leather collar and worn fabric, breathing in the lingering essence of him. *Oh, Papa.* Going back to the Mallet, to the space we'd shared for years, had perhaps been a mistake. I needed to heal and move forward, not backtrack into my pit of grief. Sobs rose to my throat, threatening to spill over.

With a wavering breath in and out, I pulled myself away from the musty coat and perched at my desk. For a writer, no pain was ever without purpose. The tears dripped down my face without permission. I instinctively walled off the grief, but as my defenses rose, I intentionally released them.

I dipped the pen in the inkwell and closed my eyes. What if someone else felt this same hurt? What if something I wrote could speak to them and make them feel less alone or bring truth into their struggle? For the sake of another hurting soul that might happen upon this installment, I braced myself over my desk and allowed the pain to rise and crest over me.

I walked again through our tower cell, mentally touching each precious object. His crooked bed. The neat row of blank books. Scattered envelopes from Marsh House Press torn open and discarded. The messy but honored stack of reader responses in their own corner. His rich voice floated back to me, and I let it play through my aching heart, slicing through me.

That desperation of being kept from the one person who loved you for yourself—that's what Jayne Windham felt right now for Charles Sterling Clavey. Maybe Lady Jayne had to watch him court other women, perhaps even marry someone, knowing that she would never be free to sink into that beloved relationship. She would crave it so desperately, just as I craved the father lost to me through death.

I understand, Lady Jayne. Oh, how terribly I understand.

Then, with my grief at its peak, I bled my pain onto the page, spreading its black inkiness in perfect swooping letters. Raw, concise phrases revealed the true hurt of fresh loss. How cleansing to cut one's own heart open and lay it on the page. Cleansing, yet terrifying. These were the feelings most people worked to hide from the outside world—even loved ones who might sympathize. And here I was, setting them down in black and white, ready to ship into a world of strangers who did not know me.

I poured out my pain until my skin warmed with the weight of emotion. Dropping the pen, I sighed and stood. Fresh air would help. I tugged open the tall window and stuck my face into the breeze. The heaviness dissipated into a pleasant afterglow. This time my writing had been good. Not waffly, look-at-me prose, but beautiful heartache and real struggle.

16

No one understood her love of reading, but to Lady Jayne, fiction was far better than real life—it always had to make sense, and real life seldom did.

~Nathaniel Droll, *Lady Jayne Disappears*

Why could I no longer meet Silas's gaze whenever I saw him? For days I avoided direct conversation with him for reasons I could not pinpoint. I craved it and feared it at the same time. Would that wonderful day evaporate into foolishness in the light of reality?

A knock at my door snapped my attention back to the moment, with the sun setting and the dinner hour approaching. "Come in."

Silas? My heart tripped a little. No. Of course he wouldn't come to my bedchamber.

Nelle slipped through the door, a cream-colored gown draped across her arms. "Two bits of news." Her lips pressed into a thin line around the words.

"One includes wearing that dress, I imagine."

"While you were out a few days ago, you kindly accepted a dinner invitation. Lady Pochard said no, but Juliette claimed it would be rude to decline, since the Naughtons attended the benefit."

"So rude." I crossed to Nelle and ran my fingertips over the satiny dress. Mauve rosebuds accented the sash and neckline. "And the other bad news?" I ached to share my experience with Silas Rotherham, but how would I phrase it? I could hear the scorn in my friend's voice. "Really—*him?*" Besides, what was there to tell? A few moments of shared conversation and a near kiss that never evolved.

"This came for you-know-who." Shuffling the dress to free one hand, Nelle drew a letter from her apron pocket and held it out. The missive was for Nathaniel Droll from Marsh House Press. I'd forgotten about the letter posted days ago on our trip to Glen Cora.

"Thank you, I'll deliver it to him." My words felt dishonest as soon as they were out.

"I'll send Annie up to help you dress." With an affectionate arm squeeze and a smile, she wished me luck and darted from the room.

Crossing to the desk, I slit open the envelope and pulled out the paper with bold writing.

We received your request to change the specified details. Unfortunately, we are unable to accommodate your wishes. We print most of your installments the minute they arrive, as we are accommodating your other demand that you be allowed to write until the last possible moment. It is a highly unorthodox practice, but we are pleased to honor the wishes of our most esteemed author. Please accept our apologies that we cannot also meet this request.

RAM

The paper trembled in my hand as I pictured them all sitting around reading the next installment in the drawing room, narrowing down their list of suspects. Would my downcast face give me away? Something must be done before the installment released.

Tugged and corseted into the cream-colored dress an hour later, I swept down the stairs to meet the others. The sight of my cousin dissipated my fear for the moment, packing it neatly away for the inevitable "later."

Juliette's drop-neck gold gown covered only what it must, and I frowned. How had I forgotten? Juliette, Jasper, the garden in the early morning. She was dressing this way for him. They were probably even attending the party to be together.

"Dear, you look radiant. I cannot wait to show you off." Juliette glided toward me and reached up to adjust tendrils of my hair. "I do hope you'll let me introduce you as my protégé."

I flexed my gloved fingers. "Only if you do one favor for me." It was time. If I didn't speak quickly, my heart would thud out of my chest.

"Of course." Her pretty red lips parted in a smile.

"Ignore that man from the benefit—the one who was not invited. He seems a dodgy sort."

Gaze hard and nostrils flaring, Juliette withdrew her hands

from where they had been twisting my curls into place. "Why would you say such a thing?"

I dropped my gaze evasively. "I know people, and he isn't a decent man. Not the type you should spend time with."

Anger froze the statuesque face. "You can have Silas all to yourself. Or any other one for that matter, but Jasper Grupp is not yours. You had your chance once. He told me all about that."

"Juliette—"

"Perhaps Mother was right about you needing to leave Lynhurst." The girl jerked her arm away and marched toward the front door. Our escorts emerged together from the library, trailing an aura of pipe smoke with them.

"Oh Silas, dear." Juliette's gloved hand slid effortlessly into the crook of his arm as they walked toward the door. She leaned close and spoke in a stage whisper that still managed to wind its way around the hall. "I was hoping you would escort Aurelie this time. It isn't that I don't adore your company, but no one else seems to care for the poor thing. I'd hate for my dear cousin to go without, when I can make a small sacrifice for her dignity. You don't mind, do you, darling?" She slid her hand from his arm and moved toward Kendrick.

He must think I'd arranged this. That I was becoming one of them, scheming and maneuvering.

Silas, who'd avoided eye contact with me until then, turned his solemn gray eyes to mine and held my gaze. "It would be a distinct honor."

It was dark before we arrived at the Naughtons' ivy-covered country home. Silas helped me from the carriage, flashing a private smile that spoke of our shared confidences.

Over the gravel drive and up the two large front steps, I held lightly to Silas's arm. Just past the bright entryway, Jasper Grupp stood folded in among the gentry as if he belonged. He wore the same suit that he had worn to Lynhurst—would anyone notice?—and lounged against the stair railing, balancing a crystal glass on his fingertips. He'd been drawn deep into a conversation with a few other men, but he tore himself away for a brief glance when our party entered. First, he pinned me with a cutting glance and wicked smile, then his eyes roamed to Juliette and assessed her with delight from jeweled headpiece to gold pointy-toed slippers.

"You can amuse yourself, can't you, Kendrick?" Juliette unhooked her arm and slipped into the throng of guests. She made a cursory stop to greet a few people, including the hostess, but veered quickly to Jasper, approaching him with coquettish posture. I turned away, helpless.

"What can I do to make you more comfortable here?" Silas's low voice tickled my ear.

"What makes you think me uncomfortable?"

He turned those riveting eyes on me, commanding honesty.

I relented with a sigh. "I'm not built for this sort of thing. Maybe not for anything in this life at Lynhurst." I certainly made a mess of everything. Including my one and only friendship within the family. "I am an expense, take up space . . . and I'm afraid I have become an immense burden to Juliette."

"Do not fool yourself. You are a gift to that girl, allowing her to preen you and talk your ear off. You are the perfect friend for her."

If only he knew.

"In fact, you are her *only* friend."

I fidgeted. "But that's not possible. She's so beautiful and desired by men and . . ."

"And lonely. Aurelie, the girl hasn't any friends outside of you. Especially in the female realm."

The weight of truth sank his words into my heart, leaving an ache. It was true. Juliette never kept company with other women, never had any females call at the house.

I'd ruined everything. Rolling my closed fan across my open palm, I glanced at the vivacious girl with the mess of beautiful ringlets down her shoulders. She was like the king with the golden touch—a blessing everyone wished for until they recognized it for the curse it was. Responsibility lay heavily on my shoulders. God did have a purpose for me in all this, and somehow I'd already failed.

When it was time, Silas tucked my hand into the crook of his arm and escorted me into a white-and-gold dining room decked with lavish paintings and statues.

"And you do have one other important purpose here, you know." He leaned in close to whisper his words as he seated himself beside me.

"What is that?"

"Imparting your remarkable stories to one very out-of-place visitor who happens to be addicted to fiction. Especially to yours."

A smile lifted the corner of my lips. He always knew the exact second it was time to rescue my heart from the heaviness of life. He could swim deep with me for long minutes, delving into important conversations on humanity and relationships, then draw me back up to skim the sun-dappled surface when my thoughts became too heavy.

"Have you heard the story of the wealthy married couple who had everything and nothing at the same time?"

His jaunty smile encouraged more.

"It was a disproportionate marriage. She was wealthy and intelligent, and he was merely wealthy. As happens in such marriages, they grew to hate each other, yet they could not bring themselves to do anything about it. After all, what would people think? So they remained, and the best they could hope for was benign apathy between them."

The story continued through a creamy clam soup and reached its satisfying ending just as servers carried out plates of goose with cranberries and garnish. My mouth watering for the tart berries, I slowed my talking.

"I'm quite happy that Juliette foisted her little protégé off on me tonight." Silas smiled as he sank a knife into his meat.

The ache of my failure returned. "I'm afraid I upset her. That's why she did it."

"You? No, no. You couldn't upset even an excitable viper."

"It was a misunderstanding. I only wanted to warn her away from this man, and she thought I wanted him for myself."

His eyebrows rose, fork pausing on the way to his mouth, then he recovered and resumed eating. "Is that so. You are stealing her gentleman, are you? Do you care for him?"

"He isn't a gentleman, and I'm not stealing him. It's the man who came to the benefit. He's a cad, and I've no idea how to convince her."

"Ah, him. The pitiful recipient of your daggered stares. Do you know, Juliette's parents have actually forbidden her to see him, on account of his undefined background and family connections, but I assume you have a more valid reason for declaring him unworthy."

Forbidden her? The words poured comfort over me. Perhaps I would not have to risk my friendship with her to warn her away from him again. "I knew him in Glen Cora, when I lived at the Mallet. He has been dressing and speaking as a gentleman, but he's poor as mud. Lives with his father in a tiny—"

"So it's a class difference." The steady words cut through my explanation, deflating it. "Tell me, Miss Harcourt. Have you become one of them so quickly?"

Heat drenched my face. "That isn't what I mean. It isn't his lack of wealth that bothers me, but the dishonesty. He lied about it." And so many other things.

"And who has not presented himself as better than he is when first meeting an attractive prospect? It's only natural to present our best selves and reveal the negatives later."

The words snuffed my spark. Reveal the truth later? These were the words of a man who'd hidden things himself. And likely he had, just as Nelle suspected. I had been fooled by his unassuming good nature. What lay underneath all that? Yet another complication to this character. Somehow I'd been fooled into overlooking the bad, just as I had with Jasper. I had a terrible habit of only seeing the good in people—especially the handsome ones.

Must I always fall into this trap?

"You do not approve of my response." It was stated simply, unapologetically, as he considered me, rolling his fork handle between two fingers.

"It gives you an air of deception that is unsettling."

His dark eyebrows drew low. "I've always been plain as day with you, Miss Harcourt. Ask me anything about myself and I'll tell you. Gladly."

"All right, then." I poked at the raisins settled atop the gelled side dish. "I want to know why you are at Lynhurst. The true reason."

The grim look of his face told me I'd struck gold. "All right, I'll tell you." He looked away. "I'm here to find Nathaniel Droll."

17

Charles Sterling Clavey never set out to do evil—he was merely deluded about what was good and what was not.

~Nathaniel Droll, *Lady Jayne Disappears*

By the time the chambermaid loosened my bodice and corset later that night, I never wanted to leave my chamber again. How could I ever face Silas Rotherham now? We'd made such a pleasant habit of talking often and deeply, sometimes alone. But now that must end completely.

Why on earth did the man want to find Nathaniel Droll? And how had he known to travel all the way to Lynhurst to conduct his search? He'd spent time here with Kendrick in his childhood—perhaps he read something about the setting that had tipped him off. But still—why spend an entire summer on the endeavor?

I might have considered divulging my secret to him, and only him, were it not for his earlier words about Jasper.

It's only natural to present our best selves and reveal the negatives later.

What would a man with those scruples do with my secret? Likely the man only wanted to line his pockets with bribe money from Nathaniel Droll—or make a name for himself by revealing the author's identity. Either way, I would never give him a spark of an idea as to Droll's true identity.

I sighed and pushed tired fingers through my hair. Holing away in my quiet chamber might not be a terrible idea all around. I did not belong among these people, and no amount of clothing or hair styling would change that. It was as if I attempted to play cribbage with a roomful of experts while I was only truly qualified to play marbles on the floor. They all played masterfully, as if they'd done it all their lives, knowing exactly when to hold cards or discard, what to reveal and what to hide. Even the facial expressions were calculated to reveal exactly what they wanted the others to know and no more.

Just as I pulled my cotton nightdress on and wrapped my dressing gown around myself, thankful for the waistless clothes, a knock made me jump. Shaking my fingers through my newly released hair, I opened the door.

"Juliette."

"I'm glad you're still awake." She brushed past in a blue dressing gown and dainty slippers and curled into one of the twin chairs, cradling a brown package in her lap. "I simply cannot sleep, and we're going to have a ladies' night. I've even found this delightful stash of peanut brittle, thanks to Nathaniel Droll." She extracted a thin square and popped it between her rosy lips, rolling it around.

"But you're angry at me."

"I've decided to forgive you." She patted the other chair and pulled it up to hers. "I'd hate to have to squeeze you out of my entire life just for one little misunderstanding. Kendrick convinced me that you meant well, so consider it part of the past."

Desperation had one positive aspect—quick forgiveness of a person's only friend. My brain tingled with exhaustion, but I pushed past it, forcing myself to remain engaged. This was my chance. Every word of warning, every revealing truth about Jasper, spun in my head.

But I was immediately overwhelmed at the memory of Silas's words—*her only friend*. The weight of that drowned out anything I'd meant to say. "You think an awful lot of him."

"That's why I cannot sleep. We've had the most wonderful time, right in front of everyone, but with no one seeing a thing."

But I'd seen it. Never before had I watched a pair flirt so intensely from across the room.

Juliette paused, studying me. "I don't expect you to understand. I knew you couldn't. I'm simply not like you." Knees to her chest, she dusted the chair arm with the fringe from her sleeve. "I don't have the capacity to merely *love* a man and be satisfied as a married woman. You will find a sweet, wholesome husband who is safe and good, and you'll happily spend your life with him, but I will never have that."

Only Juliette could make goodness sound undesirable. I accepted the candy and nibbled on it, the sweet and salty flavor melting my taste buds with pleasure. If only I knew Silas to be safe and good. My skittish heart desired to wall itself off from him, but I could not forget the tender way he'd held

Micah, or the way he'd spooned custard into Rosa's mouth. Those images would be etched in my memory forever, no matter what came of our acquaintanceship.

"I have always dreaded the idea of settling on one man and taking myself out of society completely. Being here in this house with only family about, I feel like a dead plant. The only time I'm alive is when I'm out among people, with men, and possibilities, and conversation. Just imagine if that is over forever. I could never again welcome the attention of a handsome aristocrat, never share flirty glances and interesting conversation. I'll know my entire future, every same old day of it, before I've lived it."

"So you mean to say that this new man is a passing fancy?" I could hope.

Juliette's eyes sparkled. "No, that's just it. This one is quite different. He found a wick in me I never knew existed and lit it. Every sentence that passes between us, every time his fingertips touch me, it sparks with life and color. It's addictive, and when you taste it, you realize your entire life before this had been dull as clay. Every flirtation before has been a hollow imitation of this. Even the ones that seemed promising ended up not quite satisfying and left me anxious for the next one. But with Jasper, every moment sparks and captivates. I cannot get enough, and I want that every day for the rest of my life."

Dread settled over me. A friend would speak the truth. But a friend would also encourage her friend's happiness.

This was not happiness, though. This was Jasper. I should speak up.

As I grabbed for the right words, the girl's cheeks pinked with excitement, making her a striking beauty. The same way she looked around Jasper. No wonder he found himself obsessed with her.

"Please do not think me foolish, dear cousin. One day I hope you experience this sort of breathtaking passion. You'll know it when you find it, and then you will understand what has captured me so."

But it wasn't real. Not with Jasper Grupp. It *couldn't* be. By his very nature, he was constantly in flux, donning and then discarding selves as if they were disposable. I should simply tell her everything, starting with the truth about my background and ending with what I knew of Jasper's many hidden traits—the lies, the stealing, the buried rage always ready to explode. But dissuading her could drive her toward Jasper even more. Warring desires consumed me.

Maybe a compromise. I'd keep watch on the pair, make sure Jasper only toyed innocently with her and then let her go. His interest in Juliette would likely dwindle, as it did with any pursuit. If he pushed too far, I could intervene immediately.

"I wish you'd be happy for me. I need one person to be so. This is the most amazing thing in all of life, ever. I want you to be glad for me because I'm finally alive." She hugged her legs to her chest.

I smiled with tight lips. "I'm happy to see you so fulfilled." Saying this turned my stomach, but it earned me a glowing smile from my cousin.

Support Juliette. Not the relationship with Grupp, but Juliette. As a friend.

She reached across the space and took my hands in hers. "I'm sorry I snapped before. You truly are a dear girl, and I'm glad you've come to Lynhurst."

"I've enjoyed the chance to know my cousins."

Juliette curled deeper into the chair. "Tell me a story, would you? I've heard so much about them. I'd like a romantic one, though."

I smiled, slipping back into my comfortable element. "Very well. A romantic one. Have you heard the story about a handsome man disguised as a peasant?" And this is exactly how God could make use of my stories. Fiction was not always a lie, but a truth told in parallel to real life. A pill of advice disguised in an easy-to-swallow tale.

That night, I brought both Juliette and Nelle into my prayer time, asking for God's guidance in each of their lives. *Bring them both a future that will keep their lives on the right path.*

Having woken before anyone else, Silas slit the envelope open in the front hall where Digory had handed it to him in the morning sunlight. He skimmed the thick, loopy writing, a sense of finality swirling up in him. At last, the answer to all his questions.

With a tremor of excitement, he walked out the garden door and flagged down a skinny boy weeding around a young birch. "Please, can you tell me where to find Florin cottage? It's on the estate, I believe."

"That it is." His bright eyes assessed Silas. "Take the path down a ways here, turn left before you come to the woods, and follow it around to the house. You'll see it. Just off the route."

"Thank you." He flipped the boy a tuppence and moved swiftly in the direction indicated. A breeze blew through the pine-scented forest and filled him with memories of many summer weeks spent here. How he'd loved visiting as a child and romping alone through the woods.

But when he arrived at the thatched cottage, nothing looked familiar. Flowers graced the window boxes and a collection of flagstones invited him right to the door.

He rapped lightly, then a little harder. Voices rang inside, and then the door opened. A woman, slender and natural-looking with the sweet face of innocence, looked at him with both question and hesitation in her eyes.

Beautiful, but not who he'd expected to find.

"Oh. I must have the wrong cottage. Pardon me." He dipped and spun to leave, but turned back. "Please, can you tell me where to find Florin cottage?" He showed her the paper, folding it to just show the address he sought. He couldn't reveal the rest until he knew more himself.

"Yes, this is it." She slipped through the nearly closed door, shutting it behind her.

"I have a matter to discuss with someone at this house. May I ask who else lives here?"

"Only myself, sir." But she glanced for a split second at the window behind her.

"Are you sure there's no one . . . ? It's just a small matter of business and a few questions."

"I live alone here." Then her sweet voice grew higher and faster. "I make dress embellishments for the ladies of Lynhurst Manor. A little repair work for the service staff as well. Not lately, but usually. Well, when it's needed."

He studied the guarded little face. What did she hide? Or *whom* did she hide? She stole a glance again toward the curtained window.

But he shouldn't badger the poor girl. Fear creased her

ivory forehead, lighting the pure blue eyes. If he left now, though, he'd be back at a dead end. The frustration of that idea propelled him to try again. "Is someone staying with you?"

"No, I stay alone."

"But I heard voices when I came to the door."

"I . . . speak to myself. For company." Red stained her cheeks.

He smiled. "A mark in your favor, to be sure. But I'm certain I heard two voices."

She backed against the door, eyes wide.

"Please, I am harmless, I promise you. I just need some information, and apparently you are my one way to access it."

Her eyes rounded like those of a cornered animal, and two desires surged through him—the desire to assure her and the need to follow this lead and find the answers.

In a flick of movement, the curtains yanked back and a child's face peered out the window—also not what he expected. She followed his gaze, then threw herself at the window, covering it with her slender body. "Please, oh please, she needs to stay with me. She isn't any trouble. And I need the work here. I've never stolen, never lied, always worked my hardest. She isn't any trouble."

Tears shone in her eyes, and he held up his hands, palms out. "It's all right, really. I've no reason to hurt either of you."

"Please go away."

"I mean you no trouble. I'm a guest at Lynhurst."

"I know exactly who you are, Mr. Rotherham. That's what makes me afraid—that you're a friend of the family." Her body, still plastered against the window, shuddered. "If they find out she's here . . ."

He held up a hand. "No one will ever find out from me. I promise. I'm not fond of most of them anyway." A head-jerk toward the house indicated the manor family. "All I ask is a conversation with you. May I please come in? I've already learned your secret. There's nothing more I can hurt by sitting at your table for a few moments. Just a few questions, and I'll be on my way. Promise."

With slow slides toward the door, she turned the knob behind her and backed in. Silas followed at a comfortable distance, afraid to send her sprinting through the woods.

Inside the dim but fresh-smelling cottage, he blinked to adjust his vision. The first thing he saw was small windows on the other side of the house, sunlight peeking around the edges of elaborate curtains. Next, the tiniest little person approached from her spot at the window, looking up at him with a soulful face that mirrored that of the woman who'd opened the door. When her delicate face dissolved into a sunny smile with two missing teeth, everything inside him melted into a helpless puddle. He lowered his frame to a squatty stool as the girl climbed onto another with a chipped teacup in one hand, bright blue eyes taking him in with childish acceptance.

"I'm Silas." He held out a hand, and she took his last two fingers and shook them with a timid grip.

"I'm Dahlia. Mum, it's all right to say it now, isn't it?"

"It's all right, love." The woman slid up behind the girl, cradling her blonde head. The affection between the two melted him even more. The mother reminded him of Aurelie, only softer, more pliable around the edges. Definitely a good sort.

"This is my daughter, Mr. Rotherham."

"Is the girl's father dead? That's nothing to—"

The quick dip of her head stopped him. How foolish. Of course her father was not dead. Not if she needed to hide the girl.

"Whoever he is, that man is the one at a loss right now. I, a mere stranger, have an advantage over him just sitting here with the two of you."

A timid smile tipped the corners of her mouth. "Thank you."

Questions floated to the surface, but the girl, little Dahlia, captured his attention and scattered his thoughts. With every glance he sent her direction, she smiled back with her entire face. What of her mother? Would her face light up that way when she fully smiled? It would be a personal goal to find out.

He cleared his throat. Only a few questions needed to be asked, but they seemed so invasive right now, sitting at her tiny table with her daughter. She still appeared skittish, ready to bolt or bound away with one wrong move from him.

He smiled at the child, where warm acceptance already radiated. "Might I try some tea?" The teacup she'd carried now lay abandoned on the table. She snatched it and poured invisible tea from her imaginary pot. "Of course you may. But you must dress like a *lady*."

Silas froze. The mother's horrified expression made it worse. Clearing his throat and yanking on his cravat, he forced an awkward smile. "Suppose I let your mother dress as a lady and I dress as a gentleman come to call on you both."

"That'll do nicely." The girl's blonde head gave one emphatic nod.

He lifted the tiny cup, his overly large fingers at awkward angles about the handle, and sipped the make-believe tea. When Dahlia dissolved in wonderful giggles, he never wanted to return to the business matters for fear of breaking this spell.

But eventually the invisible tea ran out, and the woman had relaxed onto a third stool, waiting for him to state his purpose. Unable to plunge into the straightforward questions that needed to be asked about Nathaniel Droll, Silas instead decided to lay before her his own carefully guarded information first.

"I am on the estate in search of someone, and it is important that I find him. I know little about the place or who lives here, since I haven't returned myself in many years." Or in the words of the man himself, *a hundred thousand stories' worth of time ago.*

"I've not been here many years, Mr. Rotherham. I probably cannot help you."

"Please. Tell me what you know about the true identity of Nathaniel Droll."

His host's lips pinched and her eyes widened at the name. "I definitely cannot help you, Mr. Rotherham. I'm sorry. I will not lie and say I know nothing, but I've made a solemn promise to keep certain facts secret."

He looked at the simply dressed woman with new respect. "By the way, I don't believe we finished the introductions. You already know who I am."

"I am Nelle. Nelle Wicke."

He took her soft hand in his and considered the beautiful face etched with wisdom. "Pleased, Miss Wicke. And now, if I tell you who I am, and what I'm about, will you consider helping me?"

"I'll agree to hearing you out."

"Fair enough."

18

Having experienced both poverty and wealth, Lady
Jayne only wanted freedom from both.

~Nathaniel Droll, *Lady Jayne Disappears*

It was Thursday. Publication day for *Lady Jayne Disappears*.
Would the family have read it by now? What would they have
guessed? I loosened the corset after the maid laced it up to
cater to the sickness attacking my stomach. *Lord, be with
me. You always have—now I need you again.* What was my
plan if they ejected me?

When I strode into the drawing room, the entire Gaffney
family perched on chairs facing Garamond, who held the
latest issue of *Lady Jayne Disappears*. He lingered over the
final page, studying the words with a frown.

His wife glared. "Maybe you'll listen to me next time.
You are sharp as custard, Mr. Gaffney, and I pray after this
you'll never forget it."

"Digory, I want every published installment written by Nathaniel Droll brought here as soon as possible." Garamond didn't even look up from the page as he issued the command with a shaking voice. His white face remained downcast.

"But, sir, Mr. Droll has been writing for years. That would be hundreds of installments."

The dinner bell interrupted, and the couples paired off to go into the dining room. Clem assumed his spot beside me, and we walked in, a pregnant silence hovering beyond the swish of skirts and scraping of chair legs on the floor. The undiscussed awareness of the new installment overpowered the room like a thick fog. I stared at the back of my chair when I reached it, focusing on the smooth wood. Silas slid through the doors then, head down in light of his tardiness. At least he had missed the reading in the drawing room.

Aunt Eudora strode in with her usual measured grace and motioned for everyone to be seated. "What a cheerful crowd," she said with a humph. "Makes one glad to join the festivities."

Glenna glanced at the other diners in muted judgment. Stress pinched Kendrick's usually carefree face. How impossible it suddenly seemed to swallow a bite of vegetables. I forced down one small bite of carrot and kept my gaze on my plate.

No one spoke through the course. Miserable silence blanketed the entrée course as well.

When a black-haired, clean-shaven server hovered behind Glenna to refresh her tea, the woman swiveled to glance at him. With pursed lips she turned back to her husband, passing him a knowing look. He shrugged.

"It could be any of the staff. Any of them." Her whisper was audible around the table but ignored by the other diners.

Aunt Eudora cleared her throat with a pointed look of warning toward her daughter. Garamond fiddled with his linen napkin.

"Well, it isn't one of us, is it?" Glenna stabbed her potato wedge, bursting the bubble of awkward secrecy as she finally addressed the whole table.

"Of course not." Kendrick downed his water and glanced around the table. "Juliette has nothing to do with books unless she's forced. Mother hasn't the time, and Father hasn't the inclination. I've been away at school, and Grandmama can barely hold a pen."

"Rotherham's only come recently, as well as Miss Harcourt," added Garamond. "But Mr. Droll has been publishing novels for years now."

"Mr. Rotherham has visited Lynhurst before." Juliette picked at an almond sliver with her fork as she spoke.

"I've not been to Lynhurst in years, and I promise you, I have not the talent or the imagination to write such novels." Silas's words fell on the diners without rebuttal, and silence reigned again for several seconds. Vegetables crunched and flatware tinked off plates.

Garamond studied me, his elfish face serious. Finally, he spoke the question hovering behind his guarded expression. "And you, child. Have you been here before?"

"If I ever was, I was too young to remember."

Oh, please. Don't ask more questions.

His eyes watched me through the next few bites as he chewed. Would I be willing to lie outright? It would be for the greater good—protecting an important secret and maintaining my place in this family.

But it would dishonor God, which would open me up to even

more potential trouble. I bit down on my spoon, wishing desperately for a way to reverse time and rewrite that installment.

After a metallic-tasting soup heavy with herbs, the family exited to the drawing room.

"Shall I serve your tea in the billiards room, sir?" Digory broke through the heavy silence as he approached Garamond.

"I don't believe so, Digory. Most of us will be retiring to our chambers early."

Aunt Eudora disappeared, as usual, and Glenna and Garamond absorbed themselves in private conversation in the chairs by the windows. The surprising thing was that Juliette cornered Silas. Or Silas cornered her, one of the two. The pair had removed themselves to the unlit fireplace when I walked in, Silas leaning on the ivory mantel. He had discarded the apathy he usually wore when talking with Juliette, and instead he leaned close, head forward, hair tickling the collar of his jacket. Surely he couldn't be as fascinated by what she was saying as he'd been when we'd . . .

Stop. Jealousy had no place in my heart when it came to Silas.

"What a lot of fuss over a book. A fictional one at that," Clem whispered as he approached. "Have you read it, Miss Harcourt?"

I looked down, twirling my finger in the fabric of my skirt.

"Likely isn't even worth your time. Look at this." He waved toward the scattered family. "Wouldn't Mr. Droll like to see the eruption his silly penny novel has caused in this house."

"I'm sure he'd be crushed to learn he was the cause of it."

Shaking his head, he departed from my side and strode out the door.

I had ruined everything. My dreams of writing were

foolish—a part of my childhood I'd have to release. Maybe I'd misunderstood God's intent with my work, and he was not behind this at all. Had I thrown my own human desires and goals into it? Surely he wouldn't have led me into such a mess.

The possibility of removing everything regarding writing sifted through my thoughts. Life would be empty. As if 80 percent of me had been suddenly and painfully carved away, leaving only a remnant of who I was.

Blessedly ignored for the moment, I perched on a flowered chair in an alcove and, with three deep breaths, sank away from the world and into God's presence. *You are sovereign, God. You have a plan, and I need to know what it is. At least, I need to know the next steps. I'll give up writing, really I will, but I need to know it's what you want of me. How do I make this right?*

For several moments I remained perfectly still, eyes closed, allowing strings of Scripture to wind through my mind. *Be still and know that I am God . . . May the words of my mouth and the meditations of my heart be pleasing to you . . . He which hath begun a good work in you will perform it until the day of Jesus Christ.* Each line of truth embedded into the fibers of my muscles, relaxing them.

And then the words came through, clear and warm.

Keep working, child. This is the way I've chosen for you to serve me.

After a closing "amen," my eyes flicked open and my vision immediately filled with Juliette, still standing with Silas across the room. In that second, an idea flared, quick and sure. Yes! I could take this terrible situation and make it *good.* The wonderful idea bombarded my self-imposed writing ban, flooding me with purpose and intent.

I made my escape while the rest of the family remained engrossed in private conversations. Ideas flooded my mind until a desire to write nearly overwhelmed me. In my chamber, I dug eager fingers into my hair, and pins tinked on the floor, my scalp experiencing the relief my heart was about to feel. I might leave Lynhurst next week, but I'd make full use of every last day spent there.

Grabbing a fresh notebook and pen, I lay across the rug and began to write madly about a new character. If my relatives were going to absorb my books with a hunger to see what traces of themselves existed in its pages, I'd give them something valuable to read.

As the scene spilled out from my heart, I prayed over and over.

Make it clear, Lord. Give me every word. Empty me of my sinful self and fill me instead with your Spirit so these words are yours. Open their eyes as they read this. Use it in the way you desire.

My pen completed the last word and then dropped onto the page, my head hitting the floor, cheek on the carpet. Mind buzzing, I lay there basking in the moment, exhausted and empty. Then I climbed into bed, fully ready for the coming day.

"If you were to guess," I asked Nelle the next morning, "what do you think will happen in the next installments?" I needed to begin planning the twist in the ending, but after pouring myself onto the page the night before, I had no steam left in my brain.

"Well, I'd expect to see Lady Jayne and Charles Sterling

Clavey admit their love for one another at some point. But I'm guessing it doesn't go well, looking at the title of the novel."

"You don't think Clavey murdered her, do you? He wouldn't."

"Oh no, of course not. I'd guess someone who doesn't want them together kills her, or scares her off."

"Why does no one want them together?" Images of my mother's letters, and Papa's lovelorn face, rose to my mind.

"We know he's a gentleman, but we know so little about her background." She leaned forward, eyes sparkling. "It's her secret that keeps them apart. I'd bet my wages on it."

I smiled, considering the wager. Little did she know how much control I had over the outcome. "Maybe. But I rather think Charles Sterling Clavey has secrets of his own. I'm beginning to think most men are that way." I caught her gaze. "Do you know, I believe you were right about Silas Rotherham. He said a few things the other day that painted his character differently. Perhaps I only thought him valiant because of his kindness toward me, but that effort only masked his true self. I should have listened to you. I think he may fit into the secret villain category after all."

"He isn't as bad as all that." She squirmed, thumb running over the corners of the napkin in her hands. "He has more than one agreeable attribute, don't you think?"

I looked at my friend, who wouldn't meet my gaze. "More than he had the last time we spoke?"

"Do you know, he is actually quite kind."

"Good, because he's had no reason to be less than that to you."

"And he is honest and hardworking too. And sweet, once you get him talking."

Something uncomfortable, much like a warning flare, niggled me. "What are you saying, exactly?"

Nelle shrugged, her downcast profile reddening into the scalp, and the truth shifted into clarity. What an odd twist. Shy little Abigail had grown attracted to Charles Sterling Clavey. It could complicate things delightfully in the book, but in real life? I smoothed my hair back and sighed. This would only muddle a situation that had already grown far too confusing.

Certainly, it would just be a passing fancy, though. Just weeks ago she'd thought him horrible. Besides, the relationship would never be allowed. An esteemed guest who likely held a sizable fortune could never court a girl in service.

And then the seed of an idea lodged in my mind, blossoming quickly into a workable, plausible plan for the ending.

The minute Nelle closed the door behind herself a half hour later, I pulled a fresh notebook from the shelf and filled two and half pages with ideas. Lady Jayne Windham was no lady at all. She'd traveled from London with her domineering chaperone and flitted about society as a woman of high breeding, but what outsiders did not know—and Clavey's family had only recently discovered—is that she was merely a maid in a London townhouse, traveling to the country while the family she served summered abroad. Clavey's family was too genteel to reveal her secret, but they would never allow their dear son to marry such a girl.

And perhaps Lady Jayne was not murdered. She simply returned to her life as little Jayne Windham the maid, and "Lady Jayne" ceased to exist. That's certainly how it had seemed to happen in real life.

My heart flooded with hope. Lady Jayne giving up her child seemed logical in this circumstance. And she did it out of love, not abandonment. Had she thought I'd be ashamed? That her low status would offer me a difficult life?

If only I could express to her now, this minute, that the only piece that might complete my life was her presence. Simply that—not a title or notoriety, but a mother. Faults and all. Oh, to fly to her this very minute and throw my love about her like an embrace. She would never wonder if her daughter accepted her, and she'd have all the affection and comfort that had been hoarded away in my little-girl heart for nearly twenty years.

My dear, sweet mother was a maid. And she thought it would matter to me. What a terrible reason to keep two people from marrying, but it had doomed the love my parents shared from the first day. Just as doomed as the budding feelings Nelle Wicke carried for Silas Rotherham.

At that thought, I curled up at my desk and touched my forehead to its cool surface. *Lord, I give this situation to you. Do not let Nelle's infatuation with Silas stand in the way of the man you have chosen for her. Guide her to the one who will be the perfect fit for her, helping her to blossom into what you designed her to be.*

My mind picked at the corner of the next page, begging to peek into the future as God had laid it out. Heart still welling with worry and hope, I flipped the notebook to the first blank page. The best thing to fill a book was raw emotion—the kind evoked when a good friend seemed smitten with the man you loved.

Not that I *loved* Silas. Admittedly, I hardly knew the many secret corners of his life, and my doubts concerning him loomed large. But once again I found myself dwelling on the images of him at Shepton Mallet and ignoring any faults.

Whatever Silas was hiding, perhaps I could accept it. Maybe it wasn't awful.

19

Dear, sweet Abigail had the sort of genuine beauty that was abundantly evident, even to the blind.

~Nathaniel Droll, *Lady Jayne Disappears*

"Aurelie, do you know any printers with a fine hand for invitations?" Juliette sat at the desk in the morning room, compiling a guest list as others lingered over lunch sandwiches.

"I've never known a single soul who knew how to do it."

I pulled my gaze from the *London Illustrated* I hid behind and snuck a glance at Silas Rotherham. He bent over his lunch beside Kendrick in the far east corner. Would he think my answer a lie, with everything he knew?

"Who did you use before, for your house parties and dinners? Perhaps there's still time to send an order away to them. At least for the place cards."

I curled further into the couch behind my paper. "Not one name comes to mind." Would the need for cover-ups never end? I didn't belong—that truth became increasingly apparent every week I spent at the home of my ancestors.

"Heavens, Juliette. Are you really going through with this dinner party?" Kendrick leaned back in his chair across the room. "I personally did not come to the country to be thrown into every social event of the summer. You can cancel my invitation, and Silas's as well."

Juliette spun in the swivel chair away from her brother and faced me. "We shall invite Alexander. Do say you'll play along and at least *pretend* to like him."

"I promise to thoroughly like whomever I like."

Silas bit into a cracker and coughed on the crumbs.

With a disgusted exhale, Juliette blew hair off her face. She rose and strode toward me, holding out her guest list. "I need to have some backups in case you find Alexander completely despicable. Which of these men are already in your circles from before?"

I accepted the list, knowing what my answer would be. None of them.

Eventually I'd simply have to tell Juliette that my acquaintances before arriving at Lynhurst, my "circle of friends," included the bottom rung of England's social ladder.

I glanced through the list at the titled names, none of which looked familiar. Except the third one. Jasper Grupp.

"You're inviting the man from the benefit?"

"Of course I am. I may be excitable, but I am not fickle." She lowered her voice. "You know exactly how I feel."

"And what address did he give you to send his invitation?" I sat forward to hand the list back to Juliette.

"His is hand-delivered." She swiveled again, more slowly, to face me and give me a warning stare. "He's traveling a great deal, staying at this hotel and that. He cannot say from one day to the next where he can be found."

Of course. "Have you ever visited him at these hotels?"

Juliette's responding glare could have stripped the pink from the rug at my feet. "Of course not," she hissed, shielding her voice from the men with her hand.

I had crossed the enemy-friend line once again. "I'm merely asking if you've ever been able to verify his story. Do you know anything of him that has not come from his own mouth?"

"His credentials need no verification."

"Certainly." What more could I say? Nothing that would not ruin our delicate friendship.

"Perhaps the man is Nathaniel Droll." This quip from Clem at the far table made me stiffen. "Such men of mystery, both of them."

Silas's soft voice carried over to us. "If that man were Nathaniel Droll, we would know it. Droll cannot remain hidden when he is among other people, for such a writer would glow brighter than lamplight among the drab people of our day."

I looked quickly back to the newspaper in my hands. And in that moment of silence, I saw it. The literary review in the *London Illustrated*, which focused on the latest installment of Nathaniel Droll fiction. My eyes were riveted to the familiar name. Fingers crushing the edges of the paper, I absorbed the words as quickly as my eyes could move back and forth, then went back to linger over them. Words like "masterpiece" and "brilliant" swirled before me, bathing my heart in warmth. One reader talked of how it had made her reconsider her relationship with a grown son, and that connection was now much improved.

But two-thirds from the bottom of the column my eyes rested on a small collection of words that burned themselves into the backs of my eyelids.

> I should like to publicly share my disappointment with Marsh House Press for continuing to publish the work of Nathaniel Droll. In his bid for increased production, Droll has diminished greatly in quality until he's left with ridiculous plots and laughable prose that even a child could create. I find Lady Jayne's distress over losing her love preposterous and, on the whole, resembling a whiny child. I admonish you that the name attached to the piece does not alone make it worthy to print in your esteemed publication.

I closed my eyes, but the words speared through the darkness and buried themselves in my heart. *Ridiculous plots. Laughable prose.* What had I written about Jayne's angst over Clavey anyway?

I'd used the pain of losing my father.

Preposterous. Resembling a whiny child.

I again skimmed the glowing reviews, but those last words pervaded any trace of peace. Tears clogged behind my eyes as I tried in vain to force what I'd seen from my mind. But in truth, I knew I'd never un-see those words. They would haunt my writing time and shape the way I saw each scene I penned.

Silas rose, brushing off his shirt front. "I would enjoy a turn about the gardens while the horses rest. Would you ladies care to join me?"

"Miss Harcourt can accompany you, Mr. Rotherham."
Juliette tucked the hair behind her ear and bent over her list
again. "I may join you later when I've finished this."

Kendrick frowned. "My dear sister, I'm sure he would
enjoy the company of a longtime friend more than an acquaintance. No offense intended toward our little cousin."
He crossed the room and dropped his final words toward
Juliette as he passed her. "Be careful or you're liable to lose
what you so easily ignore."

Silas approached us then, straightening his coat at the lapels. "You needn't worry. My feelings toward Juliette are the
same now as the day I arrived, not to be altered by a single
walk." The man approached me and offered his arm, a polite
question tilting his eyebrows. "That is, if you care to accept."

I found myself unwilling to say no, despite my desire to
run and hide in my room. I desperately craved distraction,
and conversation with one who appreciated me. "I suppose
I could. Sunshine would be a wonderful cure for a dwindling
imagination."

With an amused smile flicking over his face, he led me
through the garden doors and down the patio steps. Silence
reigned until we had passed through the flower-covered trellis
and down onto the lower patio where we'd talked before.

"I feel like I can breathe again." Silas loosened his neck
cloth an inch with one finger and smiled down at me. "Sometimes I think I should have stayed in London. At least there,
I only have to endure this sort of mess on social evenings,
and I have the day to myself."

I pointed to the rose hedges where the gardener trimmed
them into perfect red-spotted boxes. "Shall we walk that
direction? I haven't seen the roses yet." We veered casually

toward them in a wide arc. "I must admit, it is relaxing to be here among the flowers and fresh air rather than inside, always worrying about—" My better judgment cut off the end of the sentence. I should not share so much.

"It is not a life either of us were built for, is it? Dressing, speaking, behaving in the way we ought, worrying about offending rather than living comfortably and naturally. If only they could see how foolish it is, running around attempting to please strangers and acquaintances." He paused, hands clasped behind his back. "Miss Harcourt, why don't you write about that?"

Panic tingled along my spine. "About what?"

"Life at Lynhurst. Make characters of the people here and their idiosyncrasies. You spin such wonderful stories in conversation, and perhaps some of them should be written down. What a delight to readers to have this inside view of one of England's country homes."

Turning my face away, I breathed through the pounding in my temples. "I have often regretted the times I have based any stories on real life. It is a dangerous undertaking."

"But think how nice it would be if you could make a living at writing and not have to worry about pleasing your family or anyone else. Have you considered publishing?"

"Readers are often harder to please than family." So far I had not lied.

Pausing beside a hedge that hid us from view, he took both of my hands in his. "Every story you create has been wonderful and captivating. Why not reveal to the world what you can do, what you've already done, and be proud of it?"

He knew. He must know. "I was never good at receiving negative remarks. Especially about my stories."

"It isn't as if they are rejecting you personally if they do not enjoy your work."

Dipping my head, I struggled to word a response. How could I explain the heart of a writer? An artist's life and work were woven together to make up the very fabric of his being. Condemning his work was to also condemn him personally. For it was everything about me that had created the work that was under scrutiny—my experiences, the love and pain of my true heart, the culminating effort of my entire life.

I breathed deeply of the rose-tinted air. "Logically I can accept that a person may simply not like my work, but it is nearly impossible to wrap the emotional side of myself around that fact. Especially when my feelings about my own writing fluctuate so easily and often. That's how it is with any type of art."

"I see. So it is your own criticisms that have so bound you. Miss Harcourt, you can collect all the compliments in the world, but they make no difference until you believe them."

I hesitated before the three stone steps. He could not understand, for he had money. I did not have the luxury of alienating my family or my readers.

"If you will not consider publishing, perhaps you would entertain another idea I've had in mind for some days now." With gentle pressure he guided me around an outcropping of lilies toward the terrace. "I hope you will not find it presumptuous of me to ask."

Straightening my shoulders, I nodded for him to continue, searching his face for hints. In the background of my mind, answers to all possible questions raced around.

"What do you think of Miss Wicke, the little seamstress on the estate?"

Nelle? For several empty seconds, my shoes whipped grass blades. That was his presumptuous question? "She does very fine needlework."

"Come now, that isn't what I mean."

I sighed and released the information he wanted. "As a person, Nelle is even grander than her needlework. I've only been acquainted with her a few weeks, and I already love her dearly." I could not lie about Nelle.

He lifted a tangled clematis vine for me. "I think you should help her open a shop."

The jarring suggestion sparked a number of thoughts and uncertainty. "A shop. Do you think I'm made of pound notes? I have fewer resources than she does."

"I didn't say you should finance it but help her. A wild imagination is more valuable than all the money in the world with something like this."

"What makes you suggest such a thing? And why Miss Wicke?" Confusion pelted my mind at his sudden interest in Nelle, of whom he'd never spoken before.

"A suitable match—brilliant one, actually. Your colorful imagination, her delightful talent . . . Possibly even a better match than the marriages Juliette's attempting to secure for you."

I blushed, but pressed on. "I haven't the slightest idea how to open a shop. And besides, there are a few 'complications' on Miss Wicke's end that have kept her from pursuing this before. Those hindrances still exist."

"Nothing that can't be overcome by a magnificent imagination and a big heart. Both of which you possess."

An odd mix of pride and angst spun through my heart. The thought of Nelle's sweet face brought the question to my lips: *Do you know she's becoming attached to you?* This would be the perfect opportunity to warn him, but the words escaped me. If I were planted at my desk, empty pages and pen before me, I could come up with the right phrasing. There may be plenty of cross-outs and rewritten sentences, but eventually I'd craft exactly what should be said.

"It's a shame for talent that remarkable to remain hidden away."

Just like Lady Jayne, the beautiful flower covered in the black-and-white uniform of service. Or perhaps he meant me, staunchly hidden behind the *nom de plume* of my father.

"Speaking of talent hidden away, have you heard the gossip on Nathaniel Droll? I thought you'd be interested."

Instantly my face warmed and I regretted relaxing my staunch boundaries. "I've heard everything Glenna has to say about him."

"Actually I was referring to public gossip about him. It seems the man is planning to take back the rights to his work to reprint them, and he has no plans to complete Lady Jayne's story."

Fear tripped through me, head to toe, and I pictured the pockmarked man in the dusty suit with vivid clarity. I dipped my head to hide my emotions.

"Miss Harcourt, what has upset you so? You look white as a ghost."

Swift feet carried me back to my bedchamber where I pulled notebooks off the shelf and flipped through them. Nathaniel Droll had begun to rattle my brain and shake my nerves. Was he the imposter, or was I? Did he even exist? The torn-out pages with messages from Nathaniel Droll fluttered to the ground. Flipping madly through the remaining notebooks, I found one more:

> *Follow your heart. It's rarely wrong, you intelligent girl. Do not lose your life to solve the murder. All I can tell you is this: Darling Aura, fair Aura, I'm too soon dead.*
>
> *Nathaniel Droll*

Fear spiked up my back. I stared at the word *dead* over and over. Nathaniel Droll was . . .

But he'd called me Aura, just as Papa had. But why didn't I recognize the writing?

And that's when the truth filtered through my thoughts. For all the stories we'd created together, everything we'd dreamed up and put on the page, I'd never seen a single written line of his own hand. Only his voice conveyed his captivating, wild stories.

I dug through the desk like mad, pawing through odd papers and trinkets. Surely he must have written something while he lived here. He'd been creating stories since before my lifetime. But no trace of his handwriting existed in the room.

20

"But it is impossible to be in love with the wrong man," cried Lady Jayne. "For the very fact that I love him makes him the right one for me."

~Nathaniel Droll, *Lady Jayne Disappears*

Lady Jayne was ultimately a liar. That was the only way the new storyline would work. I glided through the small forest of wildflowers where Silas had left me hours before as the sunshine warmed my uncovered face.

Diving deep into the world of my story was the only way to settle my mind as it insisted on swaying to so many troubling things. My mind picked up the threads of storyline as ideas flared by force. I had to finish this story immediately and dash it off to the publisher before the imposter sent a new book to them. That required fast thinking.

For starters, Jayne Windham had come to Lynhurst pretending to be a lady, hiding who she really was. Which made her a liar. What reader would not feel betrayed by this girl they had pitied and worried over, to find her so lacking in character? It would be a difficult twist to execute. Maybe Abigail would be the heroine after all, and Charles Sterling Clavey would fall in love with her.

I briefly imagined Silas and Nelle embracing and the thought left me cold.

No. The hero loved too deeply to pass his affection around like a bag of beans. Jayne must have the spotlight in the romance thread. Brushing the heads of daisies with my fingertips, I considered the words I'd use to aptly describe my heroine as a relatable woman who sometimes had to lie.

I sighed. This changed everything, but it was lovely when a heroine had the depth of character to take over her own story, wrangling the plot away from the author. And Lady Jayne had become so real. I could almost hear the girl's voice, the way her laughter would sound—light and joyful, bubbling up with ease. It was so clear in my head.

No, wait. I listened again. The laughter was real. Bushes rustled nearby and rose-colored fabric flashed between the hedges. Juliette eased herself through the branches, lightly scratching her arm, a blush tinging her cheeks and exposed neck.

Jasper Grupp stumbled out after her, laughing and brushing leaves from his coat. The same coat he always wore. They looked up together, a perfect pair moving in unison like two startled deer, and met my gaze. Guilt washed over both their faces, hers a blushing glow and his a mottled red clear down his neck.

"This is an unfortunate meeting." Jasper's sleek voice poured out softly between us as he brushed the debris of nature from his arms. "Perhaps we should have parted ways before coming up the drive. But a gentleman never leaves a beautiful woman to find her way alone." He bowed, eyes sparkling, and kissed Juliette's gloved fingertips.

Cords tightened along Juliette's neck as she accepted the affection with a smile lighting her face. Jasper released her fingers but held her gaze.

"You needn't worry about Aurelie. She won't say a word." Juliette stepped forward and grabbed my hands, swinging them too hard. "We're chums, aren't we?" She dropped them and turned to smile at Jasper.

Two instincts battled within me—and in the end, the overwhelming desire to agree, to cling to the tenuous friendship, won out. "Of course."

Footsteps approached on the gravel path behind me, cutting off the need for further awkward conversation.

"Who might the outsider be in this gathering?" Clem approached, riding whip in hand.

"It's about to become a twosome." Jasper stepped back with a bow. "I must take my leave if I'm to reach Bristol in time for the meeting."

Anxiousness tightened Juliette's features, but her hands remained at her sides. Clem silently observed his sister, the leaf bits and twigs on her that matched those on Jasper Grupp not seeming to escape his gaze. Juliette also excused herself to delve into party preparations, leaving Clem and me alone among the shrubs and roses.

I studied the boy's lightly freckled profile. Would I find an ally in this youth? God might do such a thing, to arrange this walk so we could discuss Juliette and Jasper and reach some solution together. With a breath in and out, and a casual gait, I began. "What do you think of your sister with that man?"

Ah, but he was young. What youth of his age would care a whit about his sister's love affairs?

But his intelligent eyes sparkled. "It's a fine pairing of two like hearts."

"You think highly of your sister, I see." I flashed him a grin of camaraderie.

"I think little of my sister and who she marries, unless it happens to be Silas Rotherham. The very fact that Mr. Grupp is *not* Silas Rotherham earns him many points of favor with me."

"You dislike Mr. Rotherham?"

"On the contrary, I find him absolutely wonderful. But not for my sister. She's not deserving of such a man."

"And you know of another girl more worthy of marrying him?" The thought sent spirals of thrill through me, drawing my mind firmly on another track.

"It's not so much the one who'll marry him as the one who will call him father."

Dahlia. My chest constricted.

"He would be more than her father, though. He would be her ticket into the world."

The words scrunched my heart in a bittersweet ache—both the pairing of Silas with Nelle and the tender way Clem dreamed for the fatherless girl.

"It cannot really be that pivotal." I fought to keep my voice normalized. "Don't you think Miss Wicke just a tad overprotective? Who in Lynhurst would end her position if they knew?"

"Every one of them would. Not because *her* sin is so great— that's the irony of it—but because they fear what it will bring to light about themselves. The date of Kendrick's birth is inconveniently early. Well before our parents' marriage. And Grand-mama . . . well, her husband had more children than she did."

Why did it seem that every person in the world loved or disliked a person based mostly upon the effect they had on his or her self-esteem?

"So you want Miss Wicke to attach herself to any man, just to make herself acceptable to these people?"

"Dahlia's never been to school, never learned numbers or reading. She's never had friends outside of me and her mother. All of that because of her wretched father abandoning her. But think of how she'd glow like sunshine, being let out of that cottage to make her way. She could do anything." He shoved his hands deeper into his trouser pockets. "Juliette would never suspect a mere maid to be her competition, but that's only because she doesn't understand Mr. Rotherham in the least."

Images of Silas overwhelmed my mind. The tender look on his face as he watched the people of the Mallet. The dust on his perfect black suit. The gentle way he hunched over to feed cake to Rosa. Those images would be tucked away in a sweet, cozy part of my memory that would hold them forever, no matter who he married.

But Clem had forgotten one very important element—the very reason he wanted Nelle and Silas married in the first place.

"Miss Wicke has a great many positive attributes, and I'm sure Mr. Rotherham would eagerly appreciate them all. But she'll eventually have to tell him her secret. And convince him to accept it." Silas Rotherham, raising someone else's child? He'd be awkward and closed off. But then again, the way he'd been with Micah . . .

No. That had been a momentary experience. It was a dif-ferent matter entirely, accepting someone else's child into your intimate life and home. "She was ashamed to tell *me* about Dahlia. Think how long it would take Mr. Rotherham to uncover the secret."

His bony elbow nudged my bare arm. "I do believe he already knows." Clem's head jerked toward a lone figure in a dark suit striding with purpose down the path toward the cottage we both loved so much, with tall, slender children's books tucked under his arm. He nodded briefly as he passed, but did not slow his steps. He hardly glanced at me.

Was it possible?

"Perhaps Miss Wicke is the reason he's here this season." Clem's words revealed layers of thought already invested in this situation.

A gut punch. Maybe my prayers for Nelle had been answered. Head spinning, I willed a recovery to happen. "But they were strangers until recently. They couldn't have known each other before Mr. Rotherham's arrival." Unless he was Dahlia's . . .

But no, that was impossible.

"Nothing says he *knew* he came here for her. But he did, all the same." He hooked his fingers through his belt loops. "God cuts out the puzzle pieces, and then fits them together when it's time."

A deep breath bolstered my strength. "If God is orchestrating, Juliette cannot stand in the way."

"It is Grandmama who has the only real power to divide them. She's done it before."

My neck tightened, and I looked to my shoes. Yes, she had. Would Papa still be alive if he'd been allowed to remain with my mother? Life would have been so different for all of us.

"But you love Nelle and you know Silas better than most

of us, I can tell." Clem looked back at the cottage. "You see how perfectly he'd fit into that family."

Silas's tender face sprang to mind, and the image of him cradling the dusty child against his perfect suit. I inhaled the powdery aroma and breathed, fighting the weight of a responsibility I did not want.

And just like that, Lady Jayne realized her prayers for Abigail's future husband were already answered.

"Who on earth has lit the wick in our dear, sullen Mr. Rotherham?" Juliette breathed the words into my ear as I joined her in the drawing room after the dinner bell sounded.

"I wouldn't know." I tried to avoid looking at Silas, but I could not ignore the remarkable glow of his face. It was something new, as if he'd found a source of both epic delight and peace all from the same fountain, and he'd drunk his fill of it that day. It brimmed out of him as we walked into the dining room amid the lovely scent of herb-roasted chicken. Standing across from him, I focused on my silver-rimmed plate and linen napkin.

Aunt Eudora entered, worn face seeming heavier than normal, and the powerful surges of anger toward this destroyer of love stories evaporated to light tingles. Bitterness curled into a sickening pity for the woman so trapped by the opinions of her peers. It was sad, really. One day she'd realize how little their opinions really mattered, and what a waste she'd made of her life—and the lives of my parents and me. She lowered into her throne-chair at the head of the table, cutting the polite restraint that kept us all silent.

"Grandmama, I have two spots left on the guest list if

you'd care to invite your own acquaintances. This is to be a family event, not just my own."

Aunt Eudora squinted her buggy eyes at Glenna, then at Juliette.

"Oh, don't look so cross, Grandmama. I've asked Miss Wicke to create you an entirely new gown, and you will be there too, reigning over the door and passing judgment on everyone."

"I've no desire for such drama. That's why I sold the London house. I do *not like people*." The pop of her cane punctuated the last words.

"That isn't why the London house was sold, and you know it." Glenna patted her red lips with a linen napkin. "That sale was to pay off your scoundrel brother's debts years ago. And look at the gratitude we get for ending our social lives—I've not seen a trace of Uncle for years."

Aunt Eudora's jaw worked slowly on the dry chicken, her lips curling in disgust.

My heart beat in my throat. *Tell them, Aunt. Tell them he's gone and that he died in debtor's prison. Tell them about the daughter he left behind. Admit to them what you did to us.* Was she so vastly ashamed of her brother that she hadn't even told her family I was his child? At least she'd claimed me as a cousin, even if she had not made the exact relation clear. Pity mingled with disgust as I watched the old woman chew, loose neck skin jiggling like that of a rooster.

But as Glenna's words registered, they pricked a hole in my disgust. She'd sold the London house to pay off his debts. She'd tried to help once, even though he'd only repaid her by returning to reckless spending and gambling, and finally to debtor's prison.

"We all of us have our weak spots now, don't we?" Garamond patted his wife's fleshy arm, head tipped toward her affectionately.

She rewarded him with a glare. "Not an ounce of your abundant weakness comes from me, my darling."

Silas buried himself in conversation with Kendrick to his left, and it was the first dinner where he and I did not exchange a single word. It left me parched.

After dinner, the men departed to the billiards room and the women moved into the drawing room and perched on the couches and chairs. Juliette slipped an arm around me, leading me to sit beside her.

"It's Silas Rotherham, isn't it? He's upset you. I could nearly *see* the tension between you."

"He's done nothing distasteful toward me."

"And here I've been pushing him on you. I will not let him hurt my little protégé that way. He disregards you as if you are not good enough. Just you wait. I have the perfect antidote to a broken heart. I call it my replacement remedy."

She'd gotten all that from the little bit of interaction at dinner? Oddly, the girl had nearly pinpointed the truth. But the last thing I wanted was whatever Juliette deemed the perfect antidote to heartbreak.

"In just a few days' time, we'll have our little party. I'll make sure men are virtually *throwing* themselves at you. And of course, one man in particular I'm quite positive will capture your heart. This time, I make you a solemn vow. I will introduce you to Alexander."

"How on earth will that help?"

Her red lips curled into a coy smile. "You'll see."

21

She knew a great deal about real love, mostly because she had encountered the counterfeit too many times to count.

~Nathaniel Droll, *Lady Jayne Disappears*

I daydreamed myself to sleep, wondering about the mysterious man Juliette would introduce to me. I had a week to wait, but Juliette had handed me a spark, and the strong winds of my imagination had fanned it into a healthy fire. Thoughts of him crowded out the constant worries over everything else. What made this man so perfect for me? Somehow I couldn't unhinge myself from the desire to meet and instantly connect with another human being, the way she insinuated I would with Alexander.

The clouds rolled over Lynhurst Sunday morning, making me wish I could hibernate beneath the covers and dream about the party, but I rose and prepared for the day. Already the thrill of anticipation had loosened the twist in my gut.

"Pardon me words, miss, but you look like a sunbeam this morning, you do." The scrawny chambermaid yanked and tied my stays.

I laughed. "Why ever would you feel the need to excuse a compliment?" Perhaps Juliette's remedy had worked after all, if even the maids took notice of my positive countenance.

"The lady don't appreciate any words from me, good or bad. But your face is so open and sweet, I couldn't help speaking up."

I twisted around to smile at her. "Will you be joining us for services today, Minnie?"

"Oh no, ma'am. The bedchambers need tidying. Besides, I take me worship out to the hills so I get me fill of God's work rather than man's." Her head nod indicated the elaborate chapel barely visible outside my window.

On the heels of those words, I made a hasty decision I hoped I would not regret. "Minnie, I believe your wisdom has inspired me. Will you tell the family I won't be joining them for worship?"

"Of course, miss."

I snuck downstairs and out into the garden after Minnie left. It was a daring move, skipping the weekly tradition, but I felt a tug toward genuine worship that morning. The only way I'd experience that at Lynhurst was alone.

Swinging two muffins in my hands, I covered the yard in long strides. The heavy green dress weighed me down, but the escape buoyed my mood. Wandering to the east, where I hadn't yet been, I passed a vine-covered wall and turned right. The remains of a tiny roofless stone shack huddled in the outskirts of the woods just past the wall, its mystery and charm beckoning me. Chilly air wrapped itself around me as

I stepped into the abandoned space, crunching on the broken and half-buried litter of dishes in the former kitchen area. Lying flat on the soft grass that had once been a bedroom floor, I spread my arms and closed my eyes, basking in the solitude of the outdoors and the freshness of it. Sunshine heated my skin.

He maketh me to lie down in green pastures.

I dipped into prayer, beginning with silent worship, then exposing my heart to the One who already understood my plight.

He leadeth me beside the still waters.

Life had become so complicated, and before taking another step, I needed God to help untangle it. For countless minutes I lay there, conversation flowing freely.

"May I join you?" The deep voice burst my tryst in one heart-pounding second. "This looks like an inspired worship service."

"Mr. Rotherham." I scrambled to sit up, grass blades falling from my moist skin.

"Please, don't stop on my account. I simply wanted to find where my little friend had gone. I knew wherever it was, it would be far more spiritual than the services held in that room." A jerk of his head indicated the grand chapel striped with stained glass. "Tell me, though. What propelled you to choose such a place for your Sunday morning?" Coat flapping in the breeze, he settled into one corner of the half-missing wall and rested his elbows on his knees.

As usual, his casual body language relaxed me, and I smiled. "It seemed highly appropriate to speak with God in the place where his own creation has defeated man's." I ran my hand along the broken wall covered in moss at my back and the grass that had pushed victoriously through the remains of the floor. "Sometimes God wipes away man's pride in a burst of stormy power, but usually it's done quietly and gradually." Like my weeks spent at Lynhurst, slowly evolving and changing me, one challenge and heartache at a time.

"He seems to answer prayers the same way, doesn't he? At least, he has with mine. Not in one big powerful move, but gradually so I don't notice until I've turned around and see that I have exactly what I need."

I wiggled against the crumbling stone wall. Exactly what I needed. Yes, that summarized what I felt about Silas in moments like this. All the prayers I'd sent toward heaven since reaching Lynhurst, prayers for acceptance, for help in my most difficult moments, for easing of loneliness, were answered in Silas Rotherham.

Perhaps I should have also asked the Lord to fill the hole in my heart that ached for permanent companionship, for marriage. For romance. Instead, I'd prayed for Nelle's.

He'd notice soon if I didn't fill the silence. Back straight against the wall, I fell into the easy rut of story. The first that came to mind.

"That reminds me of something." My chin tipped up, smile spreading. "Have you heard the story about the drowning man?"

"No, but I believe I am about to."

I launched into the story of Pete, the sailor who fell overboard one gloomy night when the sea was green with storms. "'Don't fret over me,' he called to his mates. 'God will save me. I'm sure of it.' So they let him be. He paddled until his arms grew weak, and his friends began to worry. So sure was Pete of God's rescue that he would not hear of the men risking their own skin to jump in after him. Well, eventually poor Pete drowned under the foamy waves."

"God did not save him?" His skeptical frown made me laugh.

"Why, of course he did! He sent a whole host of men aboard his own ship. 'Twasn't God's fault the man rejected the help."

Silas laughed, his smile revealing the two tiny dimples above his mouth. "I see I've made the right decision. I have found more depth here in a matter of minutes than I was sure to find in that entire service."

"My father told me that story years ago, and I still find use for it so often." With the rush of memories, heat pooled in my chest. I shouldn't say more, but Silas's unchallenging calm released something in me. The pent-up truth poured out. "For years, I prayed for a rescue from Shepton Mallet. For myself and for Papa. It never seemed to come, and maybe that was best. Because now I find myself asking him for a rescue from my rescue."

"Sometimes it's a wonder God knows what to do with all our requests."

How true. I'd certainly made a mess of things with my own. "I think I know the perfect prayer." I twirled a dandelion before my face and closed my eyes. "God, give me exactly what I would ask for if I knew everything you know."

His eyes sparkled in response. "Brilliant."

"And perhaps God is already answering my request by carving out a spot for me in this house where I once did not belong. I've found friends and even a purpose. And slowly, I'm beginning to understand how to walk among my peers and to be what I ought."

"Is it really your dearest goal to belong here?"

I shrugged, neck warming. "Somewhere, at least. To someone."

He studied me, assessing my answer.

"You feel that way too, don't you?" I continued. "Like you don't belong here."

"Yes, but with one simple difference. I've no desire to. My visit here is purely practical, with no need to make friends and fit in. Soon I will return home."

"And do you feel that you 'belong' at home?"

"Depends on which room I find myself in." His soft smile expressed much. "But either way, I have plenty of books at home, which makes all the difference. I can slip into their pages, spark my mind, and not remember whether or not I belong to anyone or anything."

"That sounds like bandaging a splinter."

He shrugged, and comfortable silence settled between us, punctuated with sweet bird voices and wind in the trees.

I looked toward the towers of the great house. "I much prefer to attempt a friendship, try to fit in, rather than avoid everyone altogether."

He hesitated a moment before speaking. "Must you do such a thing? You were quite unusual, just as you were. I much prefer that to you becoming a duplicate of everyone else."

His words passed over me like a gentle breeze, holding me speechless.

"And now, since I've stolen your time with God, perhaps we should approach him together. Would you care to?" He rose to his knees and extended a hand.

I laid my hand in his, heart fluttering, and bowed my head.

With a deep, somber voice, he spoke to God, asking him to keep and protect the heart of his "little friend" from the rest of the world. Then when his voice silenced, I prayed for the family. He picked up the trail with fervent words for the future of Lynhurst. Back and forth, as if we were slowly joining into one unit, we spoke to God in words that swirled easily between us and rose to heaven.

And my heart was full to overflowing with unnamable thoughts.

I knew the service and lunch had ended when Nelle breezed by on the path. Silas had long since departed, but I hadn't been able to focus. Pushing up and brushing dirt and grass off my clothes, I ran to catch up with my friend. "Have you posted the last installment?"

"Days ago." Nelle slowed with a glowing smile. "I read it myself that night, and posted it the very next day. Now I'm dying to know what comes next."

"So am I."

"Has Mr. Droll told you the ending yet?" Nelle looked at me expectantly. "Walk with me and tell me. It's time I went home and relieved the underhousemaid who is keeping Dahlia."

"I've come to the conclusion that the fictional girl was in service, and that's why the family would not let her stay at Lynhurst. It makes the most sense. And of course, she couldn't marry Charles Sterling Clavey, because he was aristocracy, and she a maid."

Nelle frowned. "I've read that story a time or two. Droll wouldn't make it that simple."

"But it's happened so many times to everyday people. Wouldn't that make it interesting to read? People can see themselves in the story."

"I'd bet Lady Jayne has a more remarkable reason for disappearing. Something more worthy of Nathaniel Droll."

We rounded the corner toward Florin cottage in silence. Nelle gazed thoughtfully toward the light clouds above us. "Did you know even Silas Rotherham reads serial fiction?"

I lowered my head, mixed emotions rushing through me again at the sound of his name on Nelle's lips. "We've spoken of it."

"Mary, thank you again." Nelle stepped through the door and offered the young underhousemaid a brief squeeze before the girl scurried out the door. She shut the door behind us and leaned against it. "I wish you wouldn't hate him, dear friend. He is not so objectionable, once you really talk to him."

Dahlia whisked away a sheet hanging around the bed and rushed to us, her little voice trailing after her, and crashed into her mother's legs. "You were gone so long, Mum."

"You've been wonderful." Nelle laid a hand on the girl's head, drawing her close.

"You highly approve of Mr. Rotherham's character now, do you?" Even asking the question tightened a band around my ribs.

"Very dearly. Oh Aurelie, please do give up your hatred of him, as I have. You needn't adore him, but if you only hated him a little less. Will you do it for my sake?" Leading the girl, Nelle crossed the room and perched on a squatty stool at the table.

"I suppose." I sank into a seat across from the pair.

"I've been so wrong about him. He is wonderful and

genuine and sweet, even with Dahlia. And I'm a judgmental, backward woman with no sense about men."

I laid a hand on Nelle's across the table, forcing a smile. "You're a mother trying to protect her little girl."

"Will you do it, then? As my dear friend?"

"Accept Mr. Rotherham?"

"I'm merely asking you to remain agreeable and try not to hate him."

And what would she ask in the future—for me to host their wedding?

Sunday afternoon spread the family throughout Lynhurst and its grounds, allowing for a deep quiet over the house as Silas entered the patio doors into the morning room.

"Digory, you wished to speak with me?"

"Nothing urgent, Mr. Rotherham. You have a letter on the hall table, and I wanted to be sure you saw it, since you are not in the habit of digging through the household mail."

"Yes, thank you." Dropping his riding whip into the canister at the patio door, Silas strode into the hall and lifted the envelope from the marble-topped table. This one wore the seal of his parents' household. With a frown, he slit the top and extracted the single page to skim the precise writing. His father's business interests had increased and he needed Silas home before the end of summer. Reading the unspoken words surrounding the few items written about his mother, it seemed their marriage was not faring any better than when he'd left. Drama unfolded around him, whether he remained at Lynhurst or returned home, but the mysteries of the manor proved far more intriguing than any involving his own family.

"Thank you, Digory."

"Good news from home, I trust?"

With a tiny smile, he looked at the old servant. "If there was good news forthcoming from home, I'd hardly choose to summer here."

The old servant bowed his head with silent understanding. Pocketing the letter, Silas strode toward the stairs and shifted. The tight riding clothes irritated his skin. A bath would help. But at the base of the stairs, one boot on the bottom step, his attention was drawn by a slight movement in the room directly across the great hall. A new idea dawned, and he crossed to the open door.

The gold-and-yellow room held only one occupant—Lady Eudora Eustice Pochard. Little trinkets littered the surfaces and open books lay facedown on tables, indicating it was a well-used space. The room seemed to be her sanctuary when she'd had her fill of people, which likely happened often. At least a dozen clocks pinged and plunked out the seconds of passing time in the dusty old parlor untouched by maids.

"Well, don't stand in the hall gawking at me, Mr. Rotherham."

"Might I ring for some tea for you, my lady?" He slid one foot inside the room, testing.

"I'm capable of ringing for my own tea." The high back of her wheeled chair hid all but her silhouette from him. In the extreme glow of sunlight, her parched skin looked nearly white.

"Would you care for a little company?"

"Do I ever?" She rapped her crooked knuckles on the arm of her chair. "But you may come in anyway. Curiosity has brought you here, and obviously you will not leave until it is satisfied. You might as well come and gape at the worn old woman whom no one loves."

The self-pity curled his insides, but he approached quietly. "I suppose in this day a woman of my age is a spectacle. She would have been venerated at one time, but now I'm a sort of sideshow." Her hard eyes reflected in the window she faced.

"Forgive me for being so bold, Lady Pochard, but perhaps people are only respecting your wishes by avoiding your company. You've made your feelings plain."

After several clock ticks across the room, the face that was twisted with a generalized irritation turned to him. "What is it you want here, Mr. Rotherham? We both know it isn't the company of my shallow grandson or my vapid granddaughter. Are you perhaps trying to gain a financial advantage for yourself?"

"I want nothing from you or your bank account, Lady Pochard. Kendrick is a wonderful rider, and he is refreshing my equestrian skill. As for the vap . . . Juliette, she is not as unpleasant as you insinuate. She covers up an awful lot of intelligence with her attitudes."

The too-long lips curled into a smile of devilish amusement. "I do believe you could find the good in a reptile, Mr. Rotherham. What do you have to say about me, then?"

Silas compressed his lips between his teeth, mentally shuffling for exactly the right words. "You have a highly acute perception, stemming from a combination of the sharp wit you were born with and trials that would shock your family."

"A wise answer. You might even be smarter than the man who had the good sense to choose me for a wife."

"I am merely intentional about recognizing the good in

people. A little something to combat all the critics in the world."

Her amused "huh" bounced her in her chair. "I'm not sure whether to call that foolish or brilliant."

"I'd settle for obedient. It was God's idea, not mine."

Rubbing her thumb across the edge of her chair arm, she held his gaze with her glistening eyes. "My acute perception senses you have evaded my question. Why, Mr. Rotherham, are you here?" She laid each word out carefully in the dusty air between them.

Silas tensed under her scrutiny. He had no desire to tell her, but maybe she could help. Yes, he could tell her at least a piece of it. "I'm wondering about Jayne Windham. And all the scandal linked to her name."

"It seems you've been snooping about the affairs of this house already, if you've uncovered that name. There's nothing worth knowing about her."

"Then satisfy me—please. Curiosity will eat me alive."

Disapproval shot from her eyes as she examined Silas, as if deciding how much he might be worthy to know.

Before she could deny him again, he encouraged her. "Secrets are so much less powerful out in the open. Besides, I believe I have a secret you'd like to know as well. Perhaps we can trade. That is, if you are interested in knowing who has been watching your home."

Her slow grin seemed almost evil. "I thought you might know something about this Nathaniel Droll business. You're smarter than my pitiful family. And yes, I would deem that a fair bargain. My secret for yours."

"I haven't uncovered the whole story just yet, but I can tell you what I know for certain."

"In that case, I will offer you the answer to one specific question of your choosing in exchange for the piece you do know."

"All right." He crossed his arms. "How is Jayne Windham connected to Aurelie?"

"Ah, a wise use of your question." She inhaled, her taffeta dress crinkling around her ribs. "Lady Jayne was Aurelie's mother."

"So she is dead?"

"Did I say she was dead?"

"You said *was*. She *was* her mother."

"Only because she does not deserve that title any longer. No, she is most certainly not dead. That is two questions, by the way. And now, Mr. Rotherham, your secret. Who is Nathaniel Droll?"

22

Sometimes plans have the wonderful benefit of back-firing you to exactly where you needed to be in the first place.

~Nathaniel Droll, *Lady Jayne Disappears*

A bang on my bedchamber door yanked me from a deep sleep Thursday morning. While I tried to lift my heavy head from my cloud of a pillow, the door burst open and Juliette charged in, the hue of her bright blue dress hurting my eyes. Anger radiated from her face.

"Get out of bed, you coward." She slung the covers back, and cold struck my body just before the girl dragged me from the bed by my sleeve.

I tumbled and thumped onto the floor on my side, batting hair out of my face. Pain surged up my hip. My ire spiked with the pain. With my limbs tangled in my loose nightdress, I struggled to stand before my cousin.

"You are a part of this hateful Nathaniel Droll business,

aren't you?" Juliette swung a periodical at my arm, but I ducked, crumpling back to the floor. "He wrote about Jasper, and everything I told you is in here. Are you him? The one who's been spying on this house?"

Now I was fully awake, brain clear as ice water. The thin strand of our friendship had snapped. Juliette clutched the familiar green book containing the next Nathaniel Droll installment, which had released that day. I scrambled to retrieve the pieces. "Nathaniel Droll has been writing about Lynhurst far longer than I have been here." I fumbled toward restoration with my words, whatever the cost.

"Don't be clever. You know who the real man is, don't you? How else would Nathaniel Droll know my private affairs if it was not for you telling him?"

I held up my palms. "As I live, I've not met a single man since coming here that you do not know about. Nor have I spoken to anyone. When would I have had the chance? I am at Lynhurst nearly all the time." Dishonest. That's what I was. Not outright, but still dishonest. My stomach twisted, but I held my gaze steady. It was necessary—vital, really—to keep the truth quiet. Besides, I needed to keep the communication between myself and Juliette open if I was to protect her from the impending danger.

Anger contorted the girl's face, but pain etched itself in her eyes. "You were the only one I trusted with that secret. How else could it have gotten out?"

"Clem? He saw you as clear as I did on Saturday. If he did, there were likely others." I'd only written in the secret trysts, hadn't I? Nothing specific Juliette had told me. Nothing of the girl's feelings or thoughts.

Right?

Juliette hid her face behind her trembling hands, pressing her fingertips into her forehead.

I laid a tentative hand on the girl's arm. How could I help at this point? All the vindication I'd felt writing that issue faded against my desire to calm Juliette. "What will you do?"

"It's too late to do anything. Everything's been printed. Has Mother seen it yet? She mustn't. If you truly wish to help me . . ." She paced, releasing her wild curls.

"I cannot take it from her room. She'll lay hold of it eventually. But we can—"

"No! We have to get it out of her room before she sees it. I'll work out the rest later."

A thump and then a screech lifted up to us from below. "JULIETTE!" We froze.

Scrambling to her feet, Juliette ran out the door, tossing her copy of the troublesome issue at my feet. Landing in a whoosh on the fallen blankets, I prayed for the situation currently unfolding. No, *exploding*. Guilt swelled from an annoying prickle to overwhelming waves. I'd made another mess of things with my oh-so-brilliant solution. What had seemed so obvious and easy was, in reality, a complicated and tangled mess.

I flung my dressing gown around my body and tied it as I strode out the door with the installment in my hand. Only pieces of the heated conversation floated up to me as I hung over the third-story railing. Finally I snuck down to the second floor, just down the hall from the suite of rooms hosting the drama.

"I don't believe a word of it. No girl hides it if it's innocent."

How could anyone sustain that high of a pitch?

"There were other reasons."

"I do not care to hear them. Not a single one. Excuses!"

"Why won't you even give him a chance? Simply because we do not know his family background, it doesn't mean—"

"It means *everything*! You are forbidden to have anything more to do with him. Ever. No gentleman asks a lady to sneak around, dangling her reputation by a thread. I'll not have it. Not for my daughter."

"Would you listen—"

"I will not!" A thump against wood. "This conversation is over. I will not allow you to continue so foolishly."

A shuffle, then Glenna banged out of the room, open robe barely covering her nightdress. "My child. *My* child." Her plump bare feet paced across the hall. She pivoted and spotted me, and I shot up from the third step.

"I'm sorry, I was—"

"*You!*" One long finger shot out at me and I quaked on my step. "I want you with her everywhere she goes from now on. You hear me? *Everywhere!*" She balled her fists and stalked back into the bedroom. My body instantly sagged against the railing. She turned at the door. "Never allow them to be alone together. Not for a minute. And if I find you've failed, I'll personally remove you from this house, no matter what my fool mother says."

Garamond's low voice carried on beyond the bedroom wall, Juliette's not inserting itself once. Clem's freckled face peeked out of another suite down the hall, his big eyes blinking. Spotting me, he sprinted closer and crouched beside me.

"You missed the grand show." With a tiny smile, I handed Clem the leafed-through issue that had just released that morning and pointed to the section that spoke of Juliette.

He took in the story quickly, one hand cupping the back

of his neck. A frown shadowed his youthful face, making him look older.

"She's in there now with your father."

He glanced at the closed door, then back at the book with a lopsided grin. "What a pity I've missed the fun. This'll put a chain on her for sure."

"I'm to be her chaperone from now on."

He whistled. "Put a chain on you too now, didn't they? That's the end of your life."

The end of my life. Why yes, it was. I breathed slowly, keeping my face calm to hide the sudden storm rising inside. This complicated the one part of my life that truly belonged to me—my writing.

I *had* to keep working on it, though. Those issues had to be posted every week, on time. If they stopped now, when I was not to leave Juliette's sight, she'd know for sure who had written it. And then, so would everyone else.

The awkwardness of being Juliette's companion rivaled that of a three-legged race with a stranger. We stumbled over each other and invisible boundaries shifted constantly. After lunch, I hovered about the main hall, watching Juliette climb the stairs. Surely they didn't expect me to follow the girl to her bedchamber, did they? Juliette had hardly spoken to me since our forced companionship had begun.

But I had done it to myself.

"Well there, little cousin. What brings such a frown to that face?" Kendrick clopped into the hall from the main entrance, snapping riding gloves off his hands. "Juliette hasn't gone and said something brash, has she?"

"Oh, no." Spinning to face him, I composed myself. "She had a bit of a row with your parents this morning. And now I'm to chaperone her."

Movement outside the window pulled my attention from Kendrick. Was that—yes, it was Nelle. The slim figure in pale pink glided companionably beside Silas in his riding suit, their arms brushing. I couldn't look away. Nelle turned to face him, chin tipped up toward his face, as if he had just told the story of how he'd personally rescued fifty drowning children from the English Channel. Silas turned to Nelle with a glowing smile and nodded. And in that single moment, reality pivoted for me.

What if it was mutual?

Kendrick's eyebrows rose at my words. "Chaperone. Has she an appointment to call on a man today? I hadn't heard anything."

"I'm not chaperoning an outing. I'm chaperoning . . . in general."

Displeasure creased his forehead, and he strode forward, mud flaking off his riding boots. "Are you to smack her hand away from the sweets before dinner too?"

I shrugged helplessly. My disloyal peripheral vision again caught sight of the pair outside, walking together down the path to Florin cottage. They reached the trees, then Silas began jogging back toward the house. I bit my lip.

"There, now. It isn't your fault, child. We can get you out of this mess. We only need a good excuse to ease you out of your duties. What about a man, little cousin? Have you any interested gentlemen calling about? Perhaps you can claim distraction for a few hours."

I stared at the grout of the tile under my feet.

"Oh, Kendrick, that's my duty." Juliette's voice echoed down the stairs as she descended like royalty, a lighter blue dress fitting her body perfectly. How had she changed so quickly? "You'll have to trust my judgment. I have the perfect man selected, invited, and ready to be dazzled by our little cousin."

That Alexander again. Did he actually exist?

"Ah, I have a guess. Is it—" One raised eyebrow passed secret information between the siblings.

"Of course. You see it too, don't you?"

"You are a wonder at matchmaking, dear sister."

"Now do you see why we must have another party here? How else would she ever meet him if we didn't assist a little?"

How interesting that the only way I could meet my man of destiny was to have it so thoroughly planned.

"What will they have to say about this little soiree?" He jerked his head toward their parents' suite upstairs. "I heard you've earned yourself a ball and chain. No offense intended, little dear." This last sentence he spoke to me.

Juliette's chin jutted. "They are living in the last century. In modern England, a girl can marry whom she chooses, rich or poor."

"*Marry?* You'd sell yourself to that blackguard?" His face darkened. "I thought better of you, Juliette. Far better. I find it admirable of you to drag those poor souls out of the gutters of society and help them up, but bringing one into our family—a man with no background, no fortune. What can he offer you?"

"A great deal I've never had from anyone else." She yanked her gloves off each finger and tossed them on a marble-topped table in the hall.

"You can find love with any number of men. Why not choose one that also has a bit of fortune to care for you?" He strode to her and leveled his face with hers. "Do not let your girlish fantasies ruin your life, Juliette. Love is a farce."

"What do you know, you old cad? You've never tasted the lips of even a single woman. How can you judge—"

The slam of the patio door echoed through the hall. More boot clops, and Silas Rotherham strode into the open space, his dark hair wild and windblown about his ruddy face that was full of life. He paused at the sight of the gathering, riding whip against his thigh, breathing heavily as if coming in from a sprint. "My apologies at the interruption. Kendrick, the horses are ready when you are."

"Nothing of it, good friend. I've had my fill of the indoors." Saluting with his whip, Kendrick followed Silas out the garden doors to the patio.

Silas's gray eyes pierced my thoughts as I lay in bed that night. It must have been nearing midnight, but wakefulness surged through my veins. Maybe writing would help. I could dump my racing thoughts onto the page and climb back into bed within an hour.

I clambered off the bed, bare feet sinking into the rug, and threw my dressing gown around my shoulders. Perched at my desk, pen wet with ink, I stared at the blank page. Words scrambled through my brain in half-thoughts and fleeting feelings, too scattered to channel through the pen.

Jittery with tiredness, I yanked open a drawer on my left so hard that it flew out of its cavity, bouncing and tumbling across the rug. Empty note cards splayed over the floor. But what was that underneath the drawer? Stuffed up under the slider were several pieces of paper. I pulled at them lightly to avoid tearing the brittle sheets. Most were blank, some had scribbles. Bits of stories. Character names connected with surnames by lines across the page.

Sliding out page after page, I reveled in the closeness to this most precious man. Then the last page, thick and creamy with age, was sturdy enough to serve tea on. Sliding it out and turning it over, my heart pitched as I stared into the very face of Jayne Windham. Long, wild hair splayed over narrow shoulders and framed an exquisite face both serene and passionate. He'd described her so well. Had he painted this? My fingertip grazed the texture of the colorful portrait. Pink roses accented her dark hair and matched the hue of her gown.

What a beautiful mother.

What would it have been like to lean against this gentle shoulder or be kissed on the head by those sweet lips? To have that glowing face look upon me with love?

"What happened to you, Lady Jayne? Where did you go?" *And why did you not take your baby daughter with you?*

Emotion surging through me, I rose and moved about the room. She had to be found, even if the search led only to a forgotten tombstone. This woman's story had a tangible ending somewhere. Restlessness overtook me and drove me from my bedchamber, mind humming. I tiptoed down the stairs, raising the hem of my nightdress above my ankles.

With my candle's glow leading the way, I wound through the now-familiar passages to the south tower and held my light aloft. I'd been here before and nosed my way into every crevice. What did I search for this time? Evidence, perhaps, that she had been in service before coming here. But everything in the room spoke of being owned by a true lady. I ran my hand over untouched objects on her desk—blank paper, a marble-filled vase with dried flowers, a snow globe paperweight. I lifted the round ball and shook it, watching the flakes flutter down over a miniature village.

At a noise down the hall, I jerked, sending the snow globe flying. It shattered at my feet, water spidering through the cracks of the floor. Footsteps continued, echoing in some distant location of the house. Why did it seem this house never slept?

Exhaling my fear, I knelt to clean up the shards of glass, piling them into a rag. As I gingerly lifted the marble base upside down to avoid the glass protruding from the top of it, a light etching caught my eye. I held it to my candle, which rested on the floor beside me.

Dearest Jayne, my love for you is as solid as this rock.

Garamond

Shock pulsed through me and I dropped the base, watching it roll in the glass and water. Garamond. He had loved my mother too? But he was no killer. Not a chance.

Suddenly my candle began to flicker and spurt as the stub fought for life. I'd stayed there too long. Discarding the mess of glass and rags, I snatched the candle and ran back down the passageways, straining to see the grand hall somewhere ahead. But as I reached a large space of emptiness with several halls jutting off of it, my light flicked one final breath and snuffed, a trail of smoke curling up from the wick.

Standing alone in that empty chamber with moonlight

channeling down to me from every side, I blinked at each of the dark hallways. What else lay in the shadows of those long passageways? All the stories of the past swirled around me, chilling my skin as if the characters were ghosts moving about the house.

Gulping down fear, I charged down the narrowest hall. Light faded as I progressed, and the moans of the wind sounded like a song hummed by monks in a cathedral. No windows lit my way. Turning, I saw only darkness behind me in the foreign rooms. Uneven footfalls, slow and heavy, sounded deeper in the house again. Why had I done this? It was foolish. I should be in bed, safe under the covers. Rounding a corner, the footsteps sounded louder and closer.

Step quickly. Keep moving forward. Sweat prickled my skin as it broke through every pore. Was I having a heart attack? My ribs nearly broke from the rapid beating behind them. With a cry, I walked faster, praying I would not hit a wall.

Thunk. A person. I hit a person. I shifted hard to the side to soften the impact as my heart popped, then thudded. I forced myself to recover and act logically. Shuffles echoed before me as the midnight wanderer steadied himself against a wall.

Nathaniel Droll?

A match sparked to life and dove toward my face.

"It's you." Aunt Eudora. "Good heavens, child. You could kill someone at that pace."

Unless I died of fright first.

She touched the long match to a candle standing in a wall cavity and pinched out the match's tiny flame. "You have no business being about at night."

"My mind wouldn't allow me sleep." I sighed, collapsing back against the wall to still my pounding heart. "I cannot stop thinking about my mother." Ah, how stupid. My mouth clamped shut so hard after those words that I nearly bit my lip. Nerves had loosened my tongue, releasing this glib comment into the air between us.

The face tugged down by age stared at me in the candle glow, not blinking. Her eyes were green. Sharp green. "Search all you like, but she won't be found. Best save yourself the heartache now and stop looking." The old lady moved back, shadows jumping over her face.

The cotton nightdress under my robe clung to my moist skin. "You know what happened to her, don't you? You've always known."

"Go to bed, child." Sweeping past, she continued down the hall with her cane echoing against the tile. Shuff-shuff-*clock*.

I ran after the receding light. All the answers were there, bottled up in that crippled old woman. "Please, don't go." Reaching her, I grabbed the arm holding the cane, desperate. "Just tell me. Tell me what happened."

"Take the stairs quietly. They creak."

"Please."

The woman brushed off my hand like an offending tree branch and surged forward with the force of rushing water.

Helpless, I stopped in the dark hall, feet apart and mind exploding among the shadows. Tears pricked my tired eyes. My voice burst from my chest in a desperate, heartrending plea. "Why won't anyone tell me?"

The shuffling echoed down the hall, growing dimmer along with the light, leaving me alone in the dark passageway of my own dear Lynhurst Manor.

23

There is something cathartic about immediately replacing what was lost—much like binding up a splinter in one's finger to stop the ache.

~Nathaniel Droll, *Lady Jayne Disappears*

Aunt Eudora did not attend luncheon the following day. I felt her absence keenly, and wondered if I would be welcomed at the woman's bedchamber if I called to enquire after her health. A normal niece would do such a thing. But the hours passed and I could not bring myself to approach the main suite, and before long, I had become caught up in the gowns and preparations of the dinner party.

"The woman is bitter. That's why she's been missing." Juliette slid her arms into long white gloves as we talked in her suite. "She's entirely too bitter about a great many things."

I took measured steps to the full-length mirror trimmed in ivory and gold. Her lady's maid had declared me ready for the great dinner party, and I could barely move to the right or left.

When I reached the mirror, would I see a stranger reflected back? Nelle and Juliette flanked me as I stopped before the looking glass for my first glimpse of the rich purple gown with silver trim. The material fit snugly about my slender torso, gathering at my waist and spilling in rich waves and tucks to the floor. Silver embroidery peeked out of each tuck and an elaborate design curled around my waist.

Yes, it was extravagant, but I could not hate it. Not at all. The vibrant gown wrapped me in colorful beauty like an exquisite flower. Like my mother.

"Miss Wicke, I believe you've outdone yourself with this gown. And in so short a time. I'll even forgive you not following my instructions to make it blue." Juliette approached from behind in a silver gown, cupping my bare shoulders with her gloved hands. "Although I might not forgive you for making our dear girl more stunning than me."

"It isn't your dress that draws attention." I smiled at Juliette reassuringly, but the confident girl needed none of it. Her playful smile surfaced, eyes sparkling.

"It would be better in blue, as I'd ordered, but purple suits you as well, I suppose. It is the perfect look to finally introduce you to Alexander and allow your beautiful romance to begin. Miss Wicke, have we finished our supply of the blue fabric? I thought we had ordered plenty."

"Purple and blue are nearly the same."

Nelle and I exchanged quiet looks in the mirror over my shoulder, both knowing exactly why purple had been chosen, though Nelle did not realize I also had a personal connection to Lady Jayne, the woman in purple. I turned back to once again drink in the sight of myself arrayed in the magnificent gown.

"We only need trimming for your hair. Something sensational to match that exquisite dress. Something gold, perhaps?"

"But it has silver trim." Nelle fingertip-touched the perfect tresses hanging down my back. "Might I make a suggestion, my lady? Those would be perfect." She indicated a vase of fresh flowers from the gardens—hyacinth and baby's breath. Nelle crossed the room and plucked the baby's breath and arranged it in the upswept part of my hair, giving the delicate look of lace.

Juliette evaluated me at arm's length. "An impressive touch. Fine work, Miss Wicke."

But the idea had come from my own mind when I'd described my version of Lady Jayne in the final gown worn before she had disappeared. It had been, to my thinking, the grand finale of the costumes the beautiful woman had donned before she completely left the social scene she had enthralled for months. A gentle hand-squeeze communicated my thanks to Nelle for the little talisman to take me through the night.

"You'll never be able to avoid men, looking that way, Aurelie dear." Juliette surveyed me in the mirror over my shoulder. "Prepare for love and romance. At least one of us in this room shall have it tonight." With a final coy smile, Juliette retreated to her walnut jewelry case near the window and began to pick at its contents.

"How I wish I could be there to watch." A soft glow lit Nelle's kind face, lifting her lips as she spoke more freely with Juliette out of earshot. "Will Mr. Rotherham be there?"

"I'm sure he will be. They couldn't very well host a party at the house where he is a guest and not invite the man."

"What will he wear? I want to picture everything."

A knot of dread clutched my stomach. "He will wear a black suit and look very much like every other man there."

"He is *not* like other men." The soft words escaped the girl's lips. "He enjoys children, did you know that? Enjoys them a great deal. I've never seen an unmarried man take to children so quickly." She lowered her voice to the softest whisper. "I must tell you, Aurelie, he's met my Dahlia. He's met her, and he treats her as a little lady. Brings her books to read and everything. He wants her to learn as if she were in school."

I tried three times to swallow.

"He really is the finest man. You look troubled, but please trust me. I do so want you to understand about him. Will you promise to think well of him? At least a little?"

I forced my lips into a smile. "Of course. I cannot truly hate a person, after all."

"Come sometime and see the way he speaks to Dahlia. It would surprise you so, to see that side of him. He comes quite often, now that he knows of her. And I know he wouldn't tell a soul she's there."

"You must be speaking of a man, the way your cheeks are flushed." Juliette glided back to us and draped a delicate necklace about my neck. "Is it Alexander? I shall have to tell him that you were discussing him before you even met. I'm sure he'll find it wonderfully romantic."

"It was Mr. Rotherham." I couldn't bring myself to lie, even though it was tempting.

"Still?"

Chills climbed my exposed arms.

"A fine gentleman, is all." Nelle clasped the necklace and stood back, eyes cast down.

Juliette eyed the girl. "Is he, now?" Her assessing gaze flicked from Nelle to me in the mirror, causing me to heat under the thick gown. "We'll leave Silas Rotherham to whoever happens to catch his fancy. In the meantime, you will have a grand evening and meet the love of your life."

When Juliette and I swept out of the room later, Nelle clasped my arm in a whisper-soft squeeze and breathed, "Tell me everything later."

At the top of the grand staircase a half hour later, I sucked in my breath and wobbled on the top step, as if I were about to drop off a cliff. A sudden rush of fear overwhelmed me, tingling in my chest, like a fear of heights. Juliette, who had already made her grand hostess entrance, hovered near the entryway below, gesturing with arms encased in ivory gloves.

A blond man with smooth features and a devastatingly handsome face turned briefly from his conversation at the bottom of the stairs to glance up at me, then took a second more intentional look that lingered. When my gaze locked on to his, for I could not look away, his face melted into a welcoming smile that invited conversation, had we been near enough. Warmth rolled through my cheeks. Though the stairs separated him from me, an undeniable kinship passed between us.

Heat continued to pulse through me as I hovered there, looking down at the great distance between me and the main floor. White haze flanked my vision as I pictured myself tumbling down. Hiking my skirt to my ankles, I turned and fled back the way I'd come. Through long halls, I reached the other side and descended the service stairs, squishing my dress into the narrow whitewashed stairway and testing each step before blindly placing weight on each foot. With a hiss of fabric along the wall, I reached the bottom and hurried past a few startled servers and down another tunnel to the great hall and drawing room where the guests mingled.

At last, ground level. And there had been no tumble down the stairs.

First I saw Silas lingering in an arched doorway, speaking intensely with an older gentleman. I smiled a little. The words "replacement remedy" slipped into clear understanding as I looked past Silas for the blond man with the dazzling smile. Possibilities spun through my mind, lighting my heart.

Weaving through guests with a polite smile, I finally found my way to a bay window and hovered there to catch my breath, scanning the crowd for the man I'd seen. I pivoted as someone tapped my shoulder, and there he was, tall and elegant, as if he'd just ridden off the battlefield and shed his armor in the front hall.

"Would you think me overzealous if I said you lit up the room with your beauty?" He leaned intimately close, but it did not feel out of place.

"Perhaps a bit butter on bacon. And far from original." A ladies' man, he was.

"I'd only take offense to the second one. I shall work to invent a more original phrase for so extraordinary a girl."

"I am Aurelie." I held out my hand, knuckles up.

Eyebrows raised, he took it and placed a fleeting kiss on my fingers. "Truly an original, you are. I've never had a lady give me the pleasure of her acquaintance all on her own. It makes me wonder what else you are capable of."

My already-warm neck heated at the mistake. Juliette should have introduced us. Where was she?

"I am Lord Sutherland. It is a rare pleasure to meet you, Miss . . ."

"Harcourt. Aurelie Harcourt."

"Would I have seen you at the races? I don't recall glimpsing this face before." His look surveyed me from head to hem, as if trying to place me in his memory.

"I've not been to the races, so it's not likely."

"Well, what do you do with your time? I'm quite sure I've been most places in Glen Cora that are worth being, and I haven't seen you yet."

Awkward shame blanketed me. Couldn't we start with easier questions? My past could wait for later. "I read a lot of books."

"Books." His eyes lit. "Do you read the Brownings?"

"Some things. Although I much prefer her writing to his."

"Ah, I knew you would." He sipped the liquid in his glass. "I should always wish for a romance like theirs. What sort of passion must they experience together as their shared work entwines, operating in tandem. I've always romanticized the idea of sharing my work with my wife, being a partner to her in every sense imaginable."

The fervent words brought more heat to my skin, down to my lightly throbbing fingertips, although I could not say why. I studied his fair features, contemplating the chance his words held any measure of authenticity.

"Their true romance lies in the mutual sacrifice, though," he said. "She left her place in society to join his lower rung, and he cares for her in her handicapped state every day."

"I had not heard that part." The story touched me in a way that both softened my heart and excited me to write.

"What an adorable pairing." Juliette swept up behind us,

fingertips grazing my shoulder. "How nice you've met already. Lord Sutherland, this is my cousin who has been staying with us these past weeks. Aurelie dear, this is Lord Sutherland. *Alexander* Sutherland." Her red-lipped smile nearly curled off her face.

"It is my honor once again, Miss Harcourt." His bold stare made me turn away, unable to look at him directly.

The conversation pivoted hard onto a bumpy, awkward path from which I could not seem to recover. All too aware of myself and all my clumsy movements, I soon made excuses and moved away. Time to calm my racing heart.

When my roving gaze met with an approachable older lady in red and brown who smiled back, I closed the distance between us, hand extended. "What a lovely bird nestled in your hat. He looks as though he belongs."

"Why, thank you, I suppose." The woman blinked. "I beg your pardon, but I seem to have forgotten your name, young lady."

"Miss Aurelie Harcourt. I don't believe we've met before. I'm rather new to . . . well, to Lynhurst." For I was certainly not new to the vicinity.

The aged woman's eyebrows rose, creasing her powdered forehead. "Then you'll forgive my stare. You simply look familiar." Thin lips turned up in a welcoming smile. "Let's dispense with formality and simply declare ourselves introduced on our own. My fumble has earned you that much. I am Lady Duncan of Fairfax."

"Lady Duncan, it's my pleasure." I dipped a curtsey. "And please, your fumble rescued me." And smiled, wishing I knew the proper words to say next. I should have at least inherited my mother's grace to go along with this life at Lynhurst.

Wait.

Suddenly, the night lit with possibilities and great worth. "You said I look familiar, Lady Duncan. You do not perhaps mean I look like Lady Jayne Windham, do you?" *Please say yes. Oh, please.* "Several people lately have told me all about her, and I've heard we share a few similarities."

The old lady blinked wrinkled eyelids, her gloved hands poised near her waist. "Whoever would still be discussing Jayne Windham? She hasn't been to Somerset in years."

I'd done it again, hadn't I? I had said the wrong thing. I forced a quick recovery with a smile. "I find myself drawn to the stories of Lady Jayne and wondering how many are true. She was a legendary beauty, was she not?"

The woman lowered her face close to mine, her easy grin returning. "Not a single young woman liked her. That should tell you how beautiful she was." The good-natured eyes twinkled. "I liked her immediately because I have the wonderful pleasure of being taken out of the competition. By age, that is."

I laughed, delighted by my fine companion. "Surely you were not old then, but I'm glad you enjoyed her."

"Of course I did. And so did everyone else, once the initial envy wore away. She made it impossible not to be swept up in her buoyant merriment and clever witticisms. Even the hardest of hearts would sing her praises by the time she left."

"A shame she did not return, then. I heard she disappeared quite suddenly."

Her eyes flicked back and forth. "That isn't exactly the case." Her eyes glittered with a wealth of unshared gossip. "Come, I'll tell you the whole of it."

Arm in arm, we retreated to a wingback chair and ottoman that decorated a lonely corner of the large room.

"She didn't disappear outright, mind you. A lady like that could never slink away without causing a great stir in society. She disappeared, little by little. Kept great company with her room, reading books and lounging about. We saw her in the lower south tower windows when we drove up, quite pale and without her hair done, and she refused to take callers. After a while, she stopped attending events altogether, so when she left, hardly anyone noticed."

Shattered nerves. That's what happened to Lady Jayne. Depression. The disease of the heart had attacked so often at the Mallet, sucking the life and love out of a body. It always happened to the vibrant, lively ones because they could hide it until it controlled them.

"She's likely the well-cushioned wife of some member of parliament by now, neatly decorating his lounge chairs. Marriage is almost the worst that can happen to a lively girl."

Or perhaps she'd suffered another kind of death—a life sentence at the asylum. Was it possible? Too often that was the fate of those suffering from shattered nerves.

My mind shifted quickly over the notes left in my notebook. Maybe she was not killed at the time of her disappearance, but much later. And in the meantime, she had been hidden away in an asylum. That changed my list of killers tremendously.

"Has anyone ever searched for her?"

"Heavens, who has time for that?" Her words sank my heart. "But I will say, an acquaintance of mine in Danbury Square mentioned happening upon her once in London several years ago, but she claimed they never renewed their friendship. She refused to say why."

"How long ago?"

"Oh, maybe ten years. But she sees her about in London to this day, I believe."

Alive. My mother was *alive*.

Maybe.

"How ghastly." Chills thrilled up my back and into my scalp. I simply must remain at Lynhurst now. It seemed my mother was alive and able to be found.

But why did Nathaniel Droll believe she'd been killed?

24

Beautiful women often bloom for a day, like the roses, then wither into obscurity when their season ends in marriage.

~Nathaniel Droll, *Lady Jayne Disappears*

Dinner found me between Kendrick, my unofficial escort for the evening, and Juliette. Aunt Eudora presided over the head of the table, as usual, with Glenna and Garamond to my right. Chittering laughter and the clinking of silver service brought fresh delight to the dark room. I nibbled dutifully, but wished I could sweep my decadent food into a small basket to eat it later in private, when my stomach had settled. Lord Sutherland, near the other end of the table, shared a conversation with a petite brunette in a pink gown, but obvious indifference on both parts chilled the air around them.

"Garamond, have you seen Mr. Worthington?" Glenna's frantic whisper squeaked across the table nearby. "He left the room. How long has he been gone? I considered him a suspect from the beginning."

"Oh for pity's sake, Glenna." Aunt Eudora's chin jerked with disgust. "A servant leaving the room hardly makes him guilty. What do you expect, that he sneaks into the hall to write about you?"

Glenna's pointy nose lifted. "Anything suspicious is worth noticing, Mother. Unless you wish to allow this man to continue spying on Lynhurst, whoever he is."

The old woman rolled her eyes.

"I'm determined to find him *tonight*. We must put an end to this."

I bent low over my romaine lettuce, poking at the slivered almonds and cranberries. Not yet. Just a little longer. I'd made huge strides in my search tonight, and I wasn't ready to leave.

The woman finally silenced her guesses when something farther down the table distracted her. I peeked through my lashes to see her staring with a frown at Alexander Sutherland, who cut barely perceptible glances in my direction, even as the woman beside him continued to speak. Glenna directed a glare toward me that might have frozen a desert.

As the servants cleared the final dishes, Juliette stood to invite her "esteemed guests" into the large drawing room for tea and entertainment. And when she waved me on, it suddenly struck that I was one of the esteemed guests. I allowed myself to be carried forward in the thick mass of people. By changing only my outward appearance, I belonged to this class of people. A secret part of me thrilled at belonging somewhere, to something, despite Glenna's disapproval of such a thing.

In the large drawing room, chairs had been arranged before the piano in rows, and the guests dutifully filled them. Back aching from the confines of the rigid dining room chair at dinner, I stood unobtrusively near the entrance to the left of the chairs and waited.

"It's a great honor for a mother to introduce her own daughter to you this night as a very accomplished pianist, among other splendid things." Glenna stood before us, her silly, beaming face making her extravagant dress with small hanging balls of fur seem even gaudier.

Juliette played well, pale fingers flying over the keys, crossing easily one over the other. I felt glad for my vantage point to the side of the piano that allowed me to see more of this finger work than the audience could. Music spilled from the great instrument with the same ease and speed as words fell from the girl's lips. How odd, that a girl like Juliette could produce such a sound of exquisite beauty. If only I could simply perch on a bench and magically coax music from that great box anytime my heart needed the soothing melodies.

With a flourish, the girl finished, held her arched hands over the keys, and closed her eyes as if to savor the final fading tones. Hearty applause followed.

"A mother could not be more proud." Glenna rose, joy nearly bursting the seams of her dress. "Brava, Juliette. Brava!" Her rapid claps made the fur balls bounce against her round frame. "But you all know I'm a generous woman who enjoys sharing the spotlight." She gestured magnanimously with her gloved arms toward the left end of the room. "I should be honored to hear a presentation from the other hostess of the night, who I'm certain will dazzle us as well.

Ladies and gentleman, I'd like you to meet our beautiful cousin, Miss Aurelie Harcourt."

Striding directly to me, Glenna caught my wrist with one gloved hand, drawing me toward the piano with the sheer force of her confidence. "You do play, don't you, Miss Harcourt?"

"No, I—"

She wrinkled her nose in a smile of victory. "Good."

Surprise made me weak and pliant as Glenna towed me to the piano. What on earth would I do once I reached the thing? Guiding me under the chandelier meant to highlight the pianist on the bench, Glenna encouraged me with feather-waving nods and smiles.

My stomach bottomed out to my feet. Moisture gathered. Heat poured over my face from the chandelier.

Glenna tilted her head with a motherly smile. "Come now, look at the girl's modesty. What a virtuous young woman. But you must indulge us. Everyone is anxious to hear your little recital. You'll be splendid, I know it."

My knees trembled as I sat, vibrating the under-layers of my skirt. What could I do? I'd never put finger to key in my life. Before Lynhurst, I'd only seen the instrument in the illustrations of Papa's stories. Digory watched from the corner, worry stretching his face. Where was Nelle? Strangers in colorful dresses sat between me and the door, facing me expectantly, closing off escape. The smooth ivory felt foreign under my fingertips.

Oh God, rescue me. I'm frozen.

My rescue approached from behind. A few foot clops, then a dark figure slid onto the creaking bench beside me, arm against mine.

Silas's warm breath brushed my ear. "Just breathe. I'll handle the rest."

Fingers splayed over the keys, I lowered my eyes and focused on breathing. And then a deep, beautiful song began at the bottom of the keyboard, drawn out by his tanned, strong hands. My eyes flicked open and watched Silas's fingers deftly spider over the keys with the ease of a professional. In one smooth movement, his hand climbed the keyboard toward my inept fingers and slid silently, gently under them, carrying the song up the keyboard in the part I was supposed to play. He guided my hand that lay draped helplessly over his, but I felt every thud of his knuckles into my palm, every move of his fingers working over the keys.

I wanted to cry. The gentle song with rich tones sounded like heaven. The music poured forth from the open piano, and to the audience, my arms moved up and down the keyboard. The words of David of the Bible rang through me, stirring my heart to tears.

Gracious is the Lord, and righteous; yea, our God is merciful.

The Lord preserveth the simple: I was brought low, and he helped me.

Return unto thy rest, O my soul; for the Lord hath dealt bountifully with thee.

Bountifully.

I had only to ask, and God rescued. Every time.

I stole a glance at Silas, his calm face intent on the keyboard. He looked briefly at me, and I caught a glimpse of the deluge of strength and kindness stored behind the dam of his face.

And Nelle would be the one to unleash it one day.

His gentle smile engulfed me, causing my hand resting on his to tremble. The desire to kiss him, to yank out the foundation of that dam, nearly overtook me.

He carried an emotional culmination into a glorious ending, resting his fingertips on the keys as the sound swept over the room and receded like a wave. The sudden applause startled me, and I drew my hand off Silas's and jerked my gaze back toward the audience. A few in the back stood. With a quick, awkward head bow, Silas stood from the bench, twining his fingers through mine and squeezing my hand for a brief second before slipping away without a backward look. On shaky limbs, I also stood and walked into the audience without a bow, this time finding a seat. No wall would be enough to hold me upright at this point. My insides trembled like raisin pudding.

Just before I collapsed into a chair, I caught sight of Nelle in the shadows just beyond the doorway, watching the affair with rapt attention, fist to her mouth and tears in her eyes. Had she been happy to see the man she cared for helping me? Or was she afraid of losing him to me?

I should reassure her that it would not happen. But in the afterglow of the beautiful duo, I wasn't sure I could find the words to actually promise such a thing. I closed my eyes and breathed, white-knuckling the edges of my hard chair.

Best not to think of it at all. I had been wrong before. What if Nelle did not even think of Silas that way? What if I would never care for Lord Sutherland? If only I knew anything for certain—besides the fact that I deeply loved Silas Rotherham.

25

Lady Jayne dearly loved believing all surprises to be good things, but the older she grew, the more the opposite proved true.

~Nathaniel Droll, *Lady Jayne Disappears*

Whenever Juliette's eyes sparkled, it meant danger. That much I knew for sure. The girl had circulated among the guests, talking to each person individually. Keeping to my word, I had watched her throughout the night, but nothing had been amiss. Until now, that is. Jasper Grupp slipped into the room and handed his hat to Digory in one smooth move. With eyes glittering dangerously, the girl glanced at Jasper in a flutter of lashes, then returned to whomever she talked to, her eyelashes touching her cheeks.

Jasper returned her glimpses, a smile snaking over his face. A few times the glances lingered, a secret code passing between them. Juliette held her closed fan to her cheek, tapping absently as she talked to another man. Then the fan tapped her rosy lips as they curved into a smile. Frowning, I moved through the crowd toward her.

Juliette swayed just ahead of me, gliding toward her mother, and laid a hand on the bejeweled woman's powder-white arm.

"I have a surprise for you, Mother. One you'll love."

Glenna pivoted to evaluate her. "It had better not include the name 'Jasper Grupp.'"

"Oh, but it does." Her pinched-lip smile sealed the words.

My heart drummed against my ribs. I swallowed. Was it time? Should I say something? This would be it. I had to speak up right now, before they announced their engagement.

Dear Lord, give me strength. I claim the promise from James chapter 1 and ask you for wisdom. But what on earth would you have me do, Father?

Just then Lord Sutherland slid himself between me and the mother-daughter pair. "I had no idea you were such an accomplished young woman. Have you learned to play the piano on your own, as well?"

Frustrated at the intrusion, I bit my lip. "I have never in my life had a piano instructor." The deceptive truth slipped out of my tense mind.

"Outstanding." His eyes shone. "I have a Steinway at my home, gathering a rather impressive layer of dust in an un-used parlor. I would be honored to have you come and dust those keys for me with your beautiful songs. I'm positive my mother would be astounded beyond words to hear you play."

As would I. "Thank you for the kind invitation, but I'm truly not a pianist." The words rang in my ears as false modesty, but I couldn't help it. What else could I say without tangling myself in further deceptions?

Lord Sutherland persisted, the sight of his handsome face

tickling my stomach as he leaned close again, speaking intimately as one who had known me for years. "You must know I want to see you again. Would you allow it?"

"As long as you require only my company, and not a piano recital."

A realization passed through my mind as a fleeting thought amid the tension and fear—Lord Sutherland and I were not of the same world. If we married, as Juliette certainly intended, I would be a constant fake.

But was I not already that?

"You have a bargain, fair lady. Although I will not promise I'll never again request to hear your lovely music."

Silas couldn't keep his gaze from drifting in quick sips to Aurelie. Even surrounded by a flock of guests, the girl looked utterly alone. The pallor of her face, and the expression—was it fear?—gave her the look of a lost child.

Don't worry. I will watch out for you.

The Lord had placed the girl in his path for her protection, of that he was certain. That awareness drove him to keep her always in his peripheral vision every day, even as she moved about the house in relative safety.

And then there was Mr. Grupp. Who was he that Aurelie disliked him so much? When the man separated himself from the others to retrieve a drink from the side table, Silas approached and lifted a crystal goblet for himself. "I don't believe I know you, sir."

Grupp whipped his head toward Silas, surprise in his eyes as if he had not expected anyone to talk to him. "Jasper Grupp, friend of the family."

"Silas Rotherham. Unofficial escort of the hostess, Miss Juliette Gaffney."

"Are you, now?" The man riveted his full attention to Silas then, turning his whole body and assessing him critically. The scar in his eyebrow twitched. "And here I thought you belonged to Miss Harcourt."

"I am merely watching out for a woman alone in the world."

"That one can watch out for herself—believe me." His nostrils flared as he lowered his eyes. "She always has."

"You've known her a long time?" Silas wasn't sure why this should surprise him.

"A hundred thousand stories' worth of time."

Silas frowned as the sentence caught him off-guard, resonating with a recently resurrected memory. But what memory?

Jasper met his gaze then, searching. "Has she told you nothing about our history? You mustn't be very close if she's never mentioned me."

"She's said very little of you."

"I suppose she would. She has a terrible habit of overstating her good traits and conveniently forgetting the bad. She did not end our acquaintance on very good terms, you see."

He made Aurelie sound nearly dishonest.

When Jasper looked away, Silas followed his gaze to Juliette, who motioned from across the room with tiny jerks of her head and a coquettish smile.

"If you'll pardon me, I must go and make an announcement. Quite a pleasure to make your acquaintance, Mr. . . . ."

"Rotherham. And likewise."

The man parted the crowds and strode across the room

toward the grand staircase, leaving Silas to ponder the "history" he shared with Aurelie. The vague mention left too much to the imagination, and after a lifetime of reading, Silas possessed far too much imagination.

Ah, *Tempest and Trouble!* That's where I heard those words. It was a Nathaniel Droll line.

As the man took to the stairs, his arms raised to gain the attention of the crowd, his odd words from before, and the vague tie to Droll, unsettled everything Silas thought he knew.

There stood Jasper on the stairs, tall and proud. My stomach churned and I glanced about for Silas or Garamond—for that is who I had decided to alert. But Jasper's gaze caught mine and pinned me to the spot with the slightest smile and narrowed eyes, trapping me there. Why couldn't I move? He had cast a sort of spell over my brain. His look told me he'd already won.

He raised his arms. Why was Juliette not with him? Wouldn't they announce their engagement together?

"Friends, I want to thank you for the pleasure of this time together. I've met most of you, and have enjoyed—well, some of you."

A light chuckle pattered through the crowd as conversations faded and the guests turned to face the stairs. What a fake—he even spoke like one of them now.

"I have an important secret to share, and I've decided to bring it to you first, since you are the finest in Bristol society. I'm pleased to tell you that you are now gazing upon the one and only . . . Nathaniel Droll."

Gasps arose from the crowd. Low murmuring ensued.

I grabbed my throat, my breath catching. *No, no, no.* My mind screamed. Throbbed.

How dare he?

How *dare* he?

I pinned him with a look, channeling the anger inside me toward him in one powerful glare, but he did not see it. His countenance, alight with pride, swept over the well-dressed gentlemen and ladies who looked up to him. Murmurs and clinking punch glasses filled the momentary silence.

"Yes, it's true. I have kept myself anonymous for years to maintain a normal life, but I've recently been encouraged to make myself known. So there you have it, everyone. And I am pleased to make your acquaintance." With a bow, he descended the steps again into an eager throng of guests. Questions alighted from the people nearest him and conversation swelled to a heavy volume.

Juliette remained on the fringes, fan tapping her open palm. The smug look of victory said that this moment was to her a validating landmark. Several men toasted Jasper Grupp with loud cheers and sloshing glasses.

Rage boiled. My long fingernails cut into the delicate skin of my upper arm. What would I do now? What *could* I do? That *fiend.*

Anger pulsed over me with each thudding beat of my heart, exploding through my mind. Across the room and beyond the crowds, Juliette found me and winked. I met her look but couldn't smile. Aloneness wrapped itself around my middle and squeezed until I could scarcely breathe.

Speeding toward a quiet corner, I nearly collided with Silas. He jerked his glass up high to avoid spilling lemon water on me.

"Mr. Rotherham." All other words escaped me.

"Miss Harcourt. You look flushed. Are you well?"

"Quite well, thank you." Focus. Calm. Mask in place. Chin up, shoulders back, I forced my best smile forward. "And may I offer you congratulations on completing your mission. You now know the identity of Nathaniel Droll."

Considering his water glass, then me again, he smiled. "No indeed, Miss Harcourt. I'm not sure I do." Tipping his glass to me in a parting gesture, he slid into the mass of well-dressed guests, becoming simply another black-suited man at the party.

Not my rescuer this time.

When Jasper wove through the remaining guests toward the balcony, I followed him. Whipping aside the curtains with trembling hands, I grabbed his arm with the full force of my anger. "Jasper! What were you thinking?" I ached to shove him over the rail. It would barely hurt him at this height.

"I was thinking I needed to save my hide, after you so kindly roasted it for me." He dusted his shiny hat and tucked it under his arm. "You left me in a rather awkward position when you hinted to Miss Gaffney about my upbringing. I needed to offer her *some* explanation as to why I'd risen above my childhood, and it had an even greater effect on her than I'd hoped. We were carried away one day, and she convinced me that I should tell the world my grand secret."

"You promised." Anger curled through me. "We made a deal, and you broke it. I want that money back." It had obviously been spent on his suit of clothes already, but I didn't care.

"Our deal was that I would never reveal *you* to be Nathaniel Droll." Dark eyes sparked at me from the shadows veiling his face. "You tell me how I broke that promise, and I'll repay every farthing."

Heat burned behind my eyes. "You are despicable, Jasper Grupp. Do you have any idea what you've done?" Weeks of fear and anxiety all swirled together, solidifying into the form of the skinny man before me.

"I haven't hurt you, Aura dear. Not yet." He stroked my bare arm, running one fingertip along its smooth surface. Chills rose along its path. "I've only had a little fun with you. Made things difficult, as you've done for me so often."

"All those girls deserved to know the truth. I don't regret warning them about you."

He smiled, tilting his head. "You shall, my dear." He flipped his hat back onto his head and bowed. "Now, I should slip away from my adoring fans." With an easy leap, he cleared the rail and landed in the grass a half story below. One last lift of his hat and he moved forward, merging with the dark.

I stared until I couldn't see him. Where was my rescue now? The inky night felt devoid of everything good, even God. I had no plan, no desire to write, and no help from anyone.

26

It was her beauty and wit that drew people into her life, but her intentional love for the downcast that made them remain.

~Nathaniel Droll, *Lady Jayne Disappears*

Silas Rotherham strode with purpose through the courtyard at Shepton Mallet Prison, which was lightly populated with a few tired inmates. A door banged, sending a cloister of doves up from the eaves with pleasant thwacks and coos. He hadn't been sure when he'd left the house that morning what had prompted him to go there, other than the unnerving weight on his mind after Jasper Grupp's surprise. That announcement, as well as the man's words about Aurelie's character and past, had ignited a host of doubts that had never before occurred to him. Lying would not be out of the realm of possibility for the girl. She was, after all, a master storyteller.

Then, in the dark of night in his lonely bedchamber, questions had surfaced. Questions about years of royalty money and the plausibility of a prison inmate penning famous novels.

But as foolish as he'd felt then for missing the holes in her story, he felt even more so now for doubting the word of the girl he knew to be unusually pure and good, one immune to normalcy. This visit, and the talks he'd had with Rosa and the others, had only proven what he already knew. He hadn't answered his burning questions, but he'd learned several facts on this trip.

First, that Aurelie had been the same girl at Shepton Mallet that she was at Lynhurst. Despite her storytelling nature, every inch of the girl breathed sincerity and truth that left his doubts of her character utterly unfounded. Second, she often left the prison to run errands, as she was not a prisoner herself, giving her ample opportunity to post installments of Nathaniel Droll novels for whoever wrote them. And last, Aurelie had not exaggerated the state of the prisons, or the wicked schemes of the jailer to profit off his inmates. Only a few shillings stood between so many prisoners and their freedom, an easy amount to manage.

And for some, Silas would manage it that very day.

"Hello there!" he called as he reached the gatehouse.

The wiry man swung out, holding on to the bars, tattered coattails flying out after him. "Hello there, gov'nor. Find everything you need?"

"I'd like to discuss a few inmates with you." Walking among the prisoners Aurelie cared so greatly about had drawn out his protective side in a powerful way, spurring him into action. They required so little, and were given even less. "I've come across several men whose debts are to establishments no longer in business. Can you tell me why they've not been released?"

Confusion creased his pale brow. "Well, you can't go releasing a debtor just because. He still owes the money, even if there's no one to take it from 'im."

"All right, then what if you took it?"

He blinked.

"Let me see the prisoner log, please."

His whiskered face shuttered. "Are you an inspector from Her Majesty, then?"

He smiled. "No, sir. Just Silas Rotherham, ordinary man of business."

The man returned with a long book, pages curled back to the most current one. Leafing through, Silas selected a handful of inmates with whom he'd already spoken—those he felt could flourish if restored to freedom. Marks went beside their names.

"I'd like to talk to you about clearing a few debts. The ones noted in pencil there." He extended the book back to the man. "Starting with Rosa Clemens from cell block 38."

In an entire day at the Mallet, Silas hadn't attained nearly all the answers he'd hoped for, but what he had discovered proved more than sufficient. Questions still loomed about Nathaniel Droll's true identity, Aurelie's past with Jasper, and a host of other things. All he knew for certain was that if Aurelie told him that day that she were Nathaniel Droll and Grupp the imposter, he'd do anything in his power to convince the rest of the world of this as well, no questions asked.

Hours later, Silas Rotherham strode out of the gates of Shepton Mallet Prison, arm in arm with Rosa, and loaded her into the Lynhurst carriage. Together they watched from the shadows of a beech tree as eleven prisoners and their families straggled out of the gates, stumbling and gazing around as if they'd forgotten how to operate in the real world. One man paused, smiling face upturned, and stretched his arms up to receive the sunlight shining down on him outside the walls while his children chased each other around his legs. Silas had given the ratty little guard the equivalent of the price of a suit—*a suit*—for the pleasure of this moment.

He'd have paid ten times that.

As the families fanned out in different directions into Glen Cora, Silas solidified his resolve that this was only the beginning. He breathed deeply and settled back against the leather seat until the newly released families disappeared into their new lives.

And then they were on their way, the carriage lurching forward over the rough street. It seemed fitting to ride off into the sunset with his rescued lady by his side. Rosa, having no immediate place to go, had been carted off with Silas. Another fact he'd learned from this visit was that the woman across from him possessed an amazing talent in fine sewing, which had given him a most fabulous idea. He thanked God silently for his sovereignty in fitting together every piece of the puzzle, and for using Silas to bring it about.

Silas bit back a smile threatening to spill from the inside out as he watched the old seamstress hanging out the open windows of the carriage like a small child glimpsing the seaside for the first time.

"Now you'll have to promise to work hard and be a good help."

"I'll work harder than a team of oxen, 'andsome." She settled back into the seat, but her huge, gummy grin widened.

"The girl you'll be helping is quite talented, and I'm hoping you can share some of her duties. You remember how to do it?"

"You think that know-how just falls out me head? Of course I still *know how*." She humphed and shook her head.

"One more thing. And this is important. The woman has a young girl living with her—a daughter."

Before he could even tell her the details, light poured from every crease of the woman's smiling face. "A child!" She cackled in layers of joy that tidal-waved over the sound of the horses' jingling reins. "A child, a child. Oh, bless me stars."

Lights glowed in the thatched cottages they passed until they left Glen Cora, and then it was only fields and woods cast in the deep orange glow of sunset. Quite spectacular, really, when seen through the eyes of a newly freed prisoner. The acute awareness of such beauty sparkled in Rosa's eyes as she drank it in.

The sun glowed deep, shimmering red past the slender cupolas, a mere slit on the horizon when the carriage crunched up the drive to Lynhurst. He tipped the coachman for his silence on the matter, and then led the woman, who followed with surprising vigor on bowed legs, down the now-familiar path to Florin cottage.

As they came within sight of it and saw the candle glow in the shrouded homey windows, his aching feet slowed. This was Nelle's private home. It only had one room, did it not? He was asking her to share her space, her home, with a strange woman.

But in turn, Rosa would be helping, he argued with himself. Surely Nelle would see the value in that. Maybe he should offer to pay for Rosa's stay. She'd only be there until her children could be reached, unless they became fast friends and did what he hoped—opened a shop together. Rosa could be just the push Nelle needed to start a beautiful life where her artistry and skill were appreciated and rewarded financially. Where she and her daughter could leave the house to enjoy sunshine and people. Dahlia might even attend school.

Yes, this would be good for Nelle. Besides, it was too late to backtrack. Rosa stood beside him, and he had no other place to offer her. Those thoughts drove his steps right up to Nelle's door, where he knocked lightly with one knuckle. She could always say no if the imposition was too great. The sun had almost completely set, and only the candle glow from inside lit the shadowed path.

But when the door opened, and Nelle stood there in all her freshness and motherly radiance, shock on her pale face, he stiffened.

"Good evening, Mr. Rotherham." Her lovely cheeks pinked in the dim light.

Awkward silence stretched for seconds that felt like long minutes. Finally he expelled a gusty breath. "I should not be so bold as to ask you this, but I need a favor." Shifting from one foot to the other, he stepped aside and indicated the woman behind him. "This is Rosa. She does needlework and needs a place to stay. I thought you could help each other, and . . ." He paused, shoving both hands through his hair.

"Well, I should have thought further, but I did not. As is my regrettable habit."

He looked up to her pleadingly, but her gaze had already moved past him to the woman just behind, and it glowed with welcome.

"Rosa. I'm Nelle Wicke, and this is my home. Please, come in."

She stepped forward and led the woman into her candlelit cottage by the arm, the older one trotting after the younger, and somehow the pair made sense. Silas followed them in and shut the door, expelling the tension crowding his chest. He should have known it would be like this. It was *Nelle*.

He perched on a stool across from the two women, his legs tucked under the table.

After several minutes of exchanging pleasantries, Rosa burst the tension when Nelle apologized for dishes scattered about the kitchen.

"Well, it's a sight better than debtor's prison. That's where I come from. Mr. Handsome won't say it, but I will. And leave them dishes. I'll help ye with them in the morning. But for now, let me feast my eyes on the colors and chaos of family life." Leaning back, she inhaled deeply and released the breath with a smile.

The corner of Nelle's lip turned up in a half grin. "Then I'm glad to have you here, dishes and all."

"Ain't none of us perfect, and I'm the best example of that lot. Now where's your fine husband so I can make my acquaintance and pass judgment?"

Silas's muscles tensed across his back. Nelle absently swept crumbs from the table into her palm, then dusted her palms over the table. She repeated the nervous habit several times before forcing the truth out of her lips. "There is no husband." The lovely face tipped down as she spoke the words. "My daughter was . . . accidental."

With a deep frown, the old woman shoved up from the table and walked over to the bed that mother and daughter shared. Dahlia's sleeping form lay sprawled across it. Leaning close, hands clamped to her knees, Rosa inspected the tiny face flushed in sleep and shook her head. "Ain't no mistake about an angel like that, Miss Nelle Wicke."

Silas's breath caught at the sight of the girl's tiny face, long eyelashes resting on pink cheeks. What he wouldn't give to have a precious child like that to protect and encourage. How could anyone resist scooping her up and swinging her around every day, just to see her smile?

When an aura of family and home filled the room of near-strangers, Silas knew it was time to leave. He rose at a break in the conversation and excused himself. Nelle followed him to the door to see him out. Looking down into her face, he so badly wanted to take her hands in his to communicate the gratitude overwhelming him.

"I cannot tell you what it means to me that you have trusted this stranger to come into your home. You are a gem among women, Nelle Wicke." He clamped his mouth shut as the words left. He'd done it again. Why couldn't he filter things like that before he built a wall between himself and every woman he talked to? Not every thought was meant to be voiced.

He prepared for the inevitable rejection, but Nelle lit up with a gratified smile. "It is my pleasure to help you, Mr. Rotherham. A great honor, after all you've done for me. I'm only too glad." She clasped her hands in her apron. "Besides,

I can tell by the look of her that this woman can be trusted. She isn't one of them." She tipped her head toward the big house. "She reminds me of my own mother."

The muscles of his face relaxed into a smile. "If there's anything I can do for you to repay you, anything at all . . ."

She dipped her head with the thought of whatever request she wanted to make but couldn't.

"Tell me, Nelle. I'd be more than happy to do anything for you. Money, protection, whatever it is. Let me help." He resisted the urge to tip her chin up with one finger.

"I'll think about it."

27

"If you decide to love me, you must accept all of my oddities," she warned him.

"My dear," replied Charles Sterling Clavey, "if it were not for your oddities, I should have no reason to love you in the first place."

~Nathaniel Droll, *Lady Jayne Disappears*

The announcement of Nathaniel Droll's identity reached the local newspapers soon after the gathering, and by that time a plan had formed in my mind. For several long afternoons following Jasper's revelation, I buried myself in my chambers to pen a most important installment of *Lady Jayne Disappears* that included the reappearance of a minor character.

The man posing as Arthur Hobbs III again graced the Toblerone home with his presence when they opened their residence to an art exhibit for local collectors. "A man of wealth ought to have an expensive hobby, and this shall be mine," he had declared to himself as he circulated among the guests. Would any of them notice that he wore the same suit as before? He'd only stolen the one, and it must serve every purpose of his imagined existence.

The poor man had run the entire way to the event, since imaginary wealth did not pay for carriages, and found himself dangerously parched. He eagerly accepted the tiny glass of refreshment offered by a passing butler and dashed the cupful down his gullet. As he studied the art with the critical expression of the knowledgeable man he pretended to be, he became parched again and gladly accepted the next proffered glass. By the time he'd downed several, and his magnanimous hostess approached to ask his opinion on the latest DuBlanc arrival from Paris, he suddenly found that words were difficult to pronounce.

"Shtunning, my dear. Quite lovely." Why couldn't he force out the proper sounds?

Within minutes the drinks, which contained more brandy than punch, had muddied his logic and loosened his tongue. The rooms had filled to capacity by nine, and that was the moment he chose to clink fork to crystal and stand on the stair to gain the crowd's attention.

"How nice to shee all of you." The words slurred across his lips but sounded intelligent and engaging to his inebriated mind. "Let us take a moment to thank our lovely hostess, Lady Toblerone, and the talented maid who helped to squeeze her into that dress. Well done, maid." He set down the cup and clapped in broken rhythm. "Also, her chef who prepared that wonderful dinner that I only recently discovered to be lobster. To which I'm highly allergic. Lady Toblerone, you are quite the peach."

Loping to her with drunken strides, he snaked an arm around her back, dipped her backwards, and planted the sort of kiss on her that echoed throughout the room. With a cry, Lady Toblerone wrenched free and stumbled back. "Lord Hobbs, what do you mean by all this?"

Lord Toblerone approached from behind, his wiry frame guarding the poor woman.

"Pardon me, Lord Tober . . . Toler . . . blerone." Hiccup. "It seems your wife has chosen me over you. And for the record, my name is not Hobbs. It's Grupp. Jasper Grupp. Never a keener man has walked this earth. Did you know I pretend to write famous novels?"

And with that, he bowed and summarily released the many drinks he'd consumed all across the glittering shoes of his hostess.

The only way to deal with any problems in my life, it seemed, was through Nathaniel Droll. I relished skewering Jasper with my words, knowing they'd be read by England at large.

"Miss Harcourt?" A knock accompanied a muffled voice outside my door.

"Come in."

Minnie popped her round face into the room. "You're wanted in the yard for badminton."

"I'll be there presently." I rose and glanced toward the armoire for appropriate attire. Despite my lack of coordination, the idea of fresh air and exercise appealed to me after several days of near imprisonment.

But I quickly learned I was not meant to play the lively game but to watch it, along with the other women from Lynhurst. Neatly arranged in the shade with cheese and crackers and a few assorted cold meats, we idled around the wrought-iron patio table, hat brims shading our faces. I reached for another slice of Swiss cheese, reveling in the sun warming my exposed arm. Something about constant fear and turmoil made one appreciate small blessings in abundance.

"This is something we could never do in our London house." Juliette's high-pitched cheerfulness grated as the birdie popped from Silas and Garamond's side to Clem and Kendrick's and stuck in the grass.

Aunt Eudora humphed from her wheeled chair behind us, blowing out the handkerchief that covered her face.

"Don't bother to sugar the truth." Glenna's sour face grimaced in the shade. "Country life will always be a miserable prison for those meant to live in the city."

"Do you know, I've learned something rather interesting." Juliette leaned back and nibbled a cracker. "Wasn't it Uncle Woolf we were trying to save when we sold that London house? Well, as it turns out, the man remained a wastrel, despite our sacrifice on his account. How abominable! Imagine—we gave up a city life for the man, and—"

"Who on earth told you such a thing, Juliette?" Aunt Eudora's voice snapped out from her corner of the patio as her handkerchief floated to the ground before her.

Jasper Grupp. No one but that fiend would have done it.

"A good friend who happens to have inside information on the man."

"Remarkable proof that some people are simply beyond help." Glenna popped one bit of candy after another between her tiny lips.

Teeth clamped shut and grinding, I tightened my belly but said nothing. Tears threatened.

Glenna turned, fanning her red face. "Mother, what on earth put it into your head that you should even try to save that wastrel brother of yours in the first place?"

"Glenna, do not question my judgment. The same generosity that opened my hand to him will also one day open my hand to your family as I write out my will."

"But, Grandmama, he brought such disgrace to you. I heard there were even children born to unwed women of his acquaintance. Good heavens, we have little vagabond cousins running around that might show up at our door at any time, demanding to be let in." Juliette laughed. "Imagine a little urchin off the street wanting to join our family as if they could actually belong, simply because of some silly old indiscretion that tied us to them. What on earth would we do with such people?"

Vagabond. Wastrel. The words rattled around in the part of my heart that refused to acknowledge the truth about the man. All the years of writing serial novels, the money he must have earned . . . yet he allowed us to remain in Shepton Mallet.

I harshly shoved aside images of Papa throwing away his money in foolishly large amounts to secure the immediate comforts he so enjoyed, of our painfully empty tin that should have contained his savings, if he'd had any—

No. Stop. He wasn't a wastrel. *Wasn't*. Hadn't he produced the stories that captivated even the elite members of this household? Who among them had accomplished such a thing? Even penniless, Papa had created a legacy to last beyond his lifetime, and I had to remember that, no matter what they said. Clear visions of Papa's precious face rose before my mind.

"What would we do?" Glenna's narrowed eyes flicked to me. "Cast them out as soon as possible."

I forced my crossed arms into my gut. The taste of all the cheese and bread I'd consumed rose in my mouth as I dipped my head.

"There was *one*." Aunt Eudora spat out the words. "*One* child born to *one* woman. I will not hear you speak of my brother any more. There is too much you don't know."

"You mean there's *more*? How wonderfully dramatic!" Juliette clapped her hands in little pops that echoed in the shaded patio. "You shall have to tell us the whole story now, Grandmama. What became of the wretched woman and her poor child? Has the lad grown up to be as worthless as Uncle Woolf?"

I shot up, ramrod straight, chair jerking back. Anger had eclipsed my self-control, and I did not care a whit. "You know *nothing* about him! How dare you!" Or maybe it was I who did not. I breathed hard. My stiff bodice would suffocate me. No, *they* would. The tight circle of them, focused on me. Judging me.

Commotion lit up the patio as female exclamations echoed in the little space. The noise drew the maids out, cap ribbons flying behind them as they ran to assist.

Before anything worse could happen, I stole away, my slippers swishing through grass. Anger swelled against my ribs as I ran. Why? Why had I ever walked into their silly games, with courtships and flirtations, gowns and ridiculous curled hair? I'd been safe in prison. Happy. My feet thumped the ground with all my pent-up ire, carrying me toward the woods. I veered left before the tree line and ran through the grass, pumping hard against my heavy dress. Whipping around a crumbled wall, I plastered my cheek against the mossy stones, breathing hard.

Arrogant. Worthless. That's all this family was.

I should tell them. Just spit out the secret I had tucked away inside me. Then they would look at their "wastrel" uncle and his child entirely differently, wouldn't they?

Hot, angry tears poured over my cheeks.

I moved slowly among the scent of roses later that evening as darkness descended, my fingertips skimming the powdery petals. Moist breeze cooled my skin. Aloneness suddenly seemed a comfort at the moment, not a threat. It had taken enormous courage to walk inside for dinner after the upset of the afternoon, but the conversation I overheard behind the closed drawing room doors had shattered my bravery. Kendrick and Glenna voiced what I had feared from the beginning—I did not belong at Lynhurst. Aunt Eudora had obviously told them all who I was, and the truth was in the open. What to do with this odd cousin from debtor's prison who simply did not fit anywhere?

In the dim starlight, I paused to the right of the tall drawing room windows that framed the cozy family gathering inside. What *was* to be done with me? I couldn't return to Shepton Mallet without Papa. My only family was here at Lynhurst. And they thought—no, they *knew*—I did not belong.

Making my living as Nathaniel Droll tempted me beyond belief, but I did not belong in that role, either. For as much as I tried to shove my way into the identity, some unseen force pushed me back out with a power I could not combat.

Perhaps that's all this was—God pushing me firmly from this work. All the paranoia about some invisible ghost, and seeing danger in everything . . . none of this was necessary if I removed myself from the two places I was not wanted.

But if I did that, what had I left?

I moved to the trellis and stood beneath the waterfall of clematis, closing my eyes to experience the aroma and feel of the flowers more deeply. No matter what happened in the coming days or weeks, whether I stayed as an intruder or left as a homeless waif, I could enjoy this moment. No one could deny me that. I leaned against the vines twining the wooden frame, my face tipped heavenward.

I've asked for so much, Lord, and you've given it to me. Forgive me for seeming ungrateful if I ask for more, but I would dearly love a place to—

"You look as though you belong." Silas's voice rumbled over my thoughts.

My eyes winged open, my heart blasting, then recovering. "Belong . . . here?"

Something about his face seemed different as he stood quite near, as if the moon glow and quiet shadows had intoxicated him into a dreamy haze. Like he considered kissing me. But he remained in place, his gaze pinning me with quiet delight. The change unsettled me. I broke the tension by looking down at the grass now blue in the shadows.

"Among the flowers, I mean. You look like one of them."

"There is no part of Lynhurst where I belong, I'm convinced of that."

"What is it that makes you think so?"

"I'm sure they've told you what happened today. With . . . everything. My father, our past. I do believe I could have belonged here, if only they didn't care so greatly what people think of them." Hurt welled up again, swift and sharp, as I thought about what they'd said.

"Has it ever occurred to you that you are guilty of the same?"

I whipped my face up to look at him, anger pricking. "Is this another one of your word plays, Mr. Rotherham? A joke? Surely you know my character better than that."

"Then why does their disapproval bother you so?"

I dropped my gaze, studying the pink rose at my fingertips. "Because Papa deserves better."

He shoved his hands in his pockets. "I've been to Shepton Mallet again. How incredible, to hear how they love you in that place. Yet here at Lynhurst, among your own family, you fight to be accepted. What exactly is the difference?"

"The people." The answer rolled off my tongue.

"I thought so too, at first." He stepped closer, his chest nearing my face. "But after visiting your prison twice, I think the difference is in you, Aurelie."

I balled my fists. "How can you think that? I am the same,

wherever I live. No fancy clothes will ever change me, and I would think you'd know that much about me by now."

"Listen. If a boy was drowning in the English Channel and you were the only one there who knew how to swim, you'd dive right in, wouldn't you? And the last thing you'd worry about is how proper your form appeared to the watchers on the beach."

"What a question."

"You lived that way at Shepton Mallet. Passionately breathing life into those people with every action, extravagantly loving, diving in and rescuing. You hadn't time for caring what you looked like to anyone. Instead you focused on others. You saw them as real, worthwhile individuals with credible ideas and talents, and that's what makes you such an angel in their midst."

Tears gathered behind my eyes, heating my face. "I cannot live that way here. They don't want my help."

"You can always choose selflessness. Make them feel good about themselves the way you did for the people of the Mallet, rather than shaping so carefully what they think of you."

"You make me sound selfish."

"I only want you to be who you actually are."

"That person does not belong here."

He moved forward, gripping my arms, his face earnest. "You will never belong here, Miss Aurelie Harcourt of Shepton Mallet. Not one bit. And may it always be so."

"They are my family, and I have nowhere else to go. And my heart. . . my heart needs to belong somewhere. It is not a loner."

In answer he bent forward, fingertips moving up and exploring my hair as if he reveled in the tresses, nose resting atop my head. "That I know." His voice tickled my scalp until he leaned back, and it was intoxicatingly intimate.

I leaned a breath closer. *Do that again.*

"May I speak honestly with you?"

I sought his eyes. "What have you been doing since I've known you?"

This was it. The words were at the gate of his lips, ready to flood out into the night between us, mending and warming my heart. Answering my prayers. For I read the deep feelings in his expression. Eyes closed, I savored his nearness. Loneliness suddenly felt like a foreign concept.

"I find it . . . wonderful that you do not belong." His voice hitched. "The very fact that you do not fit in here, among these broken people. The fact that you do not feel comfortable. I find *you* wonderful."

Silas folded me boldly in his arms, pulling me to his chest, tightly binding together the shattered fragments of my heart for a moment of supreme peace. A small whimper of release escaped my lips. Oh, the sweet scent of him. The feel of his chest. The heady warmth of a full embrace. Stars lit the cloudless sky overhead, a beautiful backdrop to the moment. My mind swirled. Pure pleasure in the moment bound my objections.

Silas. Silas was holding me. I belonged to him for this moment.

"Your beauty outshines everyone around you, and it would even if you wore a feed sack. No one in this house has any sense, Aurelie. None at all." His words tumbled out as his lips moved tenderly along the top of my head. Was he kissing my hair? "Except for one single person who saw the remarkable beauty in you from the beginning, as I did." He loosened his hold and leaned back to look at me, his arms still supporting my back. One fingertip traced my spine over my dress. "One would think you were an angel, the way Nelle speaks of you."

Nelle. Her sweet face came to mind, a niggling ache invading the moment. Nelle, looking up at Silas in hero worship. The pair walking together as if one person. *"He has met my Dahlia and he treats her like a little lady."*

But he couldn't love Nelle. Couldn't.

I glanced up into his eyes glowing with pure affection and suddenly imagined them turned on Nelle that same way. Somehow I could picture it. Confusion ripped through me, and I stepped back, sliding out of his embrace. I needed space to right my brain.

"Please." Desperation scored his shadowed face. "Please don't go. I couldn't bear it."

Maybe I'd been mistaken about Nelle. His feelings for me were so ardent, so genuine. When I hesitated, he stepped forward again, closing the distance in one swift movement, embracing me and nuzzling my ear. Again, I was anchored firmly to his chest. His lips brushed the tip of my ear, sending chills across my scalp and down my neck. My head swam.

He leaned back to face me, searing me with his gaze. With one thumb caressing my cheek, he closed his eyes and lowered his face to mine. I anticipated it, ached for it, my lips tingling. I could let him, and sink into it with great pleasure. He wanted me. Chose me. Not Nelle—me.

But Nelle. Dear, sweet Nelle.

Nelle.

The niggling ache grew as I pictured her kind face scored with hurt and betrayal and then it engulfed me painfully.

"He really is the finest man . . . I do so want you to under-

stand about him. Will you promise to think well of him? At least a little."

The memory of her earnest face, glowing with thoughts of Silas, pulsed in my mind.

A light movement of his hand on the skin of my arm broke through my thoughts.

I couldn't think this way, so intoxicated by the nearness of him. It would be a mistake, whatever happened in that moment. I slipped back, dipping my head to avoid the kiss. My forehead skimmed his nose, and I planted my hands on his chest.

Heart brimming, I lifted my face from a safe distance and searched his eyes. "I should go inside." The confusion in my heart was mirrored on his face. Before my disloyal heart could change its mind, a door slammed open behind us and a stream of light cut across the lawn. I pulled fully away and took a step back.

He stood at the safe distance I had created, watching me with tender eyes. How easily I could sink into loving him.

But not yet. Not until the truth had been untangled, and it was clear who he belonged to. I could not make the mistake of lavishing my devotion on a man who was not wholly mine. And if Nelle had even a sliver of a chance to win him, then she should. For she needed him far more than I did.

Every hasty action in my first romance had been utterly regretted. In those moments, I'd warned myself against all rash behavior in the future, and for the first time, I listened to the advice of my past self.

I stepped forward and squeezed his hand, sealing the authenticity of my affection, and tore myself away from his presence before we could be discovered. I fled through the night with ragged breaths of clammy air, my path lit only by light streaming out of the windows.

But in the cool reality of aloneness, I berated myself. Why? Why had I done it? The thought trailed me as I ran into the house and up the stairs to my bedchamber, my haven in this foreign place. I could be deep into a kiss with him right now, tasting his lips and delighting in his embrace. I locked the door behind me in my bedchamber, but my efforts would not shut off the flow of feelings battling for control. I sank to my rug in a puddle of regret, angst, and desire and cried.

28

Too often people make a goal of avoiding mistakes.
That is a mistake in itself, for no life lesson will pierce
deep enough to remain with us unless it is preceded by
the sharpness of regret.

~Nathaniel Droll, *Lady Jayne Disappears*

I watched the moon from my window that night, knees tucked
to my chest as I curled into the wingback chair. My empty dinner tray lay on the floor beside me. It was probably good that
I hadn't known until now this tray would appear if I missed
dinner, or I'd have skipped plenty of meals before this one.

How could I show my face before them again? I had even
upset Silas now, my only true ally. Before I could break open
my heart and pray, a knock sounded on my door.

"Special delivery," called a muffled female voice.

I uncurled from the chair and rose to answer. Juliette stood
on the other side, eyes shining, holding out a cup of Danish
pieces and stewed strawberries.

Awkwardness tightened my limbs as I opened the door for my cousin and ushered her in.

"I know how you love your breakfast sweets, so I had the kitchen staff fetch a few things for you." Juliette held out the cup, smiling, then dropped her gaze. "I made some rather base comments today, and I hope you will forgive me."

With a smile, I took the cup and returned to my chair to curl into it. Juliette followed, taking the other.

"Really, I had no idea you were related to Uncle Woolf at all. Grandmama never tells us anything worthwhile, you know. She hugs her secrets to her like they're her real family. And you must believe me, I'd never have called you those things if I had known. We've gotten to know you, so it's quite different. You are not some orphan from the gutter." She reached across the expanse and touched my arm, catching my gaze with bright eyes. "I'm glad you've come to us, and I hope they never make you leave."

My face relaxed, my neck and shoulders sinking into the cushions. "Thank you."

"You are still the only one in this entire house who supports me seeing Jasper. You understand when no one else does."

When I pinched my lips, holding back the flood of thoughts, Silas's words of conviction surfaced again, washing over me as truth. I *did* care what they thought of me. Too much. I knew Jasper, and knew that nothing good would come of his relationship with Juliette, yet I chose silence in the matter. Why? To maintain my constantly tenuous friendship with this girl. To ensure I remained in this house. For *my* benefit, not Juliette's. What an utterly selfish decision.

But that would change.

"I am not exactly a supporter, you know." No, not enough.

Stronger. Courage. I inhaled. "You deserve far better. He truly is an awful person, Juliette." There. The words were out. "Gambling, lying, drinking. A lot of anger. Believe me, there is much wickedness under that gentleman's suit. I knew him before I came to Lynhurst. I even thought to help him, to bind all those gaping wounds with love."

Her little mouth pinched, eyebrows arching. "Do you truly believe you can win him this way?"

"Truly, I do not desire him. I've never wanted anyone less in my life. But I care for you, dear cousin, and I so much want you to have the best. And Jasper Grupp is far from it."

Her narrowed gaze dug under the layers of my countenance, studying carefully.

My heart nearly vibrated against my ribs. "Ask him where his real home is. Demand that he show you where he stays. It will not be in a fancy hotel or seaside inn. Ask the people who live around Shepton Mallet about him. They all know the truth. If you will not listen to me, I hope you listen to all of them."

"He is Nathaniel Droll. His fortune is likely more vast than half the shire, no matter his origins."

"Not everything is as it seems, Juliette. Believe me. The man is so far from what he claims to be." Juliette's silence bolstered my courage. She was listening. Speaking the truth was working. "And I will no longer turn my head if you go to meet him again."

Juliette held herself with marble-like posture and studied me. "You truly mean all these things?"

I nodded, hope welling in me.

"I'm glad to know the truth. I'd hate to carry on in any kind of relationship that holds falseness." Her words were wooden. Perhaps she was in shock.

I reached across our knees to squeeze Juliette's hands. The girl's fingers remained curled into her palms, my affection unreturned. Holding her back straight against the curls that spiraled down from a clump atop her head, Juliette considered me with tight features.

I released her hands. "Now, let us talk of something else. Can we plan a dinner party here? Please?" That should tempt her.

But the distance between us remained.

Juliette left within a few minutes, thoughtful silence shrouding her. When the door shut behind the girl, I fell to my knees at the window, my forehead on the chilled sill.

Thank you, God. Thank you that she listened. Please help her take it to heart. It was truly miraculous the way you opened her ears when my foolish silence was lifted. The truth really is freeing, and I thank you for that as well. Please give her the strength to break ties with Jasper and move forward. Calm Jasper's heart toward her and toward me, that he might not take vengeance on either of us.

Rising with a cleansed heart, I took to my desk and pulled down a volume from the shelf. Pleasant emotions coursed through me. If only I could channel them into my book.

The image of Juliette's face hovered as I crawled into bed later on. My purpose had solidified, and God had made clear his plans for me, like a lantern lifting to cast its light farther out along the path. I would help steer Juliette out of her relationship with Jasper, show her family how foolish they were to waste their lives pleasing people, and write books to teach people God's truths through story. No matter what Silas Rotherham thought, I would belong here one day because God did have a purpose for me.

When a knock sounded on my door the next morning, I jumped out of bed and swirled my robe about me, a greeting for my cousin on my lips. But it was not Juliette on the other side of the door.

"Nelle." Waves of bittersweet emotion washed over me as the sight of my dear friend collided with my memories of Silas the night before. The girl stood outside my door, smiling and holding up another purple dress with flowerets embroidered along the bustline and waist.

"Do you like it? You were stunning in the purple gown you wore to the party, so I had to make you another. I hope you don't mind."

"Mind?" I smiled, drawing my friend into the room, despite my aching heart. I needed a little more time to deal with my attachment to Silas Rotherham, and that was hard to do while in Nelle's presence.

"Will you try it on? I'm quite fond of this gown, and I want to see if it fits well enough. I used the same template I created for the others, but the gathers around the bodice might give it a different fit." She smiled. "Besides, I'd love to see it on you."

"Of course." Twirling my hair up to my scalp, I turned my back so Nelle could undo the buttons and ties. "About Silas. I'd like to ask you something."

"Yes?" Her quick fingers slowed.

"What—"

Bang! Bang! Pounding on my door made us jump. I walked to the door to answer, Nelle trailing behind to fix the closures on the back of my dress.

"WHAT HAVE YOU DONE?" Anger quaked Glenna's body as I flung open the door, her trembling hand waving a paper at me. "You wretched, evil girl. How dare you sneak into this house as one of our own and ruin our family. I want you *out!*" She whipped the letter across my face, spiked it onto the floor, and stalked out. "Digory!"

Gut clenched, I snatched the paper and flattened it against the wall.

I have gone to be with the man I love, and none of you can convince me I should do otherwise. I cannot stay here another day without being allowed to see him. The force between us is stronger than any of you with such simple, empty marriages could possibly understand.

My dear cousin Aurelie, thank you for showing so plainly the truth of your friendship with me. You should know that your scheming finally drove me into the waiting arms of my lover, and for that I thank you.

The smirk came through the girl's words as if she'd drawn a picture above them. My knees weakened, and I sank to the floor against the doorway. Regret washed over me in massive tidal waves. Oh, what had I done?

Silas had been right. I'd rationalized, protected my image for far too long.

At the expense of someone's future.

Why had it been so important? *Why?* So what if my family knew of my past? They knew now anyway. And Juliette—she hadn't liked me any better in the end for supporting her wrong decisions. While I had believed the fire to be completely under control, a gentle smoldering that was easily extinguished, little sparks had been gaining strength beneath the leaves until they united in one huge, engulfing fire I was helpless to stop.

"Nelle, we've got to find Juliette. She's run away with Jasper Grupp." I turned, forcing my muscles to cooperate.

"To marry him?"

"Marriage isn't likely with this man, but plenty of other catastrophes are."

With a quick nod, Nelle tossed me a hat and followed me out the door. "We should find Silas. You cannot do this alone."

My stomach clenched. "Not Silas. Maybe Kendrick. Or Digory. Yes, I'll take Digory."

"You need Silas. Kendrick is in Bristol for the day, and Digory . . . well, he wouldn't be able to stop a kitten."

Tugging me after her, Nelle ran down the stairs, leaving the letter on the floor behind us.

"Digory, where is Mr. Rotherham?" Nelle's voice reached the grand hallway before her feet did.

Before the old servant could process the request, Silas emerged from Garamond's study, a ledger book open across his palm. With quick, efficient words, Nelle summarized the events of the morning, one hand on his arm to draw him toward the entryway.

Garamond followed. "What's happening? What's this about Juliette?"

I turned to the men and focused on Garamond. "She's run away with Jasper Grupp, and we're going to find her."

"Run *away*?" He blinked in disbelief, eyes bugging out of his normally placid face.

"We'll find her, Lord Gaffney. She's only just left." I tightened my wrap and moved through the gathering crowd. I turned to whisper to Nelle. "But I will *not* take Silas Rotherham."

"Fine then." Nelle looked to the man in question, still anchored against the doorway of the study. "I'll go with Silas. You can stay here."

"Why are *you* going?" Glenna's voice reached us as she sailed down the stairs, finger pointed at me. "Garamond and I will be taking the carriage, and you will wait here. And you'll be lucky to stay another night in this house."

"Lady Gaffney, why don't you remain here and I'll take the carriage out to search." Silas popped his hat onto his head and glanced at Nelle in silent communication.

We all froze as the front doors banged open and the sound echoed through the hall. Digory's polite voice floated in, along with the punctuated staccato of footsteps on tile. Lord Sutherland brushed into the room and slowed, surveying the small crowd, an air of confidence settled easily over his shoulders. "Quite a reception. Were you expecting me to call? I'd come to speak to Juliette."

"That man has run off with my daughter!" Glenna reached the landing and pushed past the servants toward the visitor. "Lord Sutherland, you must help us find her."

"Juliette?" Lord Sutherland's smile died on his clean-shaven face. His skin blanched. "Juliette is gone? Of course I'll help. Where have you looked so far?"

"I know where to find the man." I stepped forward. "I know exactly where he lives, and where he spends his time."

"Wonderful. We'll take my carriage. Lady Gaffney, I'll make sure your daughter is returned to you if there's anything I can do about it."

One hand resting on my back, pressing the buttons into my skin, he led me toward the door. Outside, Silas loaded Nelle into Lynhurst's carriage and then with agile movements, he pulled himself up and shut the door behind him. I watched the backs of Nelle's and Silas's heads through the tiny rear window with a fleeting tug of regret.

But that was all I had time to feel. Worry clamped down again as the coachman handed me into Lord Sutherland's carriage and I settled into the leather seat facing forward.

"How did this happen? How ever did he convince her?" The man's words clipped out in the quiet air as the antsy horses surged forward.

"She's been sneaking around with him for weeks. She convinced herself she's in love with the man."

"He's a first-class scoundrel. You know that, don't you?"

"I do. But she wouldn't listen to me."

He smeared one gloved palm across his face and groaned.

I gave the coachman directions to Shepton Mallet, where he'd have to leave us. This fine carriage would never fit through the nearby neighborhood streets such as Headrow Lane. Looking at the pure white glove splayed over the handsome face made me suddenly wish I'd gone alone. What would he think of where we were going? I'd have to explain so much about my relationship to Jasper, and my past in this place. And I hadn't the energy to do it.

All of it would be overshadowed by finding Juliette, though, which would surely happen.

"How long have they been gone? Did he at least have intentions of marrying her, or did he only plan on ruining her?" Lord Sutherland's face, so perfect and confident moments earlier, now looked haggard.

I studied his agonized face, understanding for the first time. "You care for Juliette, don't you?"

"Of course I do." The words snapped out, punctuated

by his heels hitting the base of his seat. "I've known the girl since we could walk."

But he cared more than a mere neighbor would. I watched him without a word, shaping him into a hero for another novel. He'd make a fabulous one—confident and handsome, passionate and secretly devoted. I selected a handful of words I could use to display him properly in my novel while the passing moments made him fidget. If only I could pull back his exterior and look at the thoughts flying through his mind. They'd likely be wonderfully fascinating.

"Is Juliette aware of your interest?"

Emotional strain pulled his features tight, and he finally spoke. "Sometimes it is best if two people are not coupled together. Juliette and I are exactly the same. We'd eat each other for breakfast."

"Should a person only marry her opposite then?"

"It's a special kind of torture to marry a person exactly like you. Imagine all your own faults and insidious habits rolled up in another person you must live with every day. A person you must love forever. Could you promise such a thing without growing weary of them?"

Silas's gentle face appeared before my mind. Could I? It hardly seemed possible to grow weary of talking about books, walking about the gardens, and slipping into the comfortable presence of a person who understood me without explanation. And his solid handsomeness—

No. Stop.

"I understand, I think. Marriage is not always the happy ending for every love story."

Emotion twitched across his face, and instantly a powerful turmoil showed just below the surface. "The truth of the matter is, true love is not simply about obtaining the person of your dreams but making sure they obtain their dreams."

What on earth was I to do with the avalanche of feelings from this man, both spoken and silent? How did I always draw this out of people? Everyone except Silas Rotherham, it seemed, whose wall still remained in place, except for the large crack that had so recently appeared.

Contemplative silence filled the small space as we rolled over stone bridges and past muddy sheep fields. When the carriage finally turned toward town, I sat straight against the seat and watched Lord Sutherland's face. Soon he'd be immersed in my background, even if he didn't know it.

"Exactly what sort of cad is this man?"

"The kind who gets whatever he wants, in whatever way he can."

"You were one of his victims, I assume, from the look of your face."

Embarrassment pricked my skin. My chin dropped to my collarbone. "Briefly." The word came out so soft, I wondered if he heard it.

Sickly fog rolled over the stone and thatch scenery of Glen Cora. With each clop of horse hooves, moments passing without conversation, my stomach calmed and I relaxed into the springy seat back. Why did it matter at all what Lord Sutherland thought of me? It didn't, really. He was merely a neighbor. One who was possibly in love with Juliette.

Slowly, carefully, I filled in the details I knew about Jasper Grupp. I told him about the years of deceit, his poor background, the bouts of surprising rage, and most recently the lies that allowed him to attend parties with Juliette.

He considered me, cheeks tight. "I suppose you will make

a story of this. I have heard much about your wonderful tales, and this would make a winning piece. A runaway girl marrying the wrong man, the desperate race to find her . . ."

"I shall want to forget this ever happened once we are safely home again. Even if Juliette is found immediately and everything goes smoothly." The thought of writing brought a dull ache to my gut. I should have taken my head out of the clouds long ago and focused on real life. Then things like this might not have happened.

When we reached the center of town, I directed the coachman to the gates of Shepton Mallet, and we climbed out at the end of the street. Lord Sutherland walked with his hands shoved in his pockets, arms clamped to his sides, on guard against pickpockets or diseases in the air. He fit here as well as I had at Lynhurst the first night. Chest cinching painfully, I forced myself to stay calm. I'd need every ounce of my wits to combat whatever we might find at the Grupp cottage. Thankfulness swelled in me for the tall man who strode beside me and the safety he represented.

When I directed him to the correct house a few blocks from the prison, Lord Sutherland pounded on the door with his fist. A warm breeze circled us as we waited, but no one answered.

"Hello there!" A friendly voice called from the side of the house where the elder Mr. Grupp waved as he walked toward us.

"Mr. Grupp, where is Jasper? It's important." I flew down the steps to meet him, grasping his arms. "Tell me where he is."

29

The love Lady Jayne bestowed on her friends never changed them, but rather it broke through the lies and hindrances to reveal the version of them that God always intended them to be.

~Nathaniel Droll, *Lady Jayne Disappears*

"What exactly is he up to?" Lord Sutherland slumped in his carriage seat, defeated.

"Perhaps he wants a ransom or simply to ruin her. Either way, we won't have to convince Juliette he's a cad. He'll do that all on his own."

Jasper's father had given us no information except what was evident between his words—his son did not have honorable intentions. Jasper had simply disappeared yet again, his father unaware of any marriage plans. When none of Jasper's favorite haunts provided any clues, we had turned the carriage toward home as shop owners flipped their signs from "open" to "closed." The long day of searching had wearied me inside and out.

Our polite conversation ceased as the carriage lumbered up the drive to Lynhurst, leaving us wilted against our seats. Finally we reached the house and jerked to a stop. Dust swirled around the stilled carriage before I convinced myself to rise and step toward the house. Glenna slid out the front door, hatless, hand to her chest, her eyes haunted. Garamond joined her on the landing.

First, I'd have to face Glenna and the family. Then I'd have to talk to Nelle and hear every last detail of her carriage ride with Silas. Which would overwhelm me in the end?

Positioning myself safely behind Lord Sutherland, I approached the house, a resigned air of finality and impending goodbye trailing after me. Glenna surged forward with intensity and cinched my wrists, jerking me up the final step and silently asking the single, all-important question with starving eyes.

"We haven't found them." The truth soured my mouth.

The woman jerked back and collapsed into a puddle of fabric and tears on the step, her dress billowing out in the wind. Garamond knelt and cradled her, holding her head to his chest. Messy, noisy sobs echoed in the yard. I moved back. I would be the last source of comfort for the woman now.

The sobs became heaves of breath and slowed. Glenna's body stiffened as control once again fortified her. Anger shadowed her features. Like a viper the woman rose, her back straight, her face mottled and hair clinging to her skin, glaring at me with a look of venom.

"I won't give up." My heart pounded. "They cannot hide forever. I'll keep—"

"*You.*" Her snarl quivered. "You dirty prison rat. Look at the trouble you've caused, the people you have hurt. But you don't care a whit, do you?" She waved her arms and marched toward me. "So long as you have nice dresses and parties and the name of a respectable family." She spit the last words out. "Get out! And if I ever lay eyes on you again, I'll shred every—"

"Here now, dainty one." Garamond pulled at her thick shoulders from behind. "I'll not have you injured over this. Come inside and let the men deal with it."

"And you." She whirled to face her twiggy husband. "Don't you care about anything? Even your child? Take your sniveling self away and let me be."

Folding like a fan, he backed into the shadows of the house. Glenna lifted her skirt and charged toward me. Nelle appeared suddenly and slipped between us, propelling me out of Glenna's path, and together we stumbled up the steps and into the house. With firm pressure across my back, Nelle moved my stiff body into the great hall and swung me into a window bay.

"Now listen, you must stay out of sight. We'll all keep looking for the girl, but you must give up the search and remain in the shadows, understand? Promise me. I want to keep you here, and that's the only way."

Like a warmth that melted chocolate, Nelle's quiet words liquefied the tension holding me upright and I fell into her arms. "I do not deserve to stay." It was my fault. Jasper's presence, Juliette's addiction to him, their decision to escape. "Perhaps I should go."

"Not unless you want to break my heart. Oh, dear Aurelie." Nelle clasped my arms, propping me up. "This family needs you more than you could ever know. You've touched this house with that lovely healing spirit of yours. I was merely the skillful fingers attached to a needle until you came here and saw more. Now, I imagine myself as a woman, an individual with value. Perhaps even someone to be courted." She ducked her chin at this last part. "You've made my life three-dimensional, with color and purpose and hope. Even a future."

"I only saw what was already there." I squeezed the words out of a tight throat.

"But it made all the difference now, didn't it? And imagine what it could do to your family if you stay. How desperately they need you, just like I did."

Thou anointest my head with oil; my cup runneth over.

Blessings abounded where they were not deserved. Nelle's words rolled over me, gently soothing the pain of all I'd endured that day. I held my hands over my chest, where my heart welled with too many words to speak.

Finally, I found my voice. "The need is great, but my abilities are not."

"If only you saw the truth." She smiled. "I must go tell Silas you're back, but promise me you'll not leave. At least not yet. I have wonderful news to share with you soon. I'm just bursting to tell you later. There, now I've done my best to keep you here."

What sort of news? But the girl had gone, running on tiptoes toward the front door.

Silas Rotherham's figure appeared outside, striding toward the couple on the steps who were now surrounded by attentive staff members.

Silas. Nelle had called him Silas.

Pressing my fingertips against the chilled glass, I drank in the sight of them. Nelle's dear face tipped up to look at Silas. A pair. Two opposites that fit together. Then Lord Sutherland passed them on the path to the house, stopping to throw a glance of quick disapproval in their direction. His steps slowed so he could tell them something, but Silas pulled Nelle toward him as if to shield her from Sutherland's words. Bittersweet emotions tugged at me as I watched my friend, heart spilling out of the girl's face as she looked up in gratitude at the strong man beside her. How beautiful. Fitting. I could imagine Dahlia swinging between them. Tears threatened.

Turning from the window, I closed my eyes. *Thank you, if this is your answer to my prayer.* I bit my lip. *Now can you bring someone for me so my heart doesn't ache so much?*

A familiar squeak across the floor cut through the moment. A maid rolled Aunt Eudora's wheeled chair through the hall and stopped behind me before leaving us. Together we stared out the window at everyone, a heavy silence blanketing the little bay for several moments.

"Yet another mismatched couple." The voice deepened with age rang through the empty hall. "It's as if men only want the girl they must not have, simply because they cannot have her."

"You're too late, Grandmama." Clem emerged from the shadows, his eyes sparkling with victory against his pale face. "I overheard them in the carriage when they arrived, discussing their secret betrothal. Silas plans to propose to her, with or without your blessing."

I forced a delighted smile that tugged up my lips. They were to be married. Why did I suddenly feel so heavy? Because it had happened so quickly. Perhaps it was better that I had not encouraged his affections, if he was going to be this fickle.

Footfalls echoed in the hall, and then Kendrick joined us. "Have I heard right? There is a betrothal in the house?"

"It's not official yet." Clem's face pinched, almost as if he now regretted sharing the news with us, now that the information had begun leaking past our tiny gathering.

Kendrick's eyes flew to me, and I looked down at the tile, then automatically darted a glance toward the couple outside. He followed my gaze, his countenance darkening. "*Her?* Why, that little tart." He strode to the window, folding his arms. "How dare a servant presume to pair herself with a gentleman! We must forbid this. And that devious little wench is to be sent away."

Clem turned on him with a dark look. "You're only sore because he didn't choose Juliette."

"He might have, if that little Miss Wicke had not flaunted herself before him, eager to rise above her station. I, for one, will not tolerate this from a servant of Lynhurst."

"If you dare to break them apart, just so he can make the match *you* believe best for him . . ." Clem raised his balled fists.

Kendrick waved him off and strode toward the library. "Save your energy, little brother. Miss Wicke will need your help when Silas realizes what he's done. And he will—I'll make sure of it."

Rage boiled over Clem's pure face as he stalked away and marched up the stairs. I trembled where I stood on the green-and-white-checked tile in the silent moments after their retreat, a pillar supporting me.

Finally Aunt Eudora spoke. "Kendrick is right. They do

JOANNA DAVIDSON POLITANO

not belong together." She rolled toward the window and leveled a gaze at the pair. "I suppose I'll have to intervene and play *un*matchmaker yet again."

Intoxicated with emotion, I spun to face the shriveled woman. "You *cannot*." Every joint trembled. "It isn't your affair. It was never your affair!"

This was *her* fault. All of it. Not mine—hers. The unraveling began years ago, when this woman forced my parents apart and sent them each on a terrible spiral that would never fully mend. Jasper, debtor's prison, the humiliation—none of that would have happened without this woman forcing her way into love affairs as if destruction were her livelihood. Mismatched, indeed. "Servant or not, that woman has more value than you'll ever have in your wretched long life. Why must you split every couple who finds happiness? Do you really want everyone as miserable as you, or do you honestly care *that much* about what people think of your precious family and their worthless social image?"

Lace trembled atop the old woman's head, but her long face did not change. Movement to the left snapped the strain in the room, and I exhaled, stepping back. One by one, they filed into the grand hall—Glenna and Garamond, Kendrick, and several black-and-white-clothed servants. Even Digory and Lord Sutherland huddled on the fringes. I could hardly breathe.

Garamond strode forward, moving protectively around his mother-in-law. "I'm sure you'd like to retire for the night, my lady."

"Absolutely not. Age does not make me brainless. Put words in your own mouth, not mine. Tell the servants to bring up tea service with plenty of sandwiches since dinner was

313

neglected this evening. And be sure to invite Lord Sutherland to remain with Miss Harcourt until she's recovered from the strain of the all-day search."

The white-hot hatred simmered to a rolling boil and cooled with each exhale. I was to stay at Lynhurst. Just like that. I forced my breath through my nostrils, pinching my mouth shut. What had become of me? Emotions had ripped through my wall of common sense again, sending me into a passion of words that could not be withdrawn.

And that woman, limp as a doll in her chair, watched her family with detached, bug-like eyes that would never again be pretty, and clung to her bitterness as if it were her only comfort. Pity ebbed over me once again for Aunt Eudora. I had reached out a hand to comfort any number of needy souls, but this destructive woman needed it more than most. And I'd just failed her.

"Digory, I'd like you to send that little seamstress Miss Wicke around to see me." Her sharp voice commanded obedience. "I must have a word with her directly."

Eyes downcast, I slipped past the gawkers to the steps and hurried up to my bedroom sanctuary on the third floor. History was rewriting itself, despite my efforts and prayers. Poor Nelle, with her gentle soul and thirst for love that would now go unquenched.

I pulled a notebook from my shelf and dropped it onto the floor, collapsing before it. Writer's block had plagued me every time I'd attempted to create an ending for *Lady Jayne Disappears*, but now I had it. *When you cannot write anymore, do not torture yourself.* Papa had said it at least once per novel. *Instead, torture your characters.*

Heart overflowing with grief, I was ready to torture Lady

Jayne and her suitor. It was clear now where Lady Jayne had gone when she'd disappeared, and why it had happened.

I turned to my notebook, the empty page an invitation. It was all for Abigail. In the end, it was not the social differences that kept Lady Jayne and Clavey apart, but the heroine's own softheartedness.

First would be a scene in which Lady Jayne glimpsed the depth of love her dear friend felt for Charles Sterling Clavey. Did Clavey return her love? Of course he did. He saw her gorgeous heart beneath the simple clothing. Lady Jayne would then have to make the utterly painful decision to give up Charles for her, and to leave the estate because she could not erase her own feelings for the man who would be marrying her friend. Sweet Abigail, who lived in shame because of her past, desperately needed a husband who would accept that, as well as her working-class status. And he'd need to be kind and gentle and care for her with devotion. What sort of man would fit that?

Only one. And I loved him for it.

As I curled my hurting self over my notebook, writing moved quickly from idle pastime to a necessity, and I plunged into it with the desperate obsession of one clinging to a life raft. Broken, aching, I cracked my delicate heart like a fragile eggshell and poured its contents onto the page. The words flowed quickly, rich and poignant. Painful and vulnerable. Pieces of myself floated into Lady Jayne's character, and anyone who read this would see me in the pages. The scene was powerful and full of every emotion sparkling in the prism of my heart. It was exquisite in its raw beauty—the chapter I had been trying to write for days.

Finally, I had created an ending worthy of Nathaniel Droll.

30

When she accepted her own uniqueness, it was freeing. She was able to shift her effort from fitting in to
improving who she actually was to begin with.

~Nathaniel Droll, *Lady Jayne Disappears*

Silas Rotherham sprinted through puddles toward Florin cottage. In the quiet of early nightfall, the tiny dwelling looked
like a fairy-tale setting, quaint and welcoming. How did she
do it? Nelle had transformed even a humble cottage into a
homey abode.

He knocked with one knuckle, then stood back. What if
she slept already? This visit to an unmarried woman was
already inappropriate this late.

When the curtain in the window lifted, then swept back
across, he exhaled away his tension. Of course she was awake,
and he would be welcomed in. He never need fear visiting
here. The door groaned open, and Silas stepped into the
sweet aroma of cinnamon and apples.

"Mr. Rotherham." Nelle's inner glow lit up the dim room as she welcomed him in. "You'll join us, I hope. Rosa has cooked more than enough for the three of us."

Rosa's lumpy frame jerked and swayed in the midst of the steam and sizzle over the old cast-iron stove.

"Silas!" A little girl squeal came from the shadows, and before he could spot the girl, her tiny frame crashed into his shins, sending him backward. "Mr. Silas." Her gap-toothed grin, purely accepting and joyful, temporarily bandaged the wound inside him. If only girls did not grow up to be women and lose that simple ability to love without bounds.

"Mr. Rotherham, would you like to see it?" Hands in a towel, Nelle steered Silas toward a cluttered far corner of the room, with a large covered object on a stand. "Dahlia, help with the apples, please."

"I trust the money I gave you—"

"It was plenty. And honestly, you did not have to do it. I would have managed."

"It's merely a loan. I am investing in two very talented women, and I expect a quick return on it."

She smiled, tucking her lower lip between her teeth, and whipped away the canvas cloth with a dramatic flair. Underneath stood a black iron-and-wood machine, complete with hand wheel, silver attachments for thread, and a flat plate to hold the material up to the needle. Silas reached out a finger and spun the wheel, watching the needle move smoothly up and down in the middle of the plate. It really was quite an invention.

"And this will do all the work for you, so you can tend the garden and make the meals?"

She laughed, a clear and buoyant sound as if she'd recently

tasted joy for the first time. "It isn't quite that efficient, but it'll help me work faster. Oh, I cannot wait to tell Aurelie about all this. She will be more excited than anyone. I nearly told her this afternoon, but so much happened in those moments."

"I think you should reveal it to her in person, as you did for me just now." He ran one thick finger along every surface of the machine his money had purchased. Next time he'd have to bring oil and rags for maintenance.

Her two hands perched gently on his arm extended toward the sewing machine, and her voice dropped to a whisper. "Did you do it? Did you speak to Aurelie? I meant to ask you in the carriage, but . . ."

His jaw twitched. Why had he come? Now he'd have to discuss it. Relive the rejection all over again. Knots tightened across his back. He gave a brief nod and glanced down, indicating the failed outcome. "I purposely avoided bringing it up on the search this afternoon. I did not care to discuss it."

"Oh, Silas, I'm sorry." She squeezed his arm, bestowing comfort through her touch.

"You are not at fault, dear Nelle."

Her face instantly shrouded, she drew him over to a worn chair in the furthest corner from the lively kitchen and sat in it, pulling him down to kneel beside her. "You know I am. This is all because of the things I said about you when she first came. If not for that, you two might even be betrothed and happily in love right now. I tried to fix it, though. Truly. I told her all the time how wonderful of a man you are, and I thought she listened."

"There was no need."

"Of course there was. I misjudged you, like I do every man, and I was determined to fix it. This cannot be over. You'll simply have to try again."

Again? His throat cinched closed. Heat poured over him. "I don't think so. I've never been the sort to force myself on anyone." His pride could not bear another failed attempt.

"Let me speak with her. Perhaps I can convince her if I tell her everything you told me."

He rose, pushing against the chair arm to stand. "I thank you for what you've tried to do, but you needn't go any further with it. I'm long overdue to return to London as it is. The way they dismissed you today without cause, without explanation, certainly tipped the scales, and I don't care to remain. It was simply never meant to be between Aurelie and myself."

She sprang up from the chair, taking his hand in both of hers and pleading with her eyes. "Don't go. My own love story had a tragic ending, but it makes the pain a bit softer to live through the love stories of other people. Especially the ones I care for."

"Then you shall have to become the unofficial matchmaker of Glen Cora." He squeezed her hands.

"Actually, I cannot remain in this area at all. I was hoping you could help me."

"Nelle, please do not be chased away by that woman. She's sending you away over something that simply isn't true. There isn't a single gentleman here you've encouraged."

"Even if the fault is hers, I cannot bear to remain. Will you help me?"

He sighed, raking fingers through his hair. "I can help you set up near London, if you choose. I'll be able to have you there in a few days, weeks at most. Can you keep yourself nearby until I'm ready?"

"Yes. There's an old garden shed on the property where we can hide for a few days, and I'm sure the underhousemaid will bring us food." She laid a hand on his arm and smiled up at him. "And in exchange, will you please let me talk to Aurelie?"

He shook his head. "Don't worry over me. Somehow I relish the idea of returning to work. I miss it, sad as it may seem."

She frowned. "You'll still love her, you know. And you cannot escape your feelings forever, even if they are a bit messy."

Moving toward the table where dented plates had already appeared, he sighed and surveyed the little house, up to the rafters. "No, but with a pile of work and a few wonderful books, I can keep them at bay for a surprising length of time."

Drained, I crept down the stairs as the early morning sun cast hazy orange rays through the sky. After purging my soul of the beautiful ending I'd been meant to write, the one that resonated with the deepest, most private parts of me, I'd opened a blank volume and spent the entire night filling its pages with a safer, more predictable ending. I would post this one to the publisher, despite its trite storyline and lack of emotion.

Perhaps readers would hate this ending, but what of it? Nathaniel Droll was merely a fictitious name that belonged to no person, including me. The important task now was being done with the contracted novel so I could finish the real-life story it mirrored. Lady Jayne lived, and I meant to find her.

Finding no one home at Florin cottage, I carried my wrapped package back to the house and asked Digory to post it for me. "Promise you will keep this between us, will you?"

"Of course, miss." The kind smile in his watery blue eyes comforted me. "Servants have neither ears nor eyes, only hearts for their masters."

It was still early, so the family would not be downstairs for at least another half hour. Thirty minutes should be enough time to normalize my emotions.

But Clem burst in the patio doors, shattering the blessed quiet. His hard gaze cut toward me, anger marring his freckled face. "Mother was right about you." Standing tall with fury, he suddenly seemed so much older.

"I will help find her however I can."

"And what good'll it do? I'm sure Grandmama has terminated her service." He snapped off his riding gloves. "She left last night. I didn't have a chance to tell her goodbye. I'll never see her again." Tears budded at the corners of his eyes.

Service?

Nelle.

"No. You mean—Nelle is gone?"

"What did you think would happen? Once Grandmama is involved, things always go her way. You couldn't leave Silas Rotherham alone, could you? Just couldn't let Nelle and Dahlia have a family." He kicked off his boots. "Well, now he's all yours. I hope you enjoy your life."

As he made a hard pivot into the morning room, I froze in place, chest heaving with the intensity of a thousand defenses I could not voice. When would it stop? How many things could I possibly ruin in this household by my mere presence?

I was supposed to help, to heal, but instead I rained trouble and chaos on my family's home.

Standing in place, I bowed my head and wordlessly connected my soul to God. I remained in this posture, submissive and trusting, breathing slowly. Peace did not come. Instead, I felt an energy firing through my chest, compelling me to move, to act. *Go. Go find her.*

When my legs finally obeyed, I hurried into the hall and yanked my cloak off the hook. "Digory, may I use the carriage?"

"I believe Master Kendrick has use of it at the moment, Miss Harcourt." His tone was nearly apologetic. "But you may take one of the horses in the stable. Do you ride?"

Hope lifted in me. "Yes, I ride." At least, I would in a moment.

In the stable, I asked the boy to saddle one of the geldings. "Whichever one you think best for me to take into the village."

"That'd be this one 'ere, miss. He goes the longer distances. The others are better for hunting and sport."

As soon as he'd cinched the saddle under the gray-spotted horse's belly, I shoved my foot in the stirrup, hoisted myself onto the tall animal with the help of the stall, and gripped the leather reins.

"Pull back to stop, nudge the flanks with your heels to make 'im go." Flattening his wool cap to his head, the boy eyed my awkward sidesaddle posture atop the horse.

With a nod of thanks, I squeezed my eyes shut and lightly heeled the animal in the side. With a jerk back and then forward, he danced out of his stall as if he'd been craving a good run all his life. As we trotted into the yard, the boy yelled, "And don't forget, hold on tight!"

The high-stepping horse jostled me across the open lawn to the drive. With one quick jolt, the reins dropped from my hands and panic seized me. Leaning forward, I clung to his coarse mane with one hand and looped the other around the animal's neck. Determination kept me atop him, where I had to remain until I reached Glen Cora. And thus I did—barely. Perhaps I did not do everything in the way I ought, but I always completed my missions one way or another.

When I met with a dead end at the most humble rooming house in the small community, I continued on to the three others in town with the same result. As the streets filled with working-class villagers shifting into lunchtime, I checked with the local seamstress and several other places that might take a single girl—also no sign of Nelle. If the girl had come to Glen Cora, she'd hidden herself well.

After trading a few pennies for simple food in the market, I dropped into nearly every store and a few places of residence. Finding no evidence that Nelle had even shown her face there, I dragged myself back to my horse, shoulders slumped in defeat. Perhaps God prompted this trip to offer me a break, wind in my face, and the solitude of the open road.

Night descended quickly as I ended my long day of searching. As the world around me dimmed, only a few lights shone—lamplight glowing in cozy homes, a lantern bobbing in the hand of an unseen pedestrian, and the glaring light of Shrewster Arm, the lively pub with a tinny racket spilling from its open doors. How easily it must suck men in, being such a bright light in the deepening darkness.

But then the door flew open wider and the light flashed on a familiar man stumbling out of the saloon, supported by his long-suffering father. Crossing the street with hope flaring, I reached the pair and laid a hand on the older Grupp's arm as he struggled under the weight of his son. What a picture of the poor man's whole life.

"What do you want now?" Jasper's bloodshot eyes widened as he spotted me. "There's nothing left for you to take. You've gotten it all." He jerked toward me and his putrid breath rained over my senses.

"Where is she?"

"I was gonna marry the girl." He stood and threw his arms in the air before me, offsetting his balance. "Really and truly marry her. But you made me a fool, and she left."

The older man sighed. "I'm sorry, Aura Rose. You know what the drink does to his mind. I'm sure you've done nothing to him, no matter how deserving he is."

"Jasper, where is she?"

But the glaze over his eyes sank my heart. His shrug further dampened my hope. Jasper's feet fumbled the single step off the walkway and he crumpled in the street. His father grunted under his weight and I ran to help. Together we struggled to lift the man into the waiting cart as he howled at some exaggerated pain.

When we'd completed the task, I threw a wan smile toward Mr. Grupp and turned to my horse, but his heavy hand on my shoulder stopped me.

"I've been waiting for a moment to talk to you alone, but I'm afraid this is as close as we'll come. You must know something, Aura Rose. It's about your father."

I spun, every muscle tensed.

"He knew there wouldn't be an inquest or a trial because of where he died, but he wanted you to know the truth. I

think he feared for your safety. I should have told you earlier."
His haggard face hung in the shadows.

"What are you trying to say?"

"It happened while you were searching for Mrs. Danbury's daughters. It wasn't the infection that took him. He was murdered, Aura Rose, by one of his creditors. A blow to the back of his head."

31

A well-written book always revealed the complex truth about its characters, but more than anything, the basic truth about its author.

~Nathaniel Droll, *Lady Jayne Disappears*

Horse hooves pounded the road beneath me as my dress billowed out behind and the shadows of despair blanketed me with their heavy weight. Mr. Grupp had escorted Papa into death because I hadn't been there. I'd left him for two days for . . . what? Ensuring another prisoner did not die without her daughters present.

Meanwhile my own papa had died without his. Tears squeezed from my wind-burned eyes. I could have prevented it—or at least walked with him through it.

Defeat crashed over me. Every area of my life had fallen apart from my own foolish actions, and my memories of life with Papa had been my saving grace. But I'd failed there too.

The weight of my guilt only intensified after a night of

sleep, but I swept it to the side as I descended to the morning room for breakfast the next day. Somehow the night had inflamed my appetite, so I loaded a plate with all manner of hot and cold breakfast food and perched on the stiff couch to devour it. Spiced sausage tickled my senses.

"Ah, you've returned." Garamond strode into the room with his narrow chest puffed out. "I was beginning to wonder if Cook was poisoning our food, the way everyone's disappearing."

I forced a bite of stewed peach down my throat and turned to watch him devour his toast.

He slowed his chewing and considered me. "Pardon my joke. Sometimes I find I must laugh when I need to maintain my composure."

Poor man. "No word from Juliette?"

He shook his head and cleared his throat with more than necessary effort. "She's likely married to that Grupp fellow by now, and hopelessly lost to us."

I slid closer and laid a hand on his arm. "I do have one piece of good news." The words had been bottled up inside me since my late return last night when I'd found no one awake to tell. "I went in search of Miss Wicke and found Jasper. Drunk and alone. Juliette has left him."

"Willingly?"

I nodded, and he dropped his other hand over mine, expressing so much through the touch—relief, gratitude, hope.

"I feel awful about—"

"Don't." He waved it off, looking away. "Juliette has a mind of her own. Unfortunately." His eyes brushed closed and he sighed.

"Have others disappeared?"

"Rotherham has returned to London as of this morning, and I believe I heard something about our seamstress being dismissed."

"I see." Of course they'd have left at the same time. I wanted to be happy for them, truly, but the news made me feel more alone than ever. At least, out of everything, I'd done one thing right in giving up Silas for Nelle.

With a wan smile, I stood to leave, but the name *Nathaniel Droll* caught my eye in the newspaper on the side table. Casually lifting the half-folded periodical, I skimmed the boxed column that exploded with news of Jasper Grupp being an imposter.

> Mr. Droll's shrewd reply to the imposter claiming his work was to simply pen the offender into his novel and thoroughly scald him with the fire of his words. We hope he is marginalized from polite society, but not to fear, dear readers. Mr. Droll will likely find a place for him in his next novel, anticipated to release from Marsh House Press.

Pinching back a smile, I wandered into the hall, belly and heart full.

"Digory, has the latest installment of *Lady Jayne Disappears* arrived yet?" Oh how that article made me want to delight in my own words again, to read afresh what readers and reviewers had seen.

"Yes, miss, it's arrived. But I sent it with Silas Rotherham when he left. He requested every installment in the house for the train ride to London."

I frowned. "Surely a trip to London is not the length of an entire novel."

"I merely do as I'm asked, miss."

With a nod, I climbed the stairs. Closing myself in my bedchamber again, I brushed against Papa's coat as it swung past me on the back of the door where I'd hung it. The whoosh of his scent overpowered my calm, loosening from my chest the tears that had clogged there all night and morning.

After emptying my soul of them, I blotted my face with a handkerchief and pulled down the notebook containing the never-to-be-published ending showcasing my raw feelings for Silas. It was beyond time to release my hurt over Papa's true demise onto the page where it belonged. This volume would be my cathartic scrap page book, a collection of scenes and snippets written only between myself and God.

Bending the pages back to the first empty one, I dipped my pen and let it hover over the book as my feelings surfaced and simmered.

But then my eye caught the final paragraphs on the left page, and my heart stopped.

And so, leaving behind her glorious purple gowns, golden trinkets, and the title that went along with it all, Lady Jayne disappeared into the mist of early morning at the manor and ceased to exist. The house she left behind became chaos, but she walked in peace.

In due time, a little maid in Manwood Gardens returned from an extended holiday to resume her duties in the kitchen, no one bothering to ask her where she had gone or how she'd *enjoyed the experience. For in truth, she'd have been unwilling to tell them of her adventure.*

No. It couldn't be!

I blinked at the sickeningly familiar words for several seconds before my fingers dove into the previous pages, eyes drinking in the sight of them. Before me lay the safe ending—the one supposedly posted to the publisher.

Yet here it remained. And out there somewhere my most intimate, shameful thoughts traveled to Marsh House Press to be printed in little green booklets and distributed to the world.

Including ardent fans Nelle Wicke and Silas Rotherham.

I slammed the book closed on the despicable words that should not be here for me to see and jumped up. What could I do now? Mistake upon mistake seemed to hurl itself from my hands, but I would not fail in this. It must be remedied immediately.

I flew down the stairs and nearly collided with poor Digory.

"Miss Harcourt. Is there anything—"

"Yes." I grabbed his arm and caught my breath. "Yes. The train schedule. Where is the nearest station, and when might I catch one for London?"

There was still time if I arrived that very day. After that, it would be the weekend, with the publishing house closed until Monday. And Monday might be too late.

"I couldn't say, Miss. But I'll find out."

"Thank you, Digory." Flashing a brief smile, I ran for the stairs and scaled them, legs pumping under my light housedress. Why had I even written down that first ending? And why on *earth* hadn't I had the sense to realize I'd posted the wrong one?

A brown traveling gown. That would be more appropriate for London offices than my pink day dress. Struggling to change clothes without help, I berated myself again. Of all the idiotic mistakes . . .

I slipped into my white side-lace boots, yanking the ties all the way up my ankle, and set a fancy hat on my already-heated head. At the door, I paused to bury my face in Papa's coat again. *I will fix things, Papa. Your pen name will not be used to destroy a romance so like your own.* Lifting it from the hook, I flung it around myself, even though the weather hardly warranted it, and forced my notebook into its inside pocket.

What about money? Jasper had taken most of this quarter's check. I dug madly through the desk. Finding a few copper pennies, I pocketed them and nearly fell back down the stairs in my haste, tripping over the hem of Papa's coat. If those pennies were not enough for the fare, I'd have to figure out another way. Even if I had to stow away in a coal car, I would get myself to London that day and repair the wrong I'd created.

Rounding the bannister at the bottom of the stairs, I swung wide and stopped at the sight of Aunt Eudora standing in the sunlight beaming through the tall windows. Where was her wheeled chair? She looked so tiny without it. Her waist was actually quite narrow and shapely.

"Digory tells me you are traveling to London." Her voice rang through the dust-filled air. "I have decided to accompany you."

Dread settled in me like cast iron.

"Young ladies should never travel without a proper chaperone." With a pointed glare that traveled up and down the length of the oversized coat far too warm for summer, she turned and limped with the aid of a heavy cane directly to the front door. "Digory, is the carriage in the drive yet?"

"Yes, my lady." His voice echoed in the narrow hallway. "Will you allow me to fetch Mary to help—"

"What part of 'no' was not clear before? This is a private excursion."

With nothing else to be done about it, I followed Aunt Eudora into the blinding sun and allowed the coachman to elbow-lift me into the carriage. In the dark box across from Aunt Eudora, I closed my eyes.

Help me, Lord. I need to make it there today, and I need to break away from Aunt Eudora to do it. Thank you for helping me realize my mistake in time.

Hopefully.

At the tiny station, bugs zinged into my personal space, somehow intensifying the heat and anxiety swirling through me. I'd removed Papa's coat and draped its weight over my arm. The train, surprisingly sleek and sturdy, proved a welcome sight as it charged into the station. Aunt Eudora paid for both fares at the window and, with substantial help from me, led us up two steep steps and to the first pair of cushioned seats where she collapsed into one. Dare I ask why the trip was private? A lady's maid would have been helpful.

The aged woman wheezed, leaning sideways and clutching the bar in front of our seats.

"Thank you for accompanying me." The sight of Aunt Eudora struggling wrung the statement out of me, no matter how much it had complicated my plans to have her along.

Whatever the woman's reasons, the trip had cost her a great deal.

"What on earth were you thinking of, traveling alone? You have a responsibility to be at least remotely decent while living in my home." Settling forcibly into the seat once she'd caught her breath, Aunt Eudora arranged her cane as close to the window as possible.

"It never occurred to me there was anything indecent about travel."

The woman rolled her eyes. Narrow fingers picked a white handkerchief from the wrist of her sleeve, and she draped it over her face, nose tenting the material over her features. And then she was still.

Setting my hat on my lap, I relaxed into the accommodating seat cushion. A patchwork of hills stretched across the view outside the window, stone fences cutting it into sections like quilt squares. Yet here we sat, in a modern convenience about to whisk us away to London.

As the conductor shouted and swung into the first car, reality settled over me. I was on my way. This would work. All would be fixed. With noisy effort, the train gathered power and surged forward, moving faster than I had ever traveled in my life and gaining speed. The exhilaration tickled me.

In minutes, Aunt Eudora's handkerchief rose and fell with the whoosh of deep breaths. Tugging the notebook from Papa's coat, I flopped it open and steadied the ink jar firmly between my boots. This would not be a simple task, but I would do it. God had aligned everything so far, it seemed, and I would succeed in fixing my problem. I had only to polish the safe ending enough to warrant what I was about to ask of the publishers.

Forcing my mind into gear, I bent down to dip my pen in the jar and then rose to stare at the flat words that must somehow have life breathed into them. How could I possibly dive into the story and rend my heart across the page in the midst of this crowded, hissing machine? But necessity drilled through me. Write. Just write.

Then the terrible words implanted on my subconscious drifted forth, surging over my sparks of creativity in drenching waves.

Laughable prose.

Not worth reading.

Childish.

How could I do this? I was not my magnificent father and never would be. I'd been fooling myself, thinking I could write. What would come after this book? Would I ever be able to produce an entire book on my own—idea, characters, prose, and ending—that would be worth reading? With my pen poised and dripping ink into the well, I fought panic.

Then other phrases vibrated through my mind.

It isn't the writing that's so fantastic. Nathaniel Droll is only famous because no one knows who he really is.

These words dropped carelessly into conversation by Garamond now branded themselves on my mind in paralyzing clarity. I was not talented and had nothing worth writing.

Time slipped by with each double-clack of the train speeding toward London.

Lord, you've given me the words when my brain proved to be a stubborn blank slate. Now please help me do it again.

32

Among the wealthy, Lady Jayne stood out like a rebellious wildflower among perfectly trimmed hedgerows. And it was much to her benefit.

~Nathaniel Droll, *Lady Jayne Disappears*

When we stepped down into the steamy London station, a massive wooden tunnel brimming with people and moist odors, I waved away smoke and clung to Aunt Eudora with my free hand. Cinched together, we wove through the throng of skirts, parasols, and moving feet toward an arched exit. Steam rose from the brick streets, and everything—carriages, people, horses—was in a supreme, noisy hurry. Why had I ever thought I could do this alone? All of the world's people seemed to have converged in the space of several blocks, all fighting for room to move about at once.

"A hansom cab, please." Aunt Eudora touched the arm of a uniformed man.

Two sharp whistle blasts brought a sleek little carriage,

no more than a covered bench on two wheels, that seemed to satisfy my aunt. Without the aid of a coachman, I helped Aunt Eudora into the cab and climbed in, fitting neatly beside her on the seat.

"Location?" An ugly man with a crooked nose leaned down from his perch behind us.

I looked at Aunt Eudora, who watched me expectantly. Should I make up . . .

"Where might ye be going?" His firm voice blasted through my thoughts.

"Upper Ashby Street, please. Number 67." I curled down into my seat, turning away from Aunt Eudora. I counted the rapid beats of my heart, but Aunt Eudora did not speak above the clatter of hooves on brick. The vehicle jerked forward, moving fast enough for the moist breeze to whip hair across my face. Must everyone move at the speed of a racehorse in this city?

Careening around corners and between other carriages, our cab stopped at an iron fence that bordered a columned stone building of at least five stories.

"'Ere ye be, missy. 'At'll be one sovereign for the fare."

Aunt Eudora tucked the coin into the man's hand as he helped her disembark from his vehicle. As soon as our feet were firmly on the ground, the man had swung up to his post and whipped his horse into a trot again.

Now what? Take Aunt Eudora along? The plan of evading her had failed terribly.

"I'll wait here while you attend your business." Leaning heavily on her cane, Aunt Eudora stood poised and certain, as if she belonged among this rush. And perhaps she had once.

"I just need to—"

"We'll strike a bargain. You carry out your errand in peace, with no questions from me, and then you will go along on an errand of my choosing, no questions asked. Agreed?" Her old eyes glittered dangerously. Who was this woman, friend or enemy?

With a quick nod, I approached the double doors and entered a dark office building with dust floating in slender streams of sunshine. People in fine, modern clothes rushed about through a low-ceilinged space. One woman sat behind a desk, her hat tilted at a stylish angle.

"Pardon me, but I'm looking for Marsh House Press."

One thick eyebrow rose toward curly hair. "Did you read the sign inside the door? This is it. First two floors."

"Oh, I . . . Who might I talk to about . . . about books? The serials?"

Whipping through a stack of papers while she talked, the woman jerked her head toward a wide marble staircase that narrowed toward the top. "Up and to the right. You'll need to speak to Ram."

Hugging my coat and notebook to my chest, I nodded and hurried up the steps that were the centerpiece of the large open floor. *Ram.* The man who had been unable or unwilling to remove the telling details of a previous installment.

At the top, a white-tiled hall with textured walls led me to an open space with several desks spread over the floor. When a suited young man with slicked hair caught my eye and offered me a tiny smile, I approached him.

"Please, I'm looking for the person in charge of the serials." Back straight, chin up, shoulders back. I must fit in, at least until my errand was done. Then I could collapse into my train seat on the way home.

"Certainly. Right this way." Springing up, he led me to an office and knocked on the slightly open door. Even he was in a hurry, with no apparent reason. "You have a visitor, sir." He gave a gentle shove to my shoulder, then disappeared as if he'd ignited a timed bomb.

I took one step in, sliding my slender frame through the space without opening the door farther. An older man with hair forced across the top of his bald head reigned over a desk full of messy stacks of paper. Sorting and thumbing through pages, he glared at me. "I've no time for an interview. Get out." Rings of baggy skin underlined angry eyes.

"Please, sir. I only need a small favor."

"My desk is piled with a million small favors. What makes you think I have time for yours?"

"I have here—" I flipped the bulky coat around until I had access to the inside pocket that held my notebook.

"Will you *kindly* take your leave, madam?"

"—Nathaniel Droll's book."

He thwacked a pile of papers onto his desk and lifted his face. "You have what?"

"I have the last chapters of his book." I yanked it out with a flourish and another paper burst from the pocket and floated to the floor. I retrieved it with a less-than-graceful bend and stuffed it back into the pocket.

Planting spectacles on the bridge of his fleshy nose, he rose and looked at me over his desk, from plumed hat to cinched waist. "Edna!" His voice boomed past his office walls. "Bring a chair. Who are you? Has my fool son bribed you to come here as some sort of joke? If I had a shilling for every Nathaniel Droll imposter, I'd be rich all over again."

"I am Aurelie Harcourt. And I've come of my own accord."

A woman scurried in with a chair for me.

"So you are claiming to be Nathaniel Droll? Such a little snit of a girl."

"No, it's—well, yes. But this—"

Stubby hands planted on the mess atop his desk, he leaned forward and put the question plainly. "Well, Miss Harcourt. Are you, or are you not, Nathaniel Droll?"

Head down, I focused only on the steps I descended, the little white toes of my boots peeking out from the dress hem. I'd done everything I could, short of stealing back the other ending. Perhaps I should have done that. I'd been there nearly an hour, telling him the story of Papa and debtor's prison and Lynhurst, but it was a tale without an ending.

Bursting into the smoggy city air, I paused. What now?

Aunt Eudora hobbled toward me from a bench near the building, her grim face focused. "Was it a success?"

I hugged Papa's greatcoat. Yes? Maybe?

"Good heavens, you needn't reveal your darkest secrets to me. I simply asked a yes or no question."

I hesitated. "Yes. Yes, I believe it was." As much as I could hope for, anyway, with a man like Ram. I'd come away with the news that publication of my next work was guaranteed, whatever I chose to write. Even though I was not the original famous author behind the pen name, reviews had validated my writing and demand always existed for work with the Nathaniel Droll name on it.

"Now for my end of the bargain." Aunt Eudora shuffled to the edge of the street, hanging over the curb until another hansom cab jerked to a stop before us. "I will admit, this

next errand is made for purely selfish reasons on my part."
She turned to me for help up into the seat and caught my
gaze. "I do so want a relationship with my brother's child,
and for that I need to vindicate myself. So there you have
it." Her mouth snapped shut in a hard smile, eyes twinkling.

I climbed up beside her, wedging my brown skirt in beside
Aunt Eudora's dark red one.

"Location?" The driver leaned into the side of the cab.

Aunt Eudora's gloved fingers fumbled in her purse and
retrieved a torn envelope. "Greenwich. 37 Kender Place."
She turned to me. "Miss Aurelie Rosette, prepare to learn
the truth."

33

Every now and then when Lady Jayne found the answers to her most pressing questions, she earnestly wished to unlearn them immediately.

~Nathaniel Droll, *Lady Jayne Disappears*

Nerves tickled my belly to the point of pain. The interminably long carriage ride felt like forever, but was likely within an hour's span.

"This will not be a long stop."

"Are we expected?"

"Remember our bargain." A few firm pats to my knee. "No questions."

Of course there would be no questions. The woman had too many things to answer for. "It's about my mother, isn't it? Why didn't you tell me she was alive?" Years had been wasted, countless embraces lost.

"Because I didn't know until recently, when I received a letter from her. Apparently the Nathaniel Droll novel sparked recognition in her as well, and she needed to find out who wrote the installments."

The city sped by outside the cab, tall buildings melting into two- and three-story homes lined up against each other like fence posts. The horse slowed and danced to a stop before rows of yellow-brick buildings with a red door at each home. A black iron fence stood between casual strollers and the stately homes.

"This is not the time for you to ask questions. Of anyone. Do you understand?"

"But how—"

"I will ask the questions. Your task is merely to listen and learn the truth." She pushed up from the seat, back straight and arm trembling, and I handed her down to the driver. After righting herself on the walk, Aunt Eudora dropped coins in the man's gloved hand, and he sprang back to his perch.

"Please do wait for us. We shan't be long." With these parting words to the driver, Aunt Eudora led me forward. Papa's coat remained behind in the hansom.

At the door of an overly elaborate townhouse, a suited butler took our card and ushered us into the building, a marble-and-glass affair with the emptiness of a museum. Led silently to an open white-and-mauve parlor to the left, I drank in every detail of the immaculate home. Lady Jayne might have decorated this home herself, if she were the mistress here. Or if she was the maid, perhaps her own hands had cleaned the tiny baubles on every surface.

After the tea cart appeared before us, our host entered—a remarkably tall gentleman with a waxed mustache and overly large spectacles attached to a narrow chain.

"Lady Pochard." His thin lips barely moved as he spoke.

"Have we had the pleasure of an introduction?" Straightening his jacket, he seated himself across from us on an ivory-and-rose-colored settee.

"Not until now." She extended her fingertips for a kiss. "Thank you for accepting my call without notice."

I shifted on the stiff couch beside her. Had I suddenly become invisible? Or were unmarried young women not worth an introduction in this culture?

"I'm hoping you can assist me. You see, I've lost my little Mimi, and she always wanders this way."

The man blinked behind his spectacles. "I beg your pardon?"

"Mimi, my kitty cat."

A hiss of fine clothes in the distance announced the entrance of the lady of the house, clothed in a brown, well-fitted gown with ivory stripes. I caught my breath as the air tangled with the fine aroma of lilacs. And before me, straight and regal, stood an exact replica of the picture tucked in my armoire.

Lady Jayne.

I stared, jittery and frozen at the same time. After a heart-pounding moment, I forced my gaze toward the carved feet of the chairs across from us. Intensity pushed at my chest, and I lifted my head to look at the woman in quick glances, unable to bear staring directly at her.

"Ladies, my wife. Lady Genovefa Chetworth."

The woman's large brown eyes snapped toward Aunt Eudora and held, a thousand questions flicking in their depths. Her well-shaped eyebrows, thick and dark, remained still, but recognition tinged the depths of her gaze.

"Pardon my manners." Aunt Eudora crooned with the

voice of a well-practiced gentlewoman. "I've neglected to introduce my niece. This is Miss Aurelie Harcourt."

Then those amber eyes riveted to me, soaking up the sight of me in a desperate, panicked look, red lips parted.

"Dearest, these nice ladies were looking for their kitty. Mimi, did you say it was?" The man's pinched lips looked almost feminine. "What color is your little darling?"

"She is gray with a brown-tipped tail. A little white on the ears. It would mean ever so much to us." Aunt Eudora cut a glance toward the slender lady of the house. "My dear Aurelie has been hurting so much. She needs closure regarding the creature, if nothing else."

Lady Chetworth trembled where she stood, her narrow collarbone jutting above the bodice of her dress as her shoulders arched forward. When she moved, something flashed at her throat. Among all the browns and whites of her costume, a large, deeply purple amethyst jewel on a black ribbon shone against white skin.

"You see, we've come on this search because my poor niece feels she desperately needs this cat. While I find all felines perfectly loathsome creatures, using and then casting people aside on a whim, I do understand Aurelie's need to . . . rekindle a much needed connection with it. You understand."

Lady Chetworth trembled harder beside her husband, her slender hand floating above his shoulder in case she had need of it.

"Of course, of course. My Genovefa finds herself inseparable from a little white poodle she calls Woolf." He laughed. "Poor Woolf is small as a mouse and likely no meaner."

A tremor passed over me that shook my shoulders when he spoke my father's name.

"Yes, I see the irony." Aunt Eudora's low voice chilled the room. "You are lucky, Lady Chetworth, to have a dog. Much more faithful companions, are they not?"

"I have no doubt cats have their very own brand of faithfulness." The woman finally found her voice, and it was rich and melodic. "You cannot judge any creature merely by what you see, unless you can cut open the heart and look inside."

Her husband laughed in short, awkward bursts of air. "What a lot of deep conversation about pets. Lady Pochard, I shall contact you immediately if I spot a creature fitting the description of your little Mimi."

"I would be most thankful to you." She stood, her right hand grabbing and crunching mine until I stood beside her. She glanced at Lady Chetworth again. "If nothing else, I'd like to find that cat and wring its neck, for all the pain it's caused my household."

Lady Chetworth sank to the settee, handkerchief-twined fingers to her chest. This finally drew the attention of her husband, who sank beside her and grasped her shoulders. "Genny, are you ill? Shall I ring for—"

She shook her head adamantly, jarring loose a tress of long brown hair that slipped down to curl about her neck. Lady Chetworth's personal maid scurried in to hover about the little woman, freeing the master of the house to rise and escort his guests into the hall. He did so with the jovial grin of a man largely unaffected by his wife's discomfort.

"You are gracious hosts, Lord Chetworth, and we thank you again for the warm welcome. I hope we shall not have cause to visit again for the same reason."

"Good luck to you with Mimi. She will turn up. Cats always return."

"Unfortunately, that seems to be so." And with those parting words, she grasped my hand and pulled me down the steps.

I threw glances back over my shoulder. That was it? We were leaving? Ten minutes of parading my mother before me, and then I was yanked away? Surely there was more. But each step away from the house wrenched my heart with the finality of our meeting. We merely climbed back into the hansom cab waiting at the curb and settled into the seat.

"Location?"

"To the station please, sir."

I spun to face her. "You can't mean it. I'm not allowed to say a single word to her?"

"She is not deserving of it."

I stiffened. "You may judge people by their humble beginnings, but I won't. It hardly matters what she was before—a chambermaid, a dressmaker, a chimney sweep."

"Sit down, child."

"No, tell me. What was she that made her so unworthy of him?"

With a grim set to her chin, she looked straight forward. "Married."

Reality washed over me in layers as I fought to wrap my mind around what she suggested.

"She was married when she met him, and married she is now. That sort of relationship is abominable to me and to God, and I could not allow it to continue."

Tears pricked my eyes. "She tricked him, didn't she?"

"No, my dear, that is one thing she is not guilty of. Woolf Harcourt knew very well that he'd made the acquaintance of a married woman the very day he met her. My brother,

God rest his troubled soul, was never one to follow any sort of rules. Marriage vows included."

The blunt words rolled over my wounded spirit, crushing the sweetness of his memory.

"But why would he do that?" One little inch of me still did not believe it possible.

"Because he was a fanciful creature who believed in the excitement of living outside of boundaries. As if it were higher than living respectfully as one ought. Dreaming and loving always trumped decorum and morals."

She turned stiffly and twined her lace-gloved hands in mine. "I loved my brother dearly. I never wanted him to spend a day in prison, but it had to be done. He believed that living the way he did, reckless and childlike, gave him control over his own life, but in fact it did the opposite." A tear made a path through the powder on her cheek. "I tried desperately to help him, any way I knew how, but in the end, there was nothing to be done but to keep him from himself. He refused to stop seeing that woman, and it would have ruined so many lives. Including yours."

"Why could I not have remained with my mother?"

"She disappeared after your birth and your father took you off." The gloved hands smoothed my hair. "He claimed he had an idea of who could keep you, but then the dominos fell quickly and he was in debtor's prison with a complicated mess of debts. We thought he'd found you a family, a nice couple, not a . . . a *prison cell*. If I'd known, had any idea . . ." The woman's fingers flitted over my face, caressing, conveying love.

Hurt and regret and love welled in me until it spilled over, urging me toward the frail woman wracked with pain, my arms sliding around her shoulders. I pulled her to myself as the hansom bounced over the road. With each passing moment in the embrace, each breath in and out near the old, powdery face, my heart softened. Her lace-covered hands made small circles on my back.

Finally, I released Aunt Eudora and sat back to meet her gaze. "Thank you."

"I've only given you the truth, Aurelie. You are grown, and all decisions regarding that woman are now yours. But I will underscore—she is not worth your time. Scriptures tell us not to cast our pearls before swine." She smiled, patting my knee. "Do not cast your lovely heart before that undeserving woman."

In the noisy center of town, I took a deep breath of dusty air once outside the hansom and braced myself for Aunt Eudora's weight. The old woman leaned heavily, nearly toppling onto me until her feet found the brick road and steadied. As we walked, silent in the chaotic mess of people, truth vibrated against my skull. It was really over, and there was no happy ending. My mother had walked away.

Finally seated again on the cushioned train seats, hot tears burned under my eyelids. I focused on the sights of the station—wooden trusses arching overhead, oversized clocks, English flags saluting from the wall—so Aunt Eudora would not see the tears if they came.

Aunt Eudora's face turned to study me when we were seated. "Do not be hard on yourself for focusing on the good in everyone. For hoping. Rich is the man who sees value in every person, even if there is none to be found."

Sobs clogged my throat. A whistle shrilled nearby and steam poured from under the train.

"You do so remind me of another individual with that very same tendency."

"Papa." I glanced at Aunt Eudora, studying the green eyes that had seemed like such daggers before, but now only seemed sharp with the pain of life.

"Not Woolf. My brother hated with a passion when someone wronged him. Especially me. The last time I saw his eyes, they were piercing enough to cut open my chest and steal the very heart out of it." Hard pain sharpened her features, then eased slightly as she moved on. "Actually, I was referring to Silas Rotherham. He is, how did he put it? 'Intentional about recognizing the good in people.' I think you two would get on quite well."

"We enjoy each other's company." The memory of his sturdy, engulfing embrace coursed over me in a matter of seconds, leaving me weak inside. I suddenly recalled with clarity the scent of his shirt as I'd laid my face on his chest. But in my daydream of that moment, I did not push away. I sank into him and tipped my head up to melt under his gaze, to receive his love and his kiss. Perhaps I had been a fool to release love when I'd finally found it in this wretched world.

"You should know, child, that he came to me to request your hand."

I caught my breath. "He . . . when?" Despicable hope swelled in me.

"The night of the badminton game. I haven't the slightest idea what occurred between him and Nelle in the meantime, but I know with the certainty of a woman who's lived through three generations of romance under her roof that he is deeply in love with you. And that's all I'll say on the matter. It's up to you to act now." She turned to me with the wry smile of an old woman. "I'm glad we've had this little chat." With that closing, she again placed a handkerchief over her face and soon dozed, sending the piece of lace up and down with deep breaths.

Her straightforward words pushed and pulled on my heart. He'd requested my hand. *My* hand, not Nelle's. I frantically tried to put events in order and understand what this information meant, but one truth loomed over the budding hope with painful clarity—it was too late. I had rejected Silas's kiss, he had left, and now I had no idea how to change anything.

As the train stopped at the first rural station, crisp night air blew in and invaded my comfort until I struggled to wrap Papa's massive coat about me and huddle into it. Forcing my arms through the sleeves and my hands into the pockets, I stiffened as a shiver convulsed me and my hand crinkled paper in the pocket. A vague memory of this paper falling out at Ram's office returned to me, and I pulled it out in my fist. I flattened it on my leg and stiffened at the sight of Nathaniel Droll's perfect penmanship filling a tiny space in the white page, the same way it did in the notebooks. All thoughts of my failed romance dissipated in the face of these written words.

At the bottom stood the single word *Papa*.

With heart palpitating, I read the note with a consuming hunger.

Dearest one,
   It is now upon you to finish two stories—the fictional one and the real-life tale it mirrors. I trust you

to resolve both stories in the style of your own dear personality. Sending your mother's story out into the world was necessary, but it has sparked a number of events that were long in coming. I've received written threats against my life, and if you are reading this letter it means my pursuer has likely succeeded in killing me. I want you to know that if it is who I think, I deserve it. You will understand many things if you dive into the empty notebooks on the shelf and complete the story I have left to you as your legacy. There is more information in those books than one might expect. I cannot state plainly what I suspect, because it is so thoroughly entangled in the novel I mean for you to finish, so you must complete both to fully understand.

Of all the worldly wealth I've held, my hands were never richer than when they were filled with my infant daughter. You are the greatest blessing I never deserved.

My hands trembled until the paper fluttered to the floor. Tears gathered and fell. Those notes from Nathaniel Droll in the notebook were his. It was the same writing.

And the clues he'd left—they were not meant to point to Lady Jayne's killer, but to his.

34

Quite often, villains of one story were heroes in another.

~Nathaniel Droll, *Lady Jayne Disappears*

We returned well after dark, and the lack of Silas Rotherham's presence echoed about the empty halls of Lynhurst. Glenna greeted us at the door, frittering around her mother as if I had accosted the woman and dragged her to London. Kendrick observed from the shadows, keeping his distance, and the servants politely ignored me as they came and went. In a house full of strangers, I had not a single ally.

"Mr. Rotherham hasn't returned, has he?" This I voiced toward Garamond, the only one to meet my gaze.

"No, Miss Harcourt. All his belongings left with him, and he seems to have departed for good this time."

As the small crowd ebbed and flowed around Aunt Eudora, the woman visibly detached herself from her family, curling back into her bitter self. A look of stone solidified on her face. I now recognized great suffering behind those sharp eyes as I recalled the way she stated her brother's hatred for her. Years and years of pain twisted her features.

But on the heels of our return, Glenna pushed herself between us, eyes snapping, and led her mother away as if I meant to harm her.

Just like my mother, I had become an outcast at Lynhurst Manor. As Glenna settled her mother into the wheeled chair and rolled her through the echoing hall, I took myself off to my bedchamber, wishing for a warm bath to soothe my nerves. Instead, I curled into the moon glow pouring through my window and looked at my father's notes, one by one, with new eyes. To whom did they point?

I puzzled over them until I could see the words on the backs of my eyelids. Yet in the midst of everything, I couldn't stop thinking about my mother. Sliding the torn-out pages back between the notebooks, I slipped out of the room and found my way toward the south tower by the blue light of the moon, which cast deep shadows across the floor.

As I entered her chamber, the pure femininity and beauty of the forgotten room wrapped itself around me again and pulled me in. In one giant release, I collapsed on the rosette-covered bedspread, a cloud of dust puffing up around me. I coughed as it settled, then breathed in the scent of the room. Of my mother, perhaps. A lilac aroma hid beneath the fine layer of filth.

God, I've no idea what to do now. How do I figure this out?

And then, as I sat up and my eyes roved over the room, I froze. There, tall and regal, with the curtains wrapping themselves around her slender frame in the breeze, stood my mother.

35

Lady Jayne revealed her secrets—not to become vulnerable, but to avoid it.

~Nathaniel Droll, *Lady Jayne Disappears*

Time paused as we stared at one another across the room that resonated with her presence. And as I studied her large, watchful eyes, only detachment and a hard seed of hostility nestled in my heart for this wretched woman. She stepped forward out of the window bay, moving in the shadows, and paused before the bed, reaching out to finger a strand of my loose hair. "You look so much like who I used to be." Her quiet voice rolled out as smooth and pure as the beautiful gown draped over her frame. Waves of calm kept me still as my mother, the woman connected to me by heartstrings, caressed my hair, then my cheek. "What a wonder to have your own self mirrored in another person. I see a familiar fire in your eyes, behind a face that is mine. I rather hoped for your sake you wouldn't inherit the fire."

"All dangerous forces can be harnessed."

She smiled. "And your father's wit. You are a dazzling blend of two very unique souls."

"You did love him, didn't you?"

She dipped her head, the energy radiating from her down-turned face speaking more eloquently than words. "He changed my life. No, he *gave* me life."

I gulped. "And me? Did you love me?"

Her countenance softened as she lifted her eyes and traced a fingertip over the contours of my face. The glow of approval in her eyes reached inner parts of my heart never before used and ignited them. "You, my dear, are my most elaborate, flawless work of art. A stunning blend of colors from two paintbrushes meant to work in tandem."

I released a breath, wondering at the gorgeous being before me. "Everything Papa said about you . . . it's truer than I ever thought."

"What did he tell you?"

"That you were a beautiful woman with an addiction to love. He said it was your curse, and at the time I thought it a lovely curse to have."

"It depends on if you are giving or receiving it. Loving someone makes you their slave. But being loved makes you the master." Her gaze intensified. "And after a childhood like mine, I wanted nothing more than to be master."

I swallowed the angry words fighting for control over me. "And did you succeed?"

Those luminescent eyes flickered intensely as they held my gaze. "He didn't tell you of my childhood, did he? If he had, you'd know the answer simply by looking at me."

She sank down beside me on the edge of the bed that used

to be hers, and she began. "In my youth, life had beaten down my father and his pride, so he beat us down. Six women in his household, and none of us stood up to him. But soon I discovered the power of my beauty in the world outside my house, and I collected affection as some girls accumulate buttons or oranges." She gazed past me. "Even into adulthood and marriage I used the power of seduction, of withheld gratification, to survive. Until I met your father." Tears glistened and one cut a path through her powder mask. "I couldn't help loving him, no matter what I tried. Just by sheer force of who he was, he lured it out of me in a way too powerful to stop."

"But you were married to someone else."

She dropped her gaze. "I married a man rich with connections, with grand hopes he'd rise to the top, and I with him. He was well-dressed, with a gentleman's position, and I'd been born into a mill family living in a coarse, dirt-floor hovel in the country. This man provided a way out of poverty. I married and had a child with him, but after the birth, I became less and less of myself, until I was merely a body doing what it ought while my soul pined away in a separate corner. A person is never meant to survive such a separation, and it was killing me.

"And then . . . ," her eyes slid closed, "then came your father. Woolf Harcourt, that radiant prism of light and vitality. The nearer I was to his presence, the more he infused his life into me, and I constantly went back for more, never satisfied."

"How did you meet him?"

"My husband worked for his family. They were close, and saw much of each other." She gave a soft laugh. "You have no idea what it did to my heart to see them side by side every day, the flapping simpleton and the dashing, brilliant man who turned my life upside down with a simple wink. At first, it was only walks in the sunshine between Woolf and me. Soon that wasn't enough, and I needed more and more of him to feel alive.

"Your father managed to have my husband sent abroad for six months in service to his family, and our love flamed like nothing I'd ever experienced before." Her lips trembled. "But then I learned you were coming. I wrote to my husband to confess and begged him to return so that we may pass you off as his. He refused, so Woolf whisked me off to Lynhurst so I could carry and birth our baby away from the public eye."

"So that summer you spent here as Lady Jayne . . ."

"Yes, I was hiding you. I assumed the identity of 'Lady Jayne,' tight-laced my corset until it nearly suffocated me, and danced into the night as often as I could, grasping at the sunset of my freedom. When I could no longer hide my secret, I kept myself in this very room, awaiting what was to come."

"And after I was born?" I nearly whispered the next words.

Her face hardened, a cord tightening along her throat. She gulped.

When tears welled in her big, beautiful eyes and poured over her lashes, I steeled myself against the outpouring of her sorrow. "I suppose you wish me to forgive you now."

She leaned back with a soft laugh, face moist. "And what do you imagine must be forgiven? Every person has the right to freedom, to live the life implanted in the core of her being. No, child. I'm not sorry." Her eyes searched mine and the tears renewed themselves. "They'd have persecuted me if

I'd returned with a baby that could not be my husband's. I couldn't have borne it. And then he'd have come home and puttered about with his sad, mournful eyes. Every time he'd have glanced at this child, it would remind him of the love his wife shared with another man." Tears spilled down and dripped off her chin. "For a woman accustomed only to adoration, I could not bear the thought of being scorned."

My hands trembled in my lap. Pain rippled over me in terrible waves as I stared at this woman who had given birth to me yet was not even a shadow of a mother. I could not cry over her, for I felt as though she were merely the one informing me that my mother had never existed. "So you chose to leave me." My cold voice offered these words as a statement for her to verify or deny.

"If fate handed me a second life, I would do the same again. Hate me if you must."

Chill permeated my being. "Then why did you come here now? Why contact Aunt Eudora?"

Slowly she lifted a green-bound installment of *Lady Jayne Disappears* in her lace-gloved hand. "This." The pages had been well-worn by eager thumbs. "I know so well that beautiful writing, as well as the woman painted by the words. They are more familiar to me than my own home. When I read this, I knew I had to face him again."

"So it was Papa you sought?" Rejection pooled in my heart, drowning it.

"After you were born, I ran. I never intended to leave *him*, only the tangled mess in which I found myself."

Which was me.

"After things settled I sought him out, but your father had disappeared. Vanished from the earth, leaving only a letter breaking off our love. His rejection shredded me from the inside out until I hardly knew who I was anymore. For many years, I thought I'd forgotten him. But when I read this, and saw the love that glowed from every page, I knew his letter had been a lie." More tears trailed down her cheek. "So I wrote to his sister, Lady Pochard. I wanted to see Woolf again, to hear from his own lips that he does not love me, because I couldn't believe it. Not after what he wrote."

With a soft rustle of her gown, she turned to me and clasped my stiff hands. "And now you shall be the instrument that brings us together, after you once tore us apart. How fitting it should be so. Please, won't you tell me where he is?"

Steeling myself against her warm hands, I met her gaze. "He is dead."

The flat words melted her refined features and she dropped her head, shoulders shaking. "No."

"He died in debtor's prison."

She shook, slender arms vibrating with emotion. After several moments, she drew her mournful eyes up to meet mine, studying them. The silk of her caress on my arm softened my bitterness. "If you are the sort of girl I believe you to be, his death has left you utterly empty too, hasn't it? For you know as well as I that there is no one like that man. No one who understands you or loves you quite as well."

I turned my face away to hide the well of tears. Her sudden warmth collided with an overwhelming desire for Papa, and for everything familiar.

"I'm so sorry. For both of us." She breathed in the quiet space that followed for several seconds. "What happened?"

"He was murdered. I've no idea who is responsible."

"Murdered! How terrible. Surely you must have some notion of who could have done such a thing."

"He never said a word before it happened. All he left me was riddles and clues."

"Daughter, show them to me." She gripped my arms eagerly, forcing me to turn toward her. "I know Woolf inside and out. Any puzzle he has created, I can unravel for you."

I stiffened, a refusal on my lips, but her gentle touch cut it off. Her hand rubbed small circles on my upper arm, loosening my bitterness with each arc.

"Please. Allow me to do this one thing for you. My freedom has cost you much. I may be selfish, but I am not unaware."

My heart hurt with a physical ache. It could not keep up with the emotional twists and loops. With an exhale that loosened the resentment hardening me, I stood and nodded. "The notes are in Papa's room, where I'm staying. We'll need to sneak through the great hall."

Her eyes sparkled. "We absolutely will not." Rising and guiding me by the hand, she took me to a little closet just outside the south tower and forced open the too-tight door. A narrow staircase climbed straight up. "After you."

I should not have been surprised that those steps reached another door right outside Papa's old bedchamber. After a breathless climb up stairs nearly too steep to scale, we tiptoed into my room and over to the desk. Slipping the notes out from between the notebooks, I laid them all out flat on the desk, arranging them into the order in which I'd received them. Her fingertip glossed over his handwriting, emotion fanning out over her face, as if she caressed the hand that wrote these words.

"He'd been receiving threatening notes before it happened,

from what I have learned. Although he never saw fit to tell me any of it while he lived."

"Knowing your father, he had some foolish notion of protecting you."

I leaned over the pages alongside her. "What do these mean? What is he saying?"

She skimmed them, passing over each torn-out page carefully. "It's in these last emphasized sentences of each note—that is what he's trying to tell you."

"They don't make sense."

"Because they're coded." Her brow furrowed. "I know, because he used to write me these terrible sonnets where the first or last letter of each—" Her voice hitched as she studied the note before her.

"What? Who is it?"

Urgency sparked through her fingers as she flipped through the notes again and then dropped them. "It's my husband."

"Lord Chetworth? But he seemed so—"

A knock on my door cut off my thought.

"No, not him. My *first* husband." With a panicked glance toward the door, she flung herself toward the heavy drapes beside my window, disappearing into their voluminous mass.

My eye flicked over those sentences, picking out the first letters of each word, and the last letters of the third.

Go and run away—make off now, dear.
Ghosts are real, and may one never die.
Darling Aura, fair Aura, I'm too soon dead.
G-A-R-A-M—

The door flung open and I turned, shoving the papers under a notebook.

"Garamond. Lord Gaffney. What are you doing here?"

36

Hothouse flowers and hothouse women should always be left where they are. For you can never re-create or maintain the flawless environment to which they've become accustomed.

~Nathaniel Droll, *Lady Jayne Disappears*

I strode hastily toward the interloper to keep him from coming near the window. His narrow face had taken on a green cast, his eyes wide and panicked as his gaze locked on me.

"What's happened? What isn't she telling me?" Garamond's pasty face appeared even more pale as he closed the gap between us in two steps, gripping my arms. "Tell me."

"Who?" I stiffened in his grip.

"Lady Pochard said you'd been to see Jayne, as if you'd found her alive." Sweat gathered at his receding hairline and dripped down his sideburns. "Where is she? Where is my wife?" He shoved back suddenly and lurched forward, grabbing his knees as rasping breaths shook him.

My mother. He was referring to my mother.

Arm around his back, I moved quickly into helper mode, guiding him to the chair near the door and easing him into it as he convulsed. Whipping a towel off the stand, I dipped it in the washbasin and returned to smear the cool water across his head. "Shhh. Easy, easy."

His breathing slowed and the trembling of his shoulders lessened. When his neck had regained a slightly rosy hue, he drew his head up and sat back against the chair to look at me. "I'm sorry. So sorry." His haggard, fleshy face seemed aged. "You must think me mad. Please, we mustn't tell Glenna anything. She's such a delicate flower, I'm afraid it would break her."

"I shan't tell a soul."

Here he sat, the man Papa's clues pointed toward, but the weak form seemed harmless as a twig. Taking the cloth from me, he swiped his moist upper lip and blotted the rest of his face.

"Shall I ring for your man to fetch you?"

He shook his head, oily hair falling around his temples. He smoothed it back into place with both hands and centered his gaze on me. "I've only recently found out that you were the child. You were the one born to my Jayne and her . . . her lover. What have they told you? Woolf would have made up a grand story, of course."

"Actually, he told me nothing. I knew very little of my mother before coming here."

"That awful serial novel tells the whole story." His face shifted away, hands framing his haggard face. "I'd thought it was Woolf writing it, until I heard he'd died, and then I began to wonder . . ." He laughed awkwardly. "Perhaps it was his ghost. No one else knows that much about what happened. Not even Glenna."

"You've managed to keep this from her all these years?"
A wry grin flicked over his face. "And *I'm* sharp as custard,
eh?" He dropped his gaze. "She knew of Jayne, but nothing of
her unfaithfulness or disappearance. I was such a fool to think
everything with Jayne would all disappear. Quite honestly, I
never expected Glenna's interest in me to last all those years
ago, so I carried on as if Jayne had died, and that was that."

"You didn't divorce your first wife?"

He shook his head. "They told me she died after the birth.
That she had the baby and ran away and could not survive
the elements. I searched for her, but I almost couldn't bear to
see her again. Her betrayal had sliced clean through me, and
Glenna's gentle love had only begun to heal the wound. We
finally had Jayne declared dead a year later—myself and my
employer, Lady Pochard's late husband. I signed the certifi-
cate myself, but I knew it was possible she remained alive."
His shoulders shook again. "I knew it deep down."

"Then why did you sign it?"

Guilt jetted across his face, tinging his skin with crimson
hues. "I wished her dead. With Glenna suddenly in my life
and my heart, I wanted nothing more than to bury her and
never look upon her wretched face again." He gulped, staring at his clenched hands.

"If Glenna loved you, why didn't you simply tell her the
whole truth?"

"I'd have lost her for sure. I couldn't push my luck—below
her in class as I was, and with a boy of my own to raise besides."

"A boy?" My mind worked to piece it all together.

"Yes, of course, Kendrick. Just a lad when his mother
disappeared."

I simply stared up at him, speechless. He was the child

Lady Jayne had birthed with the simple husband that had sucked the life from her. That made Kendrick my half brother.

"That was another reason I'd convinced myself she'd died. What woman would abandon her child?"

Pain ricocheted through me and I dropped my gaze.

He lifted tired eyes lined with saggy skin and searched my face, his thumbs wrestling one another on his lap. "I'd ask you again what you found, but now I cannot. I no longer wish to know what has happened to Jayne." He stilled his hands and stared at them as if they were foreign objects. "It is best I do not find out, don't you agree?"

I looked involuntarily at the curtains, now blowing heartily in the wind. And as a heavy breeze lifted and twirled them, I saw the empty wall and the open window beyond. Once again she had disappeared. After a deep, cleansing sigh, I responded. "I do agree. Put it behind you and simply enjoy your family. You deserve them."

His face sank into relief. "Nothing would make me happier. I have only to keep Glenna from reading the end of Lady Jayne or stop Mr. Droll from declaring my secrets. If only I had the slightest idea who he was."

I pinched my lips and averted my eyes, my secret simmering at the surface.

When I later closed the door on the world-weary man and his burdens, Papa's notes returned to spark my memory. I stared at the chair he'd occupied. No matter what Papa had supposed in his guilt, this man was not his killer.

By Thursday, publication day for the final installment of *Lady Jayne Disappears*, my worries had turned to Silas.

The household seemed to have forgotten about the finale. Everyone except its author.

I practically assaulted Digory in the hall late that afternoon. "Might I glance through the latest Nathaniel Droll?"

Some grand announcement Lady Gaffney was to make at dinner had thoroughly upset and distracted everyone in the house. Even poor Digory. He glanced into the great hall, still empty in the sunny afternoon light, and pulled the rolled-up pamphlet from his coat pocket. "I suppose, if you read quickly. The other servants are fighting over who shall be the first among them to read it."

"Oh, I'll read it ever so quickly." I snatched it before he could change his mind. "I only wish to glance at a single page."

In the quiet of the great hall, I pulled open the familiar green paper-bound volume that determined the fate of my only romance. Flipping to the serial fiction section, my heart pounded through my fingertips, and heat flushed my face as my gaze absorbed the words I could not comprehend quickly enough.

The Tiger of Tierzan

by Raymond James Turner

(Editor's note: We break from our normal story to bring you this first issue of an exciting new series. We hope this will only heighten your anticipation for the grand finale of Nathaniel Droll's *Lady Jayne Disappears*, which will appear in the next publication.)

My breath hitched as my heart spasmed and then recovered. What were they doing? And which ending would they print? One thought rolled over my mind—I had to wait another week to know anything.

But then the grand clock in the hall bonged out the hour of dinnertime, and the family gathered in the great hall. As they wound their way into the space, the front doors opened and footsteps echoed across the open tile. I held my breath as the newcomer rounded the corner and came near. The footfall was too heavy to be Juliette's, and Jasper would not dare show his face here—would he?

Only one other man was missing from our company. I watched eagerly for his face. I had need of Silas now more than ever and a bevy of things begging to be said.

"My apologies on being tardy." Kendrick strode into our midst. "I came right away when I received your message."

Kendrick. My half brother.

"We are only about to be seated." Glenna took his arm and propelled him toward the double doors.

"Really, Mother? You're going to hold me in suspense about your grand announcement?"

"I most certainly am."

The drawing room surged with energy as we strode in. Hushed voices murmured, even among the staff, speculating about the promised announcement. An undercurrent of anticipation tingled in the air as the servants gathered to enter the dining room with us.

"And now, we go in to dinner." With a smile and a dramatic flourish, Glenna threw open the dining room doors. There on the other side stood Juliette, adorned in a gold dinner gown and yellow flowers in her upswept hair, Lord Sutherland the accessory at her side. With a cry of relief, I dropped Clem's arm and ran to her, embracing her dear figure. "I'm so glad."

"You were right about that man after all," she whispered. "But I'll never admit such things outside of this room." She winked. "Nathaniel Droll is quite an informant. He delivered all I needed to know about Jasper just in time."

And in that moment, my writerly joy was nearly complete.

The family surged around her then, forcing us apart as they fought over her with joyous chatter. It felt like a festive holiday when we at last took our seats, everyone talking eagerly.

When the gelatin was served in little crystal bowls on stems, Glenna rose and tapped her spoon against her dessert cup. "That was only the first grand announcement of the night, and now you shall have the other. And you can decide for yourselves if it has lived up to your great anticipation."

Garamond frowned, Aunt Eudora rolled her eyes, and Garamond's two sons watched with anticipation. Servants clambered over each other for space at the fringes of the room.

"In addition to the return of our dear girl"—she cinched her daughter close with one arm—"we've discovered another wonderful secret." The apples of her plump cheeks glowed as if they'd burst.

Whispers moved through the gathered crowd of servants and family. I dared not breathe.

"Together we've discovered the identity of Nathaniel Droll, who comes in a form we'd never expect. Our interloper is none other than . . ."

Nelle stumbled through the service entrance, propelled by another servant. The sight released commotion in the room.

". . . Nelle Wicke."

"Mother, that's impossible!" Clem shot out of his seat, his face red behind his freckles.

Garamond paled, his eyebrows moving up and down. Kendrick scowled. Murmurs rippled through the quiet room as Nelle huddled near the door, her face a mask of fear.

"Oh, for heaven's sake." Aunt Eudora fell back in her chair, placing her jeweled fingers over her eyes.

Glenna straightened and leaned toward the head chair. "Mother, do you not find it convenient that the little seamstress's disappearance from the estate so perfectly coincided with Nathaniel Droll installments mysteriously ceasing on the verge of the final one?"

"Are you positive?" Kendrick's stony face across the table alarmed me. "All this time, Nelle Wicke was the one writing that drivel?"

"Absolutely certain." Glenna straightened as she sank into her chair and turned to her daughter. "Tell them what happened."

"Miss Wicke was measuring my gown for adjustments last week and we began talking about Nathaniel Droll. She mentioned a little detail I hadn't remembered seeing in the story, but I thought nothing of it. Until"—the girl's eyes glowed—"that very same detail appeared in the next installment. Yet somehow Miss Wicke knew of it before it was published."

My head swam. Nelle shrank back as the servants murmured around us.

"I happened upon the little thing in the chemist's shop while I waited, and I knew I'd found the true spy as soon as I'd read it."

"No!" Nelle's voice pinched in panic. "I never—"

"And this afternoon I found her hiding in the old garden shed."

Glenna broke into the story. "Imagine that, dismissed from her position and hiding out in the shed. Watching the house and gathering material for her next installment, no doubt."

"Have you any idea what you've done to this family?" Kendrick rose, spiking his napkin on the table. "We provide your house and food, and you make fools of us all?"

"Kendrick, enough." Aunt Eudora thumped the table, rattling the silverware. "This is ridiculous. I highly doubt Miss Wicke is Nathaniel Droll. She's only lived on the estate these five or six years."

"I should have known all along it was her." Kendrick seethed at the trembling figure. "No other servant in this entire house has tried so hard to rise above her station, chumming about with one of the family, seducing a valued guest."

"Kendrick, stop this immediately." Aunt Eudora stood, leaning heavily on the white-clothed table. "You are making a fool of yourself."

"I will not! How many offenses must this girl commit before you turn her away from Lynhurst? Will you allow your own servants to publicly humiliate your family and walk away unscathed? Call the constable. If you will not deal with the matter, I will. Slandering one's employer is a punishable offense, and she'll find herself in Shepton Mallet before the day's out."

Tears pooled in Nelle's wide eyes. With quick glances toward the door, she crept toward it.

"This isn't why I brought her here." Juliette glared at her brother. "It was meant as a novelty to uncover Nathaniel Droll, not vengeance."

"Look, she tries to escape. Do you still call her innocent?"

Kendrick strode around the table to guard the exit. "You will not avoid punishment, Miss Wicke, unless you can prove to us that you did not write those things."

My stomach churned and Nelle cowered further.

"Well, speak!" He advanced menacingly.

"Stop!" I shot up, knocking my plate into my glass and rattling the silverware. "Leave her alone. She is not Nathaniel Droll." I filled my lungs with air and stared directly at the angry man. "I am."

Chaos erupted at this, servants and family alike shouting their opinions.

"Listen to me." But my soft voice was no match for the noise. Balling my fists in helpless frustration, I sprinted from the room and hiked up the stairs to my bedchamber where I fell upon my shelves of notebooks. Grabbing handfuls of them filled with notes, discarded issues, and the like, I hurried back down the stairs and into the dining room. The din had only heightened, with servants outnumbering the family. Nelle shuddered in the corner.

"I have proof." But the noise continued. "Listen to me!" When the voices did not cease, frustration welled up, tightening in my arms, until I ground my teeth and slammed the stack of notebooks with a resounding *thud* on the wood floor. The room hushed to whispers as the attention finally turned to me.

"If you insist on knowing the truth, on whom you must eject from Lynhurst, it is I. I am Nathaniel Droll. I wrote about the hidden candy, the loose corset, Juliette's secret trysts, all the spectacles of this household." I looked at them, frozen like a still-life painting—Aunt Eudora sitting placidly with her hands folded on the table, Clem watching with utter shock, Glenna with an unladylike gaping mouth. Kendrick pivoted his burning glare to me, summing me up with disdain as if he wished to scorch me with his eyes. My heart pounded and I looked away.

"You shrewd little minx." Juliette watched me with narrowed eyes. "If I didn't really like you, I'd hate you. And to think of all I've confided in you."

And Garamond. The poor little man quaked in his chair as if surrounded by a firing squadron. He stared at me, the whites of his eyes showing. Our gazes met and held, his begging and questioning at the same time. I returned it with a slight nod that promised I'd keep his secret. He visibly relaxed against his chair.

"You worthless little rat." Glenna's voice cut the stunned afterglow of my announcement. "Perhaps now you'll believe me about her, Mother."

Digory ushered Nelle silently through the service door as the attention focused on me.

"I think it was a rather ingenious repayment, considering the way you treated the girl." Aunt Eudora's voice rose across the table. "Rather than say to your face what a degrading fool you are, she simply took her revenge on a fictional representation."

"Whatever does that mean?"

"I mean, instead of announcing in front of everyone all the spiteful things you deserved to hear, she merely wrote you into her book. And then punished your character." Aunt Eudora turned in her throne-like chair to me. "I applaud your panache, dear child. You exacted revenge with elegance and wit that outshines any of us here. *Now* you remind me of your father."

And then everyone spoke at once, each trying to be heard over the others.

In the din of the crowded room, I also slipped out the side door and through the now-empty service hall. Making my way into the eerily silent great hall, I tiptoed down the narrow passage jutting off to the south. Perhaps I could still catch Nelle. A charged silence rolled through the long hall where I walked alone. It was not a calming quiet, but a terrible threat just before a storm. Boots clopped in the dark somewhere behind me and I slowed my steps, just in case. In case, what? Did I really believe Silas would return for me? What a moment for him to enter.

A door closed somewhere, a deadbolt clacking into place with an echo. Panic sizzled. I gulped as my fingers began to tremble. And suddenly it occurred to me that my father's murderer remained at Lynhurst. I moved quickly through the dark hall as a small light bobbed toward me from behind. I sped up. Finally the light dropped, as if extinguished, and the footsteps neared quickly.

I turned and ran blindly ahead, but a solid arm grabbed me and yanked me into a room thick with moldy odors and dust. Strong hands shoved me to the ground. Garamond?

But it was Kendrick, tall and hunched with anger, hovering over me with a foreboding menace to his expression. "How did you know those things?"

"What things?" I backed into the shadows, nearly toppling a dead potted ficus.

"What you said about my mother. Those disgusting lies you wrote." He advanced faster than I backed up, and my heart pounded.

"She was my mother too."

He stood before me, dangerously quiet except for his labored breathing, anger twisting his features. "I should have known it was you all this time. Only you would know about her. You, who stole her from her family."

"Please, Kendrick."

I rose and he shoved me back. "Do you have any idea—any *clue*—what you've done?" Another shove and I stumbled back onto a plush red rug, banging my elbow against the floor beyond it. "The way you wrote it. What you said about them. What you . . ." He trembled above me, loose hair shaking over his veined forehead.

"I had no idea of the real story."

He lunged, jerking me up and pinning me to the wall, his hands bruising my upper arms where he clasped them. "How *dare* you make it look beautiful." His face scowled inches from mine, sweat dripping from the point of his nose. "That disgusting, vile story between a gambler and a married woman. Between a dirty charmer and my *mother!*"

Tears poured down my temples as I leaned away.

"Do you have any idea what it was like?" His voice grew soft, his trembling fingers vibrating against the ache they'd caused in my arms. "I was eight years old when my mother plucked me off her side to spend all her time with that man who was not my father. *Eight* when she disappeared from my life forever, never looking back, because she chose to be your mother instead of mine. Does that sound like a beautiful romance to you? *Does it?*" He shook me twice.

"She didn't choose me either." I forced the whispered words past my trembling lips.

His eyes narrowed. "Liar."

"It's true. I didn't even know her name until my father began telling me the story of *Lady Jayne Disappears.*"

"You lie! You just admitted to writing those things. Do you

have any idea what you've done, the trouble you've caused? I thought it was Woolf . . ." Fire flashed across his eyes so near mine as he spoke Papa's name, and that's when the truth struck me. It pierced and then swelled with clarity through my mind. What had Papa's letter said? He'd only guessed at his killer when he'd received threats.

And he'd been wrong.

"It was you." I breathed the words in disbelief. "You killed him." Garamond wouldn't. *Couldn't.* But Kendrick . . .

His lithe body tensed, hate seeming to ooze out of his pores as sweat. "The man has enemies wherever he goes. You cannot blame me."

I studied his face, realization turning to fury. "You murdered him. He left me proof." The lie slipped out and had the desired effect before my conscience could even nip at me.

"It was an accident." He released my arms and sprang back as I crumpled at his feet. "I wanted to scare him, make him stop writing about her. But he wouldn't." Tears glistened on his cheeks in the moonlight cutting through the windows on his left. "I went to talk to him and he wouldn't say a word. Not a single word." He clutched his hair. "I poked, but he refused to react. To say anything. I poked harder and harder, but he just . . . sat there. Like a lump. A worthless lump. I charged at him, screamed in his face."

Tears thickened behind my eyes as I imagined it.

"Nothing. Like my pain, my whole life, didn't matter a speck. And then I saw a board . . ."

The doors banged open behind him, light framing a dark-suited man. "Don't you touch her." Digory moved toward us like a force and grabbed Kendrick, yanking him back in his shock.

Others crowded into the doorway, blocking the light from someone's candle in the hall. "Kendrick, what is this about?" Garamond's voice carried through the empty room.

Digory bent to help me up and together we rose, facing Kendrick, who stared at us with the whites of his eyes gleaming in the dimly lit room.

"Kendrick?"

Glenna's voice jarred him. Jerking his head toward the family, then back at me, he spun and shoved past them, charging into the dark, his panting breaths echoing back to us.

Knees buckling, I clung to Digory, who supported my weight with surprising ease and embraced me, patting my hair. Then, when my legs again solidified, we moved toward the doorway and the family I had upended with my stories.

I walked past them all and avoided their gazes, but I stopped at the formidable wall of my aunt Eudora, whose stony face studied me with all the emotion of a statue from her wheeled chair.

"I'm so sorry. For my father, for my mother . . . and for ruining your household with Nathaniel Droll."

Her grimace cracked and a smile wobbled her lips. "What will be fixed must first be broken."

37

She wore bright colors and flowers in her hair even on ordinary days because life itself, the fleeting, precious gift, was her special occasion.

~Nathaniel Droll, *Lady Jayne Disappears*

They did not find Kendrick, but somehow God provided me a buffer against fear. After the wordless embrace of my family in the wake of Kendrick's terror, I felt protected in this house. If not by them, then by God himself.

My lone footsteps echoed in the grand hall later that night as I walked about, hoping to tire myself into a long slumber. When another set of steps slapped over the tile, I turned to face Clem approaching with bowed shoulders and a grim face. "It was good of you to save Nelle that way." He paused before me, hands in his trouser pockets. "I owe you an apology."

"Certainly not." I laid a hand on his arm. "You acted out of love for Dahlia."

His shoulders hunched. "I couldn't even say goodbye to her. I've no idea where they are. I simply have to trust they're safe."

"I have a feeling Silas Rotherham will make sure of that."

"I wanted to tell you about that." He rocked back on his heels, eyes downcast. "I should have told you when I found out, but I couldn't bear to. But you deserve to know."

"What is it?"

"There was no proposal. I spoke with Nelle when I found her in the garden shed, and she told me. The only proposal Silas gave her was of a business nature. He gave her a loan for a machine that'll do her sewing so she can open a shop. I couldn't even bear to tell her I'd told everyone about their engagement."

My heart thudded into my ribs. "Truly?"

He nodded. "They were never in love. Not even when I wished it."

Hot and cold surged through me. I squeezed the boy's arm. "Silas is not her only hope, Clem. She will do well. She's quiet but strong."

Another nod, and the boy excused himself, slipping into the billiards room.

I silently drank in the truth of his words, basking in the hope they provided. They brought such relief, but sadness followed it as I remembered my rejection of the man. And the ending—oh, if only they would not abide by my request this time. That ending could change everything, if only they would print the one I'd begged them not to.

Loneliness and defeat wrapped itself about me like a blanket. Craving connection to one of my own, I found my way down the halls again to the south tower with the help of a candle. But when I stepped into the rounded chamber, I sensed only hollow disappointment. Used and discarded, this room contained only remnants of the person who had once occupied it. And that woman no longer moved about in my mind as a sweet, fragrant dream, but as something tarnished and broken.

Just like memories of Papa. The wild, joyful storyteller had large holes in his character that my daughter-eyes had always glossed over, but maturity and truth had brought reality. As well as supreme disappointment.

And suddenly, I had no one with whom to connect. I had lost Silas by my own actions and I could no longer think of my parents, either of them, with the fond sense of shared identity I once had. Looking out across the lawn, I spotted the windows of the chapel glowing with inner light. Likely Aunt Eudora's current sanctuary. Somehow those stained-glass windows mirrored what I knew of my parents—beautiful, colorful, vivid . . . and broken into a million pieces.

And then there was me, the girl with the too-soft heart and quiet life. I had no interest in the social excitement and high fashion my Lynhurst family centered their life on, but neither did I resonate with my parents' desire to chase the fleeting sensations of happiness and romance with such abandon. All of their lives were far more complicated than I'd ever guessed, and somehow I'd been born into the middle of it. Me, plain and simple me. More out of place than ever before.

God, where do I belong?

And in that very question came my answer, sweeping over me with powerful force. Sinking onto my knees on the thick rug before the bed, I rested in his presence for long moments until his familiar calm stole over me with soul-drenching peace. I basked in it, fearing nothing, grateful for all of him.

"Sometimes it's desirable to not fit into such a broken place."

Silas's words now haunted me with their truth. I did not fit into this place, and that was all right. No, more than all right. What would I be if I did belong? Selfish. Scheming. Hurtful. Broken and eventually bitter.

I wanted none of that. No wonder I'd never felt comfortable at Lynhurst. There in the south tower, with the fading day outside the window, I mentally tugged apart the character of Lady Jayne in my novel and the real woman, for no one would want such a heroine. The fictional Lady Jayne would be good and sweet and loving, everything I could want in a mother. It was so far from the truth, but it bound up the wound in me that would always exist concerning the woman. Once again fiction would smooth over the harsh realities of my world and allow me to enjoy what I could never possess.

Heavy with peace and assurance, I climbed onto the bed and dropped face-first onto the soft comforter. And like a dark blanket, exhaustion swept over me and I slept the night in my mother's room.

Morning dawned with brilliant orange and red streams of light prisming through a thick fog. I woke early with the realization that I was finished writing, possibly forever. For the final installment of *Lady Jayne Disappears* had been completed, whichever one they chose to use. Standing up in the chilly room, I gathered a shawl to myself and wrapped it around my nearly bare arms.

Running fingers through my loosened hair and removing the pins, I stretched my legs under my rumpled skirts and crossed to the armoire. An overwhelming wistfulness came over me as I fingered my mother's gowns. In a moment of spontaneity, I released one from its hanger and held it up to my own body. Yes, we certainly had the same slender figure.

Struggling to undo the stays and buttons on my own dress, and using the trifold mirror for help, I peeled the lightly moist garment from my body and slipped into a deep-amethyst-colored gown from the armoire. The bodice, ruched with tiny gold flowers, hugged my torso, and the skirt fell from my waist in a waterfall of tucks and gathers. Standing before the tall mirror inside the armoire door, I spun, arms out, enjoying the swish of the luxurious fabric. It was one of the simpler gowns in the wardrobe, and less voluminous, yet still as lavish as artwork.

Would Papa approve? Had I the patience to pile my dark hair atop my head and sprinkle it with pink roses, I would look so much like her in the painting.

Tugging the stubborn window open, I climbed onto the sill and sat to watch a fresh day awaken, nearly close enough in this first-floor bedroom to brush the grass with my fingertips. I leaned my head back to drink in the wet scent of the outdoors, and when I opened my eyes, a lone horse and rider galloped across the yard toward the stables, scattering the fog in its path. With a jerk, the horse tossed its head and pivoted in the hazy sunlight, paused, and then righted its course toward the house. Had the rider seen me?

My chest tightened. Astride the horse sat the one figure

I would never erase from my mind, for he had crept in and gently, permanently encircled my heart. The horse pounded closer and chills climbed my skin. When he neared, I saw Silas's face—that precious face, an ocean of kindness spilling from its planes.

I pushed off the sill, landing barefoot in the wet grass a half story below, but a sudden shyness rooted me to the spot. The ground vibrated with the power of horse hooves as the animal drove closer. Dancing to a stop halfway to me, the horse bucked its head, and I had a sudden memory of the elation I'd felt as I flew over the landscape on horseback. But the exhilaration from the present moment greatly eclipsed it, overwhelming me with waves of exceeding joy.

Silas dismounted in one smooth movement and led the horse forward to close the distance, his open coat flapping about him. As he neared, his face ruddy and glowing with the morning wind, he extended a worn, floppy book. "I've come to make you rewrite this." His dark hair whipped across his forehead.

Shocked into stillness, I blinked and stepped closer. "What is it?" I accepted the volume and flipped through the pages. My own curly handwriting stared back at me. It was my original ending, the one I had dreaded seeing in print. The collection of my most intimate feelings for the man now extending it to me.

"You must rewrite it. I insist."

Heat flamed through me. "How did you—"

He tossed the book in the grass beside us and caught up my hands, twining our fingers. I did not stop him. "Lady Jayne does not give up so easily. Not when her love for Charles is so powerful throughout the whole book." His fingers pulled back and then sank into my hair, reveling in the tresses as the wind blew it about. It seemed too good to be true. "If she loves him, she shouldn't let anything keep them apart."

"She chose to give him up because she thought he loved her dearest friend."

"Perhaps she was mistaken." His steady gaze pinned mine as he pulled me to him.

"Her friend needs Charles so much more than she does."

"But Charles needs Lady Jayne."

"Oh." The word came out on a single breath as I laid my head against his coat.

He tightened his embrace as if I'd threatened to run again and spoke, the heartfelt words rumbling through his chest where my cheek rested. "I love you, Aurelie. So much." The words rushed forth, as if he had to push them past a barrier. "The very fact that you do not fit in here, with these broken people. The fact that you do not feel comfortable among them."

"I shall always be out of place with wealthy society."

He bent and placed a solemn kiss atop my head. "My dear Aurelie, if you fit into this world, this very broken, selfish place, it would be *you* who was the wrong size."

Tears heated behind my eyes. Once again my Father lavished his love upon me through this man who had so often been his instrument of rescue in my life.

Silas's hands slid up my back to my shoulders and cupped them, gently moving me back to look into my face. "Rewrite the ending, dearest. For me." Shutting his eyes, he bent near to rest his forehead against mine. The sweet scent of him mingled with the cool air.

I could not bear to look directly at him, so I closed my eyes and did as he asked. I spoke through the tears that dripped down my face. "As she looked back over the house far behind her, it nearly broke Lady Jayne to give Charles up, for he had earned his way into her heart with his very character and being, and no amount of time or love from another could wrench him out. She loved him quickly and fiercely, never wanting to be without him." I sniffed and looked up at him.

He pulled back to search my face, those gray eyes now a magnet for mine.

I delivered my next sentences with all the passion welling up in me in that heady moment. "But when Lady Jayne learned he loved her too, and only her, she sprinted after him and embraced him, exploding with all the bottled-up love and longing of her heart and—"

His warm lips found mine and sealed them with a kiss that was deep and powerful, dipping me back for a fuller drink. Again his fingers dove into my hair and drew me against him, the other hand caressing my back. I released my fears and sank into it, gently pulling his face closer for more. These were Silas's hands clinging to me, holding me to him. His lips exploring my face, my neck.

When he finally moved back, still holding me close, his eyes were closed and his cheeks ruddy. "I've waited far too long to do that." And with a smile creeping over his handsome face, he pulled me to him and kissed me again, anchoring me close with the force of his pent-up passion.

When we finally parted, I laughed as my mind righted itself. Our joint shadow stretched all the way to the house in the long rays of sunrise as we stood before one another. Together we knelt and then lay side by side in the grass dotted with little white flowers, hands clasped between us. The beauty of the moment eclipsed any other thought until only peace and brilliant happiness remained.

"I never thought you would return after the way you left." The words slipped out of my giddy brain.

"It isn't every day a man is able to see his girl's love for him in black and white." He squeezed my hand, then caressed the curves and knuckles with his thumb. "You were right, you know. Books are not always an escape. Sometimes they untangle real life marvelously well."

I smiled, eyes sliding closed. "Papa would have loved you."

"Actually, he did."

My eyes flew open and I searched his for an explanation.

"We visited Lynhurst every summer of my childhood so I could see my school chum Kendrick. A delightful man named Woolf caught me up while I was in my darkest, most lonely youthful moments and kindled within me a love of stories. I loved him dearly for it and returned to see him every year, eventually more so than Kendrick."

Papa. I blinked toward the sky. His words about my controversial father balmed my heart. "You truly enjoyed him, didn't you?"

He nodded against his hand that propped up his head. "He saw something good in me when few others did. I lived my adult life by that example. Ah, and I have something else you might like." He sprang up and walked to his horse to untether a long, smooth stick. "All these years, this has been a permanent fixture in my private chamber. It was your father's walking stick. They gave it to me the summer Woolf vanished." He lay beside me on his side, propped on one elbow, and laid the stick in the grass between us, touching the rough engravings. "Together we walked, invented wild tales, and discussed books.

These are the characters from his stories. See, there is Lenny the Leprechaun, and that one is Harry the Crab."

Tears clogged my lashes and I turned away from the walking stick, grass tickling my warm face. *Thy rod and thy staff, they comfort me.* "That's how you knew to search for Nathaniel Droll at Lynhurst. You'd met him before."

"That I had. At least, I'd thought it was him."

"But what on earth drove you to search for him all summer? Certainly you didn't hope to gain anything from finding him."

"When the imposter Nathaniel Drolls surfaced, my father tasked me with finding the real man and setting the whole mess to rights. I assured him I had inside information on this author and could find the truth. My father didn't even remember discussing his newly rising publishing company with Woolf on his visits here, but I'm sure now that he must have. And then when I returned home with only some of the answers a few days ago, my father told me about this snit of a girl who'd come into his office . . ."

"Snit of a girl."

Only one person had ever called me that. The words resonated in my mind, piercing my memory. As they slid into place, I sat up. "Ram? Your father is Ram, of Marsh House Press?" Ram, short for Rotherham. Of course.

"How do you think I came by the manuscript that has not seen publication?"

"You are the publisher."

"That is correct. Years ago, when we first began Marsh House Press, this man called Nathaniel Droll sent us a few short fiction pieces. Said he was a family friend who had heard of our small press and wanted to offer us his work. We weren't in a position to turn away a capable writer, so we printed it. Eventually we had him doing longer serial pieces when the shorter ones did well. When his fiction began selling in record numbers, we signed him on for more, and created a periodical specifically for his work. We always accommodated his demands for privacy, for blank checks. We hadn't a clue of his true identity for years, other than what he'd said about being a family friend. I'm not even certain when I knew it was Woolf, but I eventually had an idea of it when I recognized the setting and the style of the tales."

I lay back again, staring at the clear sky, pondering everything, connecting the pieces with wonder. "You are the one who decided to delay the printing of the final issue."

"That I am. And with good reason." He leaned close and propped up on his elbow to brush the fallen hair off my cheek, then he kissed the spot. "I dearly hoped for a happier ending."

A smile lit me from the inside out and I gingerly touched his face with my fingertip. "And you shall have it, my dear Mr. Rotherham." But in that perfect moment, with God flooding my soul, Silas beside me, and Papa's Lynhurst Manor in the distance, my heart released its fisted hold on Nathaniel Droll. What need had I for that childhood relic? "But only in the realm of reality. I shall no longer write novels after this."

"I cannot allow that." He rolled over and sat up, his frame blocking the sun as he looked down at me. "You would cease to be Aurelie Rosette Harcourt if you stopped writing. No, you will never stop, no matter what you say. Do you realize what a tool you've been given to reach people, to impact them with truth they desperately need?"

"I'm not sure my heart can handle the critics." The honest words were wrenched from the hidden vulnerabilities I'd managed to bury just below the surface. The admission nearly brought tears to my eyes as the words of an unknown reader avalanched over me once again.

"You will. You'll bear it because there will be two of us under that load." His gray eyes penetrated as a solemn promise lit them.

I sat up then and faced him, twining my fingers with his. How could I explain? "I don't think you understand what it feels like to have strangers read your secret journal in story form and do and say anything they like about it. They rip it to shreds with their words like knives and leave you bare and . . ."

His thumb slid across my lips, slowing the flow of my words, then his hand cupped my cheek tenderly. "Aurelie. There's a boy drowning in the English Channel. And an entire beach full of people observing your every move, but God saying, *Go!*" Those gray eyes sparkled with the intensity in his heart as he framed my face with firm hands. "Now go and swim like mad."

Surely goodness and mercy shall follow me all the days of my life: and I will dwell in the house of the LORD for ever. (Psalm 23:6)

If I find in myself desires which nothing in this world can satisfy, the only logical explanation is that I was made for another world.

~C. S. Lewis

Keep Reading for a
SNEAK PEEK
at Joanna's New Book

COMING SUMMER 2018

PROLOGUE

Never let common sense stand in the way of a great
legend, they say, and there's wisdom in that. Because
on occasion, those great legends turn out to be true.

~*The Vineyard's Secret*, notebook of a viticulturist

Weston-Super-Mare
Somerset, England, 1866

"It's you, isn't it?" The gnarled old hand shot out to grab mine
across the chipped counter of the Dark Horse Inn's serving
room and anchored it there. From beneath my hooded cloak,
I met the old woman's gaze that sparkled with interest and
held a finger to my lips as the loud words of the two men
beside me ignited my curiosity. I didn't set out to eavesdrop,
but some conversations are simply too interesting to avoid
overhearing.

"I say that Tressa Harlowe's dead. It's the only explanation for it."

Especially when the topic discussed by these strangers was me. In such cases, it was like I had no choice but to absorb every word, for wasn't it my business even more than theirs? I gazed from my shadowed corner of the dim room at the greasy little man who spoke these words and thanked my lucky stars I'd lost my way in the rain and wandered into this awful place.

The brutish man beside him tore off a hunk of bread and plunged it in his mug as he answered. "Dead? Ach, no. She's too smart for that."

His mousy little companion hunched over his mug as if his frame couldn't support its own weight. "Either way, she's been away from the castle for nearly four months. It's the perfect opportunity, Hamish."

I could hardly wait to hear what opportunity my absence afforded them. I leaned forward and reached for my hot tea, drawing it into the folds of my cloak as I listened.

"So what exactly are you asking me to do, Tom Parsons?"

I breathed deeply in anticipation of the response and my genteel senses were flooded with the putrid scent of the place, the sharp aroma of cheap, greasy food and working-class men.

"I'm suggesting we avail ourselves of an abandoned treasure. No different than mining, simply digging for gold."

Hamish thunked two meaty forearms on the rough counter. "Look, you know how I feel about thieving from the rich. But I'll not go stealing from the likes of Tressa Harlowe. Much as I need that new horse, I won't do it. If that hidden fortune exists, and that's a mighty big *if*, well, then she deserves it."

"It seems everyone loves that little princess of the castle."

Tom Parsons wrinkled his nose as if he could offer no suitable reason for this affection toward me.

Princess. I nearly spit my tea onto the wood floor as laughter threatened.

"Such a lot of life packed into a little mite of a girl."

"I daresay I'd be full of life if I stood to inherit ten thousand a year." The man's narrow lips pinched with resentment. "What does that girl need with a fortune anyway? Won't she have a hundred rooms all to herself one day? I've two up, two down, and ten people to fill them."

What did he know about rooms? Little good it did to have a hundred rooms or a thousand if most were devoid of life.

Parsons spoke again, sniffing at his tea. "It'd be mad not to take such an opportunity. It's like a golden egg with no goose to guard it."

"Ach, you're a fool." Hamish threw his head back to down the last of his cider and then thunked the pewter mug back onto the counter. "She'll be back when she hears what's happened. Any day that fancy carriage of hers will come rattling down the road, spraying mud on all us common folk as she comes to claim her own."

I froze, straining to hear the rest.

What? What had happened at my home? Father's summons now seemed ominous rather than exciting.

The proprietor strode through the crowd then and approached me, his sleeves rolled up to his elbows. "There's a man willing to take you to Trevelyan's outer gates, but no further. He's by the door waiting."

I stiffened as his direct address lifted my cloak of obscurity. "Thank you, sir."

"But save yourself the trip. With all the goings-on at Trevelyan, they won't be looking for help."

Before my curiosity at these words took root, both men at the bar pivoted to face me, their two pairs of eyes seeing me for the first time. I fancied a light of recognition glowed from Hamish's face, but Tom Parsons merely observed me with a hint of annoyance at the interruption.

I rose and pushed back my shoulders, bestowing a gracious parting smile toward them both. "Good evening, gentlemen." I moved past them, holding my breath as I squeezed between the tightly packed patrons, and then turned back. "You are most correct, by the way. The fortune does exist. I'll warn you though, it's guarded by the princess of the castle, and I suggest you do not underestimate her." With a polite smile, I turned again toward the door and sailed through the crowds.

Near the exit, I approached the proprietor. "There's a man named Hamish there at the bar. Please find out where he lives and send the information up to Trevelyan." I dropped a farthing in his hand. The man would have his horse. One of the best parts of eavesdropping was discovering unexpected kindness, for it was a rarity in my world, and I delighted in rewarding it. Such was the only benefit of being an heiress.

Outside, rain poured off the metal roof of the porch, creating a curtain of wetness between me and the waiting cart. I ducked and ran to the vehicle, where a man hoisted me into the dark chamber, climbed in, and slammed the door behind us.

I had never seen the legendary fortune my father had hidden, but I'd always known of it, like one knows of the queen without ever meeting her. It had haunted me until one day in my thirteenth year when I'd been brazen enough to ask him about it directly.

"I'll tell you where it is when I'm dying," he'd said with his usual gruff dismissiveness, and I'd considered the matter resolved and did not ask again.

For at that time in my life, I believed him.

1

What you plant, you should harvest and enjoy without delay, for one never knows when his time will be up.

~*The Vineyard's Secret*, notebook of a viticulturist

I sprinted toward an abandoned barn and huddled under the eaves to wring out the ends of my sopping wet cloak and peer up at my destination. Trevelyan Castle's three towers sliced upwards through the curtain of smoggy rain, rising from the gray hills that embraced it, and I deeply dreaded what I should find there. *The matter is urgent*, said Father's missive that had called Mother and me home from abroad, and I couldn't imagine what would have made him write such a thing, for he was not one given to alarm.

When the carriage harness had broken as we'd rounded the coastal road a ways back, Mother had of course seen it as a bad omen, for she could spot bad luck in a sunny day in July. But now, with the words of that Hamish sweeping through my mind, the whole world held an eerie chill that even I could not dismiss as I neared my home and saw no one coming to meet me. The man who had taken me to the outer gates of the property was no more than a distant speck as he sped toward his own home.

A shock of utter aloneness bolted through me as the cold wind penetrated to my skin. It was not the sort of isolation that lifted in the presence of others—it sat much deeper and longer-lasting than that.

The rumble of horse hooves thudded through my reverie. On the wooded path snaking through our woods, a black-cloaked rider leaned into his massive stallion, grasping his mane as they thundered together through the rain. A shiver convulsed me and I tucked myself into the shadows and watched the ghostly figures. What was this stranger doing on our land? His beast panted closer, looming large and terrible. The rider turned to look at me, rain spraying off his dark curls under the hood, and I caught sight of nearly black eyes set in a strong, stubbled face.

Leaning back in one graceful move, the stranger reined in his horse and redirected him toward the barn where I crouched. A slash of lightning illuminated the wild eyes of the stallion as he pounded closer, and I shrank into the shadows. Willing myself to be invisible, I watched them approach, and then the horse danced to a stop in the mud outside the barn.

"What are you doing here?" The rider's voice was low and harsh as the thunder, and almost accusatory. As if *I* was the invader on my own estate.

"Walking to the castle." I had to nearly shout above the storm.

"Not very effectively. Those shoes are terrible. Get on."

I hesitated at the sight of his rain-soaked leather glove outstretched to me, but this severe man was the only human I'd seen since the driver from the Dark Horse Inn. He guided his horse under the eaves and gripped my hand, then lifted me easily onto the horse behind him at a precarious side-angle that thankfully kept me from straddling the beast in my skirts.

Propriety still shouted loud warnings at the nearness of this man I didn't know, but one glance at the steep hills before us and I slipped my arms around the breadth of his body and anchored my hands on his chest. Dignity would have to make way for safety. I leaned my rain-drenched body against his back, sinking into its solidness, and the first jerk of the horse had me nearly squeezing the life out of the man. I moved close to his ear and shouted an apology over the sound of pounding hooves and thunder.

In response he covered my hand with his, pressing it to his rising and falling chest with a remarkable combination of strength and gentleness. "Hold on as tight as you need." That rare bit of masculine tenderness surprised and comforted me as I sat atop his horse and trembled.

Thank you, God, for the rescue. I shall accept this man as your hand in human form outstretched to me. Please let it be so.

I closed my eyes as the horse's hooves found solid ground at each stumbling step and I relished the cool sea breeze on my hot face in unladylike surrender, feeling quite at home in the outdoors once more. My hair clung in wavy clumps to my cheeks, which were already slimy with mud, and a sense of urgency returned to my spirit. Mother, my little butterfly mother adorned in her own sort of gossamer wings, would be waiting in that broken-down carriage for me to send her a rescue.

The ancient groom had remained with her because of her delicate nerves, which now seemed a providential turn, for Mother never would have willingly climbed atop this massive steed. With any luck, the other carriage carrying our ladies' maids and trunks would only be an hour or so behind us, and everything would be quickly set right.

Bracing against a fresh deluge of rain, I clung to the rider, my cheek to his wet cloak, and took in the familiar scents and sounds of Trevelyan Woods. So many childhood memories, both sweet and lonely, hung about the castle and the sharply scented woods around it.

When at last we crossed the drawbridge and stopped under the red timber overhang, I relaxed my grip and peeled myself away from my rescuer. The urgent words of Father's missive swirled around me then and fear gripped me anew. I glanced at the imposing entrance for reassurance, that familiar arched doorway buried in the stone wall, and it was just as I'd left it. Nothing terrible could have happened if everything looked the same, could it? With a quick grunt, my rescuer turned and swung me to the ground.

"Thank you." I delivered the simple words with a great deal of feeling as I looked past him to the downpour we'd just galloped through. The barn that had sheltered me stood at a distance that nearly put it out of sight. "Mister . . ."

"Vance. Donegan Vance."

The man's dark eyes engaged me from atop his horse, and strangely enough, I found it hard to draw mine away. He had quite an effect on me, this stranger. I wished I could be indifferent to one I knew so little, but he held a kind of horrible fascination for me. Rain dripped off the black curls that framed his face and traveled down his jaw.

"Thank you, Mr. Vance."

He gave a brief nod of acknowledgment, and then with one mighty yank of his arm, he spun the horse and galloped away in a splash of mud and rain. It was almost like a fairy tale, being rescued this way. Perhaps that's what made the man so handsome. Impossibly so. I watched them charge back into the storm together, that unknown horse and rider, and then heaved a sigh and turned to my home and whatever awaited me there.

And suddenly, as I stood wet and chilled on the stoop of my home, hope flooded my breast as I remembered with vivid clarity the reunion I would soon experience. Whatever past sadness that had kept him captive for so many years had lifted on the eve of our departure, releasing him to embrace the daughter who had desperately craved him for all of her days. We'd lost many years, Father and I, but the short time before we'd parted had been full of reconciliation and the tender promise of a restored relationship upon my return. I'd thought of it often on our travels, with surges of sweet anticipation, and now it was here.

Delight unfurled and climbed through my mind as I pictured my life as a beloved daughter. For once, it would not be merely the pitiful dream of a lonely girl, but reality. I could dig my toes into the warm soil and sprint around the lush vineyard where he'd eye me with that twinkle of masked humor beneath his proper distain for my spritely ways. He'd enjoy me. He'd *see* me. Greater delight I could not imagine.

I stepped up to the door with the curtain of rain as a backdrop, eagerly moving away from my life of solitude to one of love and fullness. Oh, the joys we would have as we finally began to know one another. I banged on the heavy wood door with my fist, then after a pause I repeated the effort. With a clank and clatter, the door opened. Framed in the glow from indoors stood our housekeeper, who remained as unchanged as the rest of the house.

"Margaret!" I leaped into her linen-clad arms, a wonderful sense of home washing over me at the sight and smell of her. "Oh, Margaret, how glad I am to see you." I pushed back and grasped her arms, words spilling out fast and breathless. "It's been a terrible night, full of adventures of the worst sort. The carriage has broken down a ways back, and we should send someone immediately. Mother is waiting, and you know how she is. We'll have to fill her with five pots of your orange spiced tea before she will be able to tolerate life again."

Her smile stilled my words. "Oh, Miss Tressa! How sorely we needed you." She tightened her arms about me in a sort of exultant embrace as she guided me out of the storm and into the house. "You've no idea how we need your light in these gray walls these days."

As I stepped inside, I couldn't help throwing one more backward glance toward the darkened woods. To my surprise, the stranger and his massive horse had paused some distance away, watching the castle. As soon as I had stepped into the shadowy interior of the house, the man once again bent into his steed's neck and urged the animal to carry him away.

"We weren't expecting you this quick. Not at all." Into the warmth and muted candlelight of the narrow receiving hall Margaret guided me, and then to the dim gallery that needed three stories to properly display our collected portraits and statues. "This room's the only one with a fire blazing at the moment, miss, but we'll have that fixed for you."

I soaked in the warmth of the fire and smiled at this maid who had often created a sense of sunshine in my dreary life over the years, but trouble clouded her sweet face.

"It's perfectly all right if you haven't had the tart made yet for my homecoming, you know. We didn't tell you we were coming." I peeled off my gloves and removed them, placing them on the stone mantel. "I should like to see Father at once. No, I shall need a thorough cleansing first. I'm afraid I'm wearing half the mud in the forest. Is Father in his study?" My numb fingers fiddled with the buttons of my traveling cloak.

She looked down and attended to the buttons with bustling efficiency. "Let me just help you with that." She undid the fastenings and tugged off my wrap that was heavy with rain and called for John. She then busied herself with sending the groom on his errand and caring for my poor cloak, avoiding my gaze. Her high little voice seemed higher, more pinched than I remembered. "He'll have my lady brought up to the house post-haste, miss. Perhaps you'd like tea and a hot water bottle for your feet." And without awaiting my reply, she hurried through the echoey room and disappeared through the service entrance.

Then the aura of Trevelyan Castle swirled around me, as it always did when I set foot inside its great doors, stilling my bubbling excitement to a sense of awe and pure inspiration for my artist's heart. The very air seemed clouded with centuries of living, a sense of ancientness, and all the ghosts that went along with it. It was merely a house, yet I couldn't escape the feeling that the emotions, triumphs, and stories of generations had seeped into the walls and remained trapped there, their essence floating about the rooms.

With a deep sigh, I spun in a slow circle, taking in the familiar portraits on the elaborate gold-and-blue backdrop of the walls, working hard to push aside the worry that insisted on settling around my heart. Margaret had looked tense, burdened.

It was merely her shock at seeing us, wasn't it?

As I slipped down the stairs after a thorough cleansing and a relaxing toilette, a fresh life had returned to my spirit. I swept into the gold-domed drawing room with the familiar massive furniture and hurried over to Mother, who had begun to recover from her ordeal of waiting in the carriage. A sense of expectancy bubbled to the surface as I entered the familiar space. "Something exciting must have happened for him to call us home and then not even meet us. What do you suppose it is?"

She touched her fingertips to her pale forehead. "Must you be so tiresome? Like a glaring light in one's eyes. This trip has only made it worse."

I pinched my lips, knowing she was right. Trapped in town as we had been, all the life inside me had been bottled far too long and it was brimming out. All the amusement and splendor of our social season abroad had excited Mother but utterly suffocated me beyond recognition. But now I was home.

And soon I would have the delightful reunion with Father I'd played out in my head during countless lonely nights spent in foreign beds.

"I need my vials before this headache swallows me utterly. I sent Lucy to fetch them a quarter of an hour ago. Where in heaven's name could that girl—?"

Crash. Metal banged and clinked on hall tile, echoing through the house, and Mother cast her eyes heavenward with a sigh of longsuffering. "Never mind."

My unfortunate lady's maid, Lucy, peeked around the door, her frizzy hair framing the wide-eyed face with tiny heart lips pursed to hold back a flood of ready excuses and apologies.

Mother waved her in with barely veiled impatience. Even though she never lowered herself to outright anger, no one failed to miss the disapproval of Trevelyan's mistress. "Did you bring my vials?"

"I have them here." The girl hurried in and handed her the case with a quick curtsey. "Also, tea will be a bit delayed." She dropped her gaze.

"Of course it will." Mother bestowed a restrained smile upon the girl as she accepted the vials. "Perhaps you should confine yourself to the back halls while the other servants are about."

In a beat I stepped forward and inserted myself into the incident. "How wonderful of you to protect Mother's vials in the collision with the tea cart. Not a one is broken, and that is admirable." I caught the girl's eyes and flashed an encouraging, conspiratorial smile upon her, for our friendship had been forged from the plights of our common adversary. Another curtsey and the dear, pitiable Lucy hurried away with her head down and her fingers desperately picking a handkerchief from her belt to absorb her tears as soon as she was out of sight of the one who had caused them.

Still restless and haunted by the pallor that had touched Margaret's usually rosy face, I crossed the room to stand in the dying amber light cast through the tall windows. Would he come from the vineyard or from somewhere in the house? I didn't want to miss the first sight of Father. "It's been many months. Do you think he's changed a great deal?"

"In six and twenty years of marriage he hasn't had the good sense to change yet. Why ever would he start now?"

The words pinched my heart. "Oh, Mother. Can't you at least try to like him? He adores you so." If only she knew how lucky she was. Perhaps I too was on the threshold of such affection from him, now that we were home.

Finally the door slid open and our housekeeper scurried in with a fresh teacart.

"Margaret, where is my husband?" Mother spoke from her graceful lounging position on the settee, her voice whisper-soft as if even the effort of speaking drained her tired soul.

Margaret turned up the teacups and poured, nervous eyes darting about, her pleasant face lined with worry. "Amos will have to tell you the news, my lady."

Mother straightened against the floral tapestry, her elegant head tipped with sudden concern. "What? What is it? Has he had a misfortune?" Her eyes darted about. "I knew something had happened when I saw the raven. And then the branches that formed a great X . . ." She turned to me, then back to the housekeeper, speaking in a strangled, desperate whisper. "He's lost everything, hasn't he?"

"No, my lady, it isn't that." Margaret nudged the poor butler forward with her elbow. "Amos will tell it."

"I . . . I wouldn't know how to say it." Amos's long fingers worked around the empty tray he carried as he faced us.

"Come now, one of you tell me what it is or I'll dismiss you both."

Margaret sighed, heaving her rounded shoulders forward. "He's died, my lady. Nearly a fortnight ago."

Disbelief tore through me as I struggled to grasp the truth. *Died!* The awful word rolled around in my mind and settled like the steel of a knife, slicing the delicate thread of hope I'd held all this time. I fought against the loss with my meager argument. "But he sent for us."

Her face softened. "Likely before he died, miss."

It was true then. He was gone. Stiff and regal, I held my composure like a calm pond on a summer's day. But beneath my face a tempest of the fiercest proportions roiled, the power of it swaying me on my feet as it passed over me, leaving me weak and unsteady in its wake. A few deep breaths with my eyes serenely closed and the initial shock receded, but the pain had sliced deep into my belly, where it continued to turn.

Then I remembered Mother. I held my breath for a heartbeat as I awaited her reaction, one hand to my satin bodice. But I had overestimated her attachment to the poor husband who'd adored her.

Mother's beautifully sculpted lips turned down. "How unfortunate." She sank back into the gild-edged settee that accented her bright gown. "Death is always such a shame."

Dear Margaret's lips pinched in her signature look of masked disapproval, but Mother had turned her gaze to me.

"Now, we shall finally have all that fortune he's held so tightly and spend, spend, spend." Her flowery little laugh grated on my raw nerves.

I curled my hand into itself. If anger could be a noise, it whirred painfully in my ears then.

"What a glorious time we shall have. Come, let's have it brought out this minute to give all due commemoration to the event. Pray, where has he gone and put it?"

I looked about for whom she might be talking to, but her gaze remained on me. "Why, I haven't a clue where it is, Mother. I assumed you . . ."

The exultant look of her blue eyes froze into two orbs of ice. "He did not tell you?"

I shook my head, gladness and fear swirling through me that the fortune should be out of her grasp, at least for this moment. "He always said he'd tell me just before he died."

I looked at the new widow stiff with shock and the truth struck us both immediately. Here we were in this immense castle with a lavish vineyard and a staff of nearly sixty-five . . . and not a penny between us. At Father's death, we were suddenly the poorest wealthy family in all of England.

Fear blanched Mother's face and her eyes blurred behind tears. "How . . . Oh, this is the most awful . . ." Then she paused with her chin out, a picture of courage as she rose from the couch with effort, and wobbled on her feet. "I suppose we must bear it."

Springing up, I ran to her with automatic obligation and steadied her, urging her to retire. Performing my usual service to her urged me forward when I wished desperately to crumple into a heap of ashes and blow away in the wind. Shock threatened me in cold waves, but I shoved them away. "Something will turn up. There's nothing we cannot better deal with after a good rest. I'll help you to your chambers and send a maid with hot milk and Eau de Cologne for your head."

Lifeless as a willow branch, she allowed herself to be led

out of the drawing room and up the great staircase as I paused to lift a candle. Three steps up, she stopped me with a faint pressure on my arm. "You knew him best, Tressa dear. Surely you can think of some place . . . you must know something. *Something.*"

I nearly said that I did not, but shut my mouth when I realized that would be a lie. I merely lowered my gaze as images flashed through my mind. The hidden room of books, the little hints he'd dropped throughout my childhood . . .

But one image stood out among the rest so plainly I could nearly touch it. His notebooks. In those pages of his notes and observations on the vineyard he had tucked pieces of himself that could be found in no other place. On the cover were the words that had echoed with shadowy intrigue throughout my childhood: the vineyard's secret. If one were to understand where he'd hidden the fortune that had been his lifeblood, the answer would be buried somewhere in those volumes.

Yet I held my tongue on the matter. The idea of Mother's casual, judgmental gaze penetrating the private words on those pages made me cringe.

"We'll think on it later, Mother. The only thing we'll discuss tonight is getting you to bed." Climbing alongside the leaping shadows of the candlelight, I glanced about the familiar house anew, seeing it as a cavern of mystery. For somewhere in these rooms lay the entirety of Father's fortune, the great secret of the man I'd barely begun to know.

"Here, miss, let me." A little chambermaid hurried up behind me and accepted Mother's weight, looping an arm around the woman's slender frame. Surprisingly sturdy, the girl bore the weight of her mistress without trouble, so I nodded my thanks and retraced my steps down the stairs.

More tea would do wonders for the chill that had gripped me from the inside out.

In the drawing room, I paused as voices nearby arrested my attention. They wafted out from behind the service door.

"Will you tell her about the master?" Amos's voice warbled out in a fearful whisper.

It was Margaret's voice that snapped out a response. "You were there when I informed them of his death, weren't you?"

"That isn't what I mean, and you know it."

ACKNOWLEDGMENTS

My deepest thanks to all the people who read this story when it was a little baby book with a lot of growing to do: Carolyn Hill, Stacey Zink, Susan Tuttle, Sonnet Fitzgerald, Allen Arnold, Bob Davidson, Jonnie Clark, KyLee Woodley, Michelle DeBruin, and Crystal Caudill.

And to the one who pushed me with a godly blend of brutal honesty, endless encouragement, and lots of sanity checks when I was a baby writer with a lot of growing to do: my Vince. I cannot fully express how much I love you.

And mostly, to the One who loved me from the start, before I'd grown at all: God.

Joanna Davidson Politano freelances for a small nonfiction publisher but spends much of her time spinning tales that capture the colorful, exquisite details in ordinary lives. Her manuscript for *Lady Jayne Disappears* was a finalist for several contests, including the 2016 Genesis Award from ACFW, and won the OCW Cascade Award and the Maggie Award for Excellence. She is always on the hunt for random acts of kindness, people willing to share their deepest secrets with a stranger, and hidden stashes of sweets. She lives with her husband and their two babies in a house in the woods near Lake Michigan and shares stories that move her at www.jdpstories.com.

MEET
JOANNA

JDPStories.com

CPSIA information can be obtained
at www.ICGtesting.com
Printed in the USA
LVOW12*1922121017
552170LV00008B/107/P